Catherine Miller is the author
own name and other pseudonyr
in London, her career took her from producing radio
commercials to being a voiceover agent for various stellar
actors. Nowadays she writes all day at home in Surrey,
occasionally lifting her head to raise her daughter and
feed the dogs.

Also by Catherine Miller

The Archers: Ambridge at War

THE
ARCHERS

HOME FIRES AT AMBRIDGE

Catherine Miller

**SIMON &
SCHUSTER**

London · New York · Sydney · Toronto · New Delhi

First published in Great Britain by Simon & Schuster UK Ltd, 2021

This paperback edition published in 2022

1 3 5 7 9 10 8 6 4 2

Simon & Schuster UK Ltd
1st Floor
222 Gray's Inn Road
London WC1X 8HB

www.simonandschuster.co.uk
www.simonandschuster.com.au
www.simonandschuster.co.in

Simon & Schuster Australia, Sydney
Simon & Schuster India, New Delhi

A CIP catalogue record for this book
is available from the British Library

PB ISBN: 978-1-4711-9554-9
eBook ISBN: 978-1-4711-9553-2
Audio ISBN: 978-1-3985-0066-2

Typeset in Palatino by M Rules
Printed and bound by CPI Group (UK) Ltd, Croydon CR0 4YY

This book is for Barbara Carlile

THE
ARCHERS
HOME FIRES AT AMBRIDGE

SUMMER

1941

The sun do shine on the just and the unjust alike.

THOMAS HARDY
Tess of the D'Urbervilles

JUNE

Summer storms are perverse.

That June was rainless and heavy, but the breeze picking up in Ambridge whispered of mischief. Cats' tails kinked as they slept; cattle twitched beneath the moon; the numberless inhabitants of the woods hunkered down.

Jane Gilpin, climbing into her narrow bed beneath the eaves of Woodbine Cottage, felt change in the air. She ascribed it to the summer solstice, that ancient turning point when the year tips over into the future.

Her gentle nighty ritual was always the same. Hair first, wound into rags. Jane had poor hair; she knew she was sometimes referred to as 'poor Jane'.

Not due to a lack of wealth – the Gilpins wanted for nothing – but because of her myriad small disappointments.

As Jane unscrewed the cold cream, she heard whispers through her open window.

At this hour?

It was, of course, local girls flitting like spirits to St Stephen's where they would conjure up midsummer visions of their future loves. Such hope! Jane remembered doing the same thing in her youth. She remembered pretending to see something.

The gramophone playing in another part of the cottage stuck suddenly. *Love is,* it stuttered. *Love is. Love is.*

'The sweetest thing.' Jane finished the line as she padded on bare feet to her sister's room.

The sombre dead in the churchyard had no option but to put up with the village girls darting in and out of the weeping stone angels and family tombs. 'Ssh!' the girls said to one another, but their excitement was doubled, trebled, by the coming storm, by the trembling of the old yew.

Summer solstice madness was upon them.

Jane lifted the gramophone needle.

The dark hillock in the bed stirred.

'Goodnight, Blanche,' said Jane.

Blanche sat up as Jane left the room, astonished by the first word her sister had spoken to her in seven months.

Cold cream done, Jane anointed her hands with Campana's Italian Balm. She held one hand up, and was glad of her failing eyesight, because her hand looked girlish again, waxen and pale.

Beyond the window, in her cherished garden, where the plants were known to her like friends, the hydrangea shivered.

*

'Be quiet! You'll have the vicar after us.'

Some of the girls concentrated on their ritual, but there was much sniggering and pushing at the back. The bold breeze teased and unsettled them all.

They felt, not with their minds but with their electric young bodies, something approach Ambridge. Something that would prise the village from its snug bed and toss it in the air.

Her medication and sleeping draught waited on a brass tray on the bedside table. Jane laid a thin hand over her heart.

She wondered if dear old Morgan Seed was being entirely truthful with her; Ambridge's doctor was known to 'manage' his patients. 'If we take good care of your heart,' he would say, 'it'll last forever.'

But, Jane would think, *you don't know what it's been through.*

However, she took her heart pills like a good girl, and mixed her own infusion to lull her off to sleep.

More maidens traipsed past her window as Jane pulled up the coverlet and settled her pillows. They smelled of lavender.

The girls were right, she thought. *Life can be magical, if you slow down enough to notice it.*

The moment shimmers.

Ambridge is just like everywhere else, and quite different.

Love is being made, snores are rattling rafters, babies are spatchcocked in cots.

Around the dark triangle of The Green, the houses are set out simply; bordered to the south by the drowsy ribbon of the river Am, they seem unaffected by any comparison to the grandeur of Lower Loxley in the east, content in their brick and stone skins. The village hall, the church, the store, are connected not by pavements but by history, by the tread of feet on lanes that loop back on themselves and tie this village up tight.

The night is a long haul in this heat; the war is turning out to be long, too. No end in sight. They are deep in a soggy middle that has no shape. Triumph. Defeat. Both are constants.

In her panelled bedroom at Lower Loxley, Pamela Pargetter peeps out from her silk eye-mask to find that her Pekinese has thrown up violet creams on the eiderdown. 'Oh, Mavis, must you?' she sighs.

Girls, their faces wet with dew, dance around the tombstones.

An old farmhouse, to the south, beyond the bridge, feels the first punch of a storm that means business.

Above the Channel, far from Ambridge, the sky is bright with flame and a pilot kisses the signet ring on his little finger, and leaps.

Jane rolls onto her back.

Walter Gabriel wakes suddenly. He celebrated the solstice a little too well at The Bull, but that should mean a deep sleep. Something has poked him. He thinks for a moment it is his wife, but she is dead some years, a fact that sometimes assails him afresh in the small hours. Something else has woken him, something nameless, gathering out there.

Jack Archer is not asleep. Far from home, he plays cards under canvas in a desert he could not have found on a map before the war. He wonders if the dull feeling in his gut is homesickness, or the strange beef Cookie fed them earlier. He takes out that picture again, of that girl. That Peggy. *His* Peggy. If he believes she is his – despite all evidence to the contrary – he might just get through this war.

The song in the churchyard rises and is snatched by the storm:

> *Rose leaves, rose leaves,*
> *Rose leaves I strew,*
> *He that will love me,*
> *Come after me now.*

'I see him!' shrieks a girl. They all cling to one another.

A window in the vicarage flies up. 'Off with you! Before I come down there and make you!' The vicar's wife scatters them with her threat.

Jane closes her eyes for the last time.

Morgan, gently and with reverence, settled Jane's body. Nobody need know how she flailed. He invited Blanche in to pay her final respects.

'Me?' Blanche seemed to have no idea how to behave in the presence of death. 'I can't be in the same room as a corpse!' She stayed out on the small, creaky landing, face puffy above her housecoat's ostrich feathers. 'What happened? She was perfectly well last night.'

'Heart failure, I'm afraid.'

7

Morgan remembered explaining to Jane how the muscles around her heart weren't quite up to the job. She had asked if that meant her heart was broken.

Was I kind when I answered her? Morgan hoped he was. He hoped he hadn't shown the impatience he felt.

He took something from Jane's bedside table. It was Morgan's; nobody need know about it. He slipped it into his pocket, where it sat and burned all morning.

The storm had given the village a bloody nose. Mrs Endicott's cherry tree rattled; Frank Brown's flowerpots swiped off the shop's sill. Mud was drying on the road as Agnes Kaye hurried towards Woodbine Cottage, and she passed a child's swing wrapped crazily around an oak.

She barged into Jane's room on legs like hanging threads. No need to knock; Agnes may have recently scampered up a few rungs of the village's social ladder, but until her marriage the previous year she had been in service at Woodbine Cottage.

'Morning, Doc.' Agnes was vivid and quick beside rotund, avuncular Morgan. She had a lot of nose, and she poked it now into the room she knew well. 'Jane likes things just so,' she said of the woman in the bed, tidying the dressing table and tucking slippers together on the rug.

A vase was on its side. 'Mop up that water,' she ordered the too-young, no-use maid. 'Cut some roses. Miss Jane's favourite, *Madame Hardy*, big white double blooms by the sundial. What you waiting for?' she barked, and the girl ran.

When the room was to her liking she stopped and finally

looked at Jane. Agnes went still, and Morgan was about to offer his handkerchief, when Blanche overcame her morbid fear of corpses enough to rush in and take Jane by the shoulders.

'How could you do this to me?' screeched Blanche, shaking her sister's body like a rag.

Morgan dithered, but Agnes took hold of her erstwhile employer and bundled her down the stairs, where Blanche launched herself at a chaise longue.

'Oh, Crow, Crow,' she sobbed.

She had called Agnes 'Crow' in the old days, as much for her skill at collecting gossip as for her beady eyes. 'Poor Jane,' said Agnes, as Jane had known people would.

Jane had also known that they wouldn't use that epithet once they had read her will. She may well be 'Cunning Jane' then, or 'Scheming Jane'.

'Poor *me*, you mean!' Blanche drummed her heels. 'What am I to do?'

A sedative was set out by Morgan, who was not at his best around hysterical females. 'Should we . . .' he said to Agnes, after they had tucked Blanche under a blanket and drawn the curtains.

'Have you done right by Miss Jane, I mean, Jane?' Old habits die hard. 'Sent for someone to wash her, and the undertaker?' On Morgan's nod, Agnes picked up her handbag. 'Then off we toddle, Doc. Whatever she says, Blanche Gilpin is well able to look after herself.'

*

The storm was fickle. Before toying with the village, it had paused at Brookfield to deliver a vicious right hook.

The Archers stood around the rim of the crater which had, overnight, opened up outside their front door. An uncanny abyss, it swallowed their yard with one gulp.

'The mud,' said Doris. 'The cart.' All the neat sheaves of hay, primly sorted by the binder, were buried with the broken wheels. The hand-painted side that had read 'Brookfield Open Air Dairy' was in splinters. She would rally, she always did, but for now all Doris Archer could see was a year of hard graft pouring down the hole.

The children saw adventure. Phil put one toe into the chasm, as all self-respecting thirteen-year-olds must when confronted with danger.

'Stop it, you young fool,' said Dan. But he said it fondly. He was phlegmatic, puffing on his pipe and taking in the devastation with composure. 'Ah well,' he said eventually.

'Look at the milking shed.' Doris, staid and stout in her pinny, pointed. As if she wanted him to panic, to *notice*. 'The whole side's come away. It's open to the elements!'

'Yes,' said Dan.

'June's a busy enough month as it is. We shouldn't be standing around maundering over a blooming great hole.' Doris had mouths to feed, and paperwork to fill in for her billeting manager duties.

'See where the barn's listing to one side, love?'

Doris hadn't noticed that.

The collie was affronted; he barked and barked,

hopping backwards, his tail a flag. 'Don't worry, Glen,' said Christine. Aged nine she considered the dog her peer. 'We'll fix it.'

'That was a bad night,' said Doris. She had smelled the air before going to bed and flinched. She had known Ambridge would emerge into Sunday somehow different.

'Not our first bad night. Nor our last. We'll be all right.' Dan sucked his teeth. 'Have to dip into the savings.'

Doris wondered at his amnesia; they had dipped only recently. Before the war she had left the finances to Dan; now that he was distracted with War Ag and the Home Guard, she had no option but to take on more responsibility. 'If we hadn't had to give up those acres . . .'

The old gripe got Dan sighing. 'I told you, I did my best.'

Did you, Dan? Fourteen acres of prime arable land snatched away by the pickpocketing Ministry of Works to build Quartershot POW camp. Dan worked his fingers to the bone for the War Ag – an irreverent abbreviation for the War Agricultural Executive Committee which implemented the various, often maddening, wartime farming regulations – but that meant nothing when the powers that be eyed up their land. The ministries didn't talk to one another; Dan's War Ag connections did the family no good.

Doris could itemize to the shilling what that had cost them.

Dan rubbed his hands, a full stop to the maundering. 'Come on, let's get ourselves to church.'

The rest of the family dispersed, creeping around the crater, but Doris lingered in a farmyard so magically changed it was the stuff of fairy tales. *Shame I don't have a magic wand.* Farmers were always one act of God away from ruin; she was accustomed to feeling the ground shift beneath her feet. The ground actually disappearing was new, but she would cope. She had no other option.

'Mother Cat!' Christine was calling their black and white cat inside the house.

Doris hurried indoors, before Dan took it on himself to tell the child the animal was missing.

A new poster was pinned above the dried goods in the village shop: <u>YOUR</u> COURAGE, <u>YOUR</u> CHEERFULNESS, <u>YOUR</u> RESOLUTION, WILL BRING US VICTORY!

Beneath it, Frank Brown cut a piece of cheese with the care of a surgeon. He was born to shopkeeping, from his wallflower demeanour to his discretion about the status of customers' accounts. All eyes were lustfully on the square of cheddar as he weighed it with great solemnity.

'Anything else, Doris?'

'Ooh, a big pot of jam and lots of chocolate, please!' Doris handed over her coupons and enjoyed the success of her joke with the rest of the queue. 'Honestly, Frank, they'll ration sunshine next.'

'It's not fair, rationing clothes,' said Mrs Endicott, squat and comfortable in a dress fashionable in her youth. 'All these different coupons are so confusing.'

'It'll get worse,' said Frank, 'before it gets better.'

Agnes, at the end of the line, said, 'Well, thank you *very* much, cheerful Charlie.'

'It's almost closing time, ladies.' Frank's mild prompt would have no effect; the shop was the anvil on which village gossip was forged. The ladies would linger.

A young woman, the Gilpin sisters' maid, flounced through the door, open to let in the non-existent breeze. 'Tell that Miss Blanche of yours,' she said to Agnes, 'I'm leaving.' She flung her ruffled maid's cap in the air. It landed on Mrs Endicott. 'She's crazy.'

'She's not *my* Miss Blanche,' said Agnes, all a-bristle, 'and have some respect. She's just lost her sister.'

The girl, seeing she had an audience, stuck her nose in the air. 'I don't have to work for the likes of you lot no more. I'm off to the mill. They need women these days. Pays twice as well and I won't have to skivvy.'

She left genteel disgruntlement in her wake.

'I should call on Blanche,' said Mrs Endicott, whose conscience was pricking her. 'It's the Christian thing to do.' She seemed tempted to be un-Christian in this instance; Blanche did not make it easy to obey the dictum *Love thy neighbour*. There were many who felt that Jane had been slowly asphyxiated by Blanche's self-ish, incessant demands. Even the saintly Mrs Endicott had been heard to opine that Blanche 'drove her sister to the grave'. Now she said, breathless, 'I heard the deathwatch beetle *that* night, the night of the storm. I knew death would visit us.'

'You need them beams in your old house seen to,' said Agnes, but Doris thought of the chasm in the farmyard.

It was constantly in her eyeline. Glen barked down into the dark, as if something wicked lived down there, something that might crawl up and consume the whole farm.

'I do like a nice funeral,' said Magsy Deveraux. Despite the heat, the matronly woman was in coat and hat and stockings. She would never let herself down by appearing in public attired otherwise.

Death visited Ambridge more often since the outbreak of war. Doris would never become inured to it, no matter how good the sandwiches after the interment. 'Will you be there, Nance?'

Nance looked up from where she bent over a ration book. 'If Dad can spare me.'

'I'll shut the shop,' said Frank. 'Out of respect.'

'Did you hear Alec Pargetter's reading Jane's will straight after the funeral? *In public.*' There was a glint in Agnes's eye. The Crow knew the refined ladies were itching to discuss this development. 'Very odd,' she said, fishing.

Mrs Endicott bit. She usually did. 'Yes, most peculiar. Jane was such a private person. Of course, the family home will pass to Blanche . . .' She let the ellipsis trail on the floor.

To be pounced upon by Magsy. 'If that's the case, why read the will in the village hall? Most unconventional. I may attend. I may not.'

You'll be there, thought Agnes. *Middle of the front row.* Everyone knew there was going to be something fishy about Jane Gilpin's will. To Doris, she said, 'Nice that you have a land girl at last, eh?'

14

'The girl seems charming,' said Mrs Endicott, fondling an egg as she waited her turn.

'Wanda? She's a great lass,' said Doris. Wanda's baffling surname would never pass Doris's lips; she would have to practise from now until Judgement Day to pronounce Laframboise even half-right. She had prayed for a land girl, a feminine bulwark against the procession of unsuitable city fellas the Ministry saw fit to send her. But sophisticated, confident, *posh* Wanda wasn't quite what Doris would have ordered.

'Is she worth the eighteen bob a week?' asked Agnes.

'Well,' said Doris. 'It's the government who pays her.'

Unasked, Nance placed a punnet of strawberries in Doris's string bag. 'I know you like them.' She was shy about her thoughtfulness, as she was about most things.

Hates being noticed, that one, was how Doris put it. Nance's gentle palette – the straw-coloured hair, the mild blush on her cheeks – was of a piece with her personality. 'Nice to see you helping your dad in the shop, even now you're married to Morgan. There's some as would stay home and keep house.'

'She has me for that!' Magsy slapped her list onto the counter. 'Don't you, Nance, dear?' When Magsy's sister died and made a widower of Ambridge's doctor, Magsy had taken the domestic helm. 'I've kept house for Morgan for *years*, I know what he likes, you see, and it's my pleasure to look after him, well, *them*.' She beamed at Nance. The women were very different creatures, from different generations, one with the confidence of a fine pedigree, the other with a natural reserve amplified by the secret that she and her father, Frank, nursed about their own pedigree.

'Nance still has the glow of a newly-wed,' said Mrs Endicott indulgently.

'They're wed a year,' snapped Agnes. 'Hardly newly-weds. More Darby and Joan.' Nobody ever commented on Agnes's newly-wed glow, even though she had married more recently. 'Did you do anything special on your anniversary?'

'Ooh, no. The war, you know ...' The war was the universal reason, the universal excuse. Nance turned to Magsy. 'Thought I might cook dinner tonight, do some mushrooms.'

'Morgan won't so much as look at a mushroom!' Magsy seemed horrified. 'Leave the cooking to me, Nance. You relax.'

Nance fetched lard and flour and sought out a toothbrush, but she was silent. Frank said, out the back in the stockroom where no civilian was ever allowed, 'What *is* the matter, Nance?'

'Have you found someone to replace me yet, like I asked?'

Frank winced at her tone. They spent all day together, but talked so little. He missed the old father-and-daughter team, the Browns, reliable and so good to one another. He knew he had let her down; his sin of omission was branded into his skin. 'Like I said, I've been busy and—'

'I have a husband and a home to look after, Dad.'

It was so unlike his Nance to interrupt that Frank stepped back from her. 'Magsy's got all that under control.'

Nance took off her brown grocer's coat and left the back way, with no goodbye.

*

Pamela Pargetter was a spare woman, with cheekbones that could slice bread.

There was no profusion, just a restrained elegance that could make her look older than her years. Her hair was coiled chicly on her head, held in place by many pins; like everything else in her orbit, it dare not disobey the chatelaine of Lower Loxley.

Grand, confident, sprawling, Lower Loxley had been in her husband's family for generations. There were numberless windows, many ways into and out of its parade of rooms. It used to feel too large for Pamela, Alec and their son, but now that many-limbed critter, the War Effort, had reached even Lower Loxley, and they shared the house with convalescing RAF officers.

The Battle of Britain had long dwindled to a halt but the RAF still chucked planes into the air like doves. There may have been severe shortages of sugar, but there was no shortage of wounded men.

More staff were recruited. Rooms long unused were aired. A slight institutional feel pervaded the once-languid house. Her drawing room had been given over to the chaps; Pamela and Alec now shared smaller spaces, if they could be said to share anything.

His time was taken up with the Home Guard; Pamela was more concerned with overseeing laundry than she would like. The real impediment to intimacy was nothing to do with their schedules.

I won, Pamela reminded herself, at least once a day. She

had won the battle for Alec's tweedy heart; he had given up his lover. *I won.*

He was not the sort to take a mistress. He was jolly decent, upright, reliable. And yet he had fallen, head over brogues, for a local woman.

He was sad in the aftermath of the affair, but Pamela felt he blamed her for his dejection. Which was *ridiculous*; it was he, not Pamela, who had behaved badly.

She moved at speed through the grand hall with her clipboard, ticking and crossing out and hoping she wouldn't bump into Dodgy, who was a sweetheart but who did tend to hold her up, and suddenly there was Dodgy.

Squadron Leader Reginald Dodge, surely convalesced but now part of the furniture, was slow-moving and yet could pop up out of nowhere. Pamela's 'darling Dodgy' was portly and moustachioed, hardly the handsome flying ace of fiction, but he was highly decorated and respected. An eternal bachelor, he was wedded to his plane, or his 'crate', as he called it, even though his war was being fought in an RAF basement. It was sciatica that brought Dodgy to Lower Loxley, and now he stood beneath a wooden scroll and read aloud the Latin motto carved into it, forcing Pamela to stop and listen.

'*Ostenditur spes alma lux beatissima,*' he said, grandly. 'A fine motto.'

'Isn't it just?' Pamela never said the Pargetter motto aloud, for fear of revealing she couldn't pronounce Latin. She had no idea what the words meant but she had carefully restored the scroll. 'If you'll excuse me, Dodgy, I must check on the room for our new arrival.'

'Lead on, dear lady.' He followed her up the servants' stairs to an upper chamber. Beneath their feet sat a Turkish rug retrieved from the attics, soft and inviting in the glow of gilded lamps. A dyspeptic eighteenth-century Pargetter glowered from an oil portrait above the mantelpiece.

Pamela saw dust on the painting, and fluff on the rug. She would swap the dreary ancestor for a painting of Rupert Pargetter. *If I can find one.* Alec's older brother had been an artist, a dreamer, and the family disinherited him. Despite this, Alec thought of his brother as a hero, and the true heir to Lower Loxley; despite Rupert's pacifism he had volunteered to drive an ambulance in the Great War, and had fallen at Ypres. She scribbled on her clipboard.

'This for the Polish chap?' Dodgy whistled. 'Lucky him. They picked him up in the sea, you know. Head wound. Bailed out, but not before he chalked up a few bandits, including one of the German big hitters. Bloody good at flying, he was in a storm, a ten-tenths.' Perhaps he saw Pamela's look of incomprehension; he tended to lose the ladies when he lapsed into RAF slang. 'Low visibility,' he explained. 'The man's a hero.'

A black Labrador, passing the door on some doggy business, backtracked and put his head in, enquiringly.

'Not *you*, Hero,' said Pamela. 'Go find your master.' She could have added, *He's probably moping about like a wet weekend.* Alec's continued melancholy struck her as self-indulgent. The Pargetters meant something in Borsetshire, as his wider family never tired of reminding Pamela, who was not from blue-blooded stock.

But it's my self-made father's fortune that keeps this place on its feet. Nobody is ever too proud to accept money.

Alec never referred to Pamela's nouveau status; he barely referred to her at all. They lived in the ruins of their marriage; the history of war taught that ruins could be built upon; sometimes ruins were necessary in order to modernize.

But to rebuild we'd have to talk. The Pargetters were well-matched in their distaste for talk. Instead, they semaphored from adjacent hilltops. Pamela was growing lonely up there in the clouds. She had stopped putting on her filmy peignoirs, stopped spraying herself with scent in the hope he'd visit her room at night. She had come to despise the look of yearning she met in her mirror.

She realized Dodgy was talking to her. 'Sorry, what?'

'Where's little Mavis?' He shared many qualities with the Pekinese. Appetite. Fondness for naps. Spectacular flatulence.

'She's not well.' Pamela motored out of the room. 'Nothing serious.' Her chest tightened. *Get a grip*, she told herself. *She's just a dog. You can't get all silly about a dog!*

Bedtime meant different things to different people.

To the farmers of the district it meant falling, like toppled trees, as soon as it grew dark. To the RAF officers telling tall tales over brandy, it meant midnight or later.

At Homeleigh, home of Morgan and Nance Seed, it meant

the tail end of a long June evening. Still promising, still scented, the house quiet and calm.

Except for off-key hymns emanating from the kitchen. Nance whispered to Morgan, from her armchair to his, 'Magsy's staying very late tonight.'

'Is she?' Morgan didn't lift his eyes from his novel.

'It's practically time for bed.' Nance couldn't be seen to carp. Magsy was, all agreed, an angel. She was a martyr at the stake of housework, devoting herself to Morgan and his two sons. When Anthony was lost in the first days of the war, Magsy had suffered alongside Morgan, and she shared his anxiety about boastful, reckless George, currently embroiled in hush-hush military schemes in Norfolk. Nance had admired her, along with the rest of the village. She still admired her. Or tried to.

'What can she be doing at this hour?' pressed Nance.

Morgan tore himself away from Aldous Huxley. 'Washing, by the sounds of it.' The kitchen was a mystery to Morgan. Things got wet in there, he knew that. And food went in raw and came out delicious. Beyond that he was an ignoramus. 'Magsy works very hard, dear.'

'But she's not a housekeeper,' said Nance. 'She doesn't have to stay late.' Magsy had an opulent home of her own, grander than Homeleigh. The irony that she kept a staff to clean her own house yet insisted on scouring the floors of Morgan's occurred to nobody except Nance. 'Can't you suggest, dear, that it's time she went home?'

Morgan looked pained. 'She might take it wrongly,' he said.

21

Nance went back to Barbara Cartland.

'If it bothers you, dear, I'll say something . . .' Morgan stood with the book in his hand. His age showed at this hour. He was stiff.

'Are you still brooding over Jane?' Nance held out her hand and he took it. She smiled, and it fell on him like a benediction. 'You did all you could. Her heart was weak. You might feel better tomorrow, after the funeral.'

He pulled his hand away. Not a tetchy man, the movement was spiky in the summer night. 'I dread the will reading after the service,' he said. 'The spectacle of it.'

'Might Jane leave you something?' Nance imagined a trinket box or a figurine.

'She already has,' said Morgan, gruffly. The little keepsake he had spirited from her bedside table was locked in his desk.

Her husband was not himself, as the saying went. Nance, never steely, capitulated. 'Don't worry about saying anything to Magsy.' She almost smiled at his relief; Magsy's moods were mighty, like weather fronts. It was time to try another tack. She yawned extravagantly, like a silent movie actress, throwing her arms in the air. 'Ooh, I think I'll go up.' She trailed slowly to the door, and turned. 'It's such a warm night . . . I daresay I won't sleep . . .' Her coquettish look was tame by any other woman's standards. 'Morgan?' she said.

'What? Oh. Yes. Off you toddle,' said Morgan, and turned a page in his book.

*

A few miles away, over the fields and the trees that were melting into night, in another house, another woman prepared for bed.

Pamela made a duchessy tour of the bedrooms, knocking, saying a graceful goodnight, checking her guests had everything they needed.

All the British officers were in situ, all of them grateful, most of them squiffy. The new room was empty.

'Oh,' said Pamela, with the very particular diction Englishwomen bring to the word.

Dodgy, his dinner jacket flecked with cigar ash, told her he had overheard the Pole saying he preferred to sleep in the Folly.

'How eccentric of him.'

Dodgy wandered off, proclaiming over his shoulder, *'Ostenditur spes alma lux beatissima*, dear lady!'

Back in her room, unclasping the pearls that lay across her collarbone like tears, Pamela noticed a flare of yellow light down on the terrace. A struck match illuminated a man's face.

'Our eccentric Pole,' she murmured.

Presumably the man was abashed by the splendour of Lower Loxley; the Folly could be glimpsed from the house but was a world away from its comforts. Built by Alec's Great-Uncle Cedric after his Grand Tour, it was a charming oddity, grand-looking from the outside, with its pavilion styling and its tower, but spartan within. Empty stone rooms, stacked atop each other. Occasionally, when the stables overflowed, a visiting groom would be lodged there. And would complain about it.

The simplicity probably reminds him of his own cottage in Poland.

She was drawn back to the window; the terrace looked so charming in the moonlight. She was not, of course, drawn there by the airman. Dark, he was. Saturnine. Pamela was accustomed to uniforms, and to what they contained – *men*. *Just men*. She kept looking, though. At the way he walked, one hand in a pocket. Head thrown back. Looking at the stars. Looking at her window.

She stepped back.

Two floors down she heard men cry, 'Alec!' and knew her husband was home. She stepped back into her dress, did up the buttons with her economical touch, and went down to the drawing room.

Nance's nightgown was twisted up in the bedcovers. There was no respite from the heat. Sweat pooled at the back of her neck.

She thought, as she often did when alone, of who she was.

She was German.

Before Frank told her the truth about his side of the family, Nance had never thought about who, or what, she was. It hadn't needed saying. She was an English weed, happy and unobserved. Now, *I'm the enemy*.

The unhappy truth intensified her natural reserve. It was impossible not to wonder who had heard the accusation, who disbelieved Frank's rebuttal. She was aloof with her father, where once she had been doting. She missed her dad, the old version, the one who didn't lie to her. And she missed her husband, separated from her by solid British floorboards, and a world of misunderstanding.

He had his back to her when Pamela reached the chaps' drawing room. Alec was finely made from all angles, but something about his back was peculiarly *him*, thought Pamela, as she accepted a drink from a young airman.

Alec's body was a drawl, a puff of smoke. It tapered. He turned, and he smiled, but it was a social smile, such as he might bestow on a Doris Archer, or even an Agnes. She said, looking up at him over the rim of her glass, 'How are the Home Guard? All present and correct?'

'All present, at least,' said Alec. His eyes were damaged eyes, like the eyes of a dog one would find on the road. Beautiful, of course; there was an almost feminine beauty to Alec. Not that he cared; he groomed himself the way he groomed his horse. Because it was expected. The right thing to do. 'How's the invalid?'

'Mavis? A little better,' lied Pamela, who had left the fuzzy little dog up in her basket, not even stirring when her belly was rubbed. She turned away in case Alec saw her sudden anguish. He would understand; he wouldn't mock; and yet she kept her emotion from him. *Why?* she thought, vehemently and atypically.

One of the chaps – Pamela had forgotten his nickname: Spiffy? Mitzi? – said, 'Saw you on your motorbike earlier, old chap. What can you get out of her? Looks like she goes great guns.'

25

CATHERINE MILLER

Alec's eyes flickered to his wife.

Her eyebrow was raised, her expression as dry as the champagne. 'So you still have the motorbike, darling? And here was me thinking you sold it.'

'Snip snip,' said Alec. 'Out come the castrating shears.'

Talk turned to the stand-offish new chap, his glorious reputation, his rescue from the sea.

'It's the frostbite that gets you,' said Spiffy, or Mitzi.

'Terrible, the way Poland was crushed in just five weeks,' said Alec, who was both ignoring his wife and gauging her attitude towards him.

'All the Polish air aces,' said Dodgy, 'fled to France. And then France collapsed, so they're here in their thousands. Damn good fliers.'

'The ladies just swoon for them,' said oh what was his name, *Terence*, that was it. Young. Nice looking. 'I've heard that British officers put on Polish accents in bars to chat up girls.'

Dodgy asked Alec, 'So, this will reading tomorrow? Reckon the old girl's left you the lot?'

'Good God, I hope not,' said Alec, with feeling. 'It's rum reading it in front of the entire community. Dread to think how it'll go down. If you'd known Jane, well, let's just say she wasn't the type to knowingly cause gossip.'

'We didn't know her,' snapped Pamela. 'We only knew her public face, and when you're a woman, that face must be good and kind and sweet.'

'Not all women,' muttered Alec into his drink.

*

26

Still in his armchair, Magsy long gone, and the old clock in the hall about to strike one, Morgan gazed up at the ceiling, as if he could see his wife through it.

Will Nance be asleep by now? He would linger a little longer. He sipped the cocoa Magsy had left him; it was cold.

It had been foolhardy, he saw that now, to expect his second marriage to be a feather bed. More a bed of nails. His young wife had only just stopped weeping a year after the wedding, the day she discovered her family tree had roots in Germany.

Nance's sadness flustered Morgan. He was adept at comforting patients, the bereaved; kindness flowed out of him. With Nance, he couldn't work out whether she wanted him to step in or hold back. She was delicate, like a trembling branch of some flowering tree, and her reserve ran deep. She had seemed so robust when they were courting, the big pink *generosity* of her had thrilled him. She made him feel young, or at least younger, but now Morgan felt that his old, clumsy hands might break her.

After the longing glances of their engagement, the honeymoon was chaste. It would have been brutish to suggest otherwise to a girl in such distress.

And thereafter? No hand holding. No holding at all. Morgan had missed the tide and was stranded. He wondered, too often, if Nance regretted squandering her youth on him. If Morgan saw her in her slip, he backed out of the room, mumbling apologies. And Morgan was a man who would happily gaze upon his wife in her slip until the end of time. She was a masterpiece, hung in a quiet corner; once you looked closely you couldn't take your eyes off the brushstrokes.

Upstairs, the masterpiece lay face down in her pillows, unable to find a place in the bed that wasn't sticky.

He regrets marrying me, she thought. If he'd known she was German before the big day, he could have backed out, with courtesy and regret. He married her because he was a gentleman, not because he loved her.

When Nance first realized the local doctor was sweet on her, she had been perturbed and delighted. She had wanted him immediately; he didn't scare her, and men could easily scare Nance. There were no hard edges. There was gentleness.

And the house, of course. No Borsetshire woman ever married without contemplating the house that came with the fellow. Homeleigh was solid and attractive, not overly grand. She had daydreamed of how she would run it neatly and prudently, make a cosy home of it. And Morgan would make a mother of her.

Neither of these daydreams came true. Nance cursed her naivety in assuming the physical side of their marriage would simply roll out in front of them, like a length of new carpet.

The chosen spot was a little way off from the house.

Pamela reached it early on the morning of the funeral. Another blank, hot day was rolling off summer's production line just like the day before and the day before that.

She began to dig. Unaccustomed to digging, she was bad

at it. Her back hurt. The hole among the oxeye daisies and the buttercups slowly grew.

Beside the hole lay something wrapped in a tartan blanket embroidered with an 'M'. Pamela stopped digging to sob, and drop to her knees beside the little body.

'Don't, Mavis,' she begged the inert little shape. 'Come back, please.'

She wondered at her emotion. She had no practice at coping with such strength of feeling. *Thank heavens Alec can't see me, crying over daft old Mavis.*

But Mavis had been her friend, and Pamela was honest enough to admit she had few of those.

An estate man, uncomfortable in black, wandered up. 'Here, let me,' he said, but she waved him away.

'I'm perfectly capable of hard work and it's the last thing I can do for my dog.'

The man stood, and stayed, even when her tears began afresh. 'That's very touching, Mrs Pargetter. I only hope there'll be as much feeling at Miss Jane's send-off.'

Business was always brisk at The Bull on the day of a funeral.

The men gathered around the bar. Philosophical. Thirsty.

'Where's Bob?' The landlord was not at his post. 'Bob!' called Dan. His collar was too tight.

'Reckon there'll be a good turn-out?' said Joe Grundy. He was a solid boy, dark-eyed beneath bushy eyebrows. Still a teenager, he was newly married, and he staked his place among the men at The Bull and pronounced upon affairs of the day, just like them. If any of these men commented on the novelty of seeing a Methodist in the inn, he would hypothesize that an apple cider wasn't 'really' booze.

'St Stephen's'll be packed.' Dan raised himself on his toes, peering through the door to Bob's quarters. 'Bob!' he called again. 'Jane was well liked.'

'Was she?' Stan Horrobin was sour in his corner. 'Seemed batty to me.' He called for Bob, too. All the men twitched, like fledglings abandoned in a nest.

Upstairs, Bob threw back his head and the pill went down. Morgan had convinced him to accept these little props; it felt old ladyish, wrong, for a thick-necked, middle-aged heifer of a man to take medication for his nerves. Nobody must know; the small glass bottle lived in the depths of his sock drawer.

'Coming!' he shouted.

His bedroom was, like the rest of the pub's accommodation, untidy and overcrowded. Dirty washing on every surface. The ornaments his wife had favoured jostling on shelves. Hurdles of books and discarded this and that on the grubby carpet. It was a shambles, and Bob had to pick his way to the stairs.

'I say, Bob,' said Dan, when the landlord joined them. 'About time you whitewashed again in here.'

He said it genially. Dan was not diplomatic, but neither was he spiteful. He was being helpful, like he had been helpful with the men filling in his yard, making little helpful comments they hadn't seemed to appreciate either.

'If you don't like it here, Dan Archer,' said Bob, 'stay away.'

That silenced them all. Walter had been about to complain that his tankard was dirty but he simply drained it instead.

They conferred when Bob went out to the back, the consensus being that Bob was having a bad day. Another one. A man could be allowed bad days when he had lost his only son. Jimmy had fallen in Egypt. A patriot. A warrior. A boy who should never have gone further than Felpersham. He and his father shared the silence of the grave; Bob never mentioned his son.

'Reckon we'll have a lock-in!' Stan brightened. Funerals meant a long bout of drinking and crying into beer and singing and, if he could be bothered, a nice fist fight to round off the day.

Bob took up a tray and set off to gather glasses. 'You all know the opening hours. Come ten o'clock I'll shut the doors and get to my bed.'

Mouths fell open. Dan felt sure it was disrespectful not to get drunk at a funeral. 'Must be hard,' he said, venturing into marshy, emotional territory he usually left to Doris. 'Funerals and that, after losing your Jimmy.'

Bob put down the tray and turned, slowly and with intent, towards Dan. 'Mention that name again and you're barred, Dan Archer. I have no son.' He looked around at the other men. 'Got that?'

There were mumbles of assent. Bob resumed picking up empties, thumping them onto the tray.

Nobody was brave enough to break the textured silence, until Morgan said he didn't envy Alec the job of reading the will. 'I've heard it's a queer set-up.'

'I could tell you plenty,' said Walter. He puffed out his chest. 'I have a part to play in the proceedings, like.'

'You?' Stan seemed unconvinced.

'I am, what was it Alec called it, *instrumental*.' Walter, who had been called many things, was particularly pleased with that description.

'Tell us more!' said Dan.

'I would rather die than break the sacred seal,' said Walter.

'Fair enough,' said Dan.

'I'll tell you this, though,' said Walter, who some might say was disappointed by the lack of thumbscrews, 'there'll be more than one will reading.' He enjoyed the reaction this aroused. 'That's all you're getting out of me, me old beauties.'

The sun was blocked in the low doorway by a man with curling black hair, a cap in his hands. In a heavily accented voice, he asked politely for a glass of water.

Bob leaned on the counter. 'You're not meant to come in here, you POWs. Cafés, yes, but not pubs.'

'Give him some water, Bob,' said Dan. 'It's boiling out there.'

Grumbling, Bob brought the man a glass. 'You an Eyetie, then?'

'*Sì*. I am of Padua.' He thanked Bob ornately and Bob said, 'Aw, you're welcome,' and when he had gone, Stan did an impression of him.

'Surprised he didn't ask for blinkin' wine,' said Stan, irked that nobody had laughed at his impression. 'Them Italian prisoners should stay locked up. Fascists, the lot of 'em.'

32

Morgan said, 'Now, Stan, that's the government, not the people.'

Dan said, 'We use Italians on the farm. Top-notch labourers. They come from that Quartershot Camp.'

'I suppose,' said Stan, who was the only man in the room not wearing black, 'it's comical when they try to speak English.'

'Can you talk Italian, Bob?' asked Dan, with a wink at Morgan.

'Why should I? I speaks English, like what all proper men do.'

It was time. They drank up. Filed out in sombre fashion, to lower poor Jane Gilpin into the ground, and discover what she had to say to them.

Her shoes muddy from the first graveside of the day, Pamela made the long journey to St Stephen's on foot, alone. Alec had hitched a lift earlier, Hero beside him on the seat of the gig like a canine wife.

Pamela preferred nature contained in pots or walled gardens, but the hum in the hedgerow lulled her. She had found a bone beneath her dressing table, gnawed by Mavis's remaining teeth and she thought of it now. She thought so hard that it took a while for the tattoo of horse's hooves on dry earth to register. She wiped her eyes, and turned to greet the rider.

It was the Polish officer. Erect on the chestnut's back, legs curved around its belly, no saddle. The way, she assumed, he rode back in Poland. *Peasants are natural horsemen.*

He said, 'Why do you wear black on a day like today?'

'And good morning to you, too,' said Pamela. 'I'm afraid I'm on my way to a funeral.'

'I apologize.' The man leapt down, to land squarely, surely. Dust flew up from beneath his boots. 'A good friend?'

'No.' Always direct, Pamela would mourn Jane to the correct degree without insulting the old girl with mush. 'No uniform today?'

They fell into step. He led the horse. It breathed noisily, wanting to run, to be free. He gave the same impression. 'Not today.' He wore fatigues of some sort, a mustardy brown, frayed and well-worn. His English was fragrant with accent, but perfect in execution. 'I'm joining the birds.' He pointed at the sky. 'Up there.'

'Don't go too near the sun. Your wings might burn. I don't know your name.' *And yet you live in my house.* The war brought about many such peculiarities.

The man clicked his heels, like a prince in the fairy tales Pamela had never read as a child. 'Tadeusz Mier. But call me Kos.'

'If you want me to.' Pamela heard herself, so stiff, so formal. 'Does it mean something, your nickname?' She looked up at him. She looked up at very few people; she looked Alec in the eye, but never found what she wanted there. Some days there was nothing at all.

'It's Polish for blackbird.'

'Because of your hair.' Pamela raised her hand, then dropped it before he could realize she wanted to touch it.

'My ... ?' Kos's smile shunted dimples into his cheeks. 'No, because blackbirds are clumsy on the ground, but swift in the air, and fiercely territorial.'

'I'm Mrs Pargetter.' She held out her hand. 'Pamela.'

34

After shaking hands, they lapsed into silence. The horse harrumphed its impatience.

As First Lady of Lower Loxley, Pamela had a back pocket full of *bon mots* and conversation starters she could dispense from beneath a witty veiled hat, or behind a shield of cigarette smoke. It was a matter of pride that all guests at her table felt entertained. This self-contained man, however, required nothing from her; that was what he seemed to tell her as he strolled, swiping the bushes with a twig.

A fork in the road. Pamela's feet knew the way.

Kos took the other direction, and jumped on the horse. 'The airfield's this way.' The happy horse danced a little.

Shielding her eyes from the sun, Pamela said to the black outline Kos had become, 'You're not supposed to fly, I heard. Because of . . .' She tapped her forehead.

She had noticed the zigzag scar on Kos's brow. Livid and raised, the RAF sawbones who stitched him up would win no prizes for embroidery.

'Just a scratch,' said Kos.

'Won't you get in trouble?'

He reached down, bending out of the sun like a god, and held out his hand. 'Come,' he said.

'I'm sorry?'

'Fly with me.'

She laughed. 'Goodness, how? I must show my face at the funeral, then there's the will, and the house and the chaps, and well, I've never flown.'

'That,' said Kos, 'is why I ask you.'

Pamela could deal with the gauche flirting of the British officers with one be-ringed hand tied behind her back. But Kos was direct, muscular.

'You would love it, Pamela. I can tell.'

'I really don't think you can.' Pamela was not conflicted. She was too busy to jump into an aeroplane. *What would Alec say?* Over breakfast, she recalled, he had said nothing at all, the only sounds the clink of her spoon and the crack of eggs being tapped open. And then he had frowned – thunderously – over a letter he had slit open.

She had asked, 'What's that, darling?', and he had looked at her surprised, as if he believed himself alone.

'Nothing.' He ripped the letter in two with what looked like hatred.

'I can't,' said Pamela to Kos.

The horse turned. Kos looked over his shoulder at her, reining in his beast. 'If you said you didn't want to, that would be fine. But it's not true that you *can't*.'

She didn't watch him gallop away. Pamela was half-irritated. But only half. Which is half less than she usually was when a man didn't follow her script.

A funeral in Ambridge was a three-line whip.

They gathered by the lychgate of St Stephen's church, the sandstone sentry just south of the Am. Frank Brown tailing Nance, her arm through Morgan's. Dan Archer, with hay in his hair. Walter Gabriel trying to control his hiccups. All in black, like a flock of muted magpies.

'Good morning, Pamela.' Agnes took every opportunity to use the Pargetters' first names.

'Mrs Kaye,' said Pamela, hurrying to the church door to locate Alec.

He was handsome and lean in a Savile Row suit tailored to feel like armour. When Pamela took his hand he seemed surprised, but he held onto it and tucked it into his elbow. 'Dreading that damn will,' he whispered.

In a terrible hat, Doris hovered near the open grave. It reminded her of the yard at home. Beside her, Wanda, 'her' land girl, hadn't changed out of her work clothes. Tall, healthy, with bunched curls that peeked out of the front of her headscarf, Wanda wore bib and brace overalls and thick boots. She never wore the government issue wide-brimmed hat, despite Doris's warnings about the sun's wicked ways. She wore lipstick at all times, even while shovelling manure.

Doris heard herself give little coughs, little nervous *Ahem*'s around Wanda. The photograph of Wanda's family home in Bath, a pile almost as grand as Lower Loxley, unnerved her. Bossing around a girl who could buy and sell you was tricky. Doris found herself using the best napkins at dinnertime; Wanda hadn't noticed. 'Christine! Phil! Here, now!' They were being giddy, something Doris generally approved of, but not at a funeral. She asked Wanda, as she nodded 'Hello' to mourners loitering in the sunshine, 'Who was that who dropped you home last night?'

'That's my Mr Bigtime.' Wanda pumped the last ounce of

CATHERINE MILLER

fun out of whatever came her way, and was unapologetically opinionated.

'Odd, him having a fancy car with a war on. Hope there's nothing illegal going on.'

'No, Boss!' laughed Wanda. 'He's with the Ministry of Supply, setting up that ROF over Borchester way. The car's all above board, he motors up from London all the time.'

The new Royal Ordnance Facility would make munitions, and bring employment to the area. 'Funny,' said Doris, 'not to be married if he's old enough to have a big job like that.'

'You mean, *is* he married? No, he's not, Boss.'

Or so he says. For a woman who married her only beau, Doris had a deep distrust of the male sex. Dan said it came from reading too many magazines, but Doris countered it came from keeping her eyes and ears open.

'I might tell him toodle-oo soon,' said Wanda. 'I fancy getting my hands on a dashing Polish airman. They're the best pilots, you know, and so suave. Bad boys!' She nudged Christine; Christine adored Wanda and grew an inch when noticed by her. 'Make sure you go for bad boys when you're older, Chrissie. They're more fun.'

Mrs Endicott paused with them long enough to say, 'Sad day, very sad day. I'm not long for this world myself,' before chugging onwards. She had been prophesying she was not long for this world since Doris was at school.

'Bob! Join us,' called Doris, but the publican pretended not to hear, his paunch severely testing his one good suit.

He rarely dipped a toe in Ambridge waters these days, as if fearful of drowning.

The villagers processed past Alec and his wife as if they were hosts of a party. The Pargetters had a word for each, even Denholm Kaye, who shuffled behind his Agnes, barely socialized, like an old bloodhound released from his kennel.

'Marriage has changed Denholm,' whispered Pamela to Alec. The dandruff snowdrifts were cleared from his shoulders. His tie appeared to be new and his trousers were – incredibly – clean. 'Bit of a hangdog look about him, though.' She felt Alec stiffen.

His insistence that Ambridge was one big family meant he abhorred gossip.

'Does he?' asked Alec, in a low voice. 'Or just possibly does Denholm appreciate his little wife, and his hot dinners and a fire that roars up the chimney all through winter?' *Plus*, he thought but wouldn't say in earshot of ladies, *the man's probably getting his oats on a regular basis for the first time in his life.* 'Agnes isn't a bad sort, and I know there's tittle tattle that she married him for his money, but I'm sure she likes Denholm well enough.'

'Plus the will he'll make when the time comes ... Agnes will like that even better.'

Two boys stood by the grave, enjoying the Gothic rush of it. Both skinny, both shabby, their hair cut with a knife and fork. The younger one, John Perkins, was a cherub. His older brother Billy was more of a devil. The evacuees' shoving and ghostly whoo-ing drew tuts and stares, until Walter administered rough justice with a clip round Billy's ear.

'Have some respect, boys,' he said. Sole caretaker of eight-year-old Nelson since his Annie died, Walter knew what worked and what did not when it came to discipline.

Billy reacted to the mild rebuke as if he'd been shot. 'Ow, mister!'

A young woman rushed up and clipped his other ear. 'There! A matching pair for you!'

'Where'd you spring from?' Billy, both ears throbbing, looked suspiciously from his big sister to the open grave. He would believe anything of Peggy; to a ten-year-old she was all-seeing, all-knowing. Right now, she should be in London not Ambridge.

'I wondered where everyone had got to.' Peggy was slender, a summer bloom, but doughty with it. Her hair was dark and her skin was creamy, and her eyes were shrewd. 'Who's dead, Walter?'

'My lovely Miss Jane,' he said, with a deep sigh.

'Aw, shame, she was a nice old duck.'

The appearance of the vicar, Reverend Henry Bissett, signalled the start of the service in lieu of the silenced bells. All made their way to the church door, Peggy with them, saying to her brothers, 'Come on, boys.' She held out her arm to Walter. 'Let's pay our respects.'

Jane was dispatched. As expected, the vicar was pompous. As expected, Doris sang too loudly. As expected, Denholm fell asleep during the eulogy.

The coffin had made its final journey on the shoulders of local labourers and press-ganged Italian prisoners of war. The villagers had dropped clods of loamy Borsetshire soil into the grave as the vicar spoke a few words.

Uninspiring words, of an idealized person who didn't resemble the woman they knew. But Doris had nodded encouragingly at Henry, because that was what one did with vicars.

There were other fresh graves. Younger folk than Jane were beneath the turf. Doris knew both lads, and their mothers. She held back a few blooms from the wreath to lay on their resting places. She pictured them in their coffins, and her mind hopped to her Jack, sweltering in a tank.

Imagination was a curse.

Blanche was solitary at the head of the procession that left the churchyard and headed for the village hall. She had sat alone in the Gilpin pew, head down, playing with her gloves and barely answering the prayers. She acknowledged no sympathy; she told the vicar she couldn't wait to get back to Woodbine Cottage's empty rooms.

Sunday-quiet, even though it was a Friday, the villagers followed. They had to speed up when Blanche broke into a trot. She was the main attraction at the second big-ticket event in Ambridge's day.

Alec dropped Pamela's arm to overtake Blanche, get there first, doing his duty as ever.

Pamela felt Mavis at her heel and looked down but there was nothing there.

41

Folding chairs slapped down on the village hall parquet. Standing room only.

They were a-buzz, the mourners, as they watched Alec take his seat at a flimsy table set up onstage for the will reading. The set from the latest amateur production stood behind him, placing him incongruously in ancient Japan; *The Mikado* had been a smash hit, the vicar's Nanki-Poo singled out for praise.

In the front row, alone, like a signpost in a field of flattened corn, sat Blanche. Doris went to pay her respects, but was pulled aside by the vicar's wife.

Frances was inserting herself pointlessly into proceedings, directing traffic, pointing at chairs. She often complained to all who would listen, and those who would rather not, about how many tasks fell to the wife of the vicar in a country parish. She said, 'Oh, Doris, leave Blanche be. Some people can't take pity when it's offered. As if I don't have enough to be getting on with.'

That was a cue. Wearily Doris took it. 'How'd you mean?'

'We have this chap lodging at the vicarage.' Frances leaned in, rolled her eyes. 'Archie, he calls himself. Quite the character. If you know what I mean.'

Doris wanted to admire the vicar's wife. Wanted to support her. But like her? No. That was simply not going to happen. 'No, I don't know what you mean, Frances.'

Frances waggled her head, looked around as if they were passing secrets. 'He's a bit . . .' She lifted her hand and let it fall, limp at the wrist. 'You know.'

'Like I said, I really don't know.'

'That way inclined,' hissed Frances.

'I see,' said Doris, who did not see.

'Used to be a valet at The Savoy, and he was working for the major, that nice elderly chap over at Ten Elms. But that all ended a little, let's say, *messily.* I must move him on, Doris. He's a bad influence, we're a vicarage, after all.'

'I could do with another labourer, with the haymaking coming up.'

'Archie's no labourer.' Frances managed to say this darkly. 'Ask around for me, I need to offload him before something happens.'

Like what? wondered Doris, who had caught on. Before this Archie kissed the vicar over his porridge one morning? She couldn't see Henry Bissett driving anyone insane with lust.

Then Doris blushed, grateful for the hundredth time that her thoughts were her own, and nobody could hear her blasphemy. She took a deep breath and sat beside Blanche. 'How're you holding up, Blanche?'

'How'd you think? I just buried my sister.'

If Doris could hear the chatter around them, then so could Blanche. Doris willed Mrs Endicott to pipe down.

'Of course,' she was saying, in the carrying tones of the British bourgeoisie, 'Jane *must* leave her half of Woodbine Cottage to Blanche. Death won't change Jane's devotion. If only dear Morgan could have saved her!'

Blanche, without turning around, said, 'Or was it Morgan that killed her? Eh?' She laughed, a girlish peal that shocked them all. She must have known Morgan was only two rows away, now going a gentle pink in the space visible between his hairline and his beard.

Nance hung her head beside him, and Morgan thought of the souvenir he had taken from Jane's deathbed. *It's mine*, he thought fiercely. *I don't have to share it.* If Morgan truly believed that, would he examine it every other day? Turn it over in his hands. Loathe it.

Magsy rode to his defence, braying, 'If anybody killed Jane, it wasn't my dear brother-in-law. It was someone much closer to home.'

Blanche stiffened.

Other voices picked up the baton.

'Shameful to see Blanche benefit from Jane's death when she caused it!'

'Serve her right if Jane left her money to charity!'

In ancient Japan, Alec cleared his throat. The buzz stopped dead. He would do his duty, but O the pettiness of the village's preoccupation today, when Minsk and Revno had fallen to the Germans, when the besieged Red Army finally surrendered at Brest.

Lower Loxley's true heir – *I'm only the spare!* – had fallen on a First World War battlefield. He had dealt with gunfire, not prattle. And now this strange will would set them all off again.

'Get on with it!' yelled Stan Horrobin.

Alec got on with it, reading out Jane's words. There were no surprises in the *blah blah blah* of the opening statement, her name and address, her status as 'an unmarried gentlewoman'.

It was only when Alec paused, like a show horse preparing for a jump, that the audience leaned in.

Mrs Endicott, who had high hopes of a jet brooch, leaned in.

Agnes, who reckoned ten years of service might be worth a hundred quid or so, leaned in.

Even the vicar, who had many times commented on the wonderful watercolour above the mantel in Woodbine Cottage, leaned in.

Jane's words and Alec's flat, masculine delivery were ill-matched.

'I have not been talkative during my lifetime, but if you take the trouble to listen to my will it has much to say to you. Listen to the language of nature. The names of the plants in my sunny plot have always delighted me, the way they roll off the tongue. I have given them much thought in the making of my will, and I ask you to take note. In the end, a garden asks for so little but gives one so much.'

Alec outlined the estate. He made clear that Woodbine Cottage, and everything in it, had belonged to Jane, and Jane alone.

'No!' The word was shocked out of Blanche.

'Eh?' squeaked Doris.

Alec waited for quiet before carrying on.

'The first instinct of my parents was always to protect Blanche. They left the house to me, confident that I would outlive her, knowing I would stay by my sister's side and provide her with a home without burdening her with its care.'

45

All heard the accusation in that statement. Woodbine Cottage was a trap; Jane had been glued in place by the weight of expectation.

'Mother and Papa knew I would never desert my post. I was Blanche's devotee, from the moment I first tried to say her name, and mangled it with my infant mouth. To me, my big sister was not Blanche but Blabs.'

'How sweet,' said Mrs Endicott.

A few handkerchiefs were taken out, a nose or two blown.

'The nickname suited Blanche. She was lively and charming, talkative, a true blabbermouth. We were happy together in the nursery, Blabs and I. That would change, but I never left her side. Now I ask her to be patient while my final wishes are carried out.'

The hall was agog. None more so than Blanche, who quivered as she watched the top of Alec's bent, Brilliantined head.

'There are five separate bequests.' Alec laid a hand on a pile of envelopes. They were thick, creamy, pre-war quality, each stamped with a red wax seal. 'The gifts will be made at intervals, the whole process to take one year.'

The communal intake of breath drowned out Blanche's, 'You vixen!'

'Each section of the will must be read in public, and will award one plant from my garden plus one personal item. I entrust oversight of this to Alec Pargetter, a lifelong neighbour and one who will not refuse me this last favour. Walter Gabriel will be permitted to enter the garden of Woodbine Cottage to retrieve the selected plants and nurture them at his home.'

Walter called from the back of the hall. 'Ere, Mr P,' he said. 'I hope I'll be allowed to keep Miss Jane's garden nice, and all?'

'We can discuss that later,' said Alec, as Blanche shook her head. 'Jane goes on thus: The very last bequest will be the key to Woodbine Cottage.'

'The last?' Agnes's gasp was echoed around the hall. 'We won't find out for another year?'

Holding up his hand for silence, Alec went on. 'The key will go to the person who deserves it.'

'That person,' said Blanche, 'will be me.'

When Stan said he knew what *she* deserved, nobody assumed he meant the cottage.

'Sounds like Woodbine's up for grabs!' Agnes was shushed by the vicar, but there were more mutterings. Such drama in the midst of a long, hot, wartime summer was heaven sent.

Dan turned to Morgan and said, 'Surely, Jane's just making Blanche wait?'

Ladies fanned themselves. Magsy said, 'Poor Jane was something of a shrinking violet in life, but not anymore!'

Blanche stood. 'I protest,' she said. She had loosened her black coat, it swung around her like the wings of a bat. 'Jane clearly went doolally at the end. I'll contest this stupid will.'

Mild but firm, Alec's tone was one Pamela recognized from when he castigated Hero for eating cowpats. 'Im afraid there are no legal grounds to contest it, Blanche. As executor I've been instructed to allow you to remain in Woodbine Cottage until the final reading.'

'Thank you *so* much.' If looks could kill Alec would be another casualty of war.

There was a stage whisper of, 'Pargetter knows more than he's letting on,' and Pamela winced for him.

'Let's get on with the first bequest.' Alec clambered back on top of the situation. 'Walter?'

Walter made for the steps to the stage, carrying before him a crate covered over with sacking. He held it – and himself – with enormous dignity, a Ruritanian feel to his procession.

'Do not ask me what's in here,' he said. 'For I am sworn to secrecy.' He dodged a kick from Stan.

Sandwiched between the vicar and the pig man, Pamela was impressed by Alec's demeanour, his fastidiousness. Self-control was something she valued; it had been in short supply during his regrettable fling. She tried to catch his eye, ready to offer wifely endorsement. He didn't look her way. A vein in his temple stood out like knotted rope.

She wondered who knew about the affair, then scolded herself. That didn't matter. What mattered was the fact that Pamela had seen off the young pretender. *I won.*

Faces were turned towards her. Even the pig man studied Pamela. 'What?' she asked them all. '*What?*'

From the stage, Alec said, 'I repeat, the first bequest is to Mrs Pamela Pargetter of Lower Loxley.'

'How *very* coincidental!' shouted Blanche, as Pamela rose like a sleepwalker.

Walter milked his role when Pamela joined him and Alec

onstage. Like an end of the pier magician, he whisked away the sacking and produced a plant of ethereal beauty.

A slender stem, trembling in an arc, was weighed down with lanterns of hot pink. It was a burst of beauty in the utilitarian hall, a loud shout of colour and form.

'It's a bleeding heart,' said Walter.

'D'you hear that?' The vicar clasped his hands together. 'Poor Jane's bleeding heart!'

The blooms danced as Pamela took possession of the terracotta pot. 'I'll take great care of it,' she told the audience, while wondering if Jane had somehow found a window to her own heart, which had certainly bled a little in the past year. That's how Pamela would put it, if she were prone to flights of fancy. *Which I'm not.*

Walter said, 'Listen to nature, Mrs Pargetter.'

'Here's your personal item,' said Alec, and he seemed as astonished as Pamela when he handed over a hoop and stick.

'It's just a toy,' said Joe Grundy, disappointed. Beside him his Susan pronounced it 'silly!'

Blanche's chair screamed on the waxed floor as she pushed it back, and barged her way out.

'Don't she want a sandwich?' Walter was already eyeing up the buffet, laid out on a trestle table and not as tempting as in previous years. The war had a terrible effect on many aspects of British life; the proud buffet table had been hit worse than most.

Pamela found herself at the centre of a scrum.

'What's Jane trying to tell you by leaving you a plaything?' Frances was avid. 'That you should have more children?'

'Surely,' said Nance, 'Jane can't accuse you of being childish?'

By the tea urn, Frank, barely recognizable out of his shop-keeper's coat, said to the vicar, 'The Miss Jane I knew would simply leave the house to Blanche and be done with it.'

'Indeed.' Henry's mouth was full; he was on his third sandwich and still had no idea what the filling might be. 'Although Blanche did rather test her towards the end.'

Stan, his ferrety odour overwhelming the company, snarled that blood was thicker than water. 'This is a con. That Pargetter's rewritten the will so his missus gets the house.'

'Yeah.' At his elbow, Stan's wife Connie backed him up. Her pockets were full of scones. 'Birds of a feather and all that. Them as has it gets more. Them with nothing gets more of that, too.'

Agnes butted in. 'The will's a riddle, innit? Jane said listen to the name of the plant. Bleeding heart. It's the letter B!'

'B for Blanche,' said Frances.

'No, *no*.' Agnes was tetchily impatient. 'There are seven letters in Blanche, but only five will readings, see? Blanche ain't getting that house!'

The vicar's wife stopped Pamela as she passed, and relieved her of the hoop. 'I'll give this to Doris, for the evacuee kiddies at Arkwright Hall. You won't want it.'

Pamela took back the hoop. 'That would be rude, Frances. It was left to me.'

'But it's worth nothing,' said Frances.

Walter loomed over them. 'Didn't you hear the will? We have to *listen*. Maybe it's a riddle spelling out a name, maybe it's not, but one thing's for sure – Miss Jane's telling Mrs Pargetter summat.' He bent close to Pamela, his breath a heady mixture of beer and fishpaste. 'Open your ears *and* your heart, missus.'

Agnes drew Frances to one side. 'Can I have a word?' she asked, in a confidential whisper. 'About that bad influence lodging with you at the vicarage. I've had an idea.'

Broom Corner was, ironically, a corner of Borsetshire that rarely saw a broom. The Horrobin homestead looked as if it grew out of the bracken, its lopsided chimney smoking and its balding thatch held together by dirt.

Needle-thin in third-hand clothes, Connie presided over it with hopeless stoicism, appeasing her Stan and somehow getting food down the throats of her children. Now, she cleared the 'best' chair of rabbit skins and set Peggy Perkins sitting on it.

She was always glad to see Peggy; she did her best for the girl's brothers, billeted with her for over a year now. Connie's best wasn't like some other people's best, but she knew Peggy saw that she tried.

'Him giving you jip?' said Peggy, dipping into her handbag in the Stygian kitchen, and slipping Connie a pound note. Apprenticed to a dressmaker, she was the breadwinner of the family.

'My Stan? He's good as gold,' said Connie, whose bruises were, fortuitously, all beneath her clothes.

'Hmm.' In a perfect world Peggy would not allow her brothers to live in such a hole with such a man but her world was far from perfect, so she looked for the good in Connie, who tried to absorb Stan's temper and who showed the children some tenderness. Even though the boys were filthy, the pair of them.

'They behaving themselves?' Peggy fixed John and Billy with a Perkins stare.

'Billy's mad for adders.'

'What's an adder when it's at home?' Londoner Peggy had scant knowledge of rural flora and fauna. She accepted a cup of stewed tea that would not touch her lips. Connie's standards were low; Peggy pushed a dog off the table. Wizbang, the knock-kneed mongrel who followed the children from London, had no manners and less sense.

'Adders are snakes!' Billy was lit up; John shuddered.

'They're poisonous.' Stan slid in, something of a snake himself. He leaned over Peggy, brushing against her to take a slice of bread. She felt the strength of his leer through her dress. 'One bite'd kill a little morsel like you, John.'

John's head bent over like a bloom on Pamela's bleeding heart, his gold hair shining. He wished Peggy could stay; she was a totem of home, a place he feared he was forgetting. Mum's busy kitchen, and the good parlour, and his cold bedroom full of toy soldiers and knitted blankets that weighed him down at night while his parents talked downstairs. 'Would an adder really kill me?' he asked Peggy.

'Best stay away from slithery things,' said Peggy, her eye on Stan.

The other children were in and out. With no big sister to supply hand-me-downs, nine-year-old Maisie was dressed as a boy. Peggy found little Bert to be unfeasibly adorable, and saw how he wanted to be friends with her brothers, but Billy and John were a tight unit. All of them kept out of Vic's way. The teenager, just a year away from conscription, was a chip off the old Horrobin block.

'Thought your Cliff'd be home from hospital by now,' said Peggy.

'He is home, but he's out and about. Had to miss the funeral. Business, you know.'

Peggy didn't know.

Connie was obtuse about her family, even about the changeling son, Cliff, the one who never lied and loved to read and refused to kill a rabbit with his bare hands. 'Starts work next week. They're letting him go back to his apprenticeship at the printers.'

'So he won't fight again?'

Stan's laugh was a growl. 'The army's got no use for him now they've ruined him.'

In a small bedroom off the kitchen, Cliff took his ear from the door as if it had scalded him. He caught sight of himself in the mirror and threw a towel over it.

The surgeons at East Grinstead's Royal Victoria Hospital hadn't so much rebuilt his face as made a patchwork of it. He had lain still for weeks, a metal cage around his head.

Now, Cliff's curling black hair partied above the carnage of his face.

Gentle Cliff had never considered himself handsome, yet he grieved his old, commonplace features.

The right eye remained sparkling, perfect, a charming blue. His left eye was a different blue, and had the hard glitter of glass. His eyelid drooped over it. A horizontal pleat puckered his left cheek, and his mouth was pulled as if whispering an aside.

The lack of symmetry meant his face made no sense; there was a lack of bulk on the left, a lack where there should be flesh. Cliff hated to happen upon his reflection. It had taken time but he could now regard his hands without horror; the burns had healed to baby softness, and they gave him no trouble. At least, none he'd admit to. He could – *Thank God!* – still write, and he did so all day, scratching notes into a leather notebook he hid from Stan. He had ambitions to show it to the doc; Morgan took an interest, and was a different design of man to the one Cliff grew up with.

In the kitchen, John sidled closer and closer to Peggy until he was in her lap. 'We made a new friend,' he said.

'Another evacuee?' Peggy carried out her inventory of the boy as they cuddled. Healthy. Fed. Unharmed. 'Your age, or is he a big boy?'

'He's a man.'

'Eh?'

Connie scoffed. 'He's an *imaginary* friend, Peg. You know little John and his stories.'

'Phew. I was going to say!'

Looking daggers at his little brother, Billy said, 'We don't talk about him to nobody. He's our secret.'

'Fine by me,' said Peggy, and pulled Billy to her, knowing he too needed to be held despite his rowdy resistance.

'Damn embarrassing,' said Alec. 'You getting the first bequest.'

They were almost home. Pamela walked so much in the war. 'Bound to be talk,' she said.

'It compromises me. What was Jane thinking?'

The answer to that had to be *Nobody knows*. The pussycat of a woman had set the cat among the pigeons in Ambridge. Pamela held up the hoop. 'Presumably this is from her childhood, when Blanche was still Blabs and there were no adult complications.' Pamela hesitated. 'No betrayals.' She saw him flinch. He hated to be reminded of his marital misstep but she couldn't help but pick at the scab. 'I have nothing from my childhood,' she realized. All her toys had been for show, overstuffed and cumbersome. The stick that came with the hoop sat comfortably in her hand, as neat as one of her cigarette holders. 'Was she mocking me?'

'No. Not a bad bone in Jane's body.'

'Maybe not, but plenty of mischief, it would seem.'

'Come on, let's get back. I need a sit-down with Dodgy about fitting up the old cottages for fresh chaps, and I'll walk you through the new elevation for repairs to the orangery. Aren't you interviewing a parlour maid later?'

Pamela wasn't listening. She rolled the hoop. It ran away

from her, as if it was alive. She scuttled after it; she hadn't scuttled in a long while. She tried a swish of the stick. 'Ooh!' she said, as the hoop obeyed. She broke into a run and chased it down the slight slope of the road.

'Steady on,' said Alec.

A fork in the road. The hoop was inclined to take the road away from Lower Loxley. Pamela was inclined to follow it.

From the crossroads, Alec called, 'What're you up to, old girl? We have chores!'

A clip fell out of Pamela's hair, and a strand fell over one eye. She was breathless.

Nothing like a last will and testament to turn one's thoughts to the infinite.

Morgan doled out sugar pills to Mrs Endicott, both of them still in black funeral garb. He took her blood pressure and demurred gently at her theory that too much mashed potato could bring on dizzy spells.

'This knee,' she said, tapping one plump leg. 'Not a pain as such. More a tingle. But you know what they say, a tingle today, a coffin tomorrow.'

Morgan had never heard them say that. He pretended to take notes. He doodled his wife's name. Among the masculine trappings on his leather-topped desk was an arrangement of dried peonies beneath a glass dome.

They were from Nance's bridal bouquet, and were as dry as his marriage.

When he married his first wife, they had been green

together. Nance expected him to take the lead. A quiet man, a patient man, Morgan was a loyal man; in twenty years of widowhood he had never joined in with the ribald talk in The Bull. Now, having married a younger woman, he must surely be the topic in there some nights.

Marriage had changed little about Morgan's life. He still contended with Magsy's endless clucking and nursery food, while the woman he had desired for years sat, untouchable, behind glass, like the damn peonies.

Midway through Mrs Endicott's soliloquy he rose and dropped the glass dome into the wastepaper basket. 'Forgive me, go on,' he said, as the flowers crackled and disintegrated amid the shattered glass.

'My spleen, Doctor. I fear it may have fallen out in the night.'

It felt vaguely sacrilegious to catch the bus into Felpersham after burying Jane but needs must. Doris found workarounds for many of their daily needs – unravelling old jumpers to knit new ones, a not entirely successful summer dress made from an old bedspread – but Christine had outgrown her cherry-red T-bars and Doris was no cobbler.

And there was Peggy at the bus stop, fresh as an apple newly dropped to the grass. The girl made light of her visits to Billy and John, but Doris knew travel in wartime was no picnic. 'How's your mum doing?' she asked.

The brightness dimmed a notch. 'She's not doing so well, without Dad, without the boys, you know.'

A mother hen surrounded at all times by chicks, Doris empathized. 'You're a good daughter,' she said.

You wouldn't say that if you heard our rows. It was worry that made them bite at each other. Worry about the boys in what her mother called 'the wilds', and worry about her father, missing now for months on end. 'You getting yourself something nice at the shops?'

Doris marvelled at single girls. Not only had Doris no coupons to spare, but the boutiques were papered with posters exhorting her to make do and mend.

The hoop led Pamela to the airstrip.

Rarely used, it was a rich man's plaything, otherwise neglected. A plane was taxiing, very much a crate, as the airmen would say. She could see tape holding it together.

She slowed, puffing.

The plane slowed, too. Stopped.

Kos leaned out, incongruous in the minuscule window. He pushed up his goggles, and the lightning flash of his scar was livid. 'I dare you!' he shouted.

Pamela rarely listened to anybody, but now she listened to a dead woman, and looked at the hoop in her hand. It had led her here, taken her breath, undone her hair, plastered her face with dust from the road.

She rolled it towards the ticking plane.

Kos flung goggles down to her.

Behind him, a dog with movie-star brown eyes, stared out at her.

'A *dog*?' she said.

'I don't know him,' said Kos. 'But he seems nice. Get in.'

It wasn't easy in her tailored black skirt. She listened to the hoop and endeavoured not to care that Kos could see her knees. The dog budged up.

They didn't speak as the plane climbed.

Ambridge fell away, the fields around it mere shapes through the rattling glass of the cockpit.

The noise was incredible. Pamela's stomach looped the loop. The plane vibrated as if it might come apart and the dog barked non-stop.

Half an hour ago Pamela had been in the village hall. *And now I'm in the sky.* Ambridge grew smaller and smaller as they climbed.

When they landed, Pamela was exhilarated by the simple fact that she hadn't died up there. Her body was known to her for the first time in a long time; it was alive with sensation.

Kos helped her down.

It was a moment before she could walk. She didn't know that the butterflies bobbing alongside them on the way back to the house were Common Blues and Large Skippers, but they matched her mood.

She was grateful that Kos didn't need to talk.

Woodbine Cottage was at its prettiest in the gauzy lilac light of early evening. The honeysuckle was waking up, but Blanche didn't notice as she chain-smoked in a chair. She was in a whirlpool of resentment, her mind working furiously.

The villagers were all so *tentative* around her, unsure what to say about this strange calamity. No doubt some of them would be hooting over their supper: *I'd laugh if this happened to one of them!*

She took off on a tour of the cottage, punching a cushion here and kicking a table leg there. The small rooms unfolded, full of inherited furniture and paintings and antimacassars and side tables and bonbonnières and vases and decoupaged fire screens and needlepoint rugs and standard lamps with ruffled shades.

None of it is mine.

The house sat in limbo, and Blanche levitated within it.

At a noise from the garden, Blanche leaned out of a top window that winked from the thatch. 'Don't just let yourself in like that, Walter.'

'Didn't want to disturb you, Miss B. Gonna give The Greenhouse a tidy and I've brought a smashing bag of manure for Miss Jane's roses.' He held up a stinking sack with pride.

'They're not Jane's roses anymore, she's dead,' said Blanche, and saw Walter start. 'I feel quite ill with the stress of it all.'

'Owt I can do?' asked Walter, who knew the elder Miss Gilpin had the constitution of an ox.

'Yes, you can leave me be. This garden is no longer your business.'

'But it needs care! It needs love!' Walter looked over the beds of jubilant flowers and the shushing grasses and the little pond he and Jane had built together. 'Them roses need to be shown who's boss. And what about Miss Jane's poison corner?' He bent down to the belladonna, the foxgloves, the cuckoo pint. 'Regular little witch's brew she had going here.'

'The garden can fend for itself. I have to, after all.' Blanche was hungry but there was nothing in the pantry. Well, there was plenty, but Blanche had no idea how to convert any of it into dinner. The plucked chicken looked obscene.

'Let me look after the garden, please.' Walter gazed up at her, a plaintive Romeo to her bitchy Juliet. 'I'll do it for nuthin',' he said, for possibly the first time in his life.

A knock at the door set Blanche scowling again. 'Off, Walter, off you go!' she shouted, as if he was a stray mutt, before slamming the window shut.

'Henry?' she said when the front door framed the vicar in all his sloping-shouldered glory. 'I'm not up to callers.' *Especially do-gooders.*

Beside Henry stood a slim young man, well-dressed, neat as an apostrophe. 'Bear with me, dear Blanche. Do you recall we discussed finding you a maid to replace the girl who fled to the mill, well, no not a maid, perhaps, more, um, a housekeeper ...' The vicar turned to the young man. 'Oh dear, what *are* you?'

'I'm Archie.' He held out his hand, forcing Blanche to take it. 'Archie Jackson, pleased to meet you.'

They were soon indoors, on soft seats, and the vicar was rattling along his rehearsed speech. Frances had made it clear; he was *not* to return with Archie in tow. 'I can vouch for Archie's temperament, and he has an outstanding reference from The Savoy, and he comes from a most respectable family and he is honest and clean and his last appointment, with the major, well, it . . . um . . .'

'It came to a natural end,' said Archie. His accent was tinctured London, endings stressed and intonations ironed out. 'Let's leave it at that.'

'Frances does so want our spare room back, so interrogate him, dear lady.'

Before Blanche could marshal a question, Archie had some for her. What duties did she need taking care of, he wanted to know. What was the turnover of staff, were all meals included, would his evenings be free?

'I have no idea,' answered Blanche to every query. 'And I don't care.'

Archie stood. 'I'll take the position,' he said. 'Twenty-two shillings a week, and I'll see the room if I may.'

Directed upstairs, he was soon back again, taking the narrow steps three at a time. 'Oh no, that won't do. Won't do at all. I'll take the flowery one with the big brass bed.'

'That's Jane's room,' said Blanche.

'She doesn't need it, does she?' Archie rubbed his hands together. 'Now, how about I rustle us up something tasty? You look done in.' In the pantry he met the chicken. 'Ooh, lovely!' he said.

The vicar had gone. He could move very fast for a man who ate three courses at every meal.

JULY

Nance was still heavy with sleep, and sublimely comfortable deep down in the bedcovers.

Her husband's foot lay companionably against her own. Male, hairy. She moved, and as she knew it would, the old mattress dipped and rolled him her way.

'Nance,' he murmured.

The curtains were flung open.

Summer was all over the room, lighting up every corner. Magsy's portly silhouette was before them, as she chirruped, 'Up you get, lazybones! Laundry day, let me at those sheets.' She found Nance in the tumbled bed. 'We're expected at the Women's Committee, dear. Shake a leg.'

Nance fumbled to pull down her nightdress, where it had ridden up.

Morgan fled as if the bed was on fire.

'I didn't hear you knock,' said Nance. Her tone was as mild as ever, but she felt savage.

Already tugging Morgan's pillow out of its case, Magsy

didn't seem to hear. 'First Tuesday of the month, that's when my sister did the linens and that's when I do them.' She smiled at Nance. 'Most particular, she was.'

The small room, off an antechamber, next to a closet, was furnished with ad hoc furniture, no curtains at the windows. As Doris sat and waited for the other members of the Women's Committee to arrive, she kept her handbag on her knee, discomfited by how different Lower Loxley felt since the RAF moved in. Was there no North Star Hitler couldn't dislodge?

She checked the dainty watch on her plump wrist. It told her, as ever, that she was running late. She hoped Wanda had woken up by now; she had left the girl asleep where she found her, against a hayrick.

Knackered, like the rest of us, she thought. Wanda looked so peaceful, and so young, her complexion cream and jam, her limbs flung about as if she had landed from a height. Big leather gloves on her townie hands. The men had schooled her in the setting up of the sheaves; Wanda had been proud of her neat wigwam; Dan had said, 'That'll do.'

High praise indeed.

Three weeks now, for the corn to ripen. *Lucky corn*; all it had to do was sit around. Before the war, Doris would have said they'd hear the church bells three times and then the corn would be ready, but now, of course, the bells were mute.

The hole in the yard opened something up inside Doris, a similar chasm, a similar rapacious mouth. The farm was always one bad season from disaster. Every penny in the Archers' bank account was forged in their sweat; they'd raided it last year to sort the cowshed.

And now that same cowshed was missing a side wall. The flapping tarpaulin upset the cows, clever, languid animals that they were. Stating the obvious over his butty, Dan had said earlier that the shed and the barn must be patched up while the weather was still warm.

'Shall I just go and shake our money tree, Dan Archer?' Doris had asked.

Hearing his whole name in that tone of voice, Dan had hightailed it out of the farmhouse and got on with dosing lambs.

She would give him an extra sausage at dinner. To atone.

There was nobody to leave the Archers a house, no big bequest to save the day.

Doris sat up as Pamela led in the other committee members. 'Ah, Doris, there you are. We can begin.'

AMBRIDGE WOMEN'S COMMITTEE
MEETING MINUTES

Date: 1st July, 1941
At: Lower Loxley
Chairwoman: Pamela Pargetter
Present: Frances Bissett, Emmaline
Endicott, Doris Archer, Blanche Gilpin,

Agnes Kaye, Nance Morgan, Magsy Furneaux,
Susan Grundy.
Minutes: Frances Bissett

1. Pamela asked for a volunteer to take
the minutes and when nobody volunteered
she told me, myself, i.e. Frances Bissett,
spouse of Reverend Henry Bissett, to do
the honours.

2. Pamela welcomed newcomer Blanche. She
said to Blanche 'If there's anything we can
do' and Blanche said 'Like what exactly'. I
myself noted that Blanche is already out of
black, and shared with her that I was in
black for a year when my dear papa died.
Mrs Endicott said that those who are left
to live must truly live and told Blanche
her costume was most fetching. Some of us
did not agree but did not say so.

3. Pamela welcomed newcomer Susan and
Mrs Endicott began to reminisce about
Susan's wedding to Joe Grundy and then
about her own wedding and then about
weddings in general and Pamela said 'Can
we please get on?'

4. Pamela asked Doris how the billeting
of evacuees was coming along and Doris said
quite well although it broke her heart when

people told her they didn't want filthy city
children all covered in fleas. Pamela said
she hadn't anticipated such a full answer.

5. Agnes said 'Evacuees are
bomb dodgers.'

6. Doris said 'Evacuees are children.'

7. Pamela said we must plan the Harvest
Festival and Flower and Produce Show. Mrs
Endicott said 'Adolf won't stop us showing
off our marrows.' Pamela said 'Quite so.'

8. Pamela said we will combine the
Harvest Festival and the Flower and Produce
show this year. Doris said 'But why?' and
Pamela said 'Because of the war, Doris,
dear' and asked were there any suggestions
for the date and then she said it will be
on Sunday 28th September. Doris said 'That
is late for flowers and vegetables the show
will be all cabbages' and Pamela said 'Dear
Doris always the backbone of our committee'
and repeated that the Harvest Festival will
be on Sunday 28th September.

9. Agnes said do we think Jane's will
is a word puzzle, and the 'B' of bleeding
heart is for Blabs.

10. Pamela said that really wasn't our
business and could we get back to the
matter in hand.

11. Blanche said her foolish sister had made it everyone's business. Note to self: ask Henry to have a word with Blanche re: her attitude to the dear departed.

12. Pamela said 'Can we please concentrate?' and asked Doris to take charge of collecting jumble for the Arkwright Hall jumble sale and Doris said 'Jumble? We are all wearing our jumble these days!'

13. Mrs Endicott said she had heard that Stan Horrobin is taking bets on who will inherit Woodbine Cottage.

14. Blanche said 'What are my odds?' and Mrs Endicott told her she was the favourite but the Pargetters are also considered a good bet because of the first bequest.

15. Pamela said in quite a cross voice that we must all focus.

16. Nance suggested we pool spare coupons for the pregnant ladies of the parish and the poor. Agnes said 'Spare coupons are you having a laugh?'

17. Nance went all pink and said the system isn't fair because rich people can buy better clothes that last longer while the less well off buy shoddy stuff that wears out. Note to self: ask Henry to have a word with Nance re: socialist tendencies.

18. Pamela said that was all very well but who will make the bunting for the Harvest Festival.

19. Mrs Endicott said she is knitting socks for our brave boys overseas and Doris said 'Why not knit them a boat to bring them home?' and Agnes said 'hear hear' and Pamela said this did not come under the scope of the committee.

20. Doris said did anybody feel more anxious now that France has surrendered because that means the Nazis are just over the Channel.

21. Mrs Endicott said she hasn't had one good night's sleep since the war began.

22. Agnes said 'Oi Pamela aren't you going to tell us to concentrate? What are you looking at out of that window? If I didn't know you better I'd say you was eyeballing that handsome airman ooh he's a looker all right.'

23. I myself said that we were not here to indulge in lustful thoughts.

24. Agnes said 'I likes a lustful thought every now and then' and nudged Mrs Endicott rather hard.

25. Mrs Endicott said she had a nice bit of tripe in her handbag for little Mavis and where was the dear little doggie.

26. Pamela wrapped the meeting up very
abruptly and, in the opinion of at least
one person present, rather rudely.

To enter the woods was to cross a border.

Billy and John left the punishing heat behind and sank into a cooler, quieter Friday. They were ignored, the wood was busy, and they were just two more mammals going about their business.

No, *three*. Wizbang zigzagged crazily in front of them, high on the smorgasbord of scents.

Brave explorers, the boys trekked towards the shimmering city they had discovered. An owl hooted; they swivelled, but it was impossible to tell where it sat in the canopy. Cliff had told them they were tawny owls, probably babies.

It took almost an hour before they saw the sign: 'Camp 48'.

He was there, waiting, watching out for them, on the other side of a wire fence that made indentations of diamond shapes on your skin if you leaned against it. He was sheltered from the rest of Quartershot POW Camp by a long low hut, and the boys were sheltered from the rest of the world by the wood.

A tall man, drawn with a generous hand, Luca Scuderi wore chocolate-coloured battle dress and a collarless shirt. Something lit him up when he spotted Billy and John.

They hastened, feet slithering on the slope. Their friend may have been a secret, but he was not imaginary. He was flesh and blood. First encountered when the boys were building a den against the fence, Luca was now a huge part of their social diary. Different, exciting, and keen to listen, in a way no other grown-up ever was.

'I speak English all time now,' he said, as they settled down on their respective sides of the fence. It enfolded the Nissen huts like a basket full of eggs. 'I speak good, yes?'

'Oh yes, really very good,' said John.

'You're all right,' said Billy. 'Silly accent.'

'Ha! You are like my *nonna*. She want miracles too. Talk *italiano* to me, Billy. Oh? You cannot?'

They all laughed. Luca was, as they often said on the hike home, a proper card.

'What you have for me?' Luca nodded at the bag over Billy's arm.

Delicacies from Connie's kitchen were pushed through the wire. Hard bread. A stale biscuit. Two mealy apples.

Looking on, Wizbang vibrated with desire.

Accepting the gifts, Luca's warm brown eyes, the whites fluorescent, widened with Christmas glee. *'Delizioso! Grazie, ragazzi, grazie!'* His nose was a knife and his hair cleaved close to his head. He was both different to, and the same as, the men Billy and John knew.

'There is football match tomorrow,' said Luca as he demolished an apple. 'Big shouting, big happiness.'

'Are you playing?' Billy fancied himself as a footballer. He had no football, though. 'Are you any good?'

'I am great!' Luca puffed out his chest and the boys fell about. 'But no. I am not allow.'

'That's not fair,' said John. He hated to hear how Luca was ostracized inside Quartershot. Just for being a proud Italian. For not liking the rules.

Luca shrugged. He was temperate. Philosophical. Turning, he pointed to the red circle on the back of his jacket. 'This is target. So they shoot me if I escape.'

'Don't escape!' John hadn't meant to say it quite so passionately.

'Don't be daft, Luca,' said Billy. 'Tommies wouldn't shoot you in the back.' The war was simple. Good versus evil. Tommies were the good guys.

'Men are men,' said Luca. 'You see this when you are bigger.'

'Dunno if we can come again,' said Billy. 'Bit dicey.'

'Shut up, Billy!' John sat up on his knees. 'We can come again, Luca, honest!'

Billy poked his brother. 'You nearly gave the game away to Peggy. She'd kill us if she knew we were here.'

John rubbed his arm, his little chin set. Peggy's version of killing them would involve a right royal telling off, plus – *Oh, God!* – the knowledge that they'd disappointed Mum. Mum's disappointment was a more compelling deterrent than the gallows.

They all stood. Luca said, 'You do what you do.' His brown eyes were liquid, and held a universe of feeling. 'But I miss you if you are not here. You are like my sons. I see you, I think of them. Next time I show photograph.' He closed his eyes for a second. '*Scusi*. If. If. You do not have to visit old Luca.'

Billy said, 'You're not old.'

John said, 'You look like you're the same age as our dad.'

The boys had discussed this. Billy maintained Luca was nothing like Dad. John would get aeriated, insist he was, kind of.

'I am proud,' said Luca, 'to be like your dad.'

'He's in—' John nearly toppled at Billy's push.

'Hey, loose lips sink ships.'

'But it's only Luca,' said John.

'He's Italian. He's the enemy.'

'Don't be mean! Luca's someone's daddy, I mean dad!'

There was a shout from within the camp. 'Scuderi!'

'I go. Some punishment. I break silly rule. *Arrivederci.* If you no come, I understand.' He stumbled over the word until he was sure he had got it right. He turned away.

He was sad, and so were the boys as they pushed back through the wood.

Not Wizbang, though. He chased a rabbit and was happy as Larry ...

The umbilical cord that connected Doris to Brookfield was taut as she drove north through the village in the farm's bone-rattler of a truck.

Dinner dishes waited in the sink, the floor was un-mopped. Nothing got done at the farm if Doris wasn't around to check and reward. It was only thanks to her vigilance and, yes, nagging, that the hen-pecked contractors had made good progress on the yard; the ugly hole was filled in. Tomorrow they could make a start on the standing for the barn.

Now she had other business to tend to. Billeting business, the only reason Doris was using precious petrol. She braked.

House martins swooped in and out of their dried mud apartments under Broom Corner's roof, the only beings who would willingly cohabit with the infamous Horrobins.

She looked down at the little girl beside her. Irene Kosten had declined her hand when Doris met her from the train at Hollerton Junction. 'We won't stay long, dear. After this we'll go straight to your new home, promise.'

The girl gazed levelly up at her as if Doris hadn't spoken. A red-headed little thing, skinny. Doris knew the skinniest foals were the tough ones. She smiled, although she was learning that smiles didn't work on Irene.

'You again?' For Connie, this was a warm greeting. 'Checking up I ain't cooked and eaten the Perkins boys?'

'Rules are rules, Connie, I have to make my rounds. I know Billy and John are thriving,' said Doris. 'Cliff about?' She sensed the lad somewhere in the shadows of the house. When he was sick and shocked and bandaged up in the Royal Victoria hospital, it was Doris who made the journey to visit him. *We have a bond*, she thought. Doris took bonds seriously, just ask Mother Cat; the moggy's return had moved her to tears when it sashayed into the kitchen. Her pact with Cliff – unspoken but real – had some magical, almost religious link to her Jack. She was keeping Jack safe by keeping Cliff safe. *Or something like that*. 'Billy and John not about?'

'Off with their imaginary friend.'

In a pair of boy's shorts, Maisie peeked out from under the table. 'He's real,' she said. 'I followed them once.'

She was ignored, as children were. She was with Stacey, her arms about her, but Stacey was a one-man dog and was stand-offish. The dog knew it was her constancy, her watching of the gate, that had brought Cliff home from the war, and she was not to be distracted by soft little hands. Maisie gave up on Stacey and came to stand in front of Irene.

Irene took no more notice of her than Stacey did.

'I like your doll.' Maisie pointed at the large red-headed simulacrum of Irene, its clothes more luxurious than anything Maisie had ever worn.

Irene held the doll away from Maisie.

'Stan about?' asked Doris.

'Out on business,' said Connie, straight-faced.

Funny business, thought Doris.

'I can't have 'er.' Connie gestured at Irene. 'Got me hands full as it is.'

Doris almost laughed at the notion of billeting a girl with Stan Horrobin. 'This little one's for Furnivall Manor.'

'Lucky her. Lap of luxury. Queer little duck, in't she?'

'They didn't turn up to collect her, so . . .' Doris was put out. Not because of the long drive to Furnivall Manor, but because the whole country should pull together, manor houses and hovels alike. 'Ah. The man of the moment!'

Cliff had perfected entering rooms without noise. Expert in angling his face so that his good eye was towards company, the distaff side to the wall.

'Dr Seed tells me you're not going back to the printing works,' said Doris.

Rearing up, Connie said, 'Don't you have nothing better to do than gossip about the Horrobins?'

'Morgan doesn't gossip,' said Doris. 'He's concerned.'

Cliff said, 'I couldn't, I just, I'm not who I was before ... I can't explain.'

Oh yes you can, my lad! Doris knew Cliff was full of words – big fancy ones at that – but he was suffocating in this house, the words all pressed back down his gullet. She had a parachute for him; she unfurled it. 'There's a job going at Arkwright Hall, the school they've set up for evacuees. Tailor made for you. Teaching mainly, helping the kids read, and a bit of caretaking. They need someone with a love of books, someone who's kind.'

Dukes up, Connie spoke before her son could do so. 'Why let him go there and be mocked? Cliff'll stay at home, where he's safe.'

'It'd be good for him, he can—' Doris chided herself for talking over Cliff's head. *If he's old enough to get his face blown off for his country, he's old enough to make his own decisions.* 'Cliff, why not give it a try? Start building a life out there in the world?'

Connie was there again. 'Look what the world done to him, and not even a thank you! Why should we worry about the world when it doesn't care about us? Our world stretches to the end of Broom Meadow, thank you very much.'

Doris was dogged. 'Cliff? At least consider the job. They'll pay you, and there's a grand library. Might lead to something else.' Might scatter a trail of crumbs from Broom Corner, where there were no books except for the ones Cliff saved up for.

'But this ...' Cliff gestured at his face, the other side, the side Doris couldn't see.

'Won't matter a jot, love. Just roll up and tell them I sent you. Have a nice chat.'

'Nobody,' said Connie, knuckles on the table, 'is having a chat about nothing.'

'Let's be off, Irene.' Doris had forgotten the pale passive little girl. 'Oh, Connie, before I forget.' She laid a document on the table. 'Get Stan to fill in these forms.'

If Connie was a sheepdog, all the hackles on her back would have risen. *'Forms?'* she spat, as if forms were the work of the devil.

'It's a census. For War Ag. Every farm and smallholding has to set down its livestock and machinery and acreage and what have you. It'll take less than five minutes.'

'It'll take less than that. He'll chuck 'em in the fire. Your Dan and his War Ag should mind their own business. All right for you, with your hundred acres.'

One hundred and eight to be precise, and Doris could walk every inch of it. Some nights she went to bed feeling as if she'd done precisely that.

Connie was opening her beak for another rant when little Maisie screamed and ran to her.

'She hit me, Mum!'

'Irene,' said Doris, astonished, embarrassed. 'We do *not* hit our friends.'

Irene was composed. 'She mustn't touch Sukie,' she said, arranging the doll's curls.

Connie was not composed. 'The little brat!'

As Doris spirited the evacuee out of the house, Connie shouted merry hell after them. Cliff caught up with Doris, slouchy hat pulled over one eye. 'Don't mind Mam. She's noisy but she doesn't mean it. Can I cadge a lift?'

'We'll be glad of the company, won't we, Irene?' Twenty minutes of knowing Irene had taught Doris not to expect an answer.

'Might pop into The Bull,' said Cliff, leaping up into the truck. 'Have a pint.'

The casual mention of a pint made Doris want to cheer; it would be a huge step forward for Cliff to brave The Bull. *Men need their pubs*, she thought.

No kindly light spilled out as they approached the inn; blackout rules made a tight box of it. As the truck braked, the door of The Bull opened and a little tobacco-scented life leaked out, along with Alec in the dun-coloured gear of the Home Guard. Bob came out after him and handed over a box of matches.

'Cliff!' Alec rushed to greet the younger man as he jumped down from the passenger side. He pumped Cliff's hand. 'Good to see you out and about.'

Bless you, thought Doris, *for noticing him*. As Bob waddled back into his fiefdom she rolled down her window and called out, 'Your begonias're looking a bit sorry for themselves this year!'

The red and yellow and pink begonias were staples of Ambridge life: the village version of the ravens at the Tower of London. Frothy, happy, and Bob's magnum opus.

Bob went to the nearest white planter. He overturned it and shook it until the plants, earth and all, fell onto the road.

'Now now!' said Alec.

'I didn't mean anything by it, Bob.' Doris wished she had held her tongue.

He was gone, swallowed by The Bull and leaving stupefaction behind him.

Alec recovered first. 'Cliff, let me buy you a beer.'

Backing away, melting into the comfortable darkness, Cliff mumbled that, actually, come to think of it, he had to get home.

'I tried, Doris,' said Alec.

'You did,' she replied. She put the truck into gear and it nosed through the night, passing the rutted track that led to Brookfield. Doris fancied she felt the vehicle tug to make the turn, like the plodding cart horses always did.

'Gosh, it's dark,' she said to Irene. Perhaps the little Londoner was unnerved by the countryside's seamless night. The hectic machinations of haymaking done for the day, the lanes weren't silent – they were never that – but the different, other-worldly sounds of rural night would take getting used to.

Irene said nothing. Well-dressed, hair brushed, holding a small hard case, the girl nonetheless gave off a feral feel. Doris didn't hold with disliking children; one might as well dislike a flower, or a lamb. *Mind you*, she thought, *there was that one lamb that ate its twin* ...

Furnivall Manor was a black puzzle shape against the night sky. It was tall, boxy, in the way of Elizabethan taste. Older than Lower Loxley, it lacked that house's charisma. As the truck lurched up the drive, the house's beams, bandages of black across the white wattle and daub, firmed up. A grand house with no family, it lay a little too far south to feel connected to Ambridge. Leased out for parcels of time to those who could afford it, it stood aloof from village life.

Irene spoke. 'It looks empty.'

It did. 'It can't be,' said Doris. *I could've sworn they said today.* 'They'll be in, they sound like lovely people.' Although lovely people didn't write to you, ever so particular, asking for one well-behaved little girl, and then neglect to turn up and collect the aforementioned well-behaved little girl.

'They don't want me,' said Irene.

'Of course they do.' Doris foresaw herself taking Irene back to the farm. Christine would be a wasps' nest if she had to share her room with sullen Irene and the doppelganger doll.

The heavy bellpull started a clatter inside the house, but no footfall.

'They don't want me,' said Irene again, just as a well-built man in shirtsleeves appeared around the side of the house.

He was wiping his hands on a tea towel. 'Aye?' he said, and he did not say it amiably. As Doris explained, he pulled down his sleeves and did up his collar.

'Right,' he said, still with no hint of a welcome. 'Well, the family's gone to their place in London. I'm looking after the place and they said nowt to me about an evacuee.' He did not look at Irene.

'I've got the letter at home,' said Doris, feeling events slide away from her. She held tight onto Irene's hand.

'What's all this?' A woman, primly dressed in a drab uniform with a starched collar, bustled around the house, arms folded.

'Just a mix-up, Nanny, you get yourself back indoors.'

Doris explained, and Nanny said, 'Aw, poor pet!' Her accent, like the man's, had an up-and-down, bendy rhythm that Doris recognized as Geordie. 'You poor little waif and stray, let's get you indoors.'

That's more like it, thought Doris, passing the man with her nose held high.

In a lit room, with the remains of a meal on the table, Doris began to relax. It was warm, domestic. Nanny 'kept it nice', as Doris's mother might have said.

Nanny moved fast on her nun-like shoes. She put her arms around Irene before the child had a chance to recoil, and held her tight. Over her head she said to Doris, 'Don't mind Beacham. His bark's worse than his bite.'

'Are you ... ?' began Doris.

'A nanny? Yes.' Nanny laughed. 'It's not me name, it's me calling. I've always been a nanny, missus. Bairns are my life.'

Beacham's head brushed the low ceiling, but Nanny was barely Irene's height. She took Irene's suitcase, unbuttoned the girl's coat with practised, practical hands. 'I always say my brother stole all the grub when we were bairns. He barely fits in this room.'

'Something's not reet,' said Beacham. He regarded Irene as if she was a stubborn stain on washday. 'The mistress said nowt to me.'

There was no need for Doris to protest. Nanny made her case for her.

'Look, they promised this nice lady they'd take the kiddie, and we're here to keep the place ticking over until they get back, so let's step in and look after this poppet until the mistress gets bored of London.' Nanny smiled at Irene who did not smile back. 'We'll make our own fun, won't we?'

The twitch in Beacham's jaw suggested he could say more, much more, if Doris wasn't there.

'Irene's my responsibility,' said Doris. 'If you have any doubts . . .' The pull of home was a siren song in her ear. The lure of her armchair, the warm weight of Glen the sheepdog at her feet, and, if she played her cards right, a cup of tea made just the way she liked it from Dan.

'We'll call them tomorrow, sort out this sorry mess,' said Beacham. 'Send her back where she came from.'

'For tonight, pet, you can sleep in the front bedroom, the prettiest one.' Nanny took up the little case.

'Mind if I tag along?' Doris made a point of inspecting the accommodation; it varied from house to house. One Peckham four-year-old slept in an airing cupboard at Nightingale Farm. *And she loves it.*

Nanny held out a hand to take the doll.

'No!' Irene's temper flashed again.

'That's Sukie,' said Doris. 'She's special.'

Nanny bowed her head. 'I do apologize, Irene. You take very good care of Sukie, I can tell. She's *so* bonny.'

That almost got a smile out of Irene.

One push at a green baize door and the intimate cosiness of the servants' hall gave way to the soaring woodwork of the great hall. Despite July's profligate warmth, the air was chilly as they crossed the black and white chessboard of the floor. *As chilly*, thought Doris, *as the careless toffs who live here.* She was grateful that Irene would be looked after by the lower orders, and not the selfish folk who ordered up Irene like a pet kitten and then forgot to collect her.

Room inspected and found more than adequate – *Like The Ritz!* Doris thought – Nanny walked Doris to the gate. 'I can see you're worried, but there's no need. My brother ...' Here she looked over her shoulder as if he might materialize. 'He has his little ways, but he's a good man really, in here.' She struck her breast. 'And I *live* for children. Irene's in safe hands.'

It wasn't Nanny's hands Doris was worried about. She did *not* like the smell of Beacham.

Don't ask; don't tell.

That was the one rule at Lower Loxley cocktail hour. Pamela disapproved of the black market but wasn't above the occasional paddle in its oily waters. Only a fool would neglect to keep the booze flowing with a dozen chaps on the premises.

'Remind me, dear lady,' said Dodgy, 'how to make a sidecar.'

'Cognac, triple sec, lemon juice.' She was watching the door as if she was at a club and not in her own home. She had only just regained her land-legs after her flight. 'And *lots* of ice.'

The other men talked of Kos, possibly because he was the latest arrival. Possibly because his tangible glamour had ensnared them all.

'No, *no*, Dodgy, twice as much cognac as the other ingredients.'

All fingers and thumbs in his dated dinner jacket, Dodgy was at least *there*, and helping. More than Pamela could say for Alec, last seen dressing for dinner in his unending grim mood. She could blame the war, but really, the war was just weather now. She could blame the will, but Pamela knew better.

It was that letter that ate at her husband. The one he tore in two.

Chaps arrived. Compliments dusted off and handed over to the lady of the house. She looked 'charming', apparently, 'quite the thing'. One not much older than her Gerald blurted out, 'Gosh, you'll do, Mrs Pargetter!' and the others laughed.

A sexless mascot, despite the gown of draped bronze chiffon, Pamela never took the clumsy flirtation seriously. Her hair pleased her tonight, though, bouffant and pleated at the back, a diamond pin trembling in it.

Like smoke, Pamela glided through the company. When Alec joined them he didn't kiss her cheek, even though she turned it his way. Hero, sleek and dark like his owner, padded in his wake.

'I loaned old Kos a monkey jacket for tonight,' said Terence.

Pamela was watching the door again. She took a slug of her sidecar and decided that Dodgy must never be allowed behind the bar. She hoped Kos wouldn't feel too out of place among these high-born men who wore their dinner jackets and bow ties as casually as Doris Archer wore her headscarf.

'Kos,' said Terence, 'is so terrifically *moody*.'

'Proud folk, the Poles,' said someone. 'Must hurt, seeing your country butchered.'

It occurred to them all that the island they stood on was separated from the butchers by a mere moat.

An eager, crocodile-toothed pilot officer said, 'Should we mention Lwow? He must be awfully cut up about it.'

'Lwow?' Those Polish W's turned to V's in the mouth; the word was all sharp edges. Pamela asked, 'What about this Lwow?' She pumped Alec for intel daily but he was stingy, telling her she wouldn't want to know.

'The massacre, darling.' Alec put a hand on her shoulder. It was warm and she felt owned and she felt grateful. Which was peculiar; Pamela strove never to belong too completely. *His indifference is turning me into a simpering village lass.*

The chaps filled her in on the Nazi sweep of Polish intelligentsia, artists and thinkers. 'Shot. All of 'em,' said Dodgy, looking into his glass.

'Who's for another?' Pamela returned to the bottle of cognac. 'Those awful Nazis.' Such a mild insult; she called the housekeeper worse. 'Does Kos come from that part of Poland?'

'Come from it?' laughed Terence. 'Kos *owns* it!'

'Well,' said Alec, grave and paternal. 'Shouldn't say that anymore. It was all stripped from his family. His land. His castles.'

'*Castles?*' Pamela shook the cocktail shaker.

'Castles, dear heart,' said Dodgy. 'Plural! Chap's an aristocrat.' He looked past her. 'Speak of the devil! Get yourself over here, Count Tadeusz Maria Jan Mier! Did I say it right?'

'Perfectly.' Kos had brushed his hair over his scar. Wearing the dinner jacket with élan, he smelled both clean and exotic. He took a thin stemmed glass and raised it at Pamela. '*Na zdrowie.*'

Her attempt to echo the toast amused him. Pamela moved away. Sometimes magnets work that way: they repel. Kos was a little too male for her liking. Too emphatic for the frothy cocktail hour. She found Alec, slipped into position beside him.

We look so well matched, she thought. Alec made room for her in the knot of chaps who talked of the war. The towering topic, the only topic, and yet so boring. It had surprised Pamela that fear was boring.

She nodded, said 'Oh!' at the proper intervals, remembering her pique at hearing she would have to sacrifice her beloved Lower Loxley to the war effort. Her symbol of plenty, her trophy, had been shaken by the scruff of its neck. She had been plunged knee-deep into finding extra beds, ashtrays, chests of drawers, shaving mirrors ... Now she felt abashed at her annoyance; all these men wanted to do was get back to the fight.

Alec was saying, 'Heard you flew three sorties a day, old man. Took down three Messerschmitts, I heard.'

The old man was a young man. He was diffident about the Messerchmitts. His right ear was distorted and the skin around it had healed a raw red.

Pamela loathed the naked envy in Alec's voice. His adoration for the fliers was more suitable for an autograph hunter meeting a movie star. She manoeuvred him to the open French windows. They could hear bees on the terrace, whirring over the lavender like an RAF squadron. She murmured – Pamela was a murmurer, never a shouter – 'Darling, you know that young officer never talks about his heroism.'

His lips close to her ear, Alec said, 'It's hard enough that you don't think much of me as a man, but it's harder that I agree with you. Look at me, in my evening wear, slurping aperitifs.' He threw the crystal glass out through the French doors and it shattered. Some of the men looked over, but most of them didn't. 'Please never again draw me to one side and tell me how to behave, Pamela.'

'When,' said Pamela, keeping her expression light, 'did I ever say I don't think much of you as a man?'

'As if you have to say it.' Alec played the game; he smiled down upon her. Nobody would guess the golden couple were arguing. 'I know I transgressed.' They never named the woman. Never. 'I have no excuse and I don't deserve absolution. But I've tried so hard to . . . to . . .'

To what? *To love me?* Pamela braced. That was an old fear; that she was unlovable.

A voice from the terrace. A foghorn, 'Hello!'

'Blanche! Welcome.' Pamela greeted the guest she had forgotten she invited. 'Alec, a drink for Blanche.'

'Make sure it's *enormous.*' Blanche was powdered and titivated, the black ruffle on her bolero tickling her sagging jawline.

Blanche knew she had been invited out of duty; Pamela knew she knew. Pamela also knew of the strange kink in Blanche's personality. *She enjoys being where she's not wanted.*

The men's manners meant Blanche could safely be lodged with the nearest gaggle of dinner jackets. 'Such stylish hair,' said Pamela as she escaped.

'Archie did it.' Blanche clinked glasses with a man-boy with a funny ear. She stared. He blushed. She recalled Archie plying a tail comb above her meagre waves and saying, 'Let's face facts, doll. You know zero about the practicalities of life, but I do. You want the upper hand, but if you let me lead I promise to feed and water you like royalty, *and* make you so damn gorgeous all those other dames will be *green.* Trust me?'

For the first time in her life, Blanche did. She trusted Archie Jackson. The sidecar was good; one could rely on the quality of the hooch at Lower Loxley. She disattended from what the charming man-child was saying and homed in on a large beefcake by the fireplace. Now, *that* was what Blanche would call a man.

Leaving the pilot midway through a sentence, she introduced herself to Kos. 'Oh you're European, how marvellous,' she said. He kissed her hand and she tittered. 'Be gentle with me.' She put a hand to her throat. 'For I am bereaved. It's hard to lose, is it not?'

He agreed. He said nothing else. Blanche said a great deal, and looked displeased when Pamela returned to say, 'Blanche, dear, don't deprive darling Dodgy of your company,' and there was damn Dodgy, like a Labrador, ready to squire her on a circuit of the room. 'You still here, then?' snapped Blanche as Dodgy took her arm.

When Pamela looked up at Kos she felt the jolt and rattle of the plane. 'What a beautiful ring,' she said; a hostess must keep the conversation aloft.

Kos twisted the gold signet on his little finger. 'My great grandfather's. Keeps me safe.'

None of Pamela's great grandfathers could read, let alone commission gold jewellery. She peered closer at the ring. 'Is that an eagle?'

'The symbol of Poland.'

'Suitably proud and fierce. Eagles don't say much.'

'Eagles are too busy flying to chitter chatter.'

'Chit chat.' She corrected him and he liked it. Alec never liked being corrected. Married for what felt like a century, Pamela had forgotten there were other men in the world beside her husband.

A flier with his arm in a sling joined them. He was peremptory, no niceties for Pamela; she was becoming a ghost in her own house. 'Heard you're a triple ace, Kos!'

Kos inclined his head so minutely that perhaps he didn't move it at all. His body was angled to intimate that he and Pamela were a unit. He was forcing the newcomer to include her.

And yet the man did not. 'I'm getting back to number nineteen squadron, over at Duxford. You must know some of the men there. Bolshy? Cats' Eyes Colin?'

'Sorry, no.'

Men and their nicknames, thought Pamela. She heard Blanche – poor, grieving Blanche – shriek with laughter and shove Dodgy so hard he almost fell through the French windows. Where was Alec?

There he was, talking to Terence. She should join them, find an opportunity to ask her husband – discreetly – what he had been about to say, what he had tried 'so hard' to do. She leaned down to straighten a brocade cushion, found a stray wiry hair.

Pamela bit her lip. She had buried her father without a tear, but the loss of Mavis was changing her. Perhaps that said more about her father than it did about Pamela.

'My best chum bought it,' said the boy with the sling.

'Bad luck,' said Kos.

'Knew he was done for. Landed so they could salvage the plane. A goner when they dragged him out.'

So much death; the drawing room was a well-lit cemetery.

And all discussed in clipped slang. There was no telling how many of these stitched-together men would still be alive at Christmas. Pamela remembered the very first flier they took in. Mass of yellow hair around a squirrel face. Minor injuries. Died of shock overnight. She covered his face with the sheet.

'Get me to France, that's what I say.' Sling was gung-ho. 'Gimme a crack at the occupied French ports.'

Pamela said, 'German ships could play havoc with the Canadian troops making their way over.'

Sling was confounded. As if Hero had piped up. 'You're well informed.'

Pamela almost laughed; he sounded disapproving. Somebody hailed the pompous man and she was glad it was just herself and Kos once more. They both, as if on a cue, turned their backs to the room.

He responded to her questions with politeness, just subtly tinged with weariness. 'Lida. That's where I am from.'

'Pretty name.'

'It's in Nowogrodek. No longer in Poland.'

'A shame.' Pamela understated, as she was raised to do. 'The Soviets claimed it?'

'Yes. They came, they created an atmosphere of terror. That's the only word for it.' When Kos looked up at the oil painting of Lower Loxley over the mantelpiece, perhaps he felt the contrast. 'My land is bedlam now.'

'You lost everything.' Pamela didn't say she was sorry; the man didn't need to hear that.

Kos turned the signet ring. 'We have to stop the Nazis.' It

didn't sound trite. It sounded urgent. 'They must not come here and trample your paradise.'

Is Ambridge a paradise? Pamela studied the photograph Kos took from his pocket. 'This is your home?' A turreted fantasia, it was beautiful.

'They snatched it. They desecrate it.'

Lower Loxley's age and its indifference to change had made Pamela feel protected in the turmoil of war. No doubt the ladies of the castle felt the same way. 'Kos,' she said, not sure where she was going with it. He smiled at her use of his nickname and she knew, suddenly, that she had reached him without trying to. This contained man, so full of grief. She was unsure what to do with the knowledge and she left him.

It was instinctive. She beat a path to her husband and papered over what had or had not just happened with Kos; she remembered instead the letter Alec ripped in half. She leaned over a map he had unfolded at a table.

Fingers were stabbed at the site of a fresh Allied victory. Syria, at Deir ez-Zor. Pamela saw the blue line of the Euphrates slink past. So romantic sounding, these theatres of war.

'A good news day,' said Alec, 'if one ignores the dribs and drabs of setbacks.'

'The war,' drawled Pamela, 'is two steps forward and one step back. A perpetual game of Grandmother's Footsteps.'

The men laughed. They were indulgent of their dear lady.

'Grandmother's what?' said Kos from her shoulder.

You followed me! 'It's a children's game.'

'Show him!' Blanche hung off a terrified Dodgy.

'Well, it's like this.' Pamela stepped out onto the broad pale slabs of the terrace. In her modish gown she hopped through the motions of the playground pursuit. She laughed and so did the men.

Except Kos. He just watched her.

Above them a red kite swung in the sky. A fighter, the bird had no interest in the rattan loungers and the discarded glasses. He swooped into the dusk, in search of red meat.

Arkwright Hall had adapted over the centuries.

The Victorian facade hid a seventeenth-century core. The twentieth century brought squeaking waxed floors, notice-boards and the quietude of lesson time, in the house's latest incarnation as a school for evacuees.

The matron treated the young man with sympathy. Her gentleness scorched Cliff as he sat in her office. How he had longed for gentleness at Dunkirk, while the world exploded and he swam through a sea of other men's limbs; now it wounded him.

He preferred Blanche's approach. At church she had gulped, then honked, 'Your face!'

After an interview of sorts, the comfortably built matron, who may well have been hiding a sofa down her apron, stood to hand him over to 'our Lorna. She more or less runs the place.'

'You mean, I've got the job?'

'As the only applicant, Mr Horrobin, yes, you've got the job.'

Cliff sometimes forgot that men were an endangered species in Borsetshire.

He barely looked at Lorna; Cliff could hardly expect folk to refrain from staring at him if he didn't repay the favour. She was small, girl-shaped, a vague person with hair the colour of nothing-in-particular. He sensed her desire to study him, his face's unique ins and outs. He knew the exact moment when, drawing nearer to him, she realized something was off, a lack of depth to his features, that horizontal seam that made his face not so much a face as an arrangement of cold meats with no spot for the eye to politely rest. Except, perhaps, for the one, long-lashed eye.

'The children are sweet.' Lorna led him upstairs. 'Well, most of them.' She showed him a storeroom and an office and the sick bay. 'We have the odd little ruffian.' Lorna had a light touch, low to the ground. Ordinary.

A bell rang and the corridors teemed, for a minute or two, with waist-high people.

'Don't run!' called Lorna, pointlessly.

'Hello? Miss!' From the tessellated tiles of the hall, a spindly, underfed woman waved. She introduced herself as 'Nanny', and said, with a great deal more anxiety than the exchange merited, could Lorna possibly take a message to Matron? The message was rambling. 'We have an evacuee, only eight but gifted, streets ahead on reading and writing, but I won't send her here, if that's all right, I have time on my hands and I'm qualified, and to be honest . . .' Nanny looked about herself furtively. 'I'm not sure our Irene would play nicely with the other bairns.'

Frank put the handwritten notice in the shop window: *Sorry no sugar.* 'Brace yourself, Nance. The customers won't be happy.'

Of all the restrictions, it was sugar that cut the deepest. As if Adolf had personally snatched their sweeties.

'Let's hope Agnes doesn't come in.' Frank had no weapons to withstand that lady's attacks.

Nance was tallying up, stowing notes and coins in a lock-able box out in the coolest part of 'out the back'. Where they kept the meat, when they had it. 'We're down a bit.'

'It evens out.' Frank had passed along to his daughter a tendency to worry, along with a tendency for a cold to settle on the chest and what could only be described as a passion for pork pies. 'This war means more work and less income, love.' All the tracing of commodities and continual auditing by the Ministry of Food tried them both.

Hemmed in by shelves, hemmed in by rashers of bacon, by blocks of hard margarine and eggs from Valley Farm's hens and Brooke Bond tea and vegetables from myriad back gardens, sat Frank's Tick Book. The Horrobins had a section all to themselves; Mrs Endicott's name never appeared.

They were quiet by nature, the Browns. Although never this quiet, until Frank's secret had emerged to squat between them. They were altered, changed. German. Frank could sing the entire German national anthem, but he never would. He was naturalized, and loyal to this land of opportunity. He wasn't called upon to prove it; nobody believed the 'slur'. Frank would prefer to be proud of both his nations, but that wasn't allowed. Bigotry was permissible in war. It was a badge of honour.

'No sugar?' Agnes banged on the window. 'Typical of you, Frank Brown!' She carried on, as if en route to Harrods to buy her sugar there, but she'd be back. All of Ambridge was registered with the shop for their rations.

'She's a one,' said Frank.

'Mmm,' said Nance, as effusive as she got nowadays with her father.

Women – mostly women – came in and out. Ration books were stamped. Asparagus picked over. Eggs held up to the light.

Magsy came in, and told Frank, 'I was thinking, last night, as I served Nance and Morgan a lovely soused herring, that my sister wouldn't be jealous of her. Not at all. She'd approve!'

'That's nice,' said Nance. It wasn't; no second wife seeks the first's approval. But Magsy meant well. 'What can I get you?'

'Lentils. I'm doing you a cheese and lentil slice tonight. With the last of the Red Leicester. Oh, my sister loved a bit of Red Leicester. Another thing you have in common. Morgan must see a lot of her in you.'

Weighing the lentils, Nance felt herself be whittled away. Her Englishness had already been diluted. Now she was being shaved to fit a dead woman's silhouette. 'Would you ask Morgan if he could fetch me after work? Thought we could toddle off to the river now that the flowers are out.' They might work better out of doors; inside Homeleigh they were trapped in the aspic of Magsy's seamless, round-the-clock housekeeping.

'I can't, my dear. I'm off to Borchester when I leave here. I'm being ever so naughty and treating myself to a David Niven double bill at the Borchester Plaza.'

'Not to worry.' Quick and particular, Nance packed up the lentils. A lock of hair fell out of her clip. It was summertime brown, more gold than her winter plumage. 'Enjoy the flicks!' she called as she fumbled with the buttons of her overall.

She left. Walked out, just like that.

'Hey, Nance!' Frank protested but she was gone, and Agnes was there. He gulped.

Nance hurried over The Green and looked neither left nor right until she pushed at the gate with the little brass plaque that read Dr Morgan Seed MD BSc. With one hand she felt for the zip at the back of her gingham sundress. Through the front door, she slung her bag into a corner.

Nobody in the waiting room: *Excellent!*

Nance trotted to the kitchen, a room that sang of cleanliness and care. She was in her petticoat by now. She pulled out a chair and sat at the table.

Out in the hallway, Morgan hummed to himself as he approached from the consulting room.

Nance crossed her legs. Thought better of that, twisted so she was side on. Leant on her hand. No. Yes.

Then he was in the kitchen and he smiled with surprise. A

real smile. Reckless. The smile made Nance feel young, even younger than she was. She felt able, in her pink scalloped slip, to drag Morgan back to youth rather than slide with him into middle age.

She waited for him to leap.

He didn't leap. Morgan said, 'Um, Magsy said something about leaving a sandwich for me?'

'Morgan!' said Nance, and it was a plea.

The front door opened. 'Only me!' Magsy was feet away, plodding towards them on wide-fit sandals. 'Forgot my glasses.'

'Cover yourself!' hissed Morgan.

All was suddenly slapstick. Nance dropped to the floor and crawled to the pantry, to pull on her sundress. As she fumbled among the jars she heard Magsy say, 'Now that I'm back I think David Niven can wait for another day.'

The garden at Woodbine Cottage rioted in the July sun. The neat borders lost their clarity. Weeds muscled in. The foxgloves went off the deep end.

Indoors, Blanche was pressed into a chair while Archie pulled on rubber gloves and said, 'Let me at those dark roots. Can't have you showing me up all round the village.'

'So, these allergies of yours ... They're really bad enough to exempt you from fighting?'

'I offered myself but they wouldn't have me. Couldn't run the risk of me dropping dead in uniform.'

Waspish, lively, with a spring in his step, Archie had taken over. There was no notion of a job description. He lapsed into slang – 'Polari, dear, a gentleman's language' – and did everything well.

Blanche liked the new regime. He was neither an operator, like Agnes, nor a saint, like Jane. 'I expect,' she said, holding a towel tight around her neck, 'you're wondering why I'm cold-shouldered in Ambridge.' There had been few visits since Jane's death, all of them perfunctory.

'Nope.' Archie held up a hand. 'Do *not* tell me. It doesn't matter.' His grooming elevated him from weedy boy to dashing blade. Trousers creased just so. Neurotically ironed shirt. 'Out there we don't fit in. In here, *we're* the insiders, Blanchie. Let's make this joint jump so they all want to join *our* gang.'

'Well, when you put it like that . . .' Blanche, a connoisseur of secrets, couldn't winkle his past out of Archie. She had enquired casually, and avidly, and now she tried again.

He paused in his stirring of peroxide and ammonia. 'I allow you your mystery, kindly do the same for me.' He began to paint on the mixture. The room smelled like Hades. He was training her nicely; Archie had no need to ask about Blanche's past misbehaviours; the vicar's wife had told him everything.

'That photograph in your room.' As they waited for the bleach to do its job, Blanche risked a personal question about the sepia trinity of ordinary-looking people by a garden fence. 'Are they your family?'

'You don't give up, do you?' Archie sounded as if he admired her. 'That's my dad, my sis and my little brother. They don't talk to me.'

Blanche was on that like a buzzard on a baby rabbit. 'Why?'

'Why'd you think? Girly fella, that's what Dad calls me. Him and my sister, they made no bones about not wanting a fairy in the house.'

Blanche pulled in her chin. 'Are you . . . ?'

'You didn't notice? God bless your innocence, Blanche. I hardly hide it, do I?'

'So you go for men, do you?'

'I do. I love a handsome chap, me.'

'We have so much in common,' said Blanche. 'Your father disapproves?'

'You could put it like that. Dad can't see it's just about who you love, he thinks it's dirty. I'm a sinner, apparently. Freak of nature. Probably responsible for the rise of fascism if you were to look into it properly.'

They laughed. Blanche didn't offer sympathy. She said, matter of fact, 'They disowned you.'

'Exactly. Dunno why I hang onto the pic. It goes every-where with me. Oh, and this, of course.' Archie pulled down his collar and twisted so Blanche could see a white line, like a jagged seam, in his tan skin. 'Souvenir of a night out in South London. Plenty of men out there who feel the same way as my father.' He righted himself. 'My exemption was the last straw. Dad made out I was shirking.

'Am I done yet?' asked Blanche, hopefully.

'Nope.' Archie leaned against a cabinet of Delft. 'I do miss me brother. Lovely lad. It doesn't bother him, the way I am.'

'Did that silly major object to you being homosexual when you worked for him?'

'Not so much object as ...' Archie weighed her up, wondering which words to use. 'Let's just say it got him a little overexcited and my tastes do not run to fat, whiskery so-and-sos.'

'No!' Blanche shrieked. 'The old goat!'

They laughed, until Archie said, 'Mind you, it wasn't funny when he chucked me out in the street with no reference. I kept house beautifully for him. His nick-nacks have never been so pampered. God knows what story he spun to Mrs Vicar.'

'Something about moral turpitude.'

'Sounds like fun. Now, listen, Blanche, we've got to get you moving about a bit. Get the blood pumping. Jane wouldn't want you going into a decline, would she?'

'Who knows what Jane would want?'

'D'you see I put that snap of her on the windowsill? I found a nice frame in a drawer.'

'Hmm. This house is full of drawers that are full of things, but none of it belongs to me, it would seem.'

'We can say good morning and goodnight to Jane.' Archie blew a kiss at that lady, apprehensive in a pudding bowl hat. He looked at his fingernails and said, off-hand, 'I can move on, if you want. If it bothers you.'

'If what bothers me?' Blanche picked up a hand mirror and examined the pores on her nose.

'Being queer.'

'Why would it bother me?' Blanche looked at him. 'It's nobody's business but yours.'

'So . . . I can stay?'

'You don't steal, you won't murder me in my bed, of course you can stay.' She went back to her pores as Archie silently fizzed, like a shaken bottle of champagne.

'You're a queen, Blanche Gilpin,' he said.

'Just do my hair and shut up,' said the queen.

Homeleigh creaked in its sleep.

A dog barked in a distant garden. Nance thought of it as the Night Dog; she never heard it in the day. She was glad of the sound of life. She wouldn't sleep tonight; she felt as if she was still blushing.

No way of knowing how much Magsy saw. Dinner had been silent. Nance had such respect for Morgan that she tended to adopt his opinions as her own; if he found her wanton, then it followed that Nance was wanton. She was ashamed.

It wasn't fate that had brought them together; Nance had grown out of girlish notions by the time he had asked for her hand. They had both simply taken a number of left turns and a number of right turns and here they both were. She didn't need their love to be written in the stars, but she knew that Magsy had expected to be Morgan's second wife.

What if he made a mistake when he proposed to me, instead?

Beside Nance, pretending to be asleep, Morgan remembered his first wife. Solid, independent, she required no tending. He used to wish, disloyally, that she did; he'd rather like to tend a woman, make her happy through his thoughtfulness.

He would like to tend Nance, and to share what was troubling him. To show her what he took from Jane's bedside table.

Impossible. Nance, like Magsy, was as complex as a UXB. Touch the wrong wire, and they would go off, taking the roof with them.

It had occurred to Morgan that Nance might be waiting for him to do the manly thing, and see off Magsy. *But that would be cruel.* Magsy deserved something from him; she had done so much for Morgan and his sons. There was sufficient cruelty in the world without him adding to it.

He sighed but Nance didn't notice; she was too busy cringing. *I offered myself on a plate and was refused.*

Perhaps Morgan didn't want a true wife; perhaps she was more of a shepherdess to guide him into old age.

Beside her, Morgan felt the heat of her body.

She stunned me tonight, he thought.

Her beauty in the kitchen was epic. A natural phenomenon, like a rainbow or an earthquake. Taking her in his arms would have been the most natural reaction, no, the *only* reaction, mandated by God and man. *Yet I behaved as if she's forbidden.*

How to tell her, how to find the words to express the way she shook him? He had only ever made love to his wife before Nance, unless you counted the pub landlady over

Penny Hassett way, and there had been strong drink taken that night.

There was a possibility, he thought bitterly, that he had ruined everything.

The villagers filed out of St Stephen's, grateful to have survived another of Reverend Henry Bisset's services.

'Thank you for attending.' He bowed, mock-serious, to little John Perkins. 'I saw you praying hard.'

'I really like Jesus, vicar,' said John, ignoring his brother's dirty look; Billy was resistant to religion.

Next in the shuffling line, Doris said, 'Lovely homily, Henry.'

'Bit long,' said Dan, then, *'What*, woman?' when Doris stood on his foot.

Henry's white vestments shone in the July heat; he seemed ready to ascend unto the heavens. 'One can't hurry the Lord, Dan.'

'One bleedin' can if there's a roast chicken waiting at home.' Dan evaded the swipe of Doris's handbag and capered off through the gravestones.

For her part, Doris was determined to have a little word with him about his pre-church pint on Sundays. She hurried to the lychgate, nodding a greeting at Mrs Endicott, who shouted gaily, 'Remind me to tell you about my terrible rash.'

Can't wait, thought Doris. She saw a stranger, a tall man, impressive in a uniform she didn't recognize, but she was more concerned with Philip. Why did boys behave so badly in graveyards? She had civilized her son, smarmed down his hair and inserted him into long trousers, yet there he was jumping from grave to grave as if the dear departed were a game of hopscotch. 'Phil! Christine!' She summoned her chicks. Brookfield's yard was level again, but the clearing up and making good was taking an age; she needed to get home, whip off her Sunday clothes, and get stuck in.

Magsy swooped, took Doris's arm. 'I've solved the riddle of the will! Five bequests, yes? And the first letter of the first plant was a "B". Well, we all know Blanche has more than five letters, but "Blabs" has exactly the right amount.' Magsy seemed relieved; she preferred the status quo, and that had taken quite a knock since Hitler started his tantrum.

'You may be right.' Doris couldn't muster much enthusiasm for the will; she had more pressing concerns. 'Jane might have more up her sleeve, though.'

Mrs Endicott – and her rash – caught them up. Coquettish, she said, '*My* heart tells me Jane left everything to the Borchester Cats' Home.' Her little round eyes sparkled with the drama of it. 'How Jane adored those pussies. Always donating. That's where Woodbine's going – to the cats!'

Whereas Brookfield, thought Doris, *is going to the dogs*.

Alec laid down a scrappy bouquet in the corner of the churchyard. Love-in-a-mist, cow parsley, the blue planet of a hydrangea head.

No headstone yet, just a cross with Jane Gilpin's name and her dates. Most ungallant to broadcast a lady's age, he thought. He was too hot in his tweed; Pamela had been right about that.

She picked her way over to him. 'Flowers for Jane? How kind.'

'Stop, Hero!' Alec called his dog away before it dug up the old dear. 'Kos!' He looked beyond Pamela. 'Didn't see you inside.'

Kos said, 'I like English churches. This is a rather fine example.'

'Is it?' smiled Pamela, pleased she had worn her new hat. She drew back its voguish veil. 'Terribly draughty in winter.'

Kos bent to stroke Hero and Pamela pulled the veil abruptly down, lest anyone see her expression change. To one of envy. Of a Labrador.

By the gate, Doris was ambushed afresh. Frances this time. 'Come and see what one of your evacuees has done. It's *disgraceful*.' She spun Doris like a top, as Christine whined, 'Come *on*, Mum!'

'They're not *my* ...' Doris gave up and followed Frances. When the vicar's wife worked herself up like this, with the fervour of a hanging judge, there was no point reasoning with her.

The vicar stood by the church carrying Irene in his arms. The child was stiff.

'Oh!' Doris almost laughed, despite the expressions on every face. It was Sukie, the doll, in Henry's arms.

'Oh dear,' said the vicar. And then, 'Oh dear dear dear.'

Nanny wrung her hands. 'If little Maisie hadn't touched Sukie,' she began.

'My kid's allowed to touch a bleedin' *doll*,' snapped Connie. For once the sinned against and not the sinner, she turned to Doris, full of ire. 'That Irene punched my lass like a prizefighter.'

'Me nose hurts.' Maisie backed up the report. She was big-eyed, full of tears.

The prizefighter spoke. 'Give me back my doll,' she said.

The vicar looked as if he wanted to do as he was told, but his wife snatched Sukie and gave her to Nanny. 'Tell her, Nanny. Tell Irene she can't have the doll back until she mends her ways.'

'Go on,' said Irene, coolly. 'Tell me.' She hesitated. 'Tell me, Mummy.'

Doris frowned.

'I've told you, pet, over and over. I'm not . . .' Nanny sagged. 'She's not a bad girl,' she said, the words tired, like a mantra she no longer believed.

'Best get her home, Nanny love,' said Doris. No need to prolong this public spectacle; Frances would recycle the drama over teacups for the next fortnight.

'She's a pure little soul, really,' said Nanny, leading Irene away with a tentative hand on her narrow back.

'It's true what they say about city children,' said Frances. 'Wild animals.'

'Children go through bad patches,' said Doris.

'True,' said Frances, watching Irene leave by the lychgate. 'Or they can be plain bad.'

'Come now,' said the vicar.

Frances wasn't finished. 'Furthermore I do *not* care for that brother of Nanny's.'

Following Frances's line of sight to where Beacham stood smoking with the Home Guard, Doris agreed, just this once, with the vicar's wife. 'Yes, something *off* about him.'

Dan, who had been out with the Home Guard three nights out of the past four, had a boyish admiration for Beacham. None of Dan's reasons resonated with Doris: 'Handy in a fight, I'll bet! Keeps a gun in the house!' *Mind you*, she thought, *if Beacham helps the Home Guard fend off the Nazi hordes I'll forgive him.* Certainly, she couldn't see Walter Gabriel seeing off an invasion.

Pamela stood by an old tomb, a phantasmagoria of weeping angels and devastated cherubs. She traced one of the names etched into the crumbling stone.

It startled her when Kos said, 'That's why the names are engraved. So we say them aloud, and the dead aren't forgotten.'

'Do ride back with us, Kos.'

He looked at the ground. 'Leonid Bajonski. Stanislaw Obiorek. Antoni Plenkiewicz.'

'Your colleagues?'

'Yes. My brothers.'

Pamela met Kos's eyes through the veil. 'Come on, I'll pour us all a stiffener when we get back.' Under her breath, she said, 'Jane Editha Gilpin'.

'B for Bob!' Stan loved to provoke The Bull's landlord. 'Blanchie's left Woodbine to *you*, Bob!'

'She'll leave it to her sister,' said Bob, 'as is right and proper.' Living next door to the Gilpins he knew what many did not; that the sisters had not exchanged a word since November 1940. No sibling love lost there. *Blanche won't get the house*, he thought, with no desire to join in the village's incessant dissection of the will. What did it matter? Bricks and mortar, money – all was meaningless. It was only Bob's schedule that kept him going, and even that he attended to listlessly. 'The usual, Dan?' he asked.

Dan watched Bob reach up for the bottle, its dark and cloudy brown depths promising much. Dan licked his lips. You could keep your fine wines; beer was Dan's reliable, homely mistress. 'Ey!' he said, as Bob, bottle in hand, turned and went through the green-painted door that led to the stairs. 'Me beer, Bob! Me beer!'

Stan laughed at Dan's woebegone expression, but soon he, too, was calling for Bob.

'Where'd he get to?' wondered Walter. Such dereliction of duty was a sin. 'Find him, Dan,' he said.

It wasn't done, Dan knew that. He really shouldn't push at the door and enter the other world, the private quarters. Egged on by his compadres, and in the hope of finding his Holy Grail (full of nice, warm beer), Dan stole cautiously up the stairs. 'Bob?'

The rooms looked ransacked, pillaged. A chair on its side. A stove crusted with slops. Clothes underfoot like drifts of snow. A fur of dust on the shelves.

'Crikey, Bob,' muttered Dan, twisting his foot on a poker

that lay, incongruously, in the hall. He stood in the debris of Bob's life, and called him again. 'We're gasping down there, Bob, old son!'

A door left ajar showed Dan a slice of the small back room. Jimmy's room. Dan felt himself grow cold, seized by a chill that took his whole body at once. He went closer, to prove he was right, and yes, he was right. *What the ... ?*

Bob was suddenly at his side, and hustling Dan down to the bar. 'Flipping cheek of it,' he snapped, as he lifted the hinged section of the counter and propelled Dan through it.

Later, much later, in his own bed in his own tidy bedroom, Dan couldn't get his story out for Doris's reproaches.

'You sniffed about in Bob's home? I never heard the like, Dan Archer!' Houses were like heads; you had to be invited in. 'You know better than to poke your nose in other folks' business.'

'Listen, woman, will you? The place was upside down, a right mess. Except for Jimmy's old room.'

'Aw, bless him. Keeping his boy's room nice even though he can't cope with the rest of the house.' Any hint of domestic skill in a man impressed Doris, long wed to a man who couldn't boil a kettle without endangering the lives of all around him.

'That's just it, love. It wasn't tidy; it was *bare*. As if nobody had ever set foot in there.' No bed. No rug. No chair, no clothes, no shoes, no nothing. A square monastic cell. 'Remember that swimming trophy young Jimmy was so proud of? How we all cheered him on at Borchester Baths? You'd think that'd be there. But no.'

'But how'd Bob get rid of everything without anyone seeing?'

Ambridge was as much a stage as a village. In quiet places, the merest activity is seismic. Doris would have heard, on the reliable village store jungle drums, if a cart arrived to take away furniture. No clothes had been donated to the Women's Committee. It was eerie, supernatural, as if Jimmy had never existed and the village had just imagined him.

AUGUST

The stained glass of Arkwright Hall's front door glowed around Lorna. She was dim among the glass's splendour, as if the sun had faded her.

Coming up the drive, Cliff kept to the trees, like a spy.

'Good morning!' she shouted.

He was still six feet away, still handsome. Then he was five feet away and he was different.

'Another day like this and we'll all melt,' she said as he passed her. Then, to the back of his head, 'I know you can speak. You talk to your class. Is it so hard to say good morning?'A sudden clamour within the house, like a wave breaking over Arkwright Hall. Assembly was over. Children streamed over the tiled floor.

'Mr Horrobin!' A delighted child jumped up and down.

Lorna shrugged and made for her office.

'Good morning!' said Cliff, after her.

'Well, that's a start.' It had only taken a month. The new teacher made Lorna bold, not her usual self. Her father called Lorna a wallpaper stain. Her father was not very nice.

'Miss, there's a lady.' Billy tugged at Lorna with a dirty hand.

Lorna turned. Cliff turned. The lady was Wanda and she stood in the halo made by the sun streaming through the stained glass. Her smile was so broad that Lorna suspected for a second that the light was coming from Wanda, from that perfect oval of a face.

'Eggs!' The Madonna held up a basket and the moment passed, but Cliff stood, dazed, as the hall cleared and he was left with the two women.

'From Doris, for the kids.' Wanda was all movement where Lorna was still.

Not as still as Cliff, who had become a statue.

'Could I have a drink of water? I'm parched.'

'Through here.' Lorna pressed at a door. She felt abashed in front of Wanda, who was taller and wider than her, and wore her dungarees like a pirate. 'Cliff? You all right there?'

He came to and sidled off. Lorna saw him keep his right side towards the piratical posh girl.

The big tap squeaked.

'Look! Sunburn!' Wanda held out her forearms. 'Boss did warn me. How do my eyes look?'

Unthinkingly Lorna said, 'Beautiful.' Wanda laughed. 'I meant, are they all red. The chaff gets into them. You smear Vaseline on them. Works wonders but looks grim.' She

---

drained the glass and banged it down on the wooden draining board. 'Cheers.' She peered at Lorna, their noses almost touching. 'Know what you need?' She took a golden bullet from the bib of her dungarees. Two swipes and Lorna's lips were cherry red. 'Gorgeous!'

Seeing her out, Lorna saw Morgan in the porch. Whistled up to investigate ringworm, he was pep-talking Cliff. 'Make your mark, my boy,' they heard him say. 'Have confidence in yourself.'

'Good advice, Doc,' said Wanda, as she passed them.

'Do thank Doris for the eggs,' said Lorna, but Wanda was being hailed by the science master. A tall, thin paperclip of a man, he was hurrying across the drive with a bicycle. Like him, it was in need of repair but serviceable. 'As promised.' He held out the steed.

'I couldn't!' Wanda gawped.

'Can't have you slogging around, cadging lifts. Please. It's yours.'

'If you're sure. I'm getting tired of Shanks's pony.'

'I'm sure.'

'So generous,' said Lorna. She and Cliff eyeballed each other; the science master was notoriously tight-fisted.

'Perhaps,' he was saying to Wanda, as she circled him on the bike, 'we could, perhaps, have a drink together one evening, perhaps?'

'Who knows?' Wanda dinged the bell and was away. 'Thanks again!'

*

Mrs Endicott, who had never been to Piccadilly Circus, said, 'It's like Piccadilly Circus in this shop, Frank!'

Coupons needed ripping out, books needed stamping, baskets needed totting up. A flustered Canute holding back a tide of customers, Frank took Connie's blackberry crop from her with one hand and weighed out a whisper of flour for Archie with the other.

'Them's best quality,' said Connie. The soft fruit grew luxuriantly at Broom Corner. 'Don't diddle me on the price.'

'I . . .' Frank was appalled at the suggestion.

'At least they can't ration fruit,' said Mrs Endicott, who was famed for her cherry harvest. The great 'they', the faceless men from the Ministry, had them all obsessed with food. There was lust in the air for the blackberries, lewd and purple in their box.

Summer supercharged the smallholdings. Frank's shelves held strawberries and the Grundys' gooseberries and Walter Gabriel's rightly famed watercress and his giant white onions the size of bowling balls.

'Get a move on, Frank,' said Agnes, pausing before saying, 'Some of us have husbands to feed.' She liked to invoke Denholm; she liked to imagine she was envied for him. 'Where's Nance?'

I wish I knew. Frank didn't answer. 'Two and nine, please,' he said to Archie.

As Archie counted out coins, a double-chinned matron asked him how his new position was going. 'Pity you'll be out on the street when Blanche loses the cottage.'

Archie turned so speedily the woman had to step back. 'I'm used to the street, love.'

As he left, Nance arrived. They did a little pas de deux on the step.

'Where you been, love?' Frank sensed a battle brewing between Agnes and the double-chinned madam about the last of the Spam.

No answer. No nothing from Nance these days. She simply took Mrs Endicott's shopping list and went to the shelves.

'Those Nazis are at it again,' said Mrs Endicott. 'They've taken away Norway's wirelesses.'

'Plain *mean*,' said Agnes, covering the Spam with her handkerchief.

'Dad,' said Nance, reaching to a tin on the top shelf. 'I had a letter.'

She's talking to me, thought Frank, jubilant. 'Who from, love?'

'The paper mill at Waterley Cross. They want me to start next week. The new legislation comes in any minute. Even married women have to work.'

'You do work, Nance. You work here.' Frank was unruffled. 'Don't you worry yourself. I'll have a word, tell them you're needed here.'

'I applied for the job, Dad, and I've accepted it.'

Frank sliced ham as thin as a rotter's promise.

Later, as he locked up, he said, 'I can't change your mind?'

She was already gone.

*

Alec was shackled to his desk, pen in hand. It was shameful to write to this particular correspondent, but he must finish what he had started. How much simpler his brother's life had been. War was black and *big*. You lived or you died. It was the nuance of life that floored Alec.

A wood pigeon cooed throatily on the window ledge. Its deep note underlined the lack of other birdsong. Alec always noticed how the volume was turned down in high summer. The birds had sung to attract mates, and now they were too bogged down with tending to their families to waste time singing.

There was a metaphor there that Alec chose not to explore. He had never sung to Pamela, literally or metaphorically. A spasm took him; he gripped the desk and withstood it. He refused to face his sadness, his loss. He would not allow himself to care that somedays he couldn't recall the face, *her* face, a face he had never photographed in case somebody found the incriminating snap.

Pull yourself together. If he said it in Pamela's voice it generally did the trick. They must live in the pact they made. They could do it; they were made of stern stuff.

'Have you seen Gerald?' Pamela leaned into his study.

Alec slammed the desk drawer shut. A mistake: she would notice. 'Gerald?' he said, sounding shifty. Their son was home for the summer, trailing a cloud of ignominy. Some new kerfuffle about a missing postal order. Expelled from Alec's old school, Rugby, for various sins – punch-ups in the dorm, burning his homework – Gerald had been held back a year by his new establishment. They had three terms to make a gentleman of him before the war machine reached out its metallic claw; Gerald seemed already too burly for a schoolboy, like a boxer trussed up in the uniform. The boy had grown up off-stage, unwitnesed by his father. And yet he regressed to truculent childhood every other day. 'He was up a tree earlier.'

'That boy seems to spend an inordinate amount of time up trees. If you see him, tell him I'd appreciate him coming to the village with me to pick up a few bits and pieces.'

'Shopping? Not exactly a boy's dream entertainment.'

'Nor mine.' Pamela was in yellow, an elegant daffodil. 'Sad, isn't it? Mavis is more missed than Jane Gilpin.'

'Not by me,' said Alec, turning back to his embossed stationery. He relaxed; she clearly hadn't noticed him slam the drawer.

'There are mutterings.' Pamela lingered. 'About the next will reading.'

'There are always mutterings. I do wish you wouldn't listen to gossip.'

She was stung. 'I didn't say I *listened*. I'm merely warning you there's a silly rumour that Jane left Woodbine Cottage to you.'

'Me?' Alec turned so fast his hair almost moved.

'She was sweet on your brother Rupert, apparently. The village elders remember your family and Jane's maternal family, the Blairs, having hopes of a match.'

'Ye Gods, I couldn't possibly accept the cottage.' Alec stood. Paced.

He was thinner than before. *Wartime diet*, thought Pamela. *Plus the burden of running the Home Guard*. Her husband was erasing himself.

A voice from the landing made them both turn. Terence, smoking in a languid way he had surely copied from film stars, said, 'Wouldn't catch me turning down an inheritance.'

Alec scowled. There was always someone about these days. 'It would be unseemly, when others in the village have so little.'

How very Alec, thought Pamela, *to fret about something that may never happen and ignore the real problem right in front of him*.

Alec excused himself, jogged out, Hero at his heels like a shadow.

Pamela wished she hadn't noticed how he had slammed the drawer. Wished she hadn't seen him discreetly turn the tiny key before he escaped. She believed she could pick the lock; Pamela believed she could do anything and she was usually right.

The drawer co-operated, as did villagers, servants, dogs. Everything, in fact, *except my husband*.

It would be for the best if she did not read the neatly folded letters she found in the drawer. Especially that one at the bottom, torn roughly in two.

The boys passed through the striped wood. Sun. Shadow. Sun. Shadow. Billy had his bearings; that way was the camp; that way was Doris's farm.

They liked Doris. Biscuits happened around Doris,

and she was free with her hugs. Connie hugged them now and then, but she was all angles. *She's out of practice*, thought Billy.

'Can we stop,' said John. 'And read Mum's letter?'

They dropped like rag dolls onto the soft floor with Wizbang. Heydon Brook, a parched trickle, wiggled past them, sluggish in the heat like everything else.

'Dear boys,' began Billy. He had to squint; the words were like the brook, meandering, snaky. He imagined Mum writing laboriously at the kitchen table, breaking off to stir a pot or wash a plate, mislaying the pen and cursing herself. She was busy busy busy, their mum, and they loved her for it.

A scarf had come with the letter. Odd gift for August, but John loyally wore it. It was rainbow striped, made from leftovers.

Billy was halting over the misspellings and the crossings out. 'You know I hate to tell you hard things, but Dad is . . .'

'Is what? *What?*' John began to rock.

'I can't make out the word. Mum changed to pencil and it's all smudged.'

John closed his eyes.

The wood spoke to itself around them.

'Missing!' said Billy at last.

It was a relief that the word wasn't shorter, that Dad wasn't dead. Then it was terrifying. They stood up. They took off, Wizbang plunging ahead.

They couldn't tell Connie; she was funny-peculiar about

anything to do with reading and writing. Cliff was always out at Arkwright Hall. Stan? Forget it.

We'll tell Luca, thought John.

Pamela read every letter in the drawer from beginning to end.

The torn one she read first, but it only made sense once she took them all in, and her new knowledge weighed her down like wet sand.

The private detective Alec had hired had a pompous literary style. 'I understand your desire to locate the young lady in question but it is my professional duty to warn you that to proceed with this search after my exhaustive investigations may be a waste of funds.'

There was more. The child, that woman's child, she was Alec's. The child Pamela remembered, had held on her lap.

There was more wet sand. Punctilious even in subterfuge, Alec had made copies of the letters he wrote to the detective. They told how he had changed his mind after ending the affair, and rushed to his mistress's home, but she had disappeared before he could tell her that he had chosen her.

Not me.

If Pamela were a man she would rush out and find someone to punch.

Even though Billy had been most particular that they must *not* tell Luca about Dad – 'None of his bleedin' business!' – John blurted it out.

'Our dad's gone missing,' he said.

121

Luca stopped rifling through the paper bag of food they had scavenged for him. A corner of crusty loaf. A sausage. 'Oh boys. I am sorry.'

'Not your fault,' snapped Billy.

'I feel bad. Sad. Here.' Luca struck his chest.

He was a bit histrionic; Billy supposed it came with being an Italian.

'Dad's not shot or nothing,' said John.

Billy didn't correct his little brother but he wondered where this information had come from. They knew nothing more than that Dad was missing. Spinning in space somewhere, tumbling between explosions.

John went on. 'He's like you. In a prisoner of war camp, with a nice canteen and that.'

'You don't know that.' Billy heard himself sound angry and wondered why.

'No, John is right, *probilamente*.' Luca smiled at the smaller boy and John threaded his fingers through the wire.

'Dad'll join the football team!'

Luca said, 'He will make goal!'

The laughter was grateful, necessary.

Luca said, 'John, it is hot for scarf.'

'Nah, I'm fine.' John's face was pink with perspiration.

Luca was serious, as if praying, when he said, 'I hope your papa meets little boys like you. They help him and bring him *salsiccia* and kiss his heart like you do to me.'

'I ain't kissed your heart, Luca.' Billy was disgusted.

'Bad English. You know how I mean?'

'S'pose.' This was veering dangerously near to mush. Billy was fervently anti-mush. He smiled, though.

'Look. I have this to show.' From a pocket in his unseasonably thick trousers, Luca withdrew a creased photograph. '*My* boys. Luca's boys.'

Enthralled by their Italian counterparts, the brothers bent together over the black and white image of a stern man with a small boy on his knee. An older brother stood to one side. Their ages matched Billy and John if their clothes did not.

'Fancy clobber,' sniggered Billy, who wouldn't be caught dead in velvet.

'That is Vittorio, big brother. Bruno is my baby. Like you, John.'

Like me, thought John.

'Who's the bloke?' said Billy. The man was bullish, proud.

'My father. He is hard but he loves us.'

Billy felt grateful for his own grandpa, a woolly little pipe smoker who read the newspaper all day long.

'Here, in England, I am on same, um, *continente* as my sons. I love all humanity, you know old Luca, but I am glad to be in Europe, after Tobruk and South Africa. Every night I pray I see Bruno and Vittorio again.'

'Please don't cry, Luca.'

'Ah John, you have big big heart, just like my Bruno.'

'Keep it down, lovebirds,' said Billy. 'The guards'll hear.'

John whispered. 'Don't want you to get beaten again, Luca.'

Luca touched a bruise waxing on his cheekbone.

'Why'd they do that to you?' Billy hated bullies even more than mush.

'I speak up for my friend. He is small. Weak. They give him small dinner and I say *no*! They hit me because I am rebel. You are rebel, Billy, yes?'

The boy tried to look modest. Someone had noticed at last!

Abruptly vehement, Luca said, 'Never lose that, Billy.' *Bee-lee.* 'Never!'

It was thrilling how Luca could change mood so suddenly and so absolutely. Not very English, but a lot of fun.

'Dad will come home and I will see my boys again.' Luca bent to find John's eye. 'I promise.'

The grass was the perfect picnic blanket, springy and green. 'Lie down, Boss!' said Wanda from where she sprawled.

Doris's knees would crack like a twenty-gun salute if she attempted such a thing. 'Finish that milk so I can take the bottle back with me.'

Scrambling up, Wanda said, 'I'll walk with you.'

'As you wish.' There was reserve between Doris and her land girl. Wartime made strange bedfellows; Doris had never before met a young woman with no notion of the pecking order, who talked ebulliently of politics at the dinner table, who contradicted her elders and betters, aka Dan, when he brought up the Japanese army's rampage over Indochina.

Turned out Wanda had a Japanese friend at boarding school, lovely girl, lovely family, 'and the art!' Well, what Dan knew about Japanese art could be written on the backside of a dormouse so that was the end of that political debate.

'Look at the lambs go!' Wanda hung over a five-barred gate.

Doris laughed with her. Some years she was too busy to notice the daft and delirious creatures bouncing when they were turned out onto the grass left once the hay was taken.

'Not sure I can eat one after seeing them like this, Boss.'

Doris stopped laughing. Each new vegetenarian or whatever they were called was a pound less in the farmer's pocket.

'Sheep have *personalities*,' marvelled Wanda.

'So do cows.' Doris would happily allow one of her herd to run the country. You'd never see old Daisy or little Red getting them embroiled in a war.

'What do you need me to do this afternoon?' Wanda handed over her milk bottle and hauled her bicycle up from the grass.

'Maybe give the men a hand with finishing the barn. Inside needs treating.' Doris spent minutes at a time gazing up at the new barn. It had risen like a cathedral and represented money they did not have.

'When do we start on a new cowshed?'

The confidence! 'We don't.' The patchwork of salvaged offcuts would have to do. A hard winter would see it crumble; Doris knew there was one on the way.

'Don't worry, Boss.' Wanda meant well, but she was the sort of person who would inherit her grandmother's jewellery or a great-aunt's house.

'I forgot. This came.' Doris handed over a letter. She never called Wanda pet or love; Wanda's class rendered her utterly foreign to unsophisticated Doris, even though they worked shoulder to shoulder every day and ate together every evening.

'Ooh, it's from Mr Bigtime!'

'Well, I didn't think it was an electricity bill,' said Doris, watching the girl kiss the envelope. She had asked Dan last night, was it quite right, a young woman accepting a gift like a bicycle from a fellow she barely knew.

Filling his pipe with great concentration, as if he was making a watch, Dan had said, 'Don't see why not, love. You jealous?'

Doris was furious. Because he was right. A little. 'Oh, do up your cardigan, Dan Archer!' she had snapped, and his giggle into his pipe irritated her even more.

'Shall we?'

Pamela led the way to the dining room, and the usual compliments rained down around her. For the old chairs and the new cushions, for the tapering candles and the silver salt cellars, the etched crystal, the comfort, the largesse.

'Is that medallion of veal I can smell?' Dodgy was transported.

'With your favourite carrots à la king. But first, mousse savoy.'

The menu didn't seem to know there was a war on. Gerald asked why couldn't they just eat normal food.

'Gerald!' Alec repeated his son's name in a gentler tone. 'Gerald, please.' He always knew what Hero wanted – generally a snack – but Gerald's needs were a mystery. He had very little boyhood left, yet he was still a vague and foggy outline to his father. If Alec asked, 'What is it that you *want*, son?' Gerald would say only, 'For you to leave me alone.'

Ladies from Pamela's bridge club had been drafted in; she was tired, she said, of the same old village faces.

Alec liked the same old village faces.

The dresses were smart if a little behind the times. In red georgette, Pamela doubted her choice; the style wasn't very 'her'. Alec had done a doubletake at her lipstick, said, 'Crikey, old girl!' She went to her seat, complacent that the evening was going to plan until she saw the place cards. 'Oh,' she said. 'No.'

'Yes,' said Kos, holding out her chair.

'But . . .' Pamela's seating plan had put her between Dodgy and a shy new chap. Yet now the place card to her right read 'Tadeusz Mier'.

He leaned down, spoke into her ear. 'Either I sit by you or I eat in the Folly.'

Paralysed, Pamela recognized a crossroads. When he interpreted her silence as acquiescence, she was grateful.

'Champagne!' she said.

'Champagne?' Gerald was happier now.

'Not for you,' said Alec.

When Pamela looked at Alec she heard phrases from the letters sizzle in her ear. They drowned out a bridge lady's comment that the veal was 'sinfully delicious'.

Another said, 'Can't help feeling a little, you know . . . when most families are dining on Lord Woolton pie.'

They were all aware of the thrifty vegetable and potato dish that tasted, cleverly, of nothing. 'One must look after our pilots,' said Pamela. 'For myself, I'd happily dine on Welsh rarebit.' With a napkin in a silver holder, of course.

'What's that?' The way Gerald pointed at Kos's lapel with his knife made Alec wonder if his expensive education had taught him anything.

'My caterpillar badge?' Kos took it off and handed it to Gerald. 'The company that makes silk parachutes sends them to pilots who bail out.'

'Sweet,' said a bridge lady.

'Charming,' said Pamela. She said it to the company at large. She could not look at Kos. His nearness ruined her appetite. A woman bound by rules, discipline came easily to Pamela. She tutted at those who couldn't govern themselves. She had come this far by following the road signs: *I must remember that.*

As Kos leaned over and clipped his badge to Gerald's jacket, Pamela wondered if she really had come all that far. *Is my marriage such a prize?*

It was as if Marxists had broken into her head. She cut up her veal.

Dodgy was amused. 'Hear our Kos is in hot water. Found a plane and went up in it. A tremendous to-do, I heard.'

'You heard right.' Kos wasn't eating much. He was drinking, though. 'I'm grounded.'

'How aggravating,' said Alec.

'Could have been worse. At least they didn't find out I took a civilian up with me.'

Pamela's fork squeaked on her plate.

Gerald let out a grating 'ha ha!' at his mother.

One of their guests had been 'up in a plane'. As the lady described the exciting experience in the dullest of terms, Kos said, sotto voce, to Pamela, 'So you didn't tell your husband. Am I a secret?'

'I don't tell him everything.' Pamela was polite. *I mustn't say anything I can't retract.* But she wanted Kos to continue flirting with her.

If that was what he was doing. Pamela had little practice in the dark arts. As Alec's wife she was untouchable. She had always cherished his proposal – 'Look, old thing, wouldn't it be better all round if we tied the knot?' – as endearingly clumsy. Distance lent perspective; since reading the letters in his desk she characterized his proposition as something more prosaic. A merger.

There was sufficient cover for Pamela to say to Kos, 'I don't care to be toyed with.'

She looked at him then, and he looked at her.

'I like you in red. Your mouth is like Christmas.'

He left early, citing a headache.

'Bit rude,' said one of the ladies.

'Kos is a law unto himself,' said Terence, and glanced at Pamela.

Or maybe she imagined it.

War Ag census forms slithered off Dan's side of the bed and onto the floorboards in the dark.

Not enough hours in the day and not enough fuel in Dan's tank; farm life was simple, circular, and backbreaking.

Doris had to prod him twice to get him awake. He sat up and spluttered, 'Gettoutofit!' He rubbed his eyes. 'Doris?'

'You have *never* written me a love letter, Dan Archer.'

His hair a chrysanthemum, Dan fell back on his pillow. 'Did you hear me?'

'Thought I was dreaming.' Dan yawned. 'I did, Doris. I sent you a postcard from Llandudno when we were courting.'

'That one? I can quote it. Wish you were here. Weather windy. All best, Dan. You added your surname in brackets.'

Dan turned to face her. It took some doing. The mattress had seen much – lovemaking, births – and it had hills and valleys aplenty. 'What's your point, love?'

Suddenly glad that she had the sort of husband she could poke awake in the small hours, Doris kissed his forehead. 'Not sure I have one, Dan.'

Autumn

1941

The serpent hisses where the sweet birds sing.

THOMAS HARDY
Tess of the D'Urbervilles

September

AMBRIDGE WOMEN'S COMMITTEE
MEETING MINUTES

Date: 1st September, 1941
At: Woodbine Cottage
Chairwoman: Pamela Pargetter
Present: Frances Bissett, Emmaline
Endicott, Doris Archer, Blanche Gilpin,
Agnes Kaye, Magsy Furneaux, Susan Grundy,
Nanny Oldman.
Absent: Nance Morgan
Minutes: Frances Bissett

1. Pamela thanked Blanche for letting
us meet at Woodbine Cottage and said 'I
know you are all anticipating the will
reading straight after this meeting but

can we try and concentrate on the Harvest Festival please?'

2. Pamela welcomed newcomer Nanny. Nanny said she does not like leaving Irene alone for too long 'because she is um err' and Agnes said 'Spooky?' and Nanny said 'very sensitive'.

3. Mrs Endicott said 'Shouldn't little Irene be at school with the other children? It might be good for her' and Nanny said 'I don't think so she has her little ways' and I myself was glad the subject was dropped as none of us want the kiddiewinks infected with Irene's bad nature.

4. Magsy asked Blanche does it feel odd to live 'in limbo'.

5. Blanche said 'I do not live in limbo dear I live in Ambridge.'

6. Mrs Endicott said it is very modern of Nance to have a job at the mill and asked Pamela does she think Alec will inherit Woodbine like everyone is saying.

7. Pamela said she is not privy to Alec's business and could we please get on.

8. Susan said maybe Jane left Woodbine to the Horrobins and Blanche threw a pen at her.

9. Pamela reminded us we are not animals in the zoo.

10. Mrs Endicott suggested we all club together and buy Bob new begonias as the empty tubs outside The Bull are bad for morale. Doris said 'Bob's prickly these days he might be insulted.' Note to self: ask Henry to have a word with Bob re: counting blessings and trusting in the Lord.

11. Agnes asked Pamela if she was wearing lipstick. Pamela said 'That is not relevant.'

12. Mrs Endicott told a joke. Hitler and Goering are on top of Berlin's highest tower. Hitler says 'How can I put a smile on the face of my people?' Goering says 'Jump, mein Fuhrer.'

13. Everyone laughed. I myself said we should not laugh at Nazis, they are diabolical. Mrs E said 'If they do invade we should line the streets and point and laugh.' Doris said 'Everything is rationed except jokes.'

14. Pamela said 'Can we please get on?'

15. Magsy asked if we knew about the siege of Leningrad and Agnes said if Ambridge was besieged she would nip out the back of the village hall.

16. Pamela said what about the massacre at Lwow and she went on for some minutes about the atrocities in Poland until I myself had to ask if we could please get on.

17. Pamela asked for fundraising ideas. Mrs E said 'I have taken up watercolours. We could sell my paintings.' She held one up and Doris asked if it was rotting fruit and Mrs E said 'No it is a self-portrait.'

18. Mrs E said that poor dear Jane loved fundraising and Blanche said 'Oh yes my sister was all heart.'

19. Connie Horrobin joined the meeting and said it was her right to take part she was a woman wasn't she. She said 'Are you all gossiping about the will reading?' and I myself said not all of our minds are in the gutter.

20. Blanche banged on the window and said Walter Gabriel was ransacking her garden but he was there to dig up that day's bequest.

21. Mrs E said talking of Walter his marrows are outrageous and he should not be allowed to compete in the Harvest Festival Flower and Produce Show.

22. Doris said 'Why not have a fun prize for silliest looking vegetable?'

23. Blanche said 'Agnes's Denholm can enter with his face.'

24. Agnes said something I myself refuse to record here.

25. Mrs E said we should start to plan the nativity and let's hold it at Arkwright Hall this year and we must borrow a real baby this time as last year's piglet did not do and the Virgin Mary never got the stains out of her robe.

26. Connie said 'Ooh it's time for the will' and everyone rose. Quite quickly.

27. Pamela said 'Do calm down ladies it's not a matinee at the Palladium.'

28. Agnes said 'No it's better.'

The stampede from Woodbine Cottage almost knocked down Walter Gabriel as he proceeded with great ceremony towards the village hall with the plant of the moment. When Agnes tried to peek under the sacking he took evasive measures.

Pamela saw from the way Alec held his head, alone on the stage, that the stress was bearing down on him. *About the will?* she thought, with a soupçon of acid. *Or those letters?*

When he began to read out Jane's words, the hall subsided into rapt silence.

'Today's bequests are very special to me, and, I hope, to their recipient. Do listen to what these modest items are trying to say.' Alec raised his head. 'Reverend Bissett?'

Blanche swivelled to glare at the man of God, who rose and sat then rose again. His look of consternation was matched by his wife's look of glee as she shoved him towards the stage.

Alec handed over a small rectangular box. When opened, it revealed a small leather wallet. Crocodile. Tobacco brown.

'That's my father's,' said Blanche, insulted, from the front row.

'It's a sign!' said someone from the back of the hall. 'You're getting the house, Reverend!'

Then came Walter's big moment. 'Miss Jane's left you a lady orchid, Rev,' he said, handing over the pot. 'It's a wildflower, from the bottom of her lawn.' Purple, jolly, beautiful, the cone-shaped clustered petals of the wild orchid bore little family resemblance to its hothouse cousins.

'L for lady orchid!' yelled Stan.

'Told you.' A towering woman folded her arms. 'Case closed. The plants'll spell out "Blabs". Don't worry, Miss Gilpin, your house is safe.'

Blanche had no interest in opinions. Archie helped her gather her handbag and her parasol. *And my wits*, she thought.

The theories rose like steam above a fresh loaf. Blanche heard them all as she made her way out.

'The wallet means Reverend Bissett will never have to worry about money, because he can sell Woodbine.'

'Jane would want the vicar to have somewhere to live in his old age.'

'It's common knowledge,' said a florid gent, 'that spinsters develop infatuations with men of the cloth.'

As a spinster, Magsy looked as if there was much she could say on the matter, but contented herself with a speaking look at Henry's jug ears and rice pudding complexion.

The theories redoubled.

'No way is Blanche getting that house, this is a cat and mouse game,' said Joe Grundy.

'It's one of them word puzzles, whatcha call 'em?' said his little wife.

'Acronyms,' said Morgan, and heads nodded sagely.

The vicar was mobbed.

'Look inside the wallet!' was the advice of the hive mind.

'The wallet belonged to Jane's father, a man famed for his charity,' said Henry, buffeted by the feeding frenzy. 'It's a symbol. I'm quite sure there won't be any money in— Oh.'

A half-crown. He turned it over, like an Egyptologist with a find. 'Oh Jane,' he said, too quietly for any other ear to hear. He sank into a pew.

'Isn't it marvellous,' said Mrs Endicott, 'how deep and feeling our dear vicar can be!'

There had been no deep feeling when a choirboy stole a thruppenny bit from the poor box. Doris remembered how Henry denounced the boy from the pulpit as if he was Beelzebub. She was relieved when Alec shushed the crowd with a stinging comment about refraining from conjecture.

Castigated, all filed out.

Try as she might, Doris couldn't stall a fantasy that un-scrolled in her head about how it must feel to own a property like Woodbine, and sell it, and have enough money to solve all Brookfield's problems. Her own greed surprised her, and she found herself glad that she had meant very little to Jane.

I'm not in the running.

Somebody else was clearly sizing up the cottage's worth. As Doris passed Woodbine, she saw Frances pull at her husband so she could peer in through the window, with the expression of a woman mentally rearranging the furniture.

'See anything you like?' Archie made Frances jump as he piloted Blanche through the front door.

The vicar, still turning the coin through his fingers, spoke sharply. 'Come *along*, Frances.'

His tone towards his lady wife would be discussed later over many cups of tea in many different kitchens.

The noise got to her. It rang in her ears even when Nance lay in bed. The women – so many faces and names! – assured her she'd get used to it.

Waterley Cross Mill was hidden. Not bucolic, not pretty, you took the turning and there it was, a pale brick palace wedged into the surrounding greenery. Well, too workaday for a palace with that finger of a chimney poking up in rude salute, but it had the soaring dimensions of one.

Nance stood in a row of women feeding a temperamental glutton of a machine. Paper travelled through it on giant rollers, and long brushes drifted in a measured fashion across the surface, over and back.

Her fingers quickly grew nimble. She lost the fear of being rolled up along with the paper. But the noise ... someone who grew up in quiet rooms with quiet folk could never get accustomed to that.

The women were smart and lively. A legion of them, hair tucked into caps, sleeves rolled up. They sang along to Gracie Fields, and soon Nance, too, could discern the piped wireless programmes above the industrial brouhaha. The women enfolded her like a new duckling in the brood when they waddled off to the canteen and left behind the gnashing machinery.

Crossing the yard, a large woman with red cheeks, mother to a tribe and wife of an infamous good-for-nothing, pulled Nance out of the way of a coal delivery. 'Mind out, dearie!'

The mill was ravenous, and Nance a mere morsel. She wilted over her tea – the strongest she had ever tasted – and remembered how she had thought the shop to be hard work.

'You'll get used to it, petal.' Red Cheeks was called Dolly. She was an elder stateswoman, respected.

'You bloody have to,' said a girl.

'No bloody choice!' said someone else.

Unused to language like that, Nance tried not to gape. She wanted to fit in. She only found out after a week or so that her nickname was Lady Muck.

Over the tea, they discussed the world. Their world: the mill.

'She's no better than she ought,' was the view on a passing woman. 'Three months gone, mark my words.' When a man from the cutting department skipped past, they told Nance, 'He thinks he's the cheese but he's only the wrapper!'

They flew apart, laughing, then drew together again, all of them connected by some invisible feminine thread.

'Who's for another?' A brawny girl collected mugs.

Nance lifted her chin. Took a deep breath. She really did want to fit in. 'I'll bloody have another bloody cup of bloody tea.'

Everyone fell about.

'Show us your hands,' said Dolly. The women tsk-tsked in sympathy, and promised Nance she'd soon stop cutting her fingers. Well, cut them less often; all their hands were criss-crossed with old and new cuts, evil thin ones that smarted.

'You got a fella, Lady Muck?'

'I'm married. He's a doctor.'

'Ooh, posh,' said Dolly.

'Lovely clean hands, I bet!' laughed her mate.

'Bet he's proud of you, doing your bit,' said Dolly.

When Nance told Morgan about Waterley Cross he had looked not proud but astonished. 'Well,' he'd said, return-ing to his book, 'I daresay they're desperate with all the men away.'

It had exercised her mind ever since. *I can't ask him what he meant by that.* They lacked a shared vocabulary to tackle delicate questions.

The women pushed away from the table. The bedlam of the mill floor would take Nance's mind off her home life.

Archie poured sherry into ruby-coloured schooners that had only ever come out at Christmas before his arrival. At Woodbine Cottage they saved nothing 'for best'; they used the most exquisite items every day. As Archie said, 'Why not?'

'You did well at the will reading.' He sat beside Blanche on the diminutive sofa. 'Just like we planned. Straight face. Give nothing away. *Dignity*, doll.' He appraised her. 'You all right?' he asked, softer.

'I'm fine.' Blanche tipped back the Pedro Ximenez in one.

'Hmm. Nothing says *I'm fine* like drinking like a docker.' Archie took her glass. Didn't ask if she wanted a top-up. She always wanted a top-up. 'Do you miss Jane? Christ, sorry.' He shook his head. 'That's a horrible question. Of course you miss her. It's only to be expected.'

Blanche held out her hand for the glass. 'When do I ever do what's expected of me?'

They passed on the stairs, Pamela in a hurry and Alec in brogues he had owned when they met; Pargetter men bought for longevity not fashion. She paused to let him pass, and glanced into a mirror with an ugly gilded frame.

'You're in the mirror all day,' he said.

'I'm not.'

'Very well, you're not.' Alec carried on upstairs, Hero loping one pace behind.

Pamela knew she was not easy to be with. She was a pendulum, and she swung wildly when attributing blame for the morass of their marriage. Some days she blamed her own stiffness, and some days she blamed the tale told by Alec's hidden letters.

Through a small window she saw a maid cross the yard with a bundle of bedding. Pamela rarely ventured out there among the dustbins, preferring to waft along the front terrace and the ornamental parterre. Now she ran out and caught up with the girl.

'Let me.' Pamela took the bedclothes. 'Have a sit down, you must be exhausted.' She hurried on, leaving the maid speechless at this rare display of concern from the lady of the house.

The stone room at the top of the folly was small, bare, but it had an ascetic beauty. Pamela knocked and opened the rough door, and it framed Kos perfectly.

He sat on the bed, legs apart, hunched over. His head was in his hands. She dropped the bedding and went to him. 'Your head?'

He didn't answer.

Pamela lifted his chin with her finger. He resisted, then let her read his face. She saw his skin taut with pain. Was his scar throbbing? She pushed his hair back and the gesture was compassionate, but not only that. It was sensual. There were tears on his cheeks where usually she saw dimples.

The bonds that tied Pamela to the house behind her were strong; they had been tested and proved. But Kos's plight moved her, deep within, like a tide waking and rearing. She was moved by being moved; she thought she had forgotten how. Kos slipped through her defences by no other gambit than by being Kos.

He opened his arms and she stepped into them, letting him press his face to her middle. He held on as if he was drowning. As if he had just bailed out of his crate.

Uncertainly at first, Pamela stroked his big, dark head. Her hand was small against it. He was a bear. No, *an eagle*. 'Better?'

'Much.'

They stayed that way as daylight moved across the folly.

Nance didn't stop to shuck off her dusty work clothes. She marched straight to Morgan's surgery at the back of the house.

He was pleased to see her. 'Ah! The working woman, done for the day!'

'I've been thinking.'

'Yes,' said Morgan, slowly, putting down his pen.

Nance closed the door and leaned against it; Magsy was at large. 'You can divorce me if you like. After all I'm damaged goods. You didn't know I was German when you proposed. Neither did I, for that matter. So, I'm just saying, I'd understand.'

She waited like a condemned prisoner, breathing hard. When she decided to get this said, on the way home, she felt she was being noble. *Whereas what I'm really doing is testing him.*

He dithered. Very Morgan, that. 'This is . . .' He coughed. 'Nance, I'm a man of my word. I won't divorce you.'

She grappled for the doorknob and was out of the room.

'And, of course,' he said, to her back, 'I . . .'

Out in the hall, Magsy was rolling up the Persian rug; her last job of the day would be to beat it half to death out on the lawn.

Morgan could not let Magsy hear what he wanted to say to Nance. He tore a sheet from his prescription pad, turned it over and wrote it down instead. Best place to leave it would be the kitchen table. When Nance fetched the cold cuts Magsy had prepared, she would see it. And see *him*.

There had been no discussion about who would lead No. 9 Platoon, C Company, 15th Battalion of the Borsetshire Home Guard. Alec Pargetter was at the helm as they patrolled the night-time lanes. The cuffed trousers chafed, the webbing weighed him down and the triangular cap made him look, according to Pamela, like a newly sharpened pencil.

The Home Guard *mattered*; Alec knew that. Yet it felt so trifling to be marching – somewhat slowly, old Mick Lister had the flattest of feet – up and down and in and around while the real fighting went on elsewhere. His pistol sat lumpen in his holster; Alec had kept it since the Great War.

'Surely it's too old to be of use,' Pamela had said. 'But then, one could say the same about you, darling.'

He had laughed, but she was right. Two years over conscription age, Alec had pulled every string he could think of to get himself into his old regiment. Friends in the corridors of power all said the same thing – he was to sit tight, get his affairs in order, and wait until he was needed.

A war could be won or lost by then.

'All right back there?' He heard huffing and puffing as they took the turning for Waterley Cross.

'Tiptop, sir!' Chas Westenra was young, bouncy; he could march to the coast and back, but was exempted from service by dint of his job as a lens grinder.

'Good, good. Stay alert!' said Alec.

The year was turning, switching off the lights of summer, setting them on the downward slope to winter.

'Who's smoking?' The smell of Player's Navy Cut was pungent on the crisp air. 'Put it out, Grundy.' Alec thought of his goodbyes with Gerald. There was talk of the evacuated school keeping the boys over Christmas. The prospect hadn't seemed to bother Gerald.

Alec's fathering was modelled on his own father's template. He lectured, he set out expectations, he came down hard on wrongdoing. Today, though, the boy's departure had triggered a suspicion in Alec that he had missed an opportunity over the summer to improve matters. On the verge of manhood, Gerald couldn't be genuinely apathetic and sullen twenty-four hours a day; when would he show his parents something else? The rebellion, the disrespect – in between the constant chastisements, there was no time to find out anything more than the basics about his son's character.

Plus Pamela spoiled him of course, but Alec didn't feel up to having that conversation.

'All right back there, Private Sweet?' Alec had had to have a word with Arthur Sweet about his non-regulation tartan slippers; if they marched too fast he and Dan would have to carry the old chap the last couple of miles. The government required all males between seventeen and sixty-five 'capable of free movement' to join the Home Guard; the well-named Sweet, with his Santa Claus white hair, stretched that definition. Maybe the government believed patriotism and gung-ho would see off a fascist invasion.

'Yessir! Are we to patrol the mill, sir?'

'Yes, but to what end I don't know.'

Westenra chipped in from the dark. 'Maybe 'cos the mill makes maps for the RAF nowadays.'

'Right *turn*!' shouted Alec, in the ridiculous way expected of him. He thought of Pamela, how dreamy she was lately, her edges softened. And the lipstick! He relied on her to be sharp as a tack, yet she had sent him off tonight without the belt she had had mended for him.

They dispersed over the mill grounds, passing the stilled coal engines and stepping across their tracks.

'No krauts here!' yelled Westenra.

'Shall we ... The Bull?' asked Private Sweet hopefully.

They picked up the pace somewhat on the march back to Ambridge.

By late afternoon the vicar had baptized two babies. The confidence of womankind amazed Henry, bringing life into war.

He looked into and backed out of the village hall, which was crammed with more women, painting badly drawn ears of corn onto banners, moulding a papier mâché sun.

The evidence of September industry in the fields enfeebled Henry. Not that he was required to lift a finger; everyone knew his labour was of a righteous nature, far more exhausting than mere physical exertion. He went to the quietest corner of the churchyard, by the high old wall, where the Gilpins lay.

Jane's cross stood at an angle.

Henry took out the half-crown she had bequeathed him. He threaded it through his fingers. It mesmerized him as it slid back and forth. It was a wonder he hadn't worn the coin smooth by now.

'Why?' he asked the hump of earth that was slowly flattening out.

Henry glanced over his shoulder. Wouldn't do for the vicar of St Stephen's to be overheard berating dead parishioners. The sleepy bumblebees staggering in and out of the ivy that had sunk its suckers into the ancient wall gave him cover with their buzzing. The blackberries, profuse and sinister, reminded him that they grew fat and dark on the bodies he interred.

He bent closer to the grave. Fiercely, he said, 'Why torment me, Jane? You are cruel, *cruel*.' And he held up the coin like a communion host.

Underwood's sat complacent on Borchester's main thorough-fare. The store sold everything, and the war had barely dented its hushed atmosphere of plenty and order. Underwood's was forever Edwardian, and Magsy, herself slightly Edwardian, was a valued, long-standing customer.

As the manager escorted Magsy out of the emporium, a young clerk, whose legs were tired and who was worried sick about her sailor beau, attended to the list left by the for-midable Miss Furneaux.

It was written on a piece of paper from a doctor's prescription pad; customers used all sorts of paper in the spirit of making do. The girl scanned the items: '1 × stout girdle (large), 2 × worsted stockings (black), 1 × drawers (very large) (best flannel).'

She flipped the page, checking for extras; her floor manager would have her guts for garters if anything were left off the order. She raised her eyebrows. Whistled. That Miss Furneaux was a dark horse all right.

In Morgan's handwriting, cramped but precise, the clerk read, 'And of course the main reason I will never desert you is simple. I love you, my best and most precious girl.'

Peggy could hear the whirr and bustle of harvest on the far side of the hedges that hemmed her in. She hadn't planned to visit Ambridge again so soon, but a stray comment from her mother had set her on the road again.

There they were, the two of them, as if she had conjured them up. 'What you up to?'

Billy and John jumped a foot in the air. Billy hid a bag behind his back.

Peggy loved them for their transparency, with a sudden white-hot squeak of emotion. She wouldn't ask what was in the bag. *Let them have their little crimes.*

'What you doing here?' asked Billy.

'Nice welcome for your sister who's brought you both a bun.'

The buns were magnificent – iced! – and the boys ate themselves into a stupor on the grassy verge.

'I loves a bun,' said John, sombre.

Wizbang wanted to paw Peggy. She fended him off the way she fended off her dance partners at the Palais. She wondered if Jack Archer could dance. *Nah.* Then she wondered why she was wondering and transferred her annoyance with herself to Billy. 'You sure you're looking after your brother?'

'Good as gold, I am.' Billy sensed John's need to confess, to yell, *We just nicked half a loaf off Connie!* The loaf had to make it to Quartershot Camp, and into Luca's hands. 'We're not going nowhere, Peg.'

'Now, see, when you offer up information you haven't been asked for, that makes me suspicious, Billy Perkins.' Peggy had to slap at Wizbang, who was berserk with love, his dirty paws marking her skirt. He really was *very* like her dance partners. 'Did you get a letter from Mum, by any chance?'

'Don't say it,' said John. 'If Dad's dead.'

'Dead? Dad? Don't be soft.' Peggy gathered him to her, and he curled around her, his big babyish head with its thick yellow curls hot against her body. 'He's just missing, we can't say for sure where he is. He'll probably be in a camp somewhere, and there are rules about camps, so he'll be safe.'

'Camps are mean,' said John, into her neck. 'They hit you when you stick up for yourself.'

'Where you getting this from?' asked Peggy. She must manage the boys' worries, she thought, while playing a Pathé newsreel in her head of her father's body somewhere, trampled and un-mourned. 'I came here to tell you not to fret, that it'll all work out fine.'

'Dad'll escape,' said John.

'Probably.' Peggy couldn't see her dad escaping from a paper bag, but it was a useful daydream.

'How do you *know*,' said Billy, eyes narrow, 'that it'll work out fine?'

'I just do,' said Peggy.

She's like a poem.

That was what Cliff thought, the romantic boy born into a fists-up family, as he watched Wanda cycle around the side of Arkwright Hall.

Like a poem, but perfect like no poem could ever be. Not even one by his adored Emily Brontë.

The poem was sweaty as she jumped off her bike, to stand bent double, wheezing, by the step where Cliff and Lorna congregated for their mid-morning natters. Bit one-sided these natters, but Cliff was coming along.

Lorna held out a cup of water, laughing, her woodland-creature face lit up. 'What've you done to yourself, Wanda?'

'I got off to walk my bike up Lakey Hill, and Walter Gabriel came flying past me and I thought if *he* can do it so can I.' Wanda collapsed onto the step. 'But as you can see, I can't.'

Her hilarity was infectious. Lorna had never heard Cliff laugh before.

Lorna studied Cliff studying Wanda. Even his glass eye seemed enlivened by the girl. Lorna understood; a lesser person might hate Wanda for what she understood, but little

Lorna was bigger than that. 'You'll have muscles on your muscles soon.'

'Look!' Wanda flexed her arm, proud of the balled mound that appeared. 'You don't get arms like that at finishing school.' She had told Lorna about how the war saved her from the prospect of Brillantmont Academy in Lausanne.

To Lorna, who had never left Borsetshire – unless you counted travelling via literature, in which case Lorna had been *everywhere*: to Paris with Balzac and Mississippi with Mark Twain – the image of a gabled mansion filled with books and music didn't sound so bad. Certainly preferable to the hops Wanda dragged her to.

'What're you two yakking about today? Don't tell me: books.' Wanda was *not* a reader. 'Withering Heights again, I suppose.'

'*Wuthering*,' said Cliff and Lorna together.

'The most romantic book ever written,' said Cliff.

'You don't need a book to find romance. You just need a member of the opposite sex. You coming on Friday, Lorna?' Wanda was revived, sparking again. She held her hand out to Cliff, who hesitated and then took it and pulled her up. She was heavy, Wanda: packed full of life. 'Ta, Cliffy.'

'Not sure about Friday,' said Lorna.

'Don't say no.' Wanda was prettily anguished. 'Mr Bigtime's off on some stupid business trip and that corporal who took a fancy to you might be there.'

It was mythical, this pash of the corporal's; he hadn't noticed Lorna. Wanda, with naive generosity, assumed all women created a ripple in the ether the way she did, but Lorna knew she was a daisy not an orchid. Essential for background colour, but unsuited to centre stage. She didn't mind this, but she did mind that Cliff so clearly agreed.

It was all hands on deck at Lower Loxley. Called upon to do housework, Pamela did it as efficiently as she wrote letters of complaint or designed a garden or made love to Alec.

Taking a tray of china down from the chaps' rooms she paused at a round window, the one on the turning of the stair. A magic porthole, it sometimes had the power to show her Kos, and today it didn't disappoint.

He was strolling in the kitchen garden, leading with those strong shoulders, always pushing through the world even when taking his time. The shoulders shocked a *Good Lord!* out of Pamela, who had never before understood the animal nature of physical attraction.

I have kissed him, she thought. And she'd do so again. She looked furtively around, as if a passing parlour maid might read her thoughts. Watching Kos amble out of sight, Pamela was happy.

Just happy.

Kos was a jewel she had found in an old coat pocket. A violet cream she'd kept for later. It had been easier than she imagined to slip the bonds of fidelity, when the reward was life bursting into Technicolor.

The guilt was merely biding its time, she knew that. She was not the sort of woman to pursue happiness at the expense of promises made. For now, as she bounced down the stairs with the tray, passing the hoop and stick leaning against the panelling, she allowed herself to sing.

She ignored Alec's look of bafflement as she passed him.

The rain was steady, numbing, and it dripped down the back of John's neck as he and Billy squatted by the wire of Quartershot Camp, waiting for Luca to come.

'What if he's been moved on?' John's scarf had come into its own as the year cooled, but now it lay against him like a wet pet. 'What if he's been shot?' That red target on Luca's back was never far from his mind.

'Stop whingeing.' Billy swung his conker on a length of twine. It was a world-beater, his most precious possession. He was worried, too; Luca was never late. Billy was no longer wary about the Italian; he loved him just as John did. Although he'd never use such a word to describe the way he felt.

Feet slipping in the mud, Luca was there. 'Boys,' he began, urgently. 'Last week you do not come.' His big doggy eyes were sad.

'Me sister turned up,' said Billy. 'Girls ruin everything.'

'I worry. Remember, you are like my own boys. It was like Bruno and Vittorio forget me.'

Wounded, sorry, John cried, 'We could never forget you!'

A green-blue egg was produced and pushed through the wire. 'From Connie's ducks.'

After formally thanking them, Luca said, 'Do you want little adventure?'

They did.

A cart of ewes rattled past the shop, drenched to the bone. On the marshy Green lay the canvas corpse of a marquee. The weather was not being kind; at this rate the Harvest Festival would be squeezed into the village hall.

In the warm, dry shop, Agnes tweaked a bow on Irene's plait. The girl pulled away, her face dark.

'She's a credit to you,' Agnes told Nanny. She appreciated quiet children, and gave thanks she was safely past childbearing age. No patter of tiny feet in her and Denholm's cottage.

'Like a doll.' Archie winked at Irene and earned a look of disgust from the child.

'Hear that, pet?' Nanny held tight onto Irene's hand.

'Scared she'll run off?' joked Agnes.

'I am. But we're working on that, aren't we? There's been some . . .' Nanny mouthed the word. 'Stealing.'

Agnes gripped her purse tighter.

'Just a hiccup, isn't it, Irene, pet?'

Why does Nanny set herself up like that? Agnes could see that Irene never answered these fond questions. She couldn't tell if Nanny's outfit was a uniform or merely the woman's austere taste. All the handsewn ruffles and gilt buttons were saved for the girl. 'Do you do your lessons nicely for Nanny?' Agnes asked only because she was perverse; it was stamped through her marrow like a stick of Brighton rock.

'Such a quick learner.' Nanny answered for Irene. 'It's all I can do to keep up with her reading and her sums. You should see her beautiful handwriting.'

Irene snorted.

'Where's that doll of yours? Sukie, isn't it?' asked Agnes.

'Dead,' said Irene.

'Well, I never,' said Agnes.

'Mislaid, she mislaid her,' said Nanny. 'She'll turn up.'

'She's dead,' said Irene.

Archie changed the subject, and pointed to spectral white footprints on Frank's linoleum. 'You got a ghost, Frank?' Archie was on first name terms with everybody; if introduced to the king, he would call him Georgie Boy.

Frank looked reprovingly at the new girl, the second new girl since Nance stepped down. Worse than the first, she'd dropped a bag of precious flour and walked it all over the shop.

The door banged open and shuddered against the shelves. Beacham, a dripping coat over his head, leaned in and said, 'Get a move on, for pity's sake, I've no time to hang about for prattling women.'

Frank's 'Hmm' was quite an outburst for him, and Agnes said, 'Your husband's a bit of a handful.'

'He's my brother,' said Nanny, dropping her bag, flustered by Beacham's displeasure. 'I've never made it to the altar. He needs me, you see.'

'What can I get you?' asked Frank, just as Nanny yanked Irene's outstretched hand from a row of apples, red and seductive.

'Don't, dear! They're not yours,' she said.

'I mean it!' bellowed Beacham from outside.

'Oh dear, I should . . .' Nanny beetled out, and they heard her apologies.

'That Beacham needs a good kick up the arse,' said Agnes. 'Now, Frank, I'll take three rashers of bacon and I don't want them so thin I can read the headlines through 'em thank you *very* much.'

Billy and John were on the wrong side of the wire.

Smuggled through a tiny slit in the fence – 'Easy to get in,' said Luca. 'Hard to get out!' – they had seen Quartershot's simple wooden church, nothing like St Stephen's. They had sniffed the delectable fried onion whiff of the canteen. They had scampered like fox pups past unsuspecting inmates.

They were delirious.

The camp was dynamic, masculine. Dirty and exciting. Billy would pretend to be Italian if it meant he could stay. He gloried in Luca's reaction to his conker – *'Magnifico!'* – and so didn't hear John's slip of the tongue when he called Luca 'Dad'.

Nor did he see Luca's pleasure at John's mistake.

They hunkered down by a Nissen hut. They could touch Luca now, although Billy chose not to. John leaned on him. The rain persisted.

'This English weather . . .' Luca blew on his hands.

'Here.' Billy peeled off his gloves.

'You are kind, Billy, but no. What I need you cannot give.

I need money.' The food, he explained, was disgusting. He needed cash to buy contraband goodies.

'So, we can't give you money, eh?' Billy retrieved a penny from his shoe. It was earmarked for a spree at the shop as soon as gobstoppers came back.

Luca frowned. Stuck out his bristly chin. 'I cannot accept.'

'Go on!' said Billy.

'Okay.'

'Oh,' said Billy, who had expected a little more resistance.

Luca's eyes widened as he pocketed the penny. 'Hey! Maybe boys like you will help your papa to escape. Maybe he come back soon and I meet this great man and tell him of his sons' big hearts.'

'They'd have to be daring and very brave.' John knew he was neither of these. 'Can we see Bruno and Vittorio again?'

They studied the children, their Mediterranean twins. They didn't linger on the surly grandpapa, just the *ragazzi* who might, even now, be helping their dad escape.

The waiting room at Morgan's house smelled of bleach. Blanche wondered how Nance could bear a doctor's hands on her, cold over-washed paws that had touched sores and boils and *bits*.

Nothing specific brought her to the surgery. Just the opportunity to talk about herself. Magsy lurked; eventually Blanche's dog-eared manners made her lay down *The Lady* and bid her good afternoon. The magazine had nothing to tell her, anyway; Blanche didn't want to please her man by knitting him a tie, nor did she plan to embroider a pillowcase.

'I do worry,' said Magsy, 'about Morgan. He took Jane's passing very badly.'

'He probably feels responsible. Suspects she took one too many of those tablets he prescribed.'

'Oh no no no,' said Magsy. 'Nobody thinks that.'

'Everybody, from the vicar's cat upwards, thinks that.'

'Next!' called Morgan from his room.

Seated at his desk, Morgan could arrange his kindly face into a specific expression of calm interest that inspired trust in his patients. He did not do that with Blanche.

She was not to know that he was bewildered by his life. That he was angry but had nobody to be angry with, and was full of love that nobody seemed to want. Blanche assumed he was chewing over her enslavement of Jane and so she lifted her nose, because attack was Blanche's first – indeed only – line of defence.

'Look like you need a tonic yourself, Doctor.'

Morgan drew on the civility that got him through the day in that calm room, with its treatment couch and its warm rugs and its fire in the grate. 'Looking forward to Harvest Festival?' He polished his glasses with the cuff of his jacket. 'Jane always took first prize with her late-flowering hydrangeas.'

'Maybe you should enter. You and your late-flowering marriage.' Blanche assumed the worst in people; she assumed Morgan had peered over the garden fence and seen how Jane's hydrangeas stooped, desiccated and neglected.

Morgan put down his glasses. He said, and it was as if a

ventriloquist pulled his levers, for he had vowed to take this fact to the grave, 'You do know your sister killed herself.'

'She certainly did not.'

'Here.' Before the adrenaline could peter out, Morgan unlocked a drawer in his desk and took out an envelope hidden beneath innocuous receipts. 'Read this.'

It was addressed to Morgan. It had crouched in his mind, loathsome as a toad, ever since he found it on Jane's bedside table. He was already ashamed of his impulse by the time Blanche picked it up, but she held it out of his reach when he lunged across the desk.

The handwriting was so familiar to her.

My dear old friend,

I apologize for making you the keeper of my secrets.

By the time you read this I will have passed over into the next realm, and left behind all my trusted companions. Only you can know this is of my own choosing.

Shortly, I will drink a cordial made from the foxgloves that are so abundant in my garden. No doubt you know that digitalis has powerful properties. Hopefully it will disrupt my unsteady heart so that it ends me.

Thank you for all the care you have given me. You made my parents' last years bearable. We are a lucky village to have a doctor like you.

I am in my right mind and I am not distraught. I go gladly from this life, for I am too fragile a stalk to withstand the weather of this past year. Do not grieve!

Keep my secret from Henry. Our vicar may feel impelled to bar me from the graveyard.

And keep my secret, too, from Blanche, who might blame herself.

Yours affectionately,
Jane.

'We could have helped,' said Morgan, when Blanche looked up. 'If we'd only—'

'Do shut up,' said Blanche. When she rose she staggered.

She knew, as did Morgan, that she was in every line of Jane's letter.

Trestle tables swathed in crepe paper flooded The Green. Bunting flapped. The marquee listed. The rain was polite enough to pause, and the sun took over.

Cardigans were cast off and collars undone as Ambridge gathered to give thanks for the harvest, get pie-eyed on Bob's ale, and ogle Pamela Pargetter's oranges.

'Where'd she get 'em?' people asked, filing past the three fruits like Muscovites filing past Lenin's tomb. Pamela wouldn't say; she was raffling the paragons for the church fund. She panicked when she lost sight of Mavis in the crowd, before reminding herself the dog was not lost. It was gone.

Worker ants from Lower Loxley laid boards over the boggy green, so Mrs Endicott was safe to do a slow circuit of every stall, pore over every competing tuber and praise every gargantuan cabbage. She reminisced about the pomegranates handed out to the children just two years ago. She was proud of the banner she had painted, and not at all vexed that everyone mistook her sheaves of corn for dead birds.

Fiddle music, as green and as raw as the produce, got toes tapping. Walter had a mate who played a squeezebox. Dancing broke out; Wanda whirled Lorna by the waist.

'Come on, Boss!' she yelled, but Doris was on duty, righting signs and overseeing the judging. Connie was at her side, her lieutenant, in a dress Doris had 'reserved' from the Arkwright Hall jumble sale.

Sewn for a farmer's wife, it hung loosely on emaciated Connie. The younger Horrobins, Maisie and Bert, verged on clean, and Connie was gay. She ruffled John's hair when he darted past, and let out a croaky *Aw!* when he hugged her, briefly, hard. Maisie ran off to reacquaint herself with Irene, but the girl was still immune to friendship and answered none of Maisie's quickfire questions – 'Why'd you do your hair all fussy like that? Want to play hopscotch?' – until Nanny snatched up Irene's hand and said, 'Don't sneak off, anything could happen.' She gave Maisie a dirty look and Maisie gave Nanny one back, a real Horrobin special.

'Bit late in the year for a produce show,' grumbled Dan to his Home Guard cronies, by the beer tent.

'Her ladyship's decision,' said Bob, nodding in Pamela's direction. 'Her as knows nothing about farming.'

'But she knows plenty,' said Dan, 'about little hats. Why do women wear them little hats?'

Answer came there none. The men had more on their minds than Pamela's chic little bowler, such as whose round it was. It was never Stan's.

A clear Best in Show, Pamela was highly visible in tailored linen. Alec watched her tour the stalls, doing her duty by making the politest of small talk with all and sundry. He hadn't complimented her on her outfit when they left Lower Loxley and he couldn't think why not. It was churlish to be so tight-lipped; he recalled his last day with Gerald, when he could have said something poignant. *Like what, though?* Alec was not creative about compliments.

He paused to say, yes, the weather was simply *marvellous* to a woman who took in washing, and to ask a very old gentleman if he needed a seat to watch the skittles. Later he would hand the rosettes to Pamela and she would bestow them on the champion vegetable growers. Their marriage might be stiff, but it was strong, and he thanked God – that most understanding of celestial chaps, always on Blighty's side – for it.

Billy was fuming. His conker had been smashed by some chump from Arkwright Hall.

'Let's follow Cliff and his two lady friends,' whispered John. 'Like secret agents!'

That took Billy's mind off his conker. When the not-pretty lady friend bought elderflower cordial from the Women's Committee stall, something shiny fell from her bag.

'Hey, lady, you lost a—'

'Shut up, John!' Billy retrieved the penny from the mud and put it in his sock.

'That's stealing,' said John.

'It's for Luca.'

Which meant, really, it was for Dad.

Squired by Archie, Blanche was there on sufferance. He wouldn't take no for an answer. 'You have to show your face,' he'd said as he arranged her hair. She was less powdered than before, her accoutrements more polished. That didn't stop her entering the Throw the Hammer competition. And winning it.

The men stood around, bereft, as Blanche stared at her prize. *What will I do with a crate of ale?* Blanche hadn't told Archie about Jane's note. About what Jane did to herself. After all those years fetching and carrying for Blanche, Jane had handed her something heavy to carry alone.

'Have it,' she said to the men and they fell upon the beer.

Frances disseminated her theory that Woodbine would go to Henry. She had listened, she said, when the wallet spoke, just as dear Jane instructed. 'We wouldn't *want* to put Blanche out of her home,' she said, 'but we must respect Jane's wishes.'

'You could sell it and give the proceeds to the poor,' said Mrs Endicott.

'We *could*,' said Frances, uncertainly.

Shaking hands with this, that and the other person left Pamela reaching for her handkerchief. She found a folded note in it.

'I WANT YOU.'

Metal glowed in her blood. Her underused, underappreciated, whippet-thin body blazed. She was caught in a noose of desire, even though she and Kos had done little more than kiss. 'Alec!' she called before she had time to think. 'May I have a word?'

'His master's voice!' Stan saluted Alec with his tankard as Alec turned on his heel.

The dress that Wanda wore revealed to Cliff that not only did she have legs but they were possibly the best legs in England. Her Chippendale shape fascinated him. He felt Lorna look at him the way she looked at her books: contemplative, wondering. He turned his face away from her, a habit he couldn't break.

'Do excuse me.' Alec passed the trio to follow his wife to the back of the marquee. He found her by a trolley stacked with trays and tin teapots.

'I do like that outfit,' he said.

'It gives me no pleasure, Alec, to tell you that I am involved with a man.'

Alec felt as if he'd been strapped into a bobsleigh and pushed downhill. 'Involved?'

Hero lay down, oblivious.

'I believe you know what that means.'

His suspicions had been vague, more a pastime than a concern. He felt as if Pamela had declared herself to be from Mars, or that beneath the tailored linen she was a Great Dane. 'You're my wife.'

'I was your wife when *you* were involved elsewhere.'

The sterile way she described his affair always hurt Alec. It had been a source of heat, his shame only so intense because it matched the love he felt. He closed his eyes briefly, as if she had struck him. 'That's over.'

This was the perfect moment to quote the letters, but there was no time, and Pamela was as businesslike about confessing her adultery as she would be about sacking a servant. 'I'm not proud of what I'm doing. I hope you can accommodate me.'

'Accommodate you? You're not asking to borrow the bloody car!'

'No, I'm being honest with you, which is a damn sight more than you were with me.'

'It's Kos, isn't it?'

Well, who else? Dodgy? 'Yes.'

'Not such a hero, then.' Alec's dog stood at the sound of his name, then folded himself up again when ignored.

'Let's not descend into insults.'

Alec dearly wanted to descend. To find Kos – *damn foolish nickname!* – and tear his arms off. But he was not good at fighting, and besides, Pargetters set the tone and today's tone could not be brawling on The Green. 'I forbid it,' he said.

Pamela walked away. He heard her murmur, 'I forbid it!' to herself, as if he'd told her a particularly good joke.

A couple hurtled around the side of the marquee, already in each other's arms, giggling through their kiss. They sprang apart and Alec recognized the man as a tenant he had held at his baptism. 'Do carry on,' he said, and left them to it.

The marrow display was, as ever, a big draw. Agnes stood to one side, directing attention to her husband's contribution. 'A whopper, don't you agree?' she asked proudly.

'Denholm's excelled himself.' Doris, cordial in hand, browsed the vegetables. The merry wheezing of the squee-zebox, and the gaiety that hung like perfume over the show, helped her take a day off from the notebook where she totted up monies in and monies out. She held the balance in her head, always in red. Dan refused to worry about money. Doris searched for him in the crowd and saw the back of his head, over at The Bull's tent. He would be squiffy by the end of the day, and would have seen nothing of the floral wonders on display. She felt a rush of annoyed tenderness, so familiar it was like an old song.

'It can't be the vicar,' Agnes was saying. 'The will, I mean. The letters B and L can't lead to Henry Bissett.'

'Oh, that stupid will,' said Doris, who couldn't care less about it. 'I never was any good at puzzles.' She got out of the way as children – evacuees, locals, she couldn't tell – surged past, whooping. The young ones were off the leash today, and their simple high spirits buoyed Doris.

Until, that is, she wandered by Pamela's orange raffle and heard the vicar's wife say to her coterie of be-hatted ladies, 'A bicycle, rather a large gift to accept from a man so many years her senior.'

Doris butted in. She agreed with Frances, but loyalty made her say, 'There's no harm in Wanda.' The girl was a Brookfielder now.

Frances spoke without words, and the ladies all looked where she looked, to where Wanda sat, knees to her chin, laughing wholeheartedly, and showing her slip. That plain little Lorna beside her, for contrast.

Too self-confident to bother with stuffy notions of dignity, Wanda gave out the wrong signals in the buttoned-up world of Ambridge. *I'll have a word*, thought Doris, then decided she wouldn't. Wanda's laughter was like a child's. It helped, she realized, to counterbalance the drone of bad news from the wireless. The maps in the newspapers with their arrows showing Allied surges and retreats.

One of those arrows may shunt them all out of place before the fighting was over. *But Ambridge is more than a dot on a map.* They were people, not statistics. The war was everywhere, like God or the common cold, and just as oblivious to Doris's desires. Doris longed to worry about small things again, about when the partridge hanging in her pantry would be ready to eat, about whether her loaf would rise. When Jack popped into her head she would like to tut at his fella-me-lad-cockiness, instead of feeling her heart contract as she wondered would she know if his stopped beating? What if Jack was hurt, now, as she ambled around this fete? The big fat baby boy she gave birth to?

'Christine!' Doris had a sharp need to see her daughter's face. 'Love, take Irene over to play quoits with your pals.'

Christine, already disgusted by the lack of toffee apples, nixed this. 'She's a funny onion, Mum.'

Arkwright Hall's contribution, a map of Ambridge made

of rose petals, had been Cliff's idea. It didn't wear well; St Stephen's was already scented slush. Cliff cleared his throat to speak and Wanda looked at him, surprised; he didn't generally say much. Lorna's look was wry – *She's always wry*, thought Cliff – whereas Wanda was like a brook, a clean rushing brook.

He said, 'Bet this isn't like the swanky do's you're used to in your real life, Wanda.'

'This is my real life, Cliffy. You don't get nails like this *imagining* farm work. You've got me all wrong. I'm a boarding school brat, more or less abandoned by Ma and Pa. I've always fended for myself. I tell you, the Boss's shack has more home comforts than my dorm.' She waved at Doris, whose basket of produce boded well for soup at Brookfield later. Her friendship with the Boss was lopsided, but that didn't faze Wanda. She knew she confused Doris. She hoped something would shift; she missed her mother, and would like an older lady to lean against in the evenings when she was exhausted and wondering about Mr Bigtime's intentions, or where she would land after the war.

Because everything would be changed, Wanda sensed that. And she would be more changed than most. How could she marry one of the chinless wonders set out in her drawing room like a menu now that she knew how to hold a sheep while it was sheared? She didn't fit in at Brookfield, and she would no longer fit in at home.

Lorna, contemplating a stall of trinkets, found a clever little ornament made from a varnished ear of corn. She knew it would tickle Cliff, but when she turned to show him, he had moved on, following the sway of Wanda's hips to the tree where the musicians gathered.

The flower tables were a particular draw.

'I do miss Jane's hydrangeas,' said Mrs Endicott. 'Are you not allergic to flowers, Archie dear?'

Before Archie could answer, a passing boy shouted, 'He's allergic to women!'

'We're all as God made us,' said Archie. 'Isn't that right, Frances?'

The vicar's wife mumbled some equivocation.

Agnes was sly. 'What *are* you allergic to, though? Exactly?'

Mrs Endicott said, 'Allergies are a cross to bear. I once ate a ham roll that nearly killed me. You keep yourself safe, young man.'

'Oh, he does that all right,' said Agnes.

On the far edge of The Green, Morgan watched a fat Shetland pony do a pompous circuit with a child on its back. The child was Irene and Nanny wouldn't relinquish her hand, marching alongside the little horse.

His wife's arm through his, Morgan hoped his white linen jacket didn't seem foppish, or try-hard. Nance had bloomed that morning, emerging from their bedroom in a blue summer dress that foamed about her like the sea. He was in awe of women's ability to transform.

Hopefully my love note put her mind at rest. He could ask – he probably *should* ask – if Nance found his declaration reassuring, but they were not quite *there*, not on that marital high ground he had assumed would be achieved automatically.

171

A tug on his other arm. Magsy led him away, proprietorially, to gaze upon Arthur Sweet dressed up as a town crier. 'So diverting!' She was hot, in too many layers, like a present nobody bothered to open.

Morgan felt Nance's arm drop. 'I'll go say hello to my dad.' She did that, but little more.

'How's the job going?' asked Frank, polite, careful.

'Fine.' Nance half-regretted her decision to leave the shop. The babble of the mill was unsettling, and she went home every day to a comfortable house where she felt like a guest. 'New girl working out?'

'She's no Nance,' said Frank.

There were no raffle tickets left for the idolized oranges. Dodgy had bought every single one.

Feeling the villagers' eyes on him, Pamela tried to dissuade him. They were lusted after, those oranges, and he wasn't giving anyone else a chance of winning them.

'I insist, dear lady.' He seemed to think he was being gallant.

Kos was nowhere to be seen. Pamela tore off Dodgy's tickets and heard her name being called to hand out the prizes. She could not afford for her love affair to consume her; it couldn't matter whether Kos was at the show or not.

'And first place for dahlias goes to Mrs Barbara Carlile and her Lady of Pruna.' Alec and Pamela were halfway through the prize-giving. There was applause but some bitterness; Mrs Carlile won last year, too.

Pamela was gracious, Alec was grave. They were on show

every bit as much as the Lady of Pruna. He would gladly overturn all the tables – the red pontiac potato that swept the board, the swede on its velvet cushion – and ask what the blazes did any of it matter?

The world was going to hell in a handcart, and his wife was making googly eyes at a chap who was not only taller than Alec but who could barely stand under the weight of his medals. But Alec did none of these outrageous things; he stroked his moustache and found something personal to say about every prizewinner.

At least Pamela was honest with me. In her funny, cool way she had shown him trust.

Pamela saw Kos then, and the winner of the Ugliest Vegetable rosette thought her smile was for him.

The marquee stayed up. The ale ran out. The villagers drifted home, and the children followed Dodgy like the Pied Piper of Ambridge, as he distributed every single orange segment, one by one.

Ambridge is a-bed; the moment shimmers.

There are petals on The Green, trodden underfoot, the carefully constructed map of the village disrupted and unrecognizable.

In Blanche's garden, there is a moment of transition, when it shifts from civilization to wilderness. The buddleia makes its move; it invades the lawn.

Doris is glad Dan is asleep as she stares at the ceiling and does frantic sums.

Dan is glad Doris is asleep as he stares at the wardrobe and frets about census forms.

The note that Jane left behind is ripped up and rotting at the bottom of a dustbin. Why, then, can Blanche read it on the backs of her eyes when she tries to sleep?

Up a tree, Alec now appreciates why his son retreats to the cypress. Private and welcoming, it's a good spot to think. About how, once again, he only noticed how deeply he cares about a woman when she showed him her back.

OCTOBER

Doris was glad of Dan's old overcoat as she got out of the truck in front of Furnivall Manor.

The implacable billeting welfare forms must be filled in; Arkwright Hall's evacuees could be done at one fell swoop but Irene required a special trip once the farm day was over.

Night seeped into Furnivall Manor, but the servants' hall was cosy: easy to warm, as Nanny said. She yammered on about the books she and Irene read together, how they were studying Cavaliers and Roundheads.

Her chatter couldn't disguise the silence that wrapped around Irene like a cloak.

'And you've no idea when the family'll be back?'

Nanny would no more criticize 'her' family than she would criticize Irene or her brother. They were, she told Doris, 'in London for the foreseeable'.

'And what about Sukie, your lovely doll, Irene? She never turned up?'

Nanny said, as Irene stood up and walked out with a stiff

175

back, 'We don't mention Sukie. She gets cross, no, not cross, just *upset.*'

They were through the Looking Glass, in a house where adults tiptoed around the child and feared her moods.

'Come and see the dress I'm working on,' said Nanny, eyes bright like an evangelist, as they always were when she spoke of her labours on behalf of Irene. 'It's in my room.'

In what looked to Doris more like a cubicle than a bedroom – Irene still slept in palatial luxury in the best boudoir – Doris cooed politely over the sapphire blue party frock. 'I've been saving the material for something special, and there's nothing more special than our Irene.'

There was no reciprocity for Nanny's adoration; not even a hint that Irene noticed it. Irene looked through Nanny as if she was vapour. Doris glanced through another open door and saw a single bed, with male paraphernalia all about.

'My brother's room,' said Nanny, closing the door, but not before Doris had seen the silk camiknickers bunched on the rug.

Back in the kitchen, Doris asked, 'Where's Beacham tonight?'

'Out with the Home Guard. He's most diligent.'

'Does he have a sweetheart?'

'He keeps himself to himself.'

'You're sure he never brings anyone home? Because ...' Doris glanced at Irene, who had returned, but was, as ever, disattending. 'In front of the girl ...'

'My brother's a decent man. It's his fate to be misunderstood.'

'Hmm.' *I understand him all too well,* thought Doris. 'Is he, does he . . . is Beacham *kind* to you, Nanny?'

Nanny quivered. Doris had seen that physicality before. A rabbit caught in the headlights, irresolute, even though staying still meant death and to take a leap meant rescue.

A heavy tread outside announced Beacham.

'You again,' he said to Doris by way of hello. 'Come to take the kid home, I hope.'

Irene didn't register the slight.

'Oh, Beacham!' There was a touch of *tsk tsk* in Nanny's tone that bounced right off the man. 'Irene's improving every day, you know that.'

'How does Irene act up?' asked Doris, lowering her voice. 'Does she cheek you? Or what?' She watched Irene looking into the grate, the reflection of the flames the only animation in her face. 'If you'd send her to Arkwright Hall, she might make friends and—'

'I warned her.' Beacham pointed at his sister. 'Her and her strays. And now look at us.'

Apparently unable to make a move without tumult, he slammed the door as he left the room. The old settle that Irene sat on rattled, and her face showed some expression at last.

Underlit by the flames, she looked murderous.

Only Nance's second day on the forklift trucks and she was regretting her move.

She had wanted respite from the noise of the mill floor,

where the endless rolling paper trapped her in one long unfolding moment. The women had given her a headache but now she was nostalgic for their hugger-mugger warmth. Out in the yard, among the men, she was an oddity.

The gaffer had tried to guide her to an indoor job. 'There's an opening in overhauling, checking for flaws. It needs an eye for detail. You'd be perfect for it.'

She had insisted. She wanted to learn a skill, she said, and so here she was, at the wheel of a squat, heavy vehicle, picking up huge pallets with its long forks and transporting them from the carriages to the mill bays.

In theory.

'Watch out!' a man had yelled on her first morning as she almost reversed over his toes. He yelled it all the time now, even when she demurely crossed the yard on foot. 'Watch out!'

The effort came as a shock. Nance considered herself a hard worker, who'd used her hands as much as her head stocking shelves and delivering to the villagers. Driving was different. The gearstick was so stiff she needed both hands to move it.

A head popped in at her grimy cab window. She sat back in alarm. She could smell cigarettes on the unshaven fellow.

'You do know,' he said, 'you've taken a family man's job?'

'Oi!' A shout from behind him, and he abruptly disappeared.

Leaning out, Nance saw Dolly holding him by the back of his collar.

'There's a war on, sonny Jim! We're all doing men's jobs.'

He yanked himself free, even more sour now the other drivers were cheering the spectacle. They all knew Dolly. They would all put their money on her if this came down to hand-to-hand combat. 'You're the weaker sex, stay in the kitchen,' he jeered.

'Give birth to twins and then tell me who's the weaker sex.' Dolly turned away from him and he ceased to exist; he was beneath the notice of the rough-hewn empress. 'We miss you, Nance, me and the girls.'

'I miss you too!'

Nance was no adventurer and it was on the tip of her tongue to say this was a mistake, she was coming back, when Dolly said, 'We're dead proud. You're like one of them suffragettes.'

'Hardly.' Nance wasn't suffragette material; she was reversing over people's toes material.

Dolly whistled, and a man in overalls turned as if he was a dog she'd called. He was playful. 'What do you want *now*, Dolly?' He let her push and prod him over to Nance's cab.

'See this one, Nance? He's a good egg. Ted Wrigley, say hello to the nice lady.'

'Hello, nice lady,' said Ted.

Nance felt the calluses as they shook hands.

'Look out for Nance, Ted. She's one of us.'

'Will do.' He had a pout, this Ted, as if he was about to tell a joke. 'Listen, lass, a word of advice. Trousers.'

'Trousers?' Nance tensed up. 'What would Morgan say?'

Dolly rolled her eyes. 'Let Morgan say what he wants while you go off and get some trousers. Join me and the girls for a cuppa, won't you? There's larks today. Know that stringy girl from Cutting? Only sweet on some Italian POW in Packing. It's a scream.'

'Aren't they fascists, those lads?' asked Ted.

'Nah, they're like you and me. The camp don't allow the fascist ones out to work.' Dolly backed away. 'You hear me, Ted? You got your orders.'

'I'll look after her.' Ted grinned at Nance, and she reversed into the wall.

The woodland Pamela and Kos walked through belonged to her husband.

Alec would never put it that way, he'd say he was a care-taker, but Pamela had seen the deeds and it was true. The gold flash of ragwort, the powdery purple supernova of water mint, all belonged to him. Pamela couldn't name those plants, but she knew they were beautiful and just right for how she felt.

Because she was, at long last, *feeling*. Pamela felt the air on her cheek and Kos's fingers tight around her hand.

They were quiet as they delved into the wood. He had already asked her not to ask him the polite questions she directed at the other pilots; 'You are not to manage me, Pamela.'

When she praised his command of English he told her he had had an English lover as a very young man.

So racy, these Europeans. She had never had a lover. Until now. 'The vicar wonders why we never see you at church.'

'I am Catholic.' Kos looked at her, said, 'Oh. This matters?'

'Don't be silly.' But, for one second, it *had* mattered. Pamela only knew people like herself, right down to the small details. Where they went to school, what they drank. She was covered over with moss, like the folly Kos slept in. 'Do you believe?'

'In you? Absolutely.'

She bumped him with her shoulder. 'No, in Him upstairs.'

'God? Of course I believe in him. You don't?' Kos seemed to pity her a little.

'I do, I suppose ...' Just another man to keep happy, really. And ignore. She looked up at Kos. He made her feel petite, something no other man had ever managed. His broad face, with its acres for her to roam in, was intent upon her. 'How long do we have before the beastly RAF take you away from me?'

'I don't know. Despite you, despite this ...' He took both of her hands and kissed them. His lips were warm and they moved on her knuckles for a moment. 'It can't come soon enough.'

'Why this desire to fight?' Pamela smoothed always, finessed bumps in the road. Picking up a gun was a failure, she felt.

'Poland,' said Kos, 'is my mother. When I see her abused by savages who know the value of nothing, when I see her valiant but in chains, I must free her. I must fight to my last breath.'

Pamela stopped, and faced him. 'You've seen some dreadful things.' She kissed him and she knew the kiss was balm to him. This intoxicated her, that she could help him. *I can reach this man.*

181

When he grabbed her he was almost rough, yet stayed within very specific parameters they both agreed upon. She ran. He caught up. He bent her backwards like a reed. She felt the heft of him against her.

When he was done kissing, he spoke against her lips. 'The way I feel about you, that's the way I feel about Poland. The eternal woman, the everything.'

When he let her go she staggered and said, 'Goodness me.' He was colourful and emphatic in the autumnal wood. She put it down to his foreignness.

Or is it his head wound?

'You're sad,' she said. Despite the ley lines of pleasure they followed to each other, this was true.

'*Jestes smutna*. I repeat it back to you, in my language, because you are sad, too.'

'No, I just get on with life.' Pamela bumped his shoulder again. 'I have to get back.'

'Why? He won't miss you.'

'Ouch! It's possible to be *too* honest, darling. We mustn't ...' Pamela asked him if he knew the English phrase 'wipe his nose in it', and he did.

'Alec hates me,' said Kos. 'I don't blame him. If he took you from me ...'

'I can't be taken, Kos. I give myself. We must play the game.'

'How the British love a game.'

Kos strode through the ferns and bracken instead of following the flattened path. He pulled Pamela so she had to trot; she almost fell. It didn't matter to her, even though nylons were the very devil to find these days.

Lower Loxley came into view past the denuded trees.

'Alec hates being too old for the call-up,' she said. 'Makes him feel useless.'

'I feel the same. I should be in the air.'

'You men and your war.'

'I won't want to leave you behind, Pamela.'

'Well, I'm not coming with you!'

She wondered what she had done to Alec to make him want to walk towards bullets; his ache to be gone had started before her affair. Then she gasped, because Kos picked her up and swung her round.

She had heard the men gossip. Kos would return to the war effort, but would never get back in the air. The doctors would never allow it. The truth would destroy him. *But it'll keep him safe, and within my reach.*

Rendered genderless by the enormous overcoat and scarf, the figure threw pebbles at the window of Arkwright Hall's staff room.

'Wanda!' laughed Lorna when she opened the window. She came out into the cold, Cliff on her tail. 'Your scarf reaches to the floor,' she said.

'Had to wrench it off the Boss's needles.' Doris knitted when she was anxious. 'Your corporal was asking after you at the weekend, Lorna.'

Cliff nudged Lorna, and she rubbed her arm although it hadn't hurt. Not physically. 'Someone sweet on you, Lorna?' he said, reaching for his own scarf to pull over his face, only to find he had rushed out without it.

'A chap with excellent taste.' Wanda bundled Lorna's hair up and stood back to appraise the effect. 'Hides her light under a bushel, this one. You should come dancing with us, Cliff. Men are *rare*. The ladies'd go crazy for you.'

He looked stunned, as if gauging whether mickey was being taken. 'I can't, you know, I have work.'

'He's so diligent,' said Lorna. 'Looks after each kid like they're his only pupil.' She saw how Cliff loved teaching, the vocation he hadn't known he had.

'Who wants to be chained to a desk with all *this* outdoors! Come for a whizz with me, Lorna. You fit just right on the handlebars.'

Giggling despite herself – this happened a lot around Wanda – Lorna said, 'The cleaner let us down. I have to mop the floors.'

'Come on, please. I want to talk about something. *Someone.*' She looked at Cliff. 'Girls' talk, Cliffy. You understand.'

Cliff would understand anything Wanda said. Even if she spoke Swahili. 'Go on, Lorna. All work and no play ...' he said.

So Lorna clambered onto the handlebars, screaming as the bicycle lurched, hoping the kids wouldn't look out to see Miss acting the fool. The girls circled Cliff. 'Thanks for lending Lorna to me. Don't be lonely without her!'

Cliff saluted as they wobbled away, hooting. He called out, 'I'm now quite cured of seeking pleasure in society!'

'What you on about, Cliffy?' laughed Wanda, over her shoulder.

Clinging on for dear life, Lorna whispered the rest of the quote. 'A sensible man ought to find sufficient company in himself.'

There was always an appropriate saying to be found in *Wuthering Heights*.

Sunday evening, the punctuation mark to the end of each Brookfield week.

Doris eased off her church shoes. She was on one side of the fire, Dan the other. He snored; Doris knitted. A sock. A very long sock.

She used to be happy on Sunday nights. And she should have been happy that Sunday night, with Phil and Chris in their beds and Dan in his chair. Mother Cat was on her lap. Wanda was in the hut that suited her so well, despite her being a toff. Tummies were full, labours were done, and mangel-wurzels and potatoes sat piled up in the new barn.

But no Jack.

The scrape of wellingtons on the mat. 'Only me,' said Wanda. 'Come to boil a kettle for my hot-water bottle. What'll I be doing tomorrow, Boss?' She yawned into the infinity scarf she'd thrown over her dressing gown.

Dan woke, with one of those busy little coughs designed to suggest he hadn't been asleep in the first place.

'The ewes' backsides need clipping,' said Doris. She laughed at the face Wanda pulled. 'And you can help the lads get the wether lambs into the carts.' Off to market they would trundle, a price on each woolly, unsuspecting head.

The kettle took its time. 'What's a wether lamb?' asked Wanda.

Dan filled his pipe. 'Male lambs with their wotsits chopped off,' he said. 'Poor little sods.'

Nance overheard the remark, as she was meant to.

'*Sieg heil!*' said a woman in a knot of smokers outside the cutting shed.

So they knew. The secret – was it ever a secret? – had followed her from Ambridge to Waterley Cross.

Nance felt thoroughly English. The only German words she knew were the ones that cropped up in news bulletins. Unable to tell her sauerkraut from her schnitzel, when Nance met her eyes in the mirror they were the blue of the sky over Borsetshire, not Hitler's master race.

Nance hurried on, leaving the cackling women behind. A long stride was easier in her new navy-blue trousers.

Morgan had been supportive: 'My radical wife!' he'd said when she twirled, sheepishly, for him. His approval emboldened her, but now Nance slunk around the corner to the goods yard.

A man passed her. Balding. Bandy. His wife ran the canteen. 'Wouldn't mind getting you down a dark alley on your own,' he said.

Too shocked to answer, Nance watched him stroll off, whistling. The shame was not Nance's – *He's the buffoon who had the filthy thought!* – but she was tarred with it. She screwed up her mouth like she used to screw up twists of sugar at the shop. She must not cry, not in front of the men, the men who wanted to bully her back to the mill floor.

On the seat of her cab sat a biscuit. Small and pale and gorgeous on the leather.

Ted lounged against his own vehicle. 'Nowt to do with me,' he said when she looked over. He winked.

Nance clambered in. She bit into the biscuit. Sweetness exploded on her tongue. It was home-cooked; this Ted Wrigley's wife was a good baker.

She licked her lips and pulled at the gearstick. It stuck but she persevered; the big glove Dolly had given her helped. Off she went, in a smooth straight line. The men wiped their mouths and put down their mugs and watched.

Some mischievous gnat bit her. She performed a dainty pirouette.

They laughed. One of them clapped.

Ted jumped on the side of her cab, like it was a fairground dodgem, and asked for a lift to the lavvies.

Nance was having fun in her new trousers. When they passed her old chums, migrating like a herd of wildebeest from canteen to floor, she wolf-whistled.

They made a clamour. Nance was one of them, she realized. She was more than the sum of her Anglo-German parts.

'Morning Irene!'

One day the girl would answer; Doris would keep plugging away. Irene's cold skin had a sculpted look above the Persian lambswool collar of her coat. *Those patent boots are too fancy for the quagmire of The Green!*

Next to Nanny's austere costume, Doris felt positively modish in her headscarf. It had belonged to her mother, and when Doris shook it out that morning she had been assailed with lily of the valley scent, and had had to sit for a minute.

'She's looking thin,' said Doris. An inveterate feeder – of livestock and children and husband – she never saw elegance in cheekbones. She preferred padding and plumpness and good health. Very little of Irene poked out of the glad rags Nanny dressed her in, but now Doris saw the girl's bony wrists beneath the frothy lace cuffs.

'Well, we're not a champion eater, are we, Irene?' said Nanny, eyebrows mating above her tired eyes. 'I do me best, cook what she likes, but . . .'

'Happen she misses her people,' said Doris, gently.

'Huh,' said Irene.

On the far side of The Green, Archie wore one of Blanche's old furs, not giving a fig for the stares: 'I'm warm as bleedin'' toast! Why should I care?' The pompadour of his hair rose over his brow.

'Not allergic to fur, then?' Blanche leaned on him as they took their constitutional. 'Only allergic to things you don't like.' She was arch. This was how they communicated much of the time. Murmured asides.

Archie pulled away, looked her in the face. 'You haven't worked it out? I didn't tell the army I have allergies; that's just a cover story I toss to the cheap seats. I told the army I'm homosexual and they had me out of that cubicle faster than you can down a small sweet sherry.'

Blanche gaped.

Archie walked ahead, checking Blanche's vital signs as she caught him up. He dwelt in half-truths but the dim search-light of the winter sun nudged a lever that pushed a cog and now he wanted to truly show himself to Blanche. 'I mean, why would I fight for a country that spits on me? Literally. Calls me a freak. Too queer to hold a gun, apparently. Well, they can have this war without me in that case.'

Blanche said nothing.

'They want me to be ashamed. Most of the time I can ignore the insults. But sometimes ...' Blanche's silence unnerved him. He was never quite sure what these country-women did and did not know about the red meat of sexual behaviour.

They passed the shop, just as Doris and Nanny went inside.

'With you in one moment, ladies!' Frank was packing and weighing and withstanding the ache in his feet. And his heart. He missed his daughter's gentle presence. Her reliable mood, her industry.

Frank feared something had died between him and Nance, and he looked back to the years they'd quietly run the shop together as a lost golden age.

One thing was for sure, Frank couldn't care less who 'got' Woodbine Cottage and he wished his customers would stop gabbing about it. While they counted down the weeks to the next will reading in January, he couldn't give a tinker's damn whether the plants spelled out 'Blabs' or not. To Frank, they spelled out 'None of my business'.

Blanche let Archie hold Woodbine's front door open for her, and she pulled off her gloves as she felt the warmth of the house that was and wasn't her home.

'Does it change things?' asked Archie.

'Does what change things?'

'I lied to you, Blanche.'

'You felt you had to. Besides,' said Blanche, dropping to the sofa. 'A little lie now and then livens things up.'

You're a bitch, Blanche Gilpin, thought Archie, heading for the gin bottle. *But you're my bitch and I love you.*

Mrs Endicott stood outside The Bull.

She wavered. It was her patriotic duty but, oh dear, couldn't someone else do it?

October was huffy, turning its back on Ambridge. On the

last night of the month, Halloween snuffed out the moon, and the village was as dark as a coal mine.

Except for The Bull. One window threw a gold rectangle onto the path. Mrs Endicott heard ale-sodden laughter. Recognizing Dan Archer's *ho-ho-ho* she was astounded. A War Ag man abetting a contravention of the rules!

She was amazed by the effect she and her hat covered with wax fruit had on The Bull when she gathered her courage and stepped in. Her timid femininity landed on the assembly like a mallet.

'Don't mind me,' she said.

But they did mind her. They sat up straighter, those that could manage it. Bob rolled his eyes. Stan turned his back.

'The blackout, Bob.' Mrs Endicott gestured at the window.

Dan leapt up. 'Lord save us,' he muttered. There was sniggering: Mr War Ag caught napping at his post. 'There.' He settled the wooden board against the pockmarked panes.

'Anything else, Mrs E?' Bob was affable but he wanted her out. The men minded their Ps and Qs around ladies, and men who mind their Ps and Qs don't buy another round.

'Well, just *this*.' Mrs Endicott stepped forward and handed him a package wrapped in brown paper and string. 'I made this for you.'

Worrying at the knot, Bob thanked her.

'It's your Jimmy.' As Bob pulled away the paper, Mrs Endicott's tone betrayed a sudden, terrible loss of confidence in her painting.

'Cracking likeness,' said Dan, although he didn't recall

Jimmy having cross eyes. *And is that,* he wondered, *a nose?*

'What am I supposed to do with this?' said Bob.

'I thought you might ...' Mrs Endicott stuttered and backed into Dan, who spilled some ale onto the counter. 'It could remind you ...'

'Of what?' Bob slung the painting beneath the bar, and snatched up a cloth. 'You can all hang onto whatever wispy notions you have about death, so long as you allow me mine. The way I see it, when you go, you go.' He wiped away the slopped beer, as if to underline his point. 'If I have a son, Mrs E, where is he? Go on. Point him out. There's nothing left of Jimmy, and anybody who says otherwise is spinning a fairy tale.'

Alec hurried to get the door for Mrs Endicott.

'Badly done, Bob,' said Walter.

'She meant well,' said Joe Grundy.

A groundswell of comment was building, but Bob held up his hand. 'You come here to drink my beer, not teach me manners. My boy done his bit, he copped it, end of story.'

'But Bob,' said Dan. He knew Jimmy was Bob's only family.

'I don't want to hear it, Dan. And I don't want to stare at poor Jimmy's face just because some old biddy has time on her hands.' Bob never cried. The memories were fuel for anger, not grief. 'You mention my boy's name and I'll chuck every last one of you out on the street. Got it?'

They got it. Especially Dan, who had seen Jimmy's stark room upstairs.

Walter laid down the darts. Nobody felt like playing.

*

Through the magic portal – that's how Pamela had come to think of the circular window that framed the folly – she saw a candle burning.

The signal.

She readied herself to leave the house, and join whatever witches were out there celebrating their Halloween sabbath.

Mist hung over the old graves and the newer ones, the tenants companionable and silent as midnight approached. Then, if the old beliefs were true, they would rise and make mischief.

Some of the living were already doing just that.

Blanche loved being out of doors at this hour. She revelled in the liberation of darkness. Nobody expected gentlewomen to be out at night, tramping and nosing and prying.

Ambridge felt dead. Hedgehogs who had squeaked by back doors now hibernated beneath damp eiderdowns of leaves. Blanche was as silent as the sleeping animals; she had to be, to get up close to windows, and peek through slits.

When Archie encouraged her to take a 'health-giving' walk in the daytime, she resisted. Dull old Mother Nature held no interest. It was humans Blanche studied.

She recalled Jane's delight in identifying bird call, or pressing some wretched little daisy in a book. It was another example of their dissimilarity, their discord, their lack of common ground. Blanche the dark valley and Jane the sunlit uplands.

But was her sunny sister so full of secret hostility that she would turn her beloved Blabs out of her home?

Yes. Yes, she was.

Blanche was certain of that. Both sisters were extremists. Jane's rigorous sense of justice would be served by Blanche finally paying a price and having to make her own way in the world.

Such maudlin thoughts were the reason Blanche had to get out of the cottage. Halloween didn't scare Blanche; *I live with a ghost*. Woodbine was haunted; Jane was in every reflection, each shadow.

A noise, sudden and out of place, gave Blanche all the distraction she craved. It was the clang of a tool dropping.

Fleet, Blanche dashed towards the village hall. She pressed herself to it, crawling around it like a bug, and peered towards a small shed, a few yards away. Its door stood open. Within, crouched and shifting in the dark like an incubus, was a figure.

Blanche shook with excitement.

More noise. Another figure took shape in the night as it hurtled towards the shed.

'Hey!' The patrician voice sent the incubus out of the shed and running.

It ran towards the hall. Blanche drew back, and saw it was no demon, just a terrified Stan Horrobin.

He would soon reach the trees and melt; a poacher like Stan knew every gap and burrow. It was hard to catch a poacher, especially for a man as tall and wide as the one hurtling after Stan. *It's that handsome flying ace from Lower Loxley*, Blanche had time to notice, before she stuck out her foot and sent Stan sprawling.

The Polish man was upon him, pinning him to the ground.

'We need the police. Where is there a phone?' he called over his shoulder.

It could have been a witch; it was sleek enough. But it was Pamela Pargetter.

Stuffing her fist into her mouth, Blanche tried not to squeal. Halloween had delivered the scandal she craved, that irreligious night pairing the hoity-toity Pamela with a man who was most definitely and decidedly not her husband.

'I don't understand,' whispered Pamela, keeping her distance from the flailing Stan. 'What was he doing?'

'Smell that?' Kos held out a rag. 'It's petrol. See the red? That's dye, the military dye their petrol so it can't be sold. But you were straining it, weren't you, sir?'

'Mind your business,' said Stan. Still lippy, even with fourteen stone of pilot on top of him. 'Let me up and I'll deck you.'

'Deck?' Kos was amused.

'Who's she? Who's that?' Stan wriggled, tried to get a look at Pamela's dark shape.

'I mustn't be here,' said Pamela.

'Make the call, please,' said Kos. He rearranged himself on Stan's back. 'This gentleman and I are perfectly comfortable.'

I love Halloween! thought Blanche.

Over the treetops, past Stan's secret thoroughfares, in its own grounds, Furnivall Manor was quiet, stately. It did not join in with the night's superstitious tomfoolery.

The windows were blind, asleep. In one swam a wan shape. A child's face. Mutinous, fuming, it stared out at the night.

NOVEMBER

At Turnpike, Denholm Kaye was opening his mail.

Like a circus bear hunched on a tricycle, he dwarfed his small, rosewood desk. 'Invitation from the Pargetters,' he called to Agnes. 'No thank *you*!' He ripped the monogrammed card in two and aimed it at the wastepaper basket.

Agnes was in from the scullery before it landed. 'What are you thinking?' She reunited the two halves. 'Sunday lunch! At Lower Loxley!'

'I always decline.' Denholm's suit was new. His waistline was new; he had not met a fried egg for months. The old Denholm was still in there somewhere, and was not a sociable man. 'Mother never made me go out and *meet people*. The food's too fancy at Lower Loxley and Pamela makes us all talk.'

'RSV bleedin' P,' said Agnes. 'Now!'

Denholm's small, newish wife was no beauty but that bothered neither him nor her. Agnes rarely looked in the mirror, looking instead at her full pantry, her full wardrobe, and the ten-pound notes she stacked neatly under the mattress. Agnes had known want; marriage brought security.

And it brought Denholm, of course. He surrendered to all her wishes, partly because he had no ideas of his own and partly because the house was in Agnes's thrall. If she was happy, Turnpike was happy.

'No, no,' said Agnes, hands on hips. 'Add how delighted you are.'

'But I'm not a bit delighted.' Denholm reached for another sheet of paper. 'It's to celebrate the vicar's birthday.' An awful thought struck. 'Oh Lord, Aggy, we won't have to buy him a present?'

'We'll buy that so-and-so a present that'll knock his holy socks off. I'll need to get a new dress made.' Denholm's mother had been large; she'd left behind enough black bombazine frocks to keep bantamweight Agnes clad for decades. They were taken in, embellished, by a seamstress friend in Penny Hassett, from 'before'. Before Agnes's wedding, her ascent.

She directed the licking of the stamp. 'Postbox, dear,' she said, and fussed him into his raincoat and a new soft hat. She watched him lumber down the path, and ignore little Lorna from Arkwright Hall. *You have no idea how to behave, Denholm Kaye*, she thought, with a fondness that sneaked up on her and surprised her.

It had taken months to reel him in; slowly slowly catchee Denholm. Born in this house, oblivious to struggle, he didn't realize he had elevated Agnes. What he saw as tedious drawbacks to village life – invitations to Lower Loxley, for example – had the lustre of Hollywood for his wife.

They shared little. Some talk of the weather, and the war. That morning she had said, 'Those poor devils in Moscow,' and he had said, 'Another blithering siege!' Both missed the old style of news on the wireless; something about the king followed by something about the chancellor of the exchequer, and occasionally someone went over Niagara Falls in a barrel.

When he returned, windswept, from his epic trek across The Green, Agnes tried to share something real. Something that felt too cumbersome to digest all by herself.

She opened an inlaid box on the sideboard. It was lined with felt. 'I sometimes feel guilty, Denholm.'

'About what, Aggy?' He was already at one with the sofa.

'Leaving Woodbine, leaving Miss Jane and coming here to live with you.' She took an earring from the box. Opal, set in gold, it had no partner. 'She wasn't strong and ... I wasn't always kind.'

'Well, um, hmm,' said Denholm, which was as far as his philosophizing ever went.

'Just little things, you know.' Agnes held up the earring. *Little thefts.* The nickname Crow had suited her; she had stuck her beak into locked cupboards. Shame felt novel for Agnes, who went through life like a hot knife through butter. 'I'm being silly, aren't I, to feel responsible?'

His snore was her only reply.

'Denholm!' she snapped, and he jumped. 'Bath time!'

'But Aggy, I'm not remotely dirty,' he protested.

Lining up in the mill's canteen, Nance was ravenous. She would fall on the slop they served as if it was ambrosia.

Just ahead of her in the queue – they had walked companionably from the coal yard – Ted said, without turning around, 'Don't have the semolina, Nance. I've got a treat for you.'

'Fruit cake?'

'You bet.'

'That wife of yours is a marvellous cook.' Nance watched the back of his head as they shuffled forwards, the neat line of the short back and sides.

'Don't have a wife.'

'Don't tell me *you* bake those dainty little cakes!'

'My sis. I live with her, see. Her and her family.' Ted turned. He held the tray across his chest. 'You'd like her, Nance. 'Ere, she's having a do for her birthday. You should come! Decent grub, bit of dancing. End of the month. What'd you say?'

'I say I'm married, Ted.' Nance was red, the brightest shade imaginable. Ambridge's postbox. W. C. Fields's nose.

Ted frowned. 'No, you're not.' He blinked. 'Sorry, you'd know, wouldn't you, if you were married or not.'

He turned away.

* * *

The folly was a home of sorts, wherein Pamela and Kos subsisted on love.

Simple furniture, stone walls. And tonight, two crystal glasses of champagne for the lovestruck paupers, plus a dish of Turkish delight.

'No more,' said Pamela. 'It's for the guests tomorrow.'

'Ah, the vicar's birthday.' Kos lay back on the narrow cot, the sheets disarranged by their earlier antics. He wore only underpants; Pamela, having only ever lain with a man who felt naked without his cravat, was dazzled by Kos's body.

She had to balance the scales with care. Not be *too* happy. Adore Kos only as much as the strange contract she'd drawn up in her head would allow.

I was driven to this.

If she had never read Alec's letters to the private detective, Pamela would never have surrendered to temptation. Even Alec's affair didn't justify Kos; it was the search for his mistress and the existence of their secret child that legitimized her behaviour. And, of course, the sting in the tail: *I didn't win, Alec regretted choosing me.* That gave her a free hand.

And yet.

She was still Pamela. Sketched with a quick, sure and conservative hand. New money; old morals.

But also hoarse with desire for the driven, jumpy Polish man who fell out of the sky six months earlier. 'I wish we could barricade that door.'

'Alec would kick it down.' Kos reconsidered, sitting up.

'Or maybe knock politely and ask, *Excuse me, are you in there, old girl?*'

'Don't make fun of him. Please.'

'Kiss me.'

Pamela did as she was told. Kos seemed to believe she was good at kissing. 'Shall we go for a walk?'

Since the episode with Stan, they walked only at night, sticking to Lower Loxley land. Constable Jenkins had been discreet, but almost as interested in why Mrs Pargetter was out so late with a gentleman as he was in arresting his old associate Mr Stanley Blair Horrobin.

'Not tonight,' said Kos. Always sure about his wants, all he really wanted to do was to have Pamela and to fly. His two constants. 'We almost got lost by that stream.'

'Don't go on about it.' Pamela prickled when picked up on any failing, however small. 'Before you I never explored.'

'I know every leaf of my land.' Kos turned on his stomach. His face was in the pillow. 'I *knew.*'

'Darling.' Pamela laid a hand on his back.

Kos was baling out of his own life. They touched, occasionally, on his fears that there would be nothing but rubble to return home to. The other night he had pointed out to her a fox, crouching in a stark November field, shivering and beautiful.

That's you, she had thought. A vulnerable animal with no cover, for all its virile strength.

'Did you get my note?' Pamela had accrued a library of billets-doux from Kos, and felt it was time to reciprocate.

'No.' He flopped over, his face shining.

She found it easily. 'It's right here, silly. On your desk.' By Pamela's standards, the message was daring. 'Read it,' she said.

'Later.'

'No, *now*!'

Kos snatched the note and balled it up and threw it at Pamela. It struck her face. 'I read it when I wish!' He rose so quickly she had to step aside. He leaned on the desk, breathing like a mare in labour.

'If you think you can talk to me in that manner you are quite wrong.' Pamela shoved a stockinged foot into a court shoe. She paused. Hopped over to him. 'Your head?'

'I'm sorry.'

'Here.' She sat on the bed. He sat alongside her. Sometimes this worked. He bent until his head was in her lap and she stroked and petted, threading his hair through her fingers, and tracing his scar. She felt the heat of his pain.

'What did the note say?' he asked, in a dull voice.

'Read it later when you can focus again.' She had written *I am yours*. She had not felt able to add, as her pen wanted to, *forever*. 'Sometimes,' whispered Pamela, stroking, petting, 'I wonder if you truly care about me or if I'm just a symptom of your concussion.'

He was up, nose to nose. 'Then leave me,' he said. His dark hair flopped over furious eyes. 'If you think that, you insult me and yourself.'

'For heaven's sake!' Pamela could have told him then that she loved him, but she was no soppy wench so she said instead, 'Stop feeling sorry for yourself, Kos. My father knows an excellent doctor and I could—"

Kos put a finger to her lips. 'Do not manage me,' he said.

Cross-legged on the deep sill, John pulled the curtains and made himself invisible to the kitchen.

Not just a kitchen, it was an everything room, much like the cosy kitchen at home. Except Connie's kitchen wasn't cosy.

John's stomach spoke, it was so hungry. When Connie told Stan there was no pot-roast chicken, Stan shouted, 'What, on a Sunday?' and kicked her and asked her what use was she, 'you old bitch'.

His mood had been stable since his arrest at Halloween. Constant rage. Stan was angry with John and Billy, with the dogs, with the furniture. Most of all with Connie, who was *very* embarrassed about the front tooth he knocked out. John tried to make her feel better. 'Makes you look like a pirate!' he said, but he wasn't sure if that worked.

Behind the curtain, John curated his treasures.

A pebble with a hole in it. A piece of shrapnel flattened into the shape of a star. A fragile, minuscule skull.

It calmed him, when the house was ablaze with Stan's violence, to move the skull half an inch. Line it up with the star. Start all over again.

The kettle whistled. He heard Maisie humming under the table. John tried to settle into his favourite daydream. The one where Dad turned up and said, 'Right! That's it! I've come to take John and Billy home!'

A different noise stilled all the others. A thump of fist against, not wood, not wall, but flesh.

The curtain was yanked aside.

Billy dragged John out, just as Connie flew through the air like an acrobat.

Magsy sneezed in her boudoir, a dark room crammed with memorabilia of others' lives. She found time to worry about how Nance was coping without her, and cursed the cold that kept her away from Homeleigh.

Morgan was carving a chicken. Nowhere near as fancy as the vicar's birthday feast at Lower Loxley, but it was golden and snug among Maris Pipers roasted in goose fat and swimming in a gravy, of which Nance was secretly but intensely proud.

'Carrots?' Nance offered the dish. She was cheerful, she felt comfortable, as if she'd been dropped into a Nance-shaped niche. 'Do they really help you see in the dark?'

'Utter piffle, my dear.' Morgan shook out a napkin. 'The propagandists' ruse to make us grow more vegetables.'

'You did a good turn getting Cliff Horrobin in at Arkwright Hall.' Nance liked to praise her husband. Apart from Magsy's berserk bias, which he ignored, Morgan tended to go unnoticed.

'He's one of nature's teachers. Such a shame about ...' Morgan waved his fork at his face.

'He's still the same old Cliff underneath.'

'True. We'll all emerge from the war with scars.'

'When you care for Cliff,' said Nance, 'I imagine you're honouring Anthony.'

'Oh. Yes. Goodness.' They rarely mentioned his dead son, lost in the first weeks of war.

Nance patted his hand. 'Marks out of ten for the chicken?' she asked as she cleared the table.

'Ooh, nine.'

Ridiculously she was crestfallen. 'Would Magsy get ten?'

'She's been doing it longer, my dear.' Morgan headed for his chair but Nance intercepted him.

'No you don't!' She set the gramophone going.

Geraldo and his Orchestra sang of 'That Lovely Weekend'. Nance held out her arms and Morgan stepped into them. They moved around the furniture, in perfect tune with one another.

'Did your first wife cook a nice roast?'

'Very nice,' said Morgan.

'Nicer than mine?'

They two-stepped awkwardly into the piano. 'Different, my dear.'

Agnes noted how surprised Doris was to see her in Lower Loxley's drawing room. She raised her martini glass in greeting, and crossed her legs so her bombazine skirt rustled.

They sat down to what Pamela described as *'la spécialité de la maison'*; Agnes didn't speak Italian and was relieved when it turned out to be good old roast beef.

Dodgy, a perennial at Pamela's table, was vocal about the

beef's excellence. He had insisted Kos join them; Pamela, ill-suited to the role of femme fatale, didn't relish both her husband and her lover at the same table.

'Such a loner, poor chap.' Ex-public schoolboy Dodgy could imagine no worse fate than being alone. 'And that head of his ... doesn't bode well.'

So Kos was there, and Alec was there, and Pamela excused herself to fetch the dessert.

The vicar looked expectant. He hated fuss, he said, when they sang 'Happy Birthday', just *hated* it, and expected nothing, truly, but, he asked, 'Is there birthday cake?'

A delectable bottle of red was passed around. 'Sorry you have to pour it yourselves,' said Alec. 'Staff. The war, you know.'

'Terrible sacrifice,' murmured Doris.

Elegant even when bored, Alec answered Dan's enquiry after his son. 'I'm afraid Gerald's in hot water.'

'Again?' said Dan, and Doris despaired at her husband's inability to have an unvoiced thought.

The vicar said, 'One does hope Gerald won't be expelled from *this* school.'

'Yes, doesn't one?' said Alec, teeth gritted; *why must the vicar be such an ass?* 'It's serious this time. A boy's watch is missing. Belonged to his father, an heirloom. Poor man was killed in France.'

Denholm said, 'Young Gerald didn't steal it, surely?' In his Ye Olde Englande, British schoolboys were noble, upstanding fellows.

A voice from the doorway. 'He did *not*.' Pamela was back,

with a be-ribboned box. The look she threw Alec could cut a lesser man clean in two, like cheese wire through cheddar.

'I wish,' said Alec, 'I shared my wife's confidence.'

Agnes noticed Denholm's dandruff was staging a comeback as Pamela said, 'Storm in a teacup, the silly watch is simply missing.' She held up the box. 'I hope Henry will forgive me. No birthday cake!'

Doris's heart sank.

'But there *is* Turkish delight!'

Doris wiped away the drool.

The vicar delved in again and again to the box of sugared cubes, and had to be prompted to pass them around. He handed Mrs Endicott's hand-painted card to Alec. 'Kittens, I think,' he said, his mouth full of Turkish delight.

'Ah, hmm.' *Rather misshapen ones*, thought Alec. 'We seem to have lost Agnes.'

'Powdering her nose,' said Denholm, Turkish delight sticking to his dentures.

It was a big nose, but even so, the powdering was taking a while. Agnes idled on an upper corridor, along a runway of intricately patterned carpet. A small snuff box jumped – *plop!* – into her pocket.

As she re-entered the dining room, candles lit against the glowering afternoon, Pamela was saying, 'Agnes might know. The vicar's trying to track down Dorothy Hughes. Her family have a smallholding just past Brookfield. Any idea where she went?'

'The girl who disappeared?' Agnes clicked her fingers. 'Like that?'

'Indeed.' Alec was uncomfortable. The girl who was among them one minute and gone the next was not Sunday lunch fodder.

'Honestly,' said Frances, brittle, 'I can't imagine why my Henry's interested. Dorothy was nothing to do with us. Nothing,' she said, searching for her husband's gaze, 'at all.'

'Some chap got her in the family way and let her down, I heard,' said Agnes. 'Don't know who he was. You got any idea, Frances?'

The vicar's wife was taken aback by her first name on an ex-maid's lips. 'Why would I?' She was shrill.

'Her poor mother,' said Doris, 'never got over it.' Shame could wreak havoc in a small community. Consequences were worse for the poor. Doris knew neither Alec nor Pamela would ever be unfaithful, but it was unjust that they would suffer less for it.

'Kos,' said Alec, and Pamela jumped. 'Keen to rejoin your squadron, I bet?'

'I am.' Kos traced something on the tablecloth with his fork. 'I need to avenge my country.'

'Ooh!' Agnes wriggled.

'Dear me, so bloodthirsty.' Frances endeavoured always to bleach the war out of conversation.

'This house seems solid and safe,' said Kos. 'But it's built on spilled blood and could topple overnight.'

'My family,' said Alec, 'have lived here for—'

'That means nothing.' Kos didn't raise his voice. His lips barely opened as he spoke. 'There is a mad dog loose. It won't *knock*. It will break down the gates and devour us all. And here we sit eating sweets.'

Denholm put down his fifth Turkish delight. With some regret.

'When we fled Poland, and then France, we called Great Britain The Island of the Last Hope. That's why I long to set off with the RAF to Berlin.'

Agnes said, 'They're giving the Jerries a right knocking about.'

Doris wondered if German mothers worried the same way she did. *Of course they blinkin' well do!* she thought.

Alec asked, 'Are you still capable of combat, though?' He tapped his head.

Her eyes as hard as the diamonds on her fingers, Pamela stared at her husband. He must surely have heard the talk of Kos's hair trigger, how he would stand and roar at a perceived insult.

Kos did not roar. 'I expect my orders any day.' He took up the bottle of wine. 'For you?' he asked Doris, with gallantry that made her go rather silly.

'A fine red,' said Dodgy. 'What is it, Kos? Gamay? I adore a good Gamay.'

Kos frowned at the label, then put it down with a thud. 'Excuse me,' he said as he bowed, and left the room.

'Ah,' said Dodgy, who realized Kos had been unable to read the label.

Pamela knew too, and barely listened when talk turned to Jane's will.

The vicar refrained from comment; his wife did not. 'If Henry and I have to bite the bullet and accept Woodbine Cottage, so be it,' she said.

'I expect to inherit something meself,' said Agnes. 'For looking after Miss Jane all them years.'

'But a *house*?' said Frances. 'There's neither a B nor an L in your name, after all.'

'Is there a B or an L in Henry?' snapped Agnes.

Denholm said 'Blake', and they turned to look at him. 'Morgan's middle name. Morgan Blake Seed. Blake has five letters, does it not?'

'Goodness, another name tossed into the hat.' Pamela rose. 'I must attend to something.'

Agnes was truculent. 'Jane'd hardly leave her house to the doc who polished her off.'

Loudly, changing the subject, Henry read the Pargetter motto engraved on his silver napkin ring. '*Ostenditur spes alma lux beatissima.*'

'So thoughtful,' simpered Frances, 'to honour Henry's birthday with the best silver.'

'Of course,' said Alec, who knew it was the third best silver.

'What's it mean?' asked Agnes, studying her own napkin ring.

Enunciating with maiden aunt precision, the vicar translated. 'Blessed light reveals bountiful hope.'

'Most uplifting,' said Dodgy. 'My family motto is bottoms up!'

'Say that again, Reverend,' said Agnes.

Gratified by his parishioner's lurch into high-mindedness, Henry repeated, 'Blessed light reveals bountiful hope.'

B, L, thought Agnes. 'Did Miss Jane, I mean Jane, speak Latin?'

'We shared many a joke in that beautiful tongue,' said Henry.

While he burdened them with some of these jokes, Pamela was in the shadows under the stairs. Kos had her hands in his.

'The love,' he said, 'is all me. It's not sickness. It's the only good thing I have.'

'Love?'

'Love,' said Kos, emphatic.

A rapping at the front door made them retreat further into the shade. 'The staff'll get that.' Pamela put her arms around Kos's neck.

At the table, Doris's mind wandered. The tug of the farm asserted itself. She must get home and clean this, sort that. Have a chat with Wanda about Mr Bigtime and the late hours she kept. She didn't notice when Alec said, 'Please excuse me, nobody in this house seems inclined to answer the damn door.'

He saw them, two people making one shape, beneath the great staircase. His stomach tilted. He ignored them, because rules were rules.

'Beacham!' He said when he pulled open the massive door. 'Come in, old chap!' Some Home Guard business would clear his palate. A trivial problem to override his wife and the Pole in his peripheral vision. Alec noticed the little girl. 'Hello,' he said, woodenly. He was better with dogs than children.

'I'd rather not come in, sir.' Beacham's face, fine-boned and fierce, was stiff. There was an effort to the silkiness, honed by years of service in grand houses. 'It's not you I've come to see.'

Doris rehearsed silently as the others discussed Latin. *Now Wanda, it gives me no pleasure to say this* ... It was only when Dan nudged her that she looked up and heard Alec use her name.

'You have a visitor, Doris.'

Morgan was out of puff. They had danced through much of Geraldo and his Orchestra's repertoire.

Nance was energized rather than exhausted. When he suggested, with some puffing, that they take a breather, she came closer. Her embrace tightened.

Morgan stepped away. He had to undo himself from her arms. The scent of her, roses and soap, was quite lovely and so it panicked him, but his haste offended her and they were estranged once more.

All this took less time than the flap of a butterfly's wings.

Billy knew his mum would let him have it for allowing John – 'with *his* chest!' – to mess about in a damp wood. Their mum had a long list of worries, and John's chest was right up there with doodlebugs and polio.

'Luca reminds me of Jesus.' John slithered over mossy stones.

'He's not Jesus, he's a bloke. Anyhow, Jesus was wet.'

'Don't say that, Billy! Jesus is *lovely*.'

'He should escape.' Billy stopped dead as the idea struck. 'Luca, I mean. Not Jesus.'

'He could go home! Bruno could sit on his knee again!'

Bruno and Vittorio Scuderi were as known to them as intimates, their personalities loosely modelled on the boys' own: so Bruno was a sentimental boy who moped about the *casa*, while Vittorio was more robust, given to pulling Italian girls' hair.

They'd help Luca escape, they decided, as they jumped up and down. Wizbang joined in; the dog was a natural accomplice, although limited when it came to skills.

Crouched by the wire, Luca was not so enthusiastic. 'No. Too dangerous. I will not put you in danger. No no no!'

They pushed. They nagged. And he said, with a laugh, 'I surrender!' He shushed their yelps and said, 'I do it for *you*,' in his earnest way. He would, he said, crawl beneath the truck that took inmates out on work detail each morning, and roll out into a hedgerow; the hazy dawn would hide him. Luca recited a list of what he would need from them. 'Money, *i miei ragazzi*. Food. Clothes.'

Billy marvelled at Luca's ability to whistle up a plan on the spot. Almost as if he'd been planning it all along.

'Before I go home I go to Downing Street. Tell Churchill bring all dads home.'

'Especially ours,' said John.

'They won't let you talk to Churchill.' Billy didn't like fairy stories. Didn't like being treated like a kid. 'Don't talk daft, Luca.'

'Billy,' said Luca, his voice as deep as the brown of his eyes. 'You do not believe in God.'

That was true, but shocking to hear it said out loud. Billy tried, but the vicar made God sound like some narky posh geezer up in the clouds.

'We must believe in something,' said Luca. 'Or why do we live? I believe my father keep my boys safe for me. Will you believe in me, Billy?'

'Yes,' said John, although he hadn't been asked.

Billy hated being cornered. He poked the ground with his boot.

Luca stood. 'This is not good plan. Too dangerous for little boys.'

'Who's little?' Billy stuck out his chin. 'I believe in you, Luca! We'll get you to Downing Street!'

And Luca laughed, all indecision gone. He took their thruppence without comment and left them, rolling a black armband on over his coat sleeve as he turned past a row of huts.

Washing the dishes kept Nance out of the parlour and away from her husband. She washed each plate with care; Magsy would doubtlessly inspect them.

The clock in the hall ticked. Morgan gave the occasional cough. Nance imagined another house.

Ted Wrigley's sister's house. Guests everywhere, Ted bashing out a tune on the piano – 'I'm pretty good!' he'd claimed – jokes, dancing.

Nance set the roasting tin to soak.

*

214

Irene looked mulishly into the distance, little mouth set, suitcase at her feet.

'I can't do that.' Doris was chilly, standing outside Lower Loxley in just her frock.

'You must.' Beacham held out Irene's hand, jerking her forward. 'Take her!'

'Mind the child! She's a little girl, not a side of ham.'

'It's not working. She's peculiar ... you don't see it.'

'Don't talk about Irene that way. And I can't just take her back, I'm not a shopkeeper. It's your patriotic duty to look after city children.'

'Duty be damned. Take her, you fool.'

He was tall and glowering, but Doris was, well, *Doris*. 'Look, here's your sister, all upset,' she said, when Nanny staggered into view.

Out of breath, Nanny grabbed Beacham's arm. 'Don't do this. Things'll improve, I promise. It just takes patience and love.'

Clearly short on both, Beacham didn't even look at Nanny. 'Heard it all before,' he said, his burning eyes on Doris.

In Doris's experience, it fell to women to sort everything out. When Nanny said she'd take care of everything, that Beacham wasn't used to children, that it would all work out, Doris believed her.

Winter

1941–2

'Don't think of what's past!' said she.

THOMAS HARDY
Tess of the D'Urbervilles

December

Blanche had watched her sister live on her nerves, and derided her as a weakling.

Now Blanche found herself a weakling, as if Jane had handed over the baton on the threshold of the grave.

Where's Archie? When he was out, the house felt empty, without soul. Even though Blanche thrived on being the subject of gossip, life in the epicentre of speculation had its effect on her. A slow, incremental dread, a prickling at the back of her neck.

When she sat on the sofa it felt like a cloud, liable to vanish – *pff!* – at any moment. The floorboards were water. Woodbine Cottage was not the stout home the childish Blabs had played in; it was a paper house that might blow away.

Where's Archie? Christmas shopping couldn't take this long when you had nobody to buy for.

She made a sandwich and it was indescribable. Blanche threw it out for the hungry, grateful-for-anything birds. The garden was flat and bleak. Pots on their side. The sundial was cracked. She turned her back on it as Archie hurtled in.

'Was she here?' He was wild-eyed. 'Tell me!'

'Whoa there,' laughed Blanche. 'Nobody's called.'

Dropping into a chair, Archie puddled as if his bones had turned to milk. 'I saw her.'

'Her who?'

'My sister. Monica.'

Blanche whistled.

'I spotted the back of her head. Just here.' Archie touched the crown of his own head; the touch was tender. 'I was so sure. But . . .'

Blanche patted his arm. Mistresses don't pat servants' arms, but *we're different*, she thought. Let other boobies follow the rules. 'Does she know you live here?'

'We don't talk, so, no. I've been careful.'

'Why this terror, Archie? Maybe Monica just wants to catch up.'

Archie leaned down, exposed the scar at the back of his neck. 'I wasn't entirely truthful about this, doll. It wasn't some stranger down an alley. I got this in my own back yard. My dad beat the tripe out of me while Monica cheered him on.' He leaned forward, nose on his knees. 'The beatings I could take, but his disgust . . .'

Blanche wished she had a handbook for this kind of thing. She wanted to help but it was the sandwich all over again.

Archie sprang up. 'And my little brother's trapped there, listening to all the sour talk, all the hatred.'

'Your father wouldn't lay hands on him, would he?'

'Nah. It's only my "perversion" gets Dad going. If I

could just tunnel into the house and bring my brother back here.'

They sat together, the two outsiders. The woman who feared her neighbours would applaud when she was turfed out, and the boy who could never go home.

The two ladies braving the cold were on committee business.

Delivering a curtain to Arkwright Hall – it would soon be a shepherd's robe in the nativity play – they had all the necessary accoutrements for their mission. A rolled umbrella, a muff, two hats – one mink, the other felt – and coats buttoned up to the neck.

The December freeze stood no chance; Magsy and Mrs Endicott were warming their hands at the brazier of gossip.

Magsy said, 'You're right! It fits perfectly!'

'Agnes is most quick, she saw it immediately.' Mrs Endicott spoke out of the corner of her mouth, like a spy. 'The B of the bleeding heart, and the L of the lady orchid match the first two words of the Pargetter motto. And there are *five words* in it, my dear. Blessed light reveals bountiful hope.'

Magsy's breath curled in the air. 'And the very first legacy went to Pamela Pargetter.' She gave a polite *Ahem* and said, 'Of course, one must remember we are discussing Blanche's future and not playing a game.'

'Indeed, indeed,' said Mrs Endicott, whose little suede boots could hardly wait to carry her to the shop and disseminate this latest dispatch.

*

Christmas, enthroned like a monarch at the end of December, owns the entire month. With ten days to go, the mill was swathed in paper chains made from rejected anti-radar paper, the foil strips glinting. Some were scissored into patterns, like the spiderwebs Nance cycled past on her way to work.

Eleven a.m. saw her trot off to the canteen, where she slotted in at the table colonized by 'her' women. Snug between Sal, who sat the wrong way round on her chair, and redoubtable Dolly, who took her tea so strong the spoon stood up in it.

'Poor old Malta, eh?' said Nance. 'Just a little island but they've had their hundredth air raid.'

Clearly not in the mood to let the war spoil her tea break, Dolly leaned back and took Nance in. 'I remember when my skin was like yours. A bowl of cream. Ah, youth!'

'That ain't youth,' said Sal. 'That's being a new wife and getting plenty of the other.'

All cackled. Nance was nudged. So she said it, no preamble, no forethought. 'Morgan and me, we don't go to bed.'

The cackling stopped.

Dolly seemed puzzled. 'You saying you're only wed a year and you're already Darby and Joan?'

An aged member of the gang was affronted. ''Ere! Don't underestimate Darby and Joan.'

'We've never done it.' Nance felt dizzy, as if confessing to a crime, but there was no going back. 'I'm still a virgin.'

'A married virgin?' Sal was poised to laugh again. 'There's no such thing, girl.'

'You're looking at one.' A blusher by nature, Nance would

222

redden up if someone uttered a double entendre in the next county. She did not blush now. She was crying for help. And the women heard her.

'That hubby of yourn needs to step up,' said Dolly.

'Lovely girl like you, should be thanking his lucky stars,' said Sal.

How to explain that it wasn't about being lovely? Nance knew it was something deep-rooted, an ugly vine that had got hold of her and Morgan.

'I say Nance should be grateful for small mercies.' A mother of eight drained her mug. 'My old man won't leave me alone.'

Dolly was magisterial. 'I gets it once a day and if I don't I kick up a right fuss. It's good for the circulation.'

Dolly's husband was known to them all, a thick-bodied, simian little bloke who was no Clark Gable.

It was clear to Nance that 'bed' truly did come down to chemistry. *And Morgan and I have none, it seems.*

No London first night was more hotly anticipated than the Arkwright Hall nativity play.

The great and the good of Ambridge sat on slatted chairs in the school's ballroom, alongside the not so great and the downright bad.

Doris hoped the improvised stage would bear the weight of the holy family plus assorted potentates and cherubim. She had sewn the donkey's ears from an old fur tippet of Mrs

Endicott's, and the frankincense was housed in an empty Coty powder box.

Stepping onstage to lunatic applause, Lorna recited the rhyming introduction too fast. She regretted the make-up Wanda had insisted she put on, and was grateful to reach the cue for the lights to go down.

'And now we invite you to meet the wondrous babe, who is in hay in Bethlehem laid.'

The lights remained stubbornly on.

She glanced at Cliff, offstage by the switch. He was staring at the third row as if it contained the meaning of life; it contained Wanda, who was, in turn, staring at Lorna, and willing her on.

'In Bethlehem *laid*!'

The lights went off. The donkey moseyed on. It all went rather well, if you discounted the Virgin Mary bursting into tears.

Afterwards, the tea urn was mobbed. Wanda took charge, winking at Joe Grundy so that he spilled his cuppa over his one pair of presentable trousers.

Cliff marshalled his performers, praised them to the skies and consoled the Virgin Mary with, 'Just nerves, happens to Ava Gardner all the time.'

Nodding, smiling, mouthing compliments for the 'super effort, just super', Pamela and Alec said not one word to each other. Both of them tracked Kos like radar operatives, knowing exactly where he was in the room at any given moment.

Mrs Endicott had collared Kos, telling him she felt 'simply

awful' for the lovely people of Pearl Harbor, but wasn't it decent of the Americans to join the war?

Kos's dimples performed for Mrs Endicott, but he handed her neatly over to Archie, who asked her, 'How come you never pop round to Woodbine Cottage, eh?'

Before the lady could stammer an excuse, she had accepted an invitation to take tea with Blanche.

'We'll have a ball,' said Archie. He tweaked John's scarf as the boy sneaked past. 'Bit 'ot in here for that!'

John and his brother pressed on, burrowing through the crowd like moles, eager to escape to Luca. They had two more pennies, plus a string vest for his trousseau.

Over their heads, Archie spotted RAF-blue-suited Terence, and Archie threw him a look he had perfected. A coded look that lasted a heartbeat too long, but could be disowned if he was challenged about it.

Terence ignored him. He had only come to please Pamela, but now he was chatting up the pretty thing at the tea urn.

Remaining polite, Wanda wondered why men never noticed when women were busy. She needed four pairs of hands to satisfy the lust for tea, yet that RAF boy kept up his silly patter. She scanned the crowd for Him – Mr Bigtime was capitalized now – but she held out little hope. *Why would someone like him come to a kiddies' show?*

When Connie said, 'Well done, son,' she whistled through the gap in her teeth. It was small, that gap, but it had much to say. It told the village that not only did Connie's husband knock her about, but they couldn't afford a dentist.

She was grateful that Stan had missed jail for what she called his 'mix-up' with the petrol, but the judge fined him the maximum amount. One hundred and sixty pounds was the same as a million to the Horrobins.

Other heads in the room shook about the fine. Doris called it 'a crying shame' to burden a family already mired in poverty, but Blanche declared it was time Stan saw some consequences. Nobody knew she had witnessed the arrest; nobody knew Kos wasn't alone that night.

She sought out Pamela, who was glacially polite, asking Blanche how her new chap was settling in.

'What about *your* new chap?' *Ah ha!* Blanche silently exulted. *That got a reaction from the ice queen.* 'Or should I say "chaps", I mean of course your RAF boarders. Who did you think I meant?'

Doris found Connie. 'Your Maisie made a lovely wise man.'

'Whatcha want, Doris?' The 'S' whistled.

'I heard about Stan.' Doris chose her words carefully; Connie was averse to sympathy. 'It's a hard old Christmas, one way and another.' Doris had hoped to give Christine a pretty silver ring she'd seen in Felpersham, but instead the girl would receive a knitted bag to hold her childish, girlish bits and bobs. 'I'm knitting like the clappers.'

'Tell you who won't be knitting presents.' Connie looked over at Pamela, who was laughing up at a tall man, now famous as Stan's nemesis. 'Lady Bountiful over there. Why can't that Polish bugger go home?'

'He's helping us win the war.'

'Win. Lose. All the same to me.' Connie sneered at Irene as she passed with Nanny. 'That girl's too good to be in the play, I suppose.' Envy. Scorn. Connie burned with both.

'She's a very particular child.' That was the adjective Doris had decided on for Irene. She could smell fear on Nanny; the woman was a whipping boy for both her brother and her charge. 'Connie! Stop staring at Pamela. It's rude.'

'So? I *am* rude. What's she saying "yes" to, I wonder?'

Not just yes, but 'Yes! Yes! *Yes!*' If Connie could lip-read she would have been thrilled by Kos's answer of, 'Oh, my darling.'

Making the rounds, Joe Grundy licked a pencil stub and took orders for Christmas trees. 'Best quality, bargain prices.' Agnes put her name down, and the Pargetters asked for the biggest he had. War would not dim the lights of Christmas.

'I see you, you naughty boy,' said Blanche into Archie's ear. 'Making goo-goo eyes at a son of the soil.'

The farmhand in question, if washed, would be a dead ringer for Leslie Howard. 'My world's egalitarian,' said Archie, in the undertone learned in a small club down a flight of steps off Sloane Square. 'We're all the same between the sheets.'

'Satin sheets are nicer, though.' Blanche loved dipping into Archie's taboo love life. 'That Lower Loxley chap's quite a looker.'

Terence lounged, bored, against a pillar.

'Hmm. He's a conundrum. Arthur or Martha?' Archie roused himself. 'I'll stick to my farm boy. No shame in a day's work for a day's pay. Not that you'd know.' He dug Blanche in the ribs.

Homing in on his target, Archie passed Doris, who was broaching a delicate subject with the vicar's wife.

'Can't we do something for Connie? That fine really clobbered her.' Doris knew how it felt to be clobbered; she could spare very little for Connie.

'The Poor Fund, you mean?' Frances had a special face she made when discussing money. As if she was sniffing vinegar. 'That's for deserving cases. Stan is hardly that.'

'Yes, but Connie . . . you've seen her tooth.'

'God helps those,' said Frances, 'who help themselves.'

It was happening again.

There was a woman in The Bull.

Alec and Dan, in their usual seats, shared a look that asked was nothing sacred? Was there nowhere to sink a beer and make ribald remarks? And women *commented* on everything. Wanda was doing just that. Commenting. She was on her tiptoes, searching for somebody, clearly disappointed not to find him there, and then she said, 'Where's The Bull's festive spirit, Bob? You'd hardly know it was Christmas in here.'

He looked daggers, and the men hoped she'd take the hint.

She didn't. Wanda left but returned in two shakes of a lamb's tail with a basket of greenery. She set Bob to looking out drawing pins and sent Stan up a ladder with some mistletoe. 'You! You're tall,' she said to Alec. 'Pin this holly to the beams.'

The Bull was still smoky and dark when she'd finished, but it was smoky, dark and festive.

'Have something on the house,' said Bob, despite himself.

'May I pour a pint?' Wanda dipped under the counter and popped up beside Bob before he could demur. 'I've always wanted to.'

'Now now, this is *my* side, young lady.'

'But you look so tired.'

The men loudly agreed with her; the coup worked.

'Sit down before you fall down, Bob,' said Dan.

'Here, take my stool.' Walter set Bob by the fire, and dislodged Joe Grundy from his chair, who in turn dislodged Chas Westenra from the settle. Wanda pulled some substandard pints as Stan chalked up the latest odds in the Woodbine sweepstake. 'Only a month or so to the next will reading, and old Blanchie's evens,' he declared. 'Alec, you're one to four. The vicar's lagging behind since we found out about that Latin saying. Morgan's an outsider, 'cos of his name being Blake. It's a long shot but there's a pretty penny to be made if the doc romps home.'

'If you pay up,' muttered Joe.

'I'll put a tanner on Blanche,' said Wanda.

Stan took her money and rubbed the slate with his cuff. 'Wills often hold surprises. Jane's own ma left me twenty quid.'

'You?' said Dan, rudely.

'She felt sorry for me mother. Dad was at war, I was on the way, and Ma had too many mouths to feed already. She went down like a sack of spuds, just outside Woodbine Cottage, and Jane's mother come out and . . .' Stan was lost in the memory of kindness, a rare commodity in his neck of the woods. 'Blow me down if she didn't buy Ma a crib. Said she couldn't see a babby go without when her own Blanche and Jane had so much.'

'A great lady.' Dan was susceptible to such tales, especially after a pint. He'd give Doris a sloppy great kiss later. *If she lets me.*

Stan recalculated the odds; he had never been to school but he was an Einstein at calculating probabilities. 'That's how I got me middle name. Blair. Jane's mother's maiden name, you see.'

'Blair?' Wanda calculated too. 'Better put yourself on that slate, Stan. B plus L! If the next plant starts with A, Jane could be spelling your name.'

Stan had to sit down.

'Go easy,' fretted Bob as Wanda filled Walter's tankard to overflowing, and kissed him on the cheek to boot. 'Beer's not free, you know.'

The shouts at the kiss turned to shouts of welcome for the gaggle of men at the door, stamping their feet and tearing off balaclavas.

'Bwona-whatsit!' Dan liked the Italians.

'Buonasera!'

'D'you lot have permission?' Bob was cranky. 'I don't want to get into trouble.'

They did and Wanda served them and Bob said, 'Make sure you take their money first.'

'Hey, Bobby,' said one of the POWs, ruffling the landlord's hair.

'Gerroff,' said Bob.

'I come back after war,' said another dark-haired fellow, 'and marry my girl.'

There were cheers for this, and Dan bought the Italian boys a round; he couldn't afford it, but Doris need never know. *Except she knows everything.* Dan was too tipsy to care.

'What's that red circle on the back of your jacket?' asked Wanda, eyes glistening at the influx of testosterone. 'Looks like a target.'

'No no no! If we escape,' said a bright-eyed chap, 'the red circle tells the world we are prisoners of war and we are catched. But we do not escape! We fall in love instead!'

They liked being allowed out to labour, the strangers told Wanda. 'We all work, except the fascists.'

A burly man spat when she mentioned Mussolini. 'He hurts my country. I hate fascists.' He got a cheer for this, naturally. 'When I see the black armband in camp I do not talk to these men. I love my Englishmen!' he shouted suddenly, and gave Walter his second kiss of the night.

Lower Loxley, 1 × v lge tree, 8/-, payment on delivery, J. Grundy

The spruce tickled Lower Loxley's famed plaster-work ceiling.

Tomorrow the estate workers would file past it to collect a small glass of something along with their Christmas box. It was an enduring waypoint in the house's year, one Alec adored, and which his wife had embraced from the first.

Even Gerald was affected by the atmosphere. One day home from school, and already grounded for some barbarity, he was sorting through the boxes of decorations with an innocent childishness Alec had feared was gone forever.

The boy – well, man-boy; *Gerald is seventeen*, Alec reminded himself – held up a bauble. 'Look, Dad. Your favourite.'

'Your mother'll let us have it, right between the eyes.'

'For decorating the tree without her?' Gerald brought his shoulders up to his ears. 'The old dame'll blow her top.'

'And then she'll creep down tonight and rearrange it all.'

'And she'll think we won't notice,' said Gerald. 'Mama really loves the tree.'

The great door opened and Pamela was there, her arms full of packages, her hat a stovepipe creation.

'Watch out!' said Alec. 'We're for the high jump!'

Gerald leapt up and laughed, 'It's all Dad's fault!'

'What is?'

'Mother, we've only just started, honestly. You'll still get to put the angel on top.'

Pamela carried on, left them to it. 'I'm sure you'll do a lovely job.'

Gerald stared after her.

Alec put the angel back in her tissue shroud.

It gave the other men a kick to see him do it, and Nance laughed as well, so every morning Ted Wrigley handed her up into her forklift like a duchess.

Dolly and her gaggle saw them and hollered. Sal leaned into Nance's cab and whispered, 'You leapt on your old man, yet?'

'Oi, let her be,' said Dolly. To Nance, confidentially, she

said, 'She's right though, duck. You gotta take charge. Haven't you noticed it's women who run the world?'

The foremen scattered the women – 'Back to work, you lot,' – and said to Nance, 'I need you to run some parts to Hollerton Junction for me. Take someone. Hey! Ted! I'm volunteering you, mate.'

Nance hesitated.

'You can drive, can't you?' On Nance's nod, the foreman said, 'What you waiting for? Chop-chop.'

Sal was watching. As Nance passed her she said, 'Unless it's not your husband you want to leap on . . .'

'Oh, shush you.' The irreverence was catching; Nance was smiling.

With only two days to go, the approaching pantechnicon of Christmas meant nothing to the cows.

The herd needed feeding every day, come what may. Just as the new yard needed sweeping and the fences needed mending. Wanda longed to sit by the Boss's stove and unfreeze her fingers, but there was work to be done, illicit work, carried out in a shed on a far field that Doris never visited.

'She's going to love this.' Dan fiddled with a length of tubing. 'It'll be the highlight of Christmas Day.'

'You sure?' Wanda manhandled the container. 'Is it supposed to smell like that, Mr Archer?'

A Waterley Cross truck tooted its horn as it trundled past the shop.

Too beleaguered to look out, Frank called out, 'Next!' Christmas meant a full shop and depleted shelves. After the last customer left he would fall asleep over his ledger, smudging the nines and the fives. He missed Nance's neat handwriting.

'Rabbit, please,' said Mrs Endicott. She didn't want rabbit, she didn't *like* rabbit, but Frank was out of chicken and she had missed her chance for pork.

'One bunny coming up,' said Frank.

'Third Christmas at war.' Agnes thumped a poster that exhorted them all to 'win the war on the kitchen front – don't waste food!' 'No bloomin' food to waste!' she said.

Doris agreed, and wondered unpatriotically if reheating last night's mashed swede really would help defeat Hitler. 'When did we *ever* waste food?'

Watching as her rabbit was rolled up in greaseproof paper, Mrs Endicott said, 'We won't lose *you*, Frank, will we? The call-up's changing, they're taking men up to, what is it, sixty?'

'They only take them to fight until they're fifty-one,' said Frank. 'And no, Mrs E, I'm exempt. There's no other shop for miles.'

Over the ladies' heads, Archie shouted, 'Got any marg, Frank?' He wished everyone a merry Christmas. He was in high spirits. He had recently been kissed. By someone who really knew what he was doing. 'I'm gonna make this a knockout Christmas for Blanche. First one without her sister, poor love.' He rarely issued updates on Blanche's welfare; he was rarely asked for one.

Connie, by the leeks, said, 'Might be her last Christmas with a roof over her head. Happen me and Stan'll be in Woodbine next year.' She slapped Bert's hand away from the leeks. He slapped Maisie. Maisie slapped him back. Connie slapped them both.

'I never met Jane,' said Archie, 'but I trust her. Blanche is staying put.'

'Here,' said Agnes, eyes glinting. 'D'you hear about Pamela Pargetter's to-do?' She had everyone's attention. 'She's in her pony and trap, clippety-clop, giving that Polish pilot a lift somewhere. She turns her back on the trap for *one minute* and—'

'Why'd she turn her back?' Connie was a born heckler. 'Thought she was giving him a lift, not getting out?'

'May I finish? Pamela turns her back, and just like that, her bag's open and her purse is out and there's a ten-bob note missing!'

Connie said, 'Probably an Italian.'

'Or a Horrobin,' said Agnes.

1 × *medium tree to Turnpike, 4/10, payment on delivery, J. Grundy*

Agnes had been making decorations since September. The Crow picked up every glittery gewgaw she saw, and now the tree shimmered, listing a little, like Mrs Endicott in one of her more flamboyant hats. The tree was beyond taste; it was in a gaudy universe of its own. And Agnes adored it.

Standing beside it in a Fair Isle jumper, Denholm attempted a seasonal expression.

'There! Stay like that!' Agnes stared down into the Brownie box camera. She would fix this triumphant moment in her new life by using the expensive new plaything that Denholm had not sanctioned. 'Say cheese!'

Instead he said, 'How much did that camera cost, Aggie?'

On a bend in the road, at the dip of the year, sat Nance. A man's overcoat was slung over her shoulders, and the owner of the coat stood surveying the road, rubbing his hands together and blowing into them.

'Getting on for dark.' Ted sank to the verge beside Nance. The van sat, useless, where it had died. 'Snuggle up. I'm not trying nothing. It's just flippin' freezing. Pardon my French.'

It was clear he wouldn't try nothing. Ted was decent. Sensing his frustration at not being able to save the day, Nance said, 'Someone'll be along.'

He produced a rustling paper bag. 'Wanna share?' The sandwich was a loose affiliation of cheddar and good bread. 'Made it meself. The kitchen's not me strong point.'

She liked that he talked. It saved her from having to. With only one or two questions from Nance, Ted told her all about himself.

About his sister being 'a great girl' and how he went out for a bevvy with his brother-in-law to get out from under her feet. He had a soft spot for his youngest nephew: 'Not just 'cos he's the image of me, honest.' He showed her his profile. 'Do I look thirty-three? Be honest.'

'Yes,' said Nance.

He laughed. 'I'm saving up. I want a place of me own, spick and span, indoor lavvy, the lot.'

Nance had always had her own room, had never shared, never ventured outside to spend a penny. The smear of oil across his cheekbones made her think of Navajo war paint. She thought of Morgan's clean, antiseptic hands.

'Don't let the lads' comments get to you, Nance.'

'They're easing off.'

'I come down hard. Especially if they're off-colour. Not having that.'

'Thanks.' It was not embarrassing to discuss such matters with Ted. He was earthy, clean, in the way that woods are. 'Don't you have a girl of your own?' The question might give him ideas, but she needed to know.

'I did have. Went with her for years. Engaged, everything. She went behind my back with a mate of mine.'

'That's very sad.'

'Lucky escape, you mean. Thought my heart was broke at the time. Now I'm well on the way to having it broke again.'

Their knees up to their chins, their shoulders touched. 'Oh?' said Nance.

'There's this girl. I'm wild about her. Classy. Nice natured. But some lucky bugger got there before me.'

Nance couldn't pretend to misunderstand. Her head swam. It was a dare; Ted was beckoning her into the open.

They heard feet, lots of them, marching. Up they hopped.

Around the bend came No.9 Platoon. All sizes, all shapes, like Liquorice Allsorts.

'Halt!' shouted Alec, and they swarmed around the truck. The bonnet flew up and Chas Westenra rolled up his shirtsleeves.

'Soon have you on your way.' Alec was kind; Nance didn't hold with the naysayers who called him stuck-up. He was a product of his upbringing, like everyone else.

The engine growled. Ted pumped Chas's hand. When he and Nance set off again, they were quiet.

A Rubicon had been crossed. Nance felt she was betraying Morgan by enjoying the jolting journey so much, watching the bare solstice trees jog by.

She and her husband were married, but not a match.

Whereas Ted and me ... Figurines on a mantel. Solid, to be sold as a pair. Nance looked past the trees to a different life, one where she had waited, looked beyond Ambridge for a partner, and married someone like Ted.

Well, *Ted*.

She might be pregnant by now.

'Nice bunch, those Home Guard blokes,' said Ted. 'Let's hope we never need them. Can't bear the thought of German feet on British soil.'

'Yeah ...' Nance wondered how many of her own relatives might be part of an invading army, shot at by Alec Pargetter and Dan Archer.

Broom Corner, 1 × sml tree, no charge, J. Grundy
Little Maisie Horrobin was spellbound. Bert stood in awe. Just one length of tinsel snaked around the stubby little

tree, the runt of the litter, but it was a starburst of beauty in Connie's kitchen.

Billy and John, although busy gents with much on their minds, could not tear themselves away. The Christmas tree, like the moon, connected them to home. The moon shone over them in Ambridge, and Peggy and Mum in London, and Dad wherever he was.

The children sat cross-legged, lost in the glow of the tinsel and the warmth that seemed to radiate from the tree and soften everything in its reach.

Midnight galloped closer over the dreaming meadows.

Inside St Stephen's, the church glowed with expectancy and celebration. A service at night felt special, singular. The villagers would sing their way into Christmas, that trans-formative day.

There were Seeds, there were Archers, there was the surviving Gilpin. The Pargetters – even bored-to-death Gerald – were in position. Mrs Endicott stopped whispering to Agnes about the will when the vicar appeared, a touch early, in the aisle.

He whisked past the seated congregation to find his wife. Frances was titivating the bidding prayers pinned up in the porch. The village children had written out their naive wishes – 'Dear Lord please make the war stop and bring my daddy home. Sarah Swadling aged 7' – and Frances had curated them.

Her display had taken a knock from latecomers fresh from The Bull. Mick Lister had elbowed a prayer to the ground as he was carried to a pew.

'Dear Lord please fix my granddad's bad legs signed Hannah Ratcliffe aged 6' lay on the floor. Frances dusted it off as Henry hissed, 'We're missing an altar server!'

'Check the back passage,' said Frances, without looking at him. There had been words in the vestry; she was in no mood to help her husband. 'That's where the little beasts go to smoke.'

'My altar servers do *not* smoke.'

She looked at him then, with pity. 'That's where he'll be, Henry.' As she turned back to the prayers, she said, 'I found your Dorothy Hughes.'

'She's not *my* . . .' Henry stopped himself. 'Where is she?'

'In the ground.' Frances pressed a thumb tack into the board. Hard. 'She gave that baby of hers to relatives, dumped it really, then drank herself to death in Liverpool. Or was it Leeds? Somewhere unwholesome beginning with L.' She finally faced Henry but he wasn't there. She located him by following the ripple of twittered remarks.

As Henry careered across the uneven stone floor he remembered, in burnished glory, the last time he saw Dorothy Hughes.

Jane Gilpin had brought her to the back door of the vicar-age. The girl's stomach was huge, her arms and legs spindly around it. Dorothy had tried to explain her predicament, but Jane had to fill in the tearful, humiliated gaps. No, she wouldn't say who the father was. Yes, her own father had thrown her out. The canvas bag at her feet constituted her worldly goods.

'Henry,' said Jane, beseeching, 'the poor girl has nowhere else to turn.'

Frances said, 'This isn't a hotel, Jane.' She said more than that. She said that Dorothy had been spotted drinking outside The Bull. She spoke of Dorothy's 'reputation'.

'I've given her ten shillings, all I have in the house,' said Jane. 'If she can't stay here, then could you spare a little from the Poor Fund so she can take a room somewhere?'

When Dorothy looked out into the night she didn't seem to have much faith in this notional room; as a farmer's daughter she had never ventured out of Ambridge.

'The Poor Fund,' Frances said, 'is for deserving cases. Isn't that right, Henry?'

Caught, *pinioned*, he had said, 'Dorothy, let me give you something from my own wallet.' He took out a note.

'Ten shillings?' Shocked, Frances laid her hand on his arm.

'All right, five,' he said.

Frances snatched the wallet. Picked through it. 'There.' She handed Dorothy a half-crown. To Henry she said, 'Agreed?'

Judas had added a kiss, but Henry merely nodded.

A little hysterically, Jane said, 'Surely we can—'

'Now now, Jane,' said Henry. 'Don't upset yourself.' He handed Dorothy her bag. Very polite. Most concerned.

Frances said, 'God helps those who help themselves.'

Now, as midnight breathed down his neck, Henry scrabbled for the new wallet, the *old* wallet, that Jane had given him. He fell to his knees in front of the slotted metal box that bore the sign 'Poor Fund'.

Doris and Dan watched in astonishment as the vicar pushed notes and coins into the slot. Shillings bounced and rolled. He rounded them up, shoved them in.

Dan said admiringly, 'Well, if that's not the spirit of Christmas, I don't know what is. Well done, Reverend!'

'Ta *da*!' Dan lowered Doris's present into the rubble of wrapping paper and ribbon.

'Ooh!' said Doris. Then, 'What is it?'

Wanda and Christine kept in their giggles. Just.

'What is it?' said Dan. 'It's only your very own barrel of potato beer, old girl!'

'Ooh,' said Doris again, with slightly less energy.

Woodbine Cottage was sweet with woodsmoke, and bright with the tinsel Archie wore instead of a tie. He gave Blanche a lambswool cardigan and she gave him a leather-bound diary.

There was booze from the moment they opened their eyes, and at about noon he asked her if she was doing all right. 'You seem fine, doll, but this day must be hard on you.'

'You mean the will?' said Blanche.

'Well, no.' Archie glanced at her as he introduced par-boiled potatoes to spitting fat. 'I mean, your first Christmas without Jane.'

'I prefer Christmas with you.'

'You are *peculiar*,' said Archie.

Wanda slipped away to her shack. After the shining fug of the kitchen it was cold and she would soon slip back to the farmhouse; today of all days the Boss mustn't be allowed anywhere near the dishes in the sink.

For now she needed to be alone to unwrap the small box Mr Bigtime had given her the night before. History had taught her that the smallest boxes from her father were the ones her mother treasured most.

She thought of her father then, of his ship and its peril, and Wanda allowed herself to wallow for the precise time it took one tear to travel down her face.

The gold bracelet coiled in the box was simple. Mr Bigtime had taste.

Small birds took off in a great clatter from bare trees.

'That means an owl's about,' said Billy to his brother. He knew lore like this now. Back in London he had known about bus routes and which pubs gave you a farthing for collecting bottles. He recited the bus routes at night; owl stuff wouldn't do him any good when he got home.

Luca had given up on them, was walking away when they reached the wire. 'You come!' he said, all relief. He rolled something off his sleeve and stuffed it into his coat pocket. 'Tell me of your turkey.'

'Blimey, Luca, we're not billeted at Buckingham Palace,' said Billy.

Right up against the wire, as if willing his little body through it, John said, 'Wish we could take you home with us, Luca.'

'I wish this too.' Luca put his fingers through the wire. Wizbang licked them. 'But I protect the weak and so I not allowed to eat dinner with nice British people.'

'We got you a present.' John sizzled with happiness. 'Go on, Billy.'

Billy suppressed a smile; the gift would knock Luca's socks off. 'Ten bob!' He pushed the folded note through the wire. 'Ten whole shillings!'

'*Bene*.' Luca tucked it away.

'It's a lot, innit?' Billy felt their offering had been dealt with too speedily. They'd been through a lot to get that money.

'Next I need bike.'

'A bike?' As there was no Peggy around to clip an ear, Billy said, 'Bleedin' hell, Luca.'

'Good clothes, too.'

John bit his lip. He hated to think what Jesus must be making of this casual talk of thieving. *And on his birthday, too.*

Glasses were gathered. A jug rinsed. The potato beer transferred via the most unhygienic length of tubing Doris had ever met in in her life.

'You first, love,' said Dan.

He's so happy. 'Chin-chin!' said Doris. She held the beer to her lips. She took it away from her lips. 'Dan, love, I can't,' she said.

'Smells like old long johns,' said Christine.

'Old long johns,' agreed Phil. 'That somebody died in.'

The vicar, pleasantly full of delicious things, turned the small painting on its side. 'What do you think it is? A nature scene? Or a modern abstract work?'

Frances peered closer at Mrs Endicott's present. 'Dear God!' she said, pulling back as if the painting had scorched her. 'I think it's *us*!'

It was that pocket of Christmas Day that nobody knows what to do with. There had been wine, feasting, card games, but now Lower Loxley was at a loose end.

On one side of the fire, Alec sat in an armchair that threatened to swallow him. On the other side of the fire sat Dodgy. Before the war, Alec would have been sitting opposite his wife.

And I would have been bored.

His previous, pre-war self he remembered as perpetually petulant, ungrateful. What he wouldn't give to be bored again.

'Your vicar was twitchy at the midnight service,' said Dodgy. 'Does he always lose his thread like that?'

'No. Perhaps he was unwell.'

Between asking the question and hearing the answer, Dodgy had fallen asleep.

Alec stole away. He encountered a chap in the hall, puffing on a pipe. Another labouring down the stairs on crutches. There were chaps simply everywhere.

He didn't know he was looking for Pamela until he found her.

Purposeful as ever, striding along the top corridor. Fixing an earring. She stopped when she saw him, and Alec wondered why. He wondered where she had been, where she was going. This interest in her was new, feverish.

She said, 'Should I suggest bridge?'

'How much longer is he staying?'

'Who?'

'Who'd you think, Pamela?'

'Why not ask him?' She made to pass him but Alec stepped into her path. 'Alec!' She sprang back. Any touch was abhorrent to her, it would seem.

As if I'm a mangy dog.

He said, 'I'm doing my best.' The words came out like bits of rope, chewed on and spat out. 'There's only so much a man can put up with under his own roof.'

'Nothing happens under your roof.'

'I don't mean ... *that*.' The image in his head, of Pamela and Kos conjoined, appalled him. 'Look here, I put a stop to things when it got too much. I did that for you, Pamela.'

Her eyes, always clever, looked dangerous. 'Don't pontificate. You're in no position to lecture me. Did I ever corner you like this? Did I?'

'You were a model of restraint.'

'Funny how even your compliments sound like slurs. Like you're disappointed in me.'

'I'm not, truly I'm not.' Alec could hear chaps doing chap things in their rooms. He hoped nobody was listening. 'You're my wife, Pamela.'

'And that says it all, doesn't it? It really is the up and down of us, the height, the width. You can name what I am, but you can't describe me.'

Alec saw no tears. Heard no passion. She confused him. 'What do you want me to do?'

Pamela took her time. She might have told him she wanted him to stop lying about how his affair ended. She said, instead, 'I want you to leave me alone.'

Tears, thought Alec, seeing her eyes change. He jumped out of her way. There must not be a scene.

Stan wore the tinsel from the tree like the laurels of a conquering Caesar. He had conquered his stockpiled beer, and his wife.

Cliff put down *Wuthering Heights* and concentrated on the Gothic horror closer to hand. He took Maisie and Bert off his mother's hands, off to his room for a story. They were still crying about the trampled Christmas tree.

They would soon grow out of that. They would soon learn crying made no difference.

Christmas Day was almost done, and Doris still couldn't get the taste out of her mouth.

Who'd have thought the self-effacing potato, supporting player at every Brookfield dinner, could turn on her like that? She rehearsed how she'd tell Jack about it, acting out Dan's pride and the expression on the kids' faces. She knew how his apple-shaped face would crease up.

So much to tell him; no doubt she'd forget half of it. Mostly Doris just wanted to check him over, the way she frisked newborn lambs, make sure he was all there.

The longing, the not-knowing, was suddenly so acute that she had to lean on the back of a chair. If she kept thinking of her boy among the bullets she would be on her knees, and then the Big Top would collapse on them all. The Archers. Her labourers. Wanda.

The memory of St Stephen's the night before lingered too. Not Henry's eccentric sermon, but the scene afterwards.

Beacham had not attended church; possibly he was unused to village life, didn't realize such an absence would be noted. Nanny and Irene, the child all gussied up in velvet, shook the vicar's hand in the porch, as Doris and her posse shuffled along behind, willing them to get a move on.

At all costs they had to reach the vicar before Mrs Endicott, who was bursting to reel off her yuletide afflictions.

At the vicar's side, Frances nodded and smiled, smiled and nodded, until suddenly she stopped doing both and tore a bidding prayer from the notice board. She thrust the scrap of paper at Irene, pushing it against the child's chest so hard that Doris started forward to say, 'Frances! Control yourself!'

'What is it?' said Henry, who looked as if he wanted

to press a lever in the stonework and eject himself from the porch.

'Disgusting!' spat Frances. 'In the house of God. Read this!' She flapped the bidding prayer, then read it herself, in a voice that shook with fury. 'Dear God, please make the vicar's wife's knickers fall down in front of everyone, signed Irene Kosten aged 8.'

'Oh, Irene.' Nanny looked at her ward as if the girl might tear off her velvet and reveal a body covered in wolf fur. 'It's just her little joke,' she said lamely to the other worshippers.

'Dear Frances's knickers,' murmured Mrs Endicott.

'Chastise her, Nanny!' ordered Frances, pointing at Irene, who stared dourly into the middle distance. 'You're afraid of the girl, aren't you?'

'Now, Frances,' began Doris, ready with oil to throw on troubled waters.

But Frances had hit her stride and would not calm down. 'That child's a bad seed, I tell you.'

'Our Irene is—' Nanny got no further.

'I'm not your Irene, don't say that.' Irene's voice was clear and unhurried. 'You're not my mother. You're nobody's mother.'

The leave-taking of midnight service had gone awry. Folk didn't know what to say, or how to design their facial expressions. The vicar said, 'Why not take the child home, Nanny? It's late.'

The villagers said muted goodnights and peeled off to

their homes, none of them certain of what they had just witnessed.

Now, at Brookfield, putting out the lamps, Doris wondered where Nanny had learned to attach herself to people who didn't want her? That brother of hers had schooled her to expect little in the way of kindness. Pain is passed on down family lines as surely as property.

It niggled at her, like a thistle in her corset. *I made a mistake billeting Irene at Furnivall Manor.*

A pall of unease hung over the manor's trio: Beacham, Nanny and Irene were a sinister tableau, angled towards Doris, lit like a melodrama.

Doris gave herself a talking-to. She was a mere billeting manager, a tiny cog in a vast machine. Yes, the machine wobbled and some days it rattled so hard you feared it might blow a gasket, but it carried on.

Ambridge would carry on through its harsh winter, like it always had, and emerge into spring more or less in one piece.

So Doris hoped.

Christmas is done; the moment shimmers.

Tomorrow will be different, no special shine in the air.

Connie is glad. She mistrusts special days; they turn to chaos. As soon as the buses are running again, she'll take one to visit that moneylender who knows her so well.

In the vicarage, Henry wakes, disoriented, in the spare room. Banished there, he watches Boxing Day creep over the sill.

Alec lies awake, grimly grateful for the raising of the conscription age. He's in the running now; how he longs for the anonymity and purpose of battle. One of those bullets may have his name on it, long though that name is: Alec Cedric Charles de Vere Pargetter.

John says his prayers. 'God bless me and Billy and Peggy and Mum and Dad, oh and Wizbang, and Connie and Cliff and Vic and Maisie and Bert and Luca and Bruno and Vittorio and their granddad.' He can't do it; he can't leave anyone out. 'And Stan I suppose.' He hopes Jesus will understand about stealing the ten bob from Pamela. 'Sorry,' he whispers.

JANUARY

Pamela was not accustomed to creeping, or sneaking, or tip-toeing. 'This will not *do*!' she said, as she ran in a crouch to the back door of her house.

'Does it matter if Alec sees you?' said Kos, infuriatingly tall and obvious behind her. 'He knows you're no longer his.'

'When have I ever said that? And the staff certainly don't need to know where I lay my head.' Pamela was careful to keep her forays to the folly below the servants' radar. She was unsuccessful in this, but would live and die without knowing it.

There was something on the back step, a curious, out-of-place something. Pamela tossed it, with a tut, into the lavender.

'It looked like it was laid down carefully, a pagan offering,' said Kos.

Pamela turned to tell him to please keep his voice down and not to prattle about 'offerings'. She kissed him, instead,

Home Fires at Ambridge

and held onto him, and felt his strength and her own need
and said, 'I adore you, you know.'

'I do know,' he said.

AMBRIDGE WOMEN'S COMMITTEE

MEETING MINUTES

Date: 5th January, 1942
At: The Cherries
Chairwoman: Pamela Pargetter
Present: Frances Bissett, Emmaline
Endicott, Doris Archer, Blanche Gilpin,
Agnes Kaye, Nance Morgan, Susan Grundy,
Wanda Laframboise.
Minutes: Frances Bissett

1. Pamela welcomed Wanda to the
committee. Pamela thanked Mrs E for letting
us meet at The Cherries. Magsy said 'Such a
light room, with every comfort' and Agnes
said 'Bit chintzy if you ask me' and I
myself thought that nobody did ask her but
said nothing.

2. Doris said 'War Christmasses aren't
the same' and Pamela said 'Yes well
Christmas can't solve everything and today
we really must get on and not stray from

253

committee business.' She said the nativity catering was a triumph and I myself was too modest to mention my tarts but Mrs E had no such qualms about her possets.

3. Pamela asked for suggestions for the Valentine's Dance. Doris said 'Pink crepe and lots of it.'

4. Pamela said the local band is still staggering on and she will book them.

5. Mrs E suggested we ban alcohol. Agnes said 'Don't you want nobody to come?'

6. Blanche said 'Oh go on and gossip about the will you know you want to' and Pamela said 'Not at all' and Mrs E said 'Blanche you must feel terrible knowing Stan may well inherit your house' and Magsy said Jane would not hand the keys to such a devil and Blanche said 'If I don't inherit Woodbine I don't care if it goes to Stan or Greta Garbo' and Mrs E said 'Having Stan as a neighbour might bring on one of my collapses, my last one was triggered by a saucy butcher's boy' and I myself said 'I have asked Henry to pray that Jane's next plant does not begin with an "A"' and Doris said 'Perhaps Jane's will is making the point that we should all be more charitable to one another' and Agnes said 'Ha that

shut you all up didn't it' and Pamela said
'May we please get on?'

7. Mrs E said 'I still think Jane might
favour the cat's home. Oh sorry Pamela' and
then she told us she is painting a view of
The Green to auction for the church fund
and there were no comments whatsoever.

8. Connie Horrobin arrived late. I
myself told her she mustn't feel she *has* to
attend. Doris said 'Please stay Connie you
are invaluable.'

9. Agnes asked if we had seen the grey
heron standing in the village pond and we
all agreed it is a most noble bird. Agnes
said 'I have not seen it since Saturday'
and Connie said 'It has more sense than to
hang around in this dump.'

10. Wanda asked who will we dance with at
the Valentine's Dance as 'there are hardly
any fellows left' and Pamela assured us all
Lower Loxley's RAF fliers will attend and
Wanda said 'Oh I do like a man in uniform.'
Note to self: ask Henry to have a word with
Wanda re: the maidenly virtues.

11. Mrs Endicott invited Pamela to tea
on the 19th January but Pamela said 'Sadly
I am in London that day and may we please
get back to business?'

12. Connie said 'Ooh London all right for some.'

13. Magsy said 'I am very annoyed with Japan for declaring war on the Netherlands, surely they barely know one another?' and Doris said it was like Felpersham declaring war on John O'Groats and said she couldn't stop thinking about the poor boys who had no gripe with anyone but had to kill other poor boys and Pamela said 'That is indeed a tragedy but not within the remit of this committee' and asked if anyone could spare a punch bowl for the Valentine's Dance.

14. Nance left early to go back to work. She was wearing trousers. Actual trousers.

15. When Nance was gone Magsy said 'I admire Nance greatly for helping the war effort but what about The Husband Effort? Isn't a woman's place beside her husband?'

16. Connie said 'You ain't never had one.'

17. Agnes said 'Borrow Stan for a week, Magsy, see if you can get the hang of it.'

18. Magsy said 'Oh I am just old-fashioned and don't like to see Morgan neglected. Not that Nance neglects him. I imply nothing.'

19. Connie said 'Who dobbed my Stan into Constable Jenkins for poaching I know it

was one of youse it was only one measly
rabbit' and Susan said 'Wasn't me' and
Connie said 'No well that's because your
Joe is always setting traps but he never
gets in trouble. Horrobins get the blame
for everything in Ambridge' and I, myself,
said 'If the cap fits' and I will not set
down the words used thereafter by Connie.

20. Pamela said 'Do you know I found a
stone with a perfect hole in it on my step
this morning.'

21. Agnes said 'Now who is straying from
committee business?' and Wanda said 'I hope
you kept it' and Pamela said 'I threw it
away' and declared the meeting over.

The robin was ubiquitous in his red jacket.

One hopped alongside Alec and Hero as they walked into the day, into the second week of the new year. He was glad the blanket of Christmas had lifted, that Gerald was no longer under his eye, that he and Pamela were not thrown together so often in jagged silence. Relishing the metronome *tramp-tramp* of his feet on the hard ground, he tipped his hat at the clutch of old biddies outside the shop but didn't break step.

Something fell out of the sky. A peregrine. It plummeted and twisted, intent and deadly. Then it rose like a firework, something small in its mouth.

If Alec saw a metaphor, if Kos was the bird and Pamela the prey and he, as ever, a bystander, then he kept it at bay with the stiff upper lip passed down to him by his celebrated forebears.

Arkwright Hall sat cosy beneath a milk-white sky.

The children were grumpy. 'They want it to snow,' said Cliff.

Lorna sat at a desk, he stood by the window. 'All we're getting this year is frost.'

'A bone-hard *no*,' said Cliff. 'You and your chum go out at the weekend?'

'You mean Wanda?'

'Well, yeah.'

'She had a date. That Mr Bigtime.'

Lorna would never step out with such a flashy individual. *Then again, such a flashy individual would never ask me.* She doubted Mr Bigtime's intentions; Victorian novels had taught her to beware of his type.

'That's not a serious affair, though.' Cliff breathed on the window and drew his initials in the fog. 'Is it?'

'Why don't you ask her?' Lorna took off her glasses and rubbed the bridge of her nose. 'Sorry. That came out rude.'

'No, it didn't.'

'It's just, I'm not Wanda's social secretary, Cliff. Do you like her?'

'She's a nice girl.'

'That's not what I'm asking.'

There was silence, except for Lorna turning the pages of the register.

Cliff said, 'I suppose I might like her a little.'

The tip of Lorna's pencil broke. She wiped the glasses that, according to her merciless little brothers, made her look 'swotty'. 'Then tell her so.'

'Me?'

'Yes, Cliff, *you*.'

'I don't know what girls like to hear.'

Lorna, who was a girl, knew the truth of this.

Cliff said, 'I told her she looked pretty the other day. Because she is, isn't she?'

'Wanda's very pretty,' agreed Lorna.

'I said her face looked just right poking out of her hair.'

'That's how you put it?'

'Yes. Why?'

'When I think of all the poetry you read, Cliff! A woman needs a tailored compliment. One that proves you've really looked at her.'

'Oh God.'

'Think of what you like best about her.' Lorna risked a look at Cliff. He was frowning, intent on the frigid world outside the window, so she could safely stare. 'Maybe the way the hair falls on her brow. Or the soft colour of her eyes. Or the way her face feels like home.' Cliff turned and she went back to the ledger. 'Or something.'

Cliff looked past her. 'We were just talking about you.'

Wanda was at the door. 'I've got a puncture, Cliff! Any chance ...?'

He was on it, happy to be of use. The girls watched him from the window. They both knew Wanda could mend her own puncture.

'Look at this.' Wanda held out her wrist to show Lorna not Mr Bigtime's gold chain, but a Perspex bangle. 'Some chap I danced with once – *once* – made it for me.'

'Another lovelorn swain.'

Wanda pushed Lorna. Laughed. 'Boys are so silly. He works at that aircraft factory, this is made from windscreen material. It's a snake, see, with its tail in its mouth.'

Cliff was back, wiping his hands, just as Lorna said, intrigued, 'A snake eating itself.'

'Like the world,' said Cliff.

'You two say the queerest things,' laughed Wanda.

All was calm, or as calm as a wartime mill could be, until the shouts began by the gate.

It was Ted. He yelled before he threw the first punch. Something like – there was disagreement later – 'You take that back!'

Nance left a stack of paper in mid-air on her forks and went running with the rest of them. Some went for the sport, others to ensure it didn't go too far.

The two men rolled on the ground, grunting, passionate. Ted got a few blunt, hard punches in. No reach of course; they were intertwined like lovers.

Dolly shouted, 'Are you mad, Ted Wrigley?'

Nance said nothing. Her breathing was quick. She knew two tell-tale dots of red were growing on her cheeks.

Ted's face was dusty, his braces undone.

She heard him say, 'She's a lady, you blaggard!'

The other man, his nose pouring blood – Nance had to look away – was her tormentor-in-chief. His mouth, usually a geyser of dirty jokes, was split.

'Ted'll kill 'im,' muttered one of the men, and brawny fellows, the ones who always had to intervene, waded in and pulled the combatants apart. The foreman despaired operatically, then forgave them the moment they stood up.

Ted spat on the floor and rammed his hat back on.

Nance watched him.

And Dolly watched Nance. 'You be careful, you,' she said, before she hurried back to the mill floor.

The open-top Wolseley Hornet took the road south and left Ambridge behind.

Kos drove fast, as if expecting the world to make way for him. 'Glad you said yes?' he shouted above the noise of the engine.

'Keep your eyes on the road!' Pamela's scarf flew off and was lost. Her nose was like ice. 'Yes, I'm glad,' she gasped.

It had taken her a while to agree. She'd given in at the nativity play, grateful to Kos for attending just to please her. Something had crushed the root of her hesitancy – maybe it was Alec's judgemental scorn about her affair, when in reality he had driven her to this, and was still lying about the extent of his own infidelity.

I can't hurt a man who regrets staying with me!

Yes, it was reckless, but perhaps it wasn't wrong. *Kos is kind and I am lonely.* She wondered where that word had sprung from. Pamela had not been raised to study her feelings, and certainly not to wallow in negative ones.

Kos grabbed her hand and kissed it. She felt it, even through the glove, and she laughed as they ate up the road.

Clattering, rowdy, the pillar box red Hornet passed carts and gigs with a toot of its horn. Pamela didn't ask how Kos got hold of the car; the aces were a law unto themselves.

An inn appeared at the right moment, and they fell upon the offered bread roll and crumbly pale cheese as if it were manna from heaven.

'Try my beer,' said Kos.

'I've never tasted beer, and I never intend to.' Pamela enjoyed how he enjoyed her exaggerated femininity. She knew he liked her masculine side, too, the male Pamela that made decisions. She knew he liked *her*.

The barmaid noticed Kos. The woman mopping the floor noticed Kos. *I have lassoed a stallion.* Alec was more a of a nervy racehorse; perfect to lead around a parade ground but never to be ridden bareback.

They would stay overnight in London. Despite her midnight visits to the tower, Pamela had remained true to the letter of marital law, if not the spirit. That could not hold, not with Kos wanting her so much.

She would give herself. Pamela Pargetter had discovered late in life that she couldn't, after all, resist temptation. *Before now I have never been truly tempted.*

Back on the road, she talked of Gerald, shouting, really, because of the wind. 'This accusation of stealing the watch, it rumbles on and on, like Jarndyce versus Jarndyce.'

He's not listening. Kos had no children, and he lived in the moment, a great unfurling now, as befitted a man with a dangerous way of life.

Pamela folded Gerald away; he belonged to her other life. It was a relief to stop cantering back and forth over the same terrain; she and Alec could not agree. He would groan, 'I've ruined my son,' infuriating Pamela, who saw such outpourings as self-pity dressed up as confession. 'There must be something we can *do*,' she would counter. They must find the key to their son, chivvy him back to the straight and narrow before he was tossed into the war.

The short January day gave way. The Hornet roared towards the capital, which had the sheen of Sodom and Gomorrah for trainee adulteress Pamela.

When Kos talked of his home, the wind snatched half the words away. Pamela listened hard, never asking him to repeat himself, careful not to dam his stream of consciousness.

'They have a word for it. *Intelligenzaktion*. They want to eradicate the thinkers who might lead Poland out of the darkness. They round people up like dogs. Late in thirty-nine, they took me.'

'You?' Pamela wondered if she heard right.

'Along with teachers, writers, priests. My uncle, an old man, he was a judge.' Kos shook his head. 'Now he is nothing at all.'

'They want to wipe out Poland,' said Pamela. 'Pretend it never existed.'

'The Nazis are a death machine,' said Kos. 'It eats humanity.'

Pamela drew her fur stole around her neck. She leaned against Kos. He said, 'There were mass executions. I saw one.'

Oh, my love. 'Where?'

'I will never say the name of that place.' Kos put his foot down. 'Nearly there,' he said.

Meanwhile, back in Ambridge, No. 9 Platoon sat in the village hall, cleaning their weapons.

The Webley was a pleasingly Wild West style of gun; Alec enjoyed its neat action, how it unfolded. Beside him, old Arthur Sweet cleaned something that wouldn't look out of place on the Bayeux Tapestry.

'That Beacham,' said Arthur. 'You know he's an ex-con?'

'What?' Alec never asked his men personal questions. 'You mean, a criminal?'

By the stove, Beacham pulled a long pin out of a rifle.

'Takes one to know one, sir. Yes.' Arthur nodded gravely. 'I've served at Her Majesty's pleasure.'

'Good gracious.' Another human opening up like an onion.

'Misspent youth.' Arthur's youth was far behind him now. 'I learned my lesson. Look at Beacham now, look!'

'What am I looking at?' Alec watched Beacham take up a bowl of 'stew'; with unidentified meat swimming in it, Alec could only think of the dish in inverted commas.

'The way he's eating. One arm around his bowl, shovelling it in. That's how we ate inside.'

'Flimsy evidence, Arthur, to hang a theory on.'

'Then look at his bearing, sir.' Arthur's skull was pale like an eggshell through the sparse white feathers of his hair; he was what Agnes would call a 'clean old man'. 'Very upright for a bloke what never served in the military. It's a feeling, really, and it's never let me down. Us old lags, we give each other the nod when we realize. Jail's not something you shout about, but Beacham, he didn't like it, sir, not one bit, when I gave him the nod.'

'If he's paid his dues we should respect that.' Alec didn't want to hear any of this. 'As we do with you, Arthur.'

'I paid me dues all right, for stealing that cheque book.' Arthur's eyes went dreamy. 'Then of course there was that washing line and the brassiere ...'

Alec rose suddenly, to fend off any more revelations about Arthur's adventures in lingerie. He had assumed, wrongly it turned out, that No. 9 Platoon was above gossip.

Over his stew, Mick Lister called to Alec. 'Sir, who'd you think will get Woodbine Cottage?'

'I have no idea.' Privately Alec still clung to the hope that Jane would leave the house to Blanche, as a well-brought-up Englishwoman should.

'Women.' Beacham banged down his bowl and wiped

his mouth on his sleeve. 'They're a mystery. Like cats. Never know what way they'll jump.'

'Jane was no cat,' said Alec. *More of a mouse*. But mice could be unpredictable too; with only a fortnight to go before the next instalment of the will, Alec dreaded what he might find in the third stiff envelope.

It was the job of a leader to join his men in danger, so Alec helped himself to stew. He chewed – and chewed – and meditated on his own position in life. Hands tied. No say in his own will; Gerald would certainly be the next caretaker of Lower Loxley. *Ye Gods*.

Alec had no hankering after a hero's death; he hadn't led a hero's life, after all. If he were to die, either choking on his stew or in some chaotic battle, he wouldn't leave much of a void. Gerald wouldn't mourn. And Pamela … Alec would do what was asked of him, even if all that was asked for now was to head up this Home Guard ragbag.

'Pint, Alec?' suggested Dan, as he screwed the lid back on his tin of polish.

'Why not? The lady wife's in London until tomorrow.'

'You lucky dog,' said Dan, who keened like a kitten if Doris spent a night away from Brookfield. 'Family business?'

'Yes, family business.' Alec was careful never to join dots that might make for a distressing picture, so he ignored the fact that he hadn't seen Kos all day. 'Hero!' he called, and the black Labrador was there.

*

The pillowslip needed darning. Head bent over her stitches, Nance added a row of forget-me-nots along the hem.

The clock ticked. Her husband read the paper. Nance was tired enough to retire, but she liked the parlour in the lamplight. She liked how comfortable Morgan looked, like a symbol of plenty. 'I reckon,' she said, and he lifted his head to listen, 'that any of the women at the mill could run the country and make a good fist of it.'

'Oh ho!' Morgan was amused. 'A parliament of petticoats.'

'If they can handle six children on no money surely they can handle the budget.'

'Indeed!' Morgan was avuncular.

Ted was not avuncular.

Nance stabbed her thumb with her needle. More and more she twinned the two men in her mind. Pros and cons. The forget-me-not bloomed red with her blood. 'I'm learning a lot at the mill,' she said. 'About life, how it's lived.'

'Don't we live life here, my dear?' Morgan added, with a small laugh. 'When you're here, that is.'

'I'm always here.'

'Not since you started your little job.'

Why must my job be little? Nance enjoyed the chink of her pay landing in the jar in the pantry. Building something. 'I do shorter hours than at the shop.'

'But the shop was different.' Morgan moved, settled himself. Perhaps he felt the change in the atmosphere. 'It didn't take you away so ... completely.'

'Take me away? Did you marry me to be here, like the

furniture? Someone to tend you in your dotage?' The words, born in a dark part of Nance, were out before she could censor them. They thudded into the bookshelves like a round of ammunition.

He said, 'I'm not so addled I need *tending*, Nance. What a way to address me.'

'Don't you ever think I need . . .' She threw down the pillowslip, once so promising and now stained with blood. *The only way there'll ever be blood on our bedlinen.*

'My dear!'

Nance recognized the tone. The one he used for difficult patients. He was *handling* her.

Ted never handled her.

'I apologize,' said Morgan, 'if I've upset you.'

'You didn't.' Nance's anger fell away. She was ungrateful, a brat, when she wanted to be a woman. Morgan's woman. 'It's me who should apologize.' She wanted to call him darling, or even beloved, but they were not intimate enough for endearments.

'I lost a patient today.'

'No! Who?' Nance kneeled in front of Morgan.

He told her. A little person of little importance, whose decline had been hard. 'I made him comfortable. That's the limit, often, of what I can do.'

'I'm sure it helped.' Nance was earnest, looking up into her husband's face.

'That's kind, my dear.'

It was the way he patted her hand – so courteous, so

neutered – that sent her out to the porch to hide her face in the cold. Just in time to see Alec and Dan stroll past in their Home Guard rig-out.

They tipped their caps and said 'Good evening!' and when they passed she leaned back against the house and undid the buttons of her blouse and let the air slap her skin.

Doris didn't have to wait up for Dan but she did so.

He'd have had an ale or two. As she knitted she imagined him scheming all the way home, rehearsing romantic sweet nothings only to abandon them all and chirrup, 'How about a spot of the other, Doris, my darling?'

No Rudy Valentino, her Dan. But would Rudy know when to wean a calf, or to spread muck from the cattle sheds on the fields so nothing was wasted? *He would not.*

That night Doris felt at ease, held in place by the life that teemed on the farm, even in midwinter. By the ham she had boiled. By the rag rug she had finished. By the cat and dog sharing an uneasy armistice by the stove.

The worries would descend again, but for now she floated above them. She liked to refer to the family's history when she grew anxious, mouthing a homily along the lines of, *We've been through worse.*

Lately, those comparisons had failed her. By an epic margin, the war was worse than anything Doris had faced before, even the first war. It was more global, more relentless. And slimy, like the moat of debt that circled Brookfield.

One more strange storm and perhaps the whole farm

would subside. Feather beds, sleeping children, her mother's teapot, all of it down into the chasm.

Doris had worked on the same row of Fair Isle for a week. Knitting. Unpicking. Knitting. Unpicking. She threw it aside. She would tidy instead, until Dan got home.

Putting everything in its place helped her hang onto that sense of rightness. Her best wooden spoon, the one that leapt into her hand when she made batter. The cat's bowl. The biscuit tin.

As she swept the already-clean floor, the missing doll at Furnivall Place popped into her head. It snagged in her thoughts, like a lost child. *Sukie*, that was its name.

She stacked Christine's homework on the table. *Naughty girl*, she thought, fondly, when she found *Encyclopaedia of Flowers* tucked into her mathematics book. *All that time I thought she was slogging away at her sums and the little minx was reading the book Wanda gave her at Christmas.*

Doris flicked through it, then closed it. Since Jane's will, plant names seemed sinister.

And besides, she'd heard Dan's whistle out in the yard.

Pamela stepped over a sandbag.

Her patent leather heels made a forgotten noise on the wet London pavement. They crushed no frost, and her padded shoulders brushed no catkins as she led Kos to her favourite luncheon spot.

She held onto him as they crossed Piccadilly, close together beneath her umbrella. There was no need to hide; nobody knew them. She had not visited her family because why would she? She had fled rather than left her father's many-roomed house in Chelsea.

The couple were relaxed in London, or as relaxed as Kos could ever be. He was passionate. He buttered his toast passionately, tied his shoelaces passionately.

The previous evening, in a divinely comfortable bed at the blacked-out Savoy, he had made love to Pamela passionately.

It was so bright a moment, as if somebody had thrown paint on her body. She would never forget it; it would never fade. Alec's lovemaking was her benchmark in such matters; it was rare, and *keen* rather than wanton.

Alec did not intoxicate her. Didn't fill her nostrils. She didn't want to touch Alec, and gloat over every inch of him. Naked, Kos was so beautifully made that he seemed clothed.

Pamela was jittery as they passed shop windows criss-crossed with blast tape. She was also, if she would only look a little closer at herself, happy. 'Here we are!' she said.

'This place is *green*,' puzzled Kos, taking in Fortnum and Mason. 'It looks like a jewel box.'

They hurried past a canopy to where a doorman held a gilded door open for them. They didn't notice the young woman sheltering from the rain, gazing at the Display-Only chocolates in the window as she ate a cheese roll.

Peggy caught sight of her bedraggled reflection and sighed. The little things mattered to her. That she smelled nice, and dressed well, and that her hair didn't look like a dead rat.

A tidal wave had pushed in the windows of her small ter-raced house when the news came about her father. Missing! *What a word.* Like he was a sock lost on laundry day. Not in his rightful place. Stuck somewhere. One thing was for sure: Dad was nowhere nice.

The dreary reflection in Fortnum's window was not the Peggy the world was allowed to know. In the eight minutes it would take to walk back to the dressmaker's studio she would rebuild the haughty, shimmering girl everyone expected, her joie de vivre filling out the drab utility shape of her dress.

A treat lay in her handbag. A letter from that Jack Archer. It wouldn't make scintillating reading, probably one long moan about food and the heat and his boots. But there'd be cartoons in the margins and his regard for her would float off the page. Why he took the time to write to a girl who gave him zero encouragement she couldn't imagine. He dropped hints – 'Would be nice to have a sweetheart to come home to!' – which she ignored. *I've got bigger fish to fry.* But even Mum, in her haze of anxiety, had noticed how Peggy ran to the doormat at the sound of a letter dropping onto it.

She put away the last bite of the roll in its crumpled bag. It'd do for later. Peggy was familiar with hunger.

Two floors above, Pamela ordered for herself and Kos. 'Split lobster roll for two.' They would peruse the patisserie trolley after that.

And after that? Back to the tent they had made of the bed in The Savoy for more adventures. She would fall off another cliff with him, the wind whistling through her hair.

The ring on her finger spoke to her, and she twisted it.

'You like it?' Kos was pleased with himself, dimples exploding.

'I adore it. But ...' Pamela saw he hated to hear 'but'; he was an all-in man. 'You told me once this ring keeps you safe. I'd rather have you in one piece than have this on my finger.'

'If I make sure you're always with me, then we'll both be safe.'

'You long to leave, though.' That hurt her, in a dull way.

'I *have* to leave. Honour demands it. Leaving what I love ... It's demanded of me, it doesn't mean I like it.'

Pamela twisted the eagle ring.

He loves me.

An inappropriate whiff of sulphur met the vicar as he left Arkwright Hall.

The fields were newly spread with dung. The wheel of the year – mucky at times – rotated calmly. 'Cliff!' He hailed the young man and offered one of his performatively sincere handshakes. 'So good to see you settling in here, getting over your, um ...' Henry tapped his own face.

The untouched side of Cliff's face went pink, deepening the contrast between that and the taut left-hand side. 'Thanks,' he said, limply. The vicar had never improved matters for a Horrobin; Cliff saw how he held his nose when dealing with Connie.

'We all have our cross to bear.' The vicar leaned back on his heels, ready to let forth. 'Was it not Jeremiah who said "Heal me, O Lord—" '

'Cliff!' Lorna yelled from inside the building. 'Quick! You're needed!'

'Sorry, Vicar.' Cliff shrugged.

'God bless, dear boy,' said Henry.

Lorna yanked Cliff into a storeroom. They waited for the vicar's footsteps to recede before erupting with laughter and tumbling out again.

'*What* a bore,' said Lorna. 'He's been talking to the seven-year-olds about Jesus, and he made him sound like a bank manager.'

'The main object of religion,' said Cliff, taking a pile of books from Lorna and following her upstairs, 'is not to get a man into heaven but to get heaven into the man.'

They smiled then, pleased, as they always were when they quoted Thomas Hardy to one another. Lorna topped him, as she so often did. 'That man's silence is wonderful to listen to.'

'Is that from *Under the Greenwood Tree*?' Cliff was smug when she nodded. He skipped down a step, and jumped back up on Lorna's other side.

'You don't have to do that – keep your good side to me.' Lorna's voice was tiny, dormouse-like. But clear as a bell. 'Both sides are good as far as I'm concerned.'

He ignored that. 'I went to Stinsford, once, to visit Hardy's grave.'

'I've always wanted to see it!'

'You should.' Cliff did not – or perhaps he was unable

274

to – translate the plea on Lorna's face because instead of saying *Let's go there together* he said, 'Only his ashes are buried at Stinsford. His heart's in Poets' Corner at Westminster Abbey.'

'No, Cliff, his heart's in his writing. You still …?'

'Yes.' Cliff was curt. He clearly regretted mentioning his scribbled poems.

'You going to the Valentine's Dance?'

He stopped dead, as if she had struck him.

'Sorry, I just …' Lorna wasn't sure what she was apologizing for. 'Me and Wanda are going, it'll be a giggle.'

'And the giggling will be at my expense.' Cliff stared at Lorna as if she had turned into someone else. 'I was never much of a one for dancing, and now the lasses will queue up to turn me down.'

'No need to snap at me,' said Lorna, in her mild way. She took the books from him and he jogged disconsolately down the stairs.

When he reached the bottom, Cliff called her name.

Lorna turned, a smile blossoming. 'Yes?'

'Is Wanda really going to the dance?'

'Yes.' The smile died a natural death.

No longer a solemn occasion, the will readings provided great entertainment for Ambridge. Jane herself had been erased by the hubbub. *Until we get to the last one*, thought Doris, taking her seat in the village hall. Something deep and animal within Doris, beneath the headscarf and the sensible hair, tingled and told her Woodbine wouldn't go to Blanche.

She hoped she was wrong.

Dressed to the nines – maybe even the tens – Blanche was in fur. She felt for Archie's fingers.

He squeezed her hand. Blanche wondered if this was why women took husbands, to have a warm body by their side, his sword hand free to see off infidels. Dictatorial Blanche readily gave in to Archie. When he'd said, 'No doll, not the blue worsted, today we're in *mink*,' she'd known he was right.

Eyes bored into her. Susan Grundy was studying Blanche as if she planned to describe her to the authorities; Magsy was more expert at concealing her interest, but still, Blanche felt the pressure of the village's scrutiny. She could wheel round and announce, 'Jane killed herself, you know!' *That* would provide the red meat they were after.

They would all blame me.

Jane would have found her way to death even if Blanche had never been born; Blanche was responsible for herself, warts and all, and Jane's death was Jane's fault. *Not mine.* Blanche squeezed Archie's hand again. *Definitely, absolutely not mine.*

Agnes fidgeted. 'Can we get cracking? Only I have my *new dining table* to polish.' She cast around to see who had heard; saw Connie's rolled eyes and was satisfied.

'No show without Punch,' said Dan. 'Walter hasn't turned up with the plant yet.' He nudged his wife. 'See her?' They both looked at Nanny. 'Her brother was in prison.'

'Beacham?' Doris was sharp. 'What for?' She recognized Dan's expression; he felt he'd gone too far, broken some chaps' charter. 'Well?'

'I don't know and it's not our business, love.' He, in turn, recognized his wife's expression: the ferret-down-a-hole look that meant she wouldn't give in until she got what she was after. Wondrous when she was on your side. Not so wondrous right now. 'We all deserve a second chance.'

'But I billeted a young girl with him!'

'Happen it's Beacham who should look out with *that* little madam.'

Boiling with curiosity, Doris knew she was condemned to wonder pointlessly about Beacham's crime; a Mrs Nobody from Nowhere couldn't discover whether it involved violence. *That's the big question.* Now, someone like Pamela Pargetter, two rows ahead, *she* would have resources, friends in high places.

And talking of Pamela, the woman was changed somehow. Laughing with that bobby dazzler of an airman, she seemed years younger. Possibly she had been prescribed a tonic by Morgan, who really should prescribe some for his wife, because things were going the other way for Nance.

From the stage, Alec too noticed the change in Pamela. He determined to have a word; people would talk. He leaned over the wax seal again, pretending to study it. What would he say? *Do stop being so happy, old girl?* He could infer she was making a fool of herself but that wouldn't be true.

The envelope brought to mind the one he'd posted on his

way to the village hall. A final cheque to the private investi-gator. His desperate attempt to claw back the sunshine of last summer was futile. *If people don't want to be found, one should let them be.* It had been ignoble to attach a silent proviso when he recommitted to his marriage. *Thank heavens Pamela knows nothing about the detective.*

For her part, Pamela was relieved she'd found a way to make Kos laugh. He had been in shock for days, unable to share what troubled him until finally he said, his lips against her hair, the words wrenched out of him in staccato bursts, 'They're really doing it. The Jews. They're sending the Jews to a labour camp. A place called Chelmno. The Nazis have no shame and no fear. They'll exterminate every last one.'

She had watched him seethe. Felt the crackle of his anger and impotence. She'd held him all night as pain beat time in his head. It had been like an exorcism, something infernal jumping inside him.

'Where's Walter?' asked Joe Grundy to the room at large.

'You needn't wait if you're busy, Joe,' said Blanche, grandly. 'I doubt *you've* inherited anything.'

At the back, Nance joined in with the laughter. Next to her, Connie smelled of dogs and sour milk. Nance almost lost her nerve, but if she could drive a forklift she could face Connie Horrobin. 'I wondered,' she said, opening a bag, 'if you could use this dress? It's too small for me.'

Unfolded, it was the colour of heather. 'You in the family way or what?' Connie sniggered, then put her hand over her mouth to cover the shameful lack of tooth. The dress was nicely finished, warm to handle.

'I heard about your troubles, Connie. I'd like to help.'

'It's all right for some.' Connie's favourite incantation. 'My Stan makes one wrong move and we're in hock for years, over some silly petrol. *You*, you marry the doc and you're in clover, no matter how many patients he buries.'

Nance hadn't expected thanks, but neither had she expected to be mown down.

Connie grabbed the dress and balled it up. 'Ta,' she said. Very, very quietly.

The crowd parted and in strode Walter, wooden crate in his arms.

'We can begin,' said Alec gratefully.

Had a pin dropped it would have sounded like a gong as Alec broke the wax seal.

After the B of the bleeding heart and the L of the lady orchid there were those who expected an A, tipping the scales towards Blabs.

And towards Stan, whose middle name – Blair – had never meant so much to him as it did today. And towards Morgan Blake Seed. Middle names were being dusted off in more than one family.

There was Jane's usual admonition to listen to nature, by now a mere aperitif to the main course. When Alec read out the words, 'My third bequest is to Bob Little, landlord of The Bull and long-standing neighbour,' there was a groundswell of surprise. *Bob! Bob? Bob. Bob!* The room filled up with the word, as if the villagers were songbirds stuck on the same note.

'He ain't here.' Connie was always pleased to deliver bad news.

'We'll press on,' said Alec. 'This is the first part of Bob's bequest.' He reached below the desk and held up a spade.

Nobody said a thing because nobody knew what to say.

Blanche laughed. She stopped when Archie bumped her shoulder with his. 'Shush, doll,' he said.

'An, um, unusual item, to be sure.' Alec floundered. He patted the table and Walter set down the box and unveiled a large, potted twig.

'Eh?' said someone.

'What the devil is that?' asked someone else.

'It's deciduous,' said Walter loftily, defensive about the juvenile plant. 'Not much to look at just now, but come June it'll be covered in great pink trumpets, all ablaze. It's an—'

'Azalea!' Agnes recognized the unpromising plant.

'A for azalea!' hollered Stan. 'B, L, A! Blair! It's gonna be me! I'm in the money!'

Blanche swayed but didn't swoon; she knew she was being watched. Relief made her light-headed; B, L, A spelled three-fifths of her childhood nickname. She was still in with a chance.

'May I interject?' Magsy stood up. 'That, Alec, is a *rhodo-dendron*. Which means the new letter is an R.'

'B, L, R?' Stan was on it like Wizbang on a dropped sausage. 'That don't spell nothing!'

'No, *no*,' insisted Frank. 'It's an azalea. It's an A.'

'Well said!' yelled Blanche.

'With respect,' said Mrs Endicott, popping up. 'That is a rhododendron.'

Agnes, disappointed that she could mangle neither an A nor an R into a clue that pointed to her good self, pulled herself up to her full four-foot-eleven and said, loudly, clearly, 'Blessed light reveals bountiful hope.' That got everyone's attention. 'If that's a rhododendron, Woodbine goes to the Pargetters.'

Public opinion leaned her way. Alec, who had suffered nightmares of neon alphabets for the past week, left the hall head down, like a murderer leaving the Old Bailey.

Blanche followed. 'It's B, then L, then *A*,' she said, to anybody who would listen. 'Blabs!'

The vicar was doubtful. 'Not if one uses the Latin name for azalea.'

'Oh, who cares about the Latin names for plants?' Blanche pushed Henry out of the way.

'Me,' said Walter quietly, from where he stood with the pot. 'Me and Miss Jane. *We* care.'

The Bull was empty, all the drinkers gone. Even Stan, who'd had to be winkled out of the snug like a tick in a dog's ear.

Bob sat at one of the rough little tables and eyeballed the azalea. Or was it a rhododendron?

It used to be a palace, The Bull. Humming like a top, it spun merrily while it served Ambridge and lined Bob's pockets.

Whitewashed walls. Lines of bottles. Those renowned begonias massed in their tubs outside. The scrape of a fiddle and Bob's mum giving them a song when the mood took her.

Tonight the fire was dead in the grate; Bob felt no need to sweep the ashes.

The whisky bottle gasped when he opened it; it was beyond the wallets of most of Bob's customers. He intended to get properly, steaming, wildly drunk. No wise publican finds respite in his wares, but where had wisdom got Bob?

He didn't bother with a glass. He took the bottle out into the yard, along with the shovel.

His legacy was no heirloom. It had flummoxed his customers.

But not Bob. He listened to it and understood.

'You saw, Jane,' he said. He looked up at Woodbine Cottage, and that lady's bedroom window winked at him through bare branches. 'You blinkin' well saw me.'

Alec dreamed.

Nazis paraded him past The Bull in his underpants. From the crowd, his brother Rupert watched, and held up a spade, ready to dig Alec's grave.

When Alec woke up, swaddled in his sheets, he reached out but there was nobody in his bed. There never was.

He listened out for snores from Pamela's room. Nothing. Either she had found a cure for the brass band noises she made at night, or she was in the folly.

FEBRUARY

If you squinted, the village hall could be in Paris. Or Rome. Or some other exotic city none of them had ever visited.

'A lot of pink.' Dan took in the crepe banners, and the ruched tablecloths over the inevitable trestle tables. 'A *lot*.'

'It's dreamy.' His daughter Christine was only allowed to stay for an hour, but what an hour that would be, in this room that vibrated with romance. The pink lampshades, the big pink heart on the back wall cut from a satin eiderdown, the *atmosphere*. 'Just right for St Valentine's Day.'

The lemonade was pink, too, and she took a glass from the hatch that separated the wonderland from the pedestrian kitchenette.

'Where's the band?' Agnes was in bombazine again, this time with a white Peter-Pan collar.

'They let us down.' Doris spoke fast, before Agnes could complain. 'Luckily Mrs Endicott has stepped in to delight us.'

'Not that old—' began Agnes as the lady herself flopped

onto the piano stool with a merry, 'Evening all!' She fanned out her sheet music. 'All the old favourites.'

'Some new ones, too?' asked Doris, hopefully; the committee's reputation hung on these events. Her corset was at her, beneath the dress she had ironed in her wellies an hour ago. She looked around for Dan; her philosophical husband, who whistled his way through the hard times, had stopped pooh-pooh-ing her money fears.

They counterbalanced each other. When one drooped, the other stood tall. Now they drooped together; did that mean Doris was right to fret, that they really were drawing nearer to a precipice?

In the kitchenette, Nance smeared fishpaste on thirty slices of wafer-thin bread. 'Will this be enough?'

'Heavens, no,' said Pamela, fresh from crushing a mutiny among land girls drafted in to nail bunting to the beams. Marshalling, organizing, she buzzed, sparks flying from her long white fingers. Through the hatch she called, 'Alec! Fetch the *men!*' ·

The men were fetched. Lambs to the slaughter in RAF blue. Alec had explained to the Lower Loxley contingent that when his wife invited one to a dance, one attended said dance, even if one would rather eat one's own feet.

The room began to fill, revellers self-conscious in their finery.

'Are we ready?' simpered Mrs Endicott from her perch.

Up a ladder, titivating a display of paper roses – *If you want something done properly, do it yourself* – Pamela called, 'Do begin!' Clambering down, Pamela felt two hands around her waist lift her from the ladder.

'People will see,' she whispered.

'Let them,' said Kos, setting her on the parquet as Mrs Endicott put her hands to the keys and the dance lurched into life.

'Who'd have thought it?' Archie twirled Blanche, who screeched with pleasure. 'The old dame's a regular Glenn Miller.'

Mrs Endicott gave 'Indian Summer' her all, and couples took to the floor, gliding in formation, just missing each other, turning, laughing. The dance was an old friend come to jolly them out of introspection. The dance was anti-war, anti-Hitler, and pro-getting-your-mitts-on-the-opposite-sex. 'Frenesi' followed, and then a lady from over Bramble Park way leaned on the piano and joined in with 'My Blue Heaven'.

'We danced to this at our wedding,' said Susan to Joe.

'That we did,' he said.

They were light on their feet, in accord, the Grundys. Poor they might have been but, while the music played, they were creatures of glamour. Their marriage was turning out to be tempestuous; some said they were growing up together. A lampshade had been hurled before they left the farmhouse, but there had been kissing and cooing and making up. Susan, greedy, bouncing Susan, was glad her man was exempted from the call-up; his place, she felt, was with her.

Applause shook the night outside, where men already smoked, and some kissing had already gone on in the shadows.

Lorna and Wanda chatted to a man who looked like a kid yet installed radar in mosquitoes. Overhearing, Agnes goggled: 'How'd they make the radar small enough?' and the man patiently explained that the 'Mosquitoes' he worked on were planes.

Then he asked Wanda to dance, and made a wall-flower of Lorna.

'Ooh, "Cheek to Cheek"! Now, this is an old one,' said Dan, quick-stepping with Doris.

'Don't talk about your wife like that!' called Archie.

Even the vicar was dancing. He held Frances carefully, as if she might bite.

Billy, full of fishpaste, could barely contain his disgust at the utter soppiness of it all. He told John, 'I'm never having a girlfriend.'

'Me neither,' said John, who was more or less certain he would marry Christine Archer. Or Wanda. Or both of them. Or Lorna.

'Why does Peggy have to ruin everything?' Billy watched his sister swing by in Terence's arms. 'Always bloomin' turning up.'

John felt safer with Peggy in the village, even though it meant they couldn't visit Luca until she returned to their mum and the bombs. They had a necktie for him, and a handful of coppers.

Peggy threw them a look over Terence's shoulder. Nothing specific, just an all-purpose look that might halt some abomination in its tracks. She would have a word with Connie about schooling; she knew Connie sent them only intermittently to Arkwright Hall. *I'll insist; they're turning into barbarians.* This was her second dance with Terence. *He better not be getting any ideas.* Men tended to get ideas about Peggy. The only idea she had was about that big slab of Polish workmanship who wasn't dancing with anybody.

'Me next!' leered Stan, through the hatch.

'Friend of yours?' asked Terence.

'He's nobody's friend,' said Peggy.

Mrs Endicott soldiered on at the piano, and Agnes considered it her moral obligation to dance with every man in uniform. Nance collected plates and ladled out punch, loving the feel of her dress floating about her legs. Trousers were all very well, but she felt womanly tonight.

She flew solo: Morgan had been called away to a baby impolite enough to arrive two weeks early. A voice in her ear said, 'May I have this dance?'

Turning, playful, Nance took a step backwards when she recognized Ted. Groomed and handsome, a different Ted. 'How'd you ... you don't live here.'

'That joker made me come.' Ted jerked a thumb at a man leaning against the wall. He had been to The Bull by the look of him. 'Me brother-in-law.' Ted pursed his lips. Wondering, clearly, how this would go down with Nance. 'Heard me talk about me new pal at work, and made me come to Ambridge to take a look at your house and that.'

It was meant to be flattering. 'But, Ted ...'

'I saw your hubby earlier.'

CATHERINE MILLER

The parquet bounced beneath their feet; there were many hobnail boots on the dancefloor.

'Bit old, isn't he?' Ted was pitying, as if Nance had bought shoddy goods at a drapers.

There was offence taken. There was shame felt. *Morgan looks decrepit to a strapping specimen like Ted.* Nance said, 'Being older isn't a failing. You're born when you're born and that's that.'

'Didn't mean nothing by it.'

'Don't treat my husband like a joke, Ted Wrigley.'

'Ooh!' Ted stepped back, hands up in surrender. Keeping it light even though she had unleashed his surname and all men knew what that meant. 'No, c'mere, hold on.'

Determined, Nance pushed through the swing door to the kitchenette where he couldn't follow.

Watching through the hatch as Nance banged down a tray, Ted heard his brother-in-law snigger. 'Shut *up*,' said Ted. His eyes, long-lashed, looked bruised and ready to cry.

Dan sidled up to Beacham. 'You been strong-armed here, and all?'

Arms folded, Beacham kept his gaze on Nanny and Irene, both as staid and demure as postulant nuns. 'I'm keeping an eye.'

'On them two hellraisers?' Dan laughed, then stopped, because Beacham didn't find it funny.

'You don't know what she's capable of,' he said.

A sturdy goddess, Wanda was in gold pleats, a comb holding up a waterfall of curls. Her nails were painted but her hands were covered in scratches. 'Boss, he's coming!' she

288

squealed at Doris. 'Making a special trip from London just for me.' Then she was off, a bright flash in the one-two-three, one-two-three sea of dancers.

Doris stood on her toes, searching for and finding Pamela, who was jiving, after a fashion, with Walter, whose bow tie was red to match his nose. Catching Pamela's eye, Doris nodded to a corner wreathed in smoke, and Pamela nodded back, and stepped away from a deflated Walter.

The talk in the men's corner was of the inevitable, imminent Allied surrender to Japan. 'A real blow,' said Kos. When he spoke, the men listened; he never talked for the sake of it.

His voice was nails down a blackboard to Alec, the banging of a rusty can. *I hate him.* He could do nothing about this base impulse. Alec rarely encountered men who incited his envy; Kos had him in kinks with the green stuff.

Talk turned to the labour camps in Singapore. 'There is much information that has not reached the newspapers,' said Kos.

Dan, Alec, Dodgy – all had heard whispers of Tommies, ribs like greyhounds', worked to death.

'A stain on history,' said Dodgy, unusually grave.

'The worst camps,' said Kos, 'are on *my* soil.'

'What d'you make of it?' Terence turned to Alec.

The deference the men gave Alec was for borrowed clothes. He was only the second son; the real lord of the manor was Rupert; his wife's real husband, it would seem, was Kos. *I own nothing. Nothing at all.* He excused himself, a little curtly, just before Pamela landed among them.

289

'Were you invited in order to sit in the corner gossiping like old women?' she asked. 'Or were you invited to dance with the ladies of Ambridge?'

'Oh,' said Dodgy, jumping up.

'Um,' said Terence.

'Yes, *oh, um*,' said Pamela. 'Off you go. Compliment their frocks. Refresh their drinks. Think you can manage that?' She knew Kos was desperately trying not to grin.

The men could, they assured her, manage that.

Lorna swayed on the edge of the action, waving at Wanda and resigned to Cliff's absence.

Hands closed over her eyes. 'Guess who?'

Her breath fled. 'Cliff!' She turned. 'You said that you weren't coming!'

He handed her a pink lemonade. 'Seemed a shame to miss all this.'

Lorna's face tingled where his fingers had touched it.

'Plus,' said Cliff, 'have to keep an eye on my dad.'

'Yeah.' Lorna hoped the word conveyed how well she understood. Her own home life was similar to Cliff's, albeit with better furniture. Her mother had the money for a dentist when Lorna's father knocked out a tooth. 'You dancing?' The pink lights reflected in her glasses.

'Me? Nah. I'm like you, not much of a one for dancing.'

'Well, I . . .' Lorna would dance if she was asked. 'Glad you came, anyway.'

'Couldn't let Wanda down. She makes everything fun, doesn't she?'

Lorna bit down on her straw.

A flourish at the piano and Mrs Endicott sat back, exhausted. The place erupted like the Albert Hall.

Beneath the cheers and whistles, Lorna said, 'I don't know why I bother with you, Cliff Horrobin,' but he didn't hear.

An unlikely hero emerged. Propelled to the piano by Agnes, Denholm was a serviceable stand-in as Mrs Endicott declared she simply must rest; a second cousin had dropped down dead after excessive exposure to the keys.

Cliff found Wanda. 'So, Mr Bigshot turn up?'

'You know that's not his name.'

'Mr Bigtime's not his name, either.'

'True.' Wanda's sunniness was ironclad.

Dipping in and out of the hall like a fox, Archie skirted the RAF corner – the men had regrouped; they kept a keen look-out for Pamela – and swept Blanche into the dance.

Dodgy lit a cigar and asked Terence, 'What's eating you, old man?'

'That fellow.' Terence was tracking Archie. 'He's a damn fairy. Written all over him.'

'Seems like a good egg, though.'

Archie was cheek to cheek with Blanche. There were tuts. Doris said, loudly enough for the judgemental Greek chorus to hear, 'We must take our pleasures where we can during war.'

Blanche laughed like a child, like the Blabs she once was. She knocked Agnes's port and lemonade out of her hand as she staggered to her chair. 'Sorry, Alec,' she said, when she found him there, waiting. 'My dance card is full.'

Alec was mortified at broaching a delicate subject. 'It's my duty to give you an inventory of the contents of Woodbine Cottage. I'm afraid you have to go through it for me, and clarify that the list is correct.'

'My one night off from mourning and you burden me with this?'

Having seen little of this mourning, Alec was regretful but firm.

When a woman behind them said loudly, 'Hope she gets nothing, gave her poor sister a terrible life, she did,' Blanche looked for Archie, her protector, her bright comet, her partner in crime. Thoughts of the will never left her; above the dirge Denholm made of 'Moonlight Serenade', she heard the pounding refrain of BLR, BLR, BLR.

Peggy was a public service; she danced with everyone. She kicked up her heels when Mrs Endicott returned to the front line. She shook her hips and wriggled her shoulders and felt her real age once more for the time it took to dance to 'Happy Days are Here Again'.

Her partner? Joe Grundy would remember those three minutes for the rest of his life.

Turning Mrs Endicott's sheet music, Lorna was an island, entirely of herself. She watched Cliff, as he kept his 'good' side to the hall, sipped his punch, ever close to Wanda yet never touching her. Lorna blamed Emily Brontë for her hopeless devotion to Cliff, even as she quoted *Wuthering Heights* to herself.

Haunt me, drive me mad, but don't leave me.

By the door, Nance checked the watch Morgan gave her for Christmas. Five hours since he left home to take part in something miraculous: while she lindy-hopped with Archie, he was welcoming a new life.

Locked into virginity, Nance couldn't know if she would ever be tested in that way, swim in the pain she felt was her due.

In from the cold, Ted dashed a cigarette away. 'Friends?' He looked about ten years old when he said that, despite the ale on his breath.

'Friends.' It was flattering, in its way, that Ted should undertake a fact-finding mission about her. *But I mustn't encourage him.* She shook her head when he pestered her to dance.

He was being frank. Saying it without saying it. *Ted's interested in me.* Something woke inside Nance. 'I'm a married woman,' she blurted out, in the middle of a blameless tale of Ted's about his brother-in-law being 'a bleedin' menace to society'.

Ted stared. Wellness personified, his eyes were clear, and surprisingly beautiful, as if topped up with light for this special night. 'Don't you think I know that?' He sounded desperate even as he observed the niceties; no onlooker would know their conversation was red-hot. 'But where is he, then, this husband of yours?'

'Working. He works hard.'

'We all do.' Ted looked away. The strand connecting them lay slack.

Nance feasted on his profile.

'You teasing me, Nance?'

'I'd never do that.'

He left her, heavy-shouldered, as if furious with the air around him. 'I'm off. Nothing for me here, is there?'

He gave Lorna a surly 'Sorry' as he bumped into her. She took Nance's glass, said, 'You all right?' Maybe it was the pink lighting but the doctor's wife looked tearful.

'Let me help,' said Nance, and they went about together, gathering up crockery. The dance was scheduled to end in half an hour. Mrs Endicott had given her all.

'Make yourself useful.' Lorna came across Cliff. 'Round up the ashtrays.'

'You reckon she's keen on him? This Mr Bighead?'

The big cheese had turned up, to be welcomed like a returning hero.

'How'd I know?'

'You're her mate. She can't, like, *love* him, can she?'

'I said I don't know!'

Wounded briefly – *Lorna's always so sweet!* – Cliff saw a face through the bright rectangle of the hatch. Wanda was animated, talking to someone out of view in the kitchenette.

He hovered. He strained to listen. Because over the chords of 'Casa Loma Stomp' he had heard the word 'love'.

'When did you know you were in love, Boss?'

Doris laughed. 'Never thought about it. Dan was Dan and I was me, and that was that.'

'But romance, Boss? Passion?'

'None of your business, young lady.' What went on

between Doris and Dan in their big brass bed was private. And precious. 'This Mr Bigtime, he's a good bit older than you.'

'Doesn't matter.'

'Why not step out with a younger chap?'

'Like who?' Wanda turned the gold bracelet on her wrist.

Doris craned her neck and saw Archie slip out of the main door. 'That Archie.' Doris didn't quite believe in homosexuality. 'Or Cliff. He's one of nature's gentlemen, and he's making his own way in the world.' Doris trusted the damaged; they knew about pain; they were not theorists. 'You could do a lot worse than Cliff.'

Cliff almost fled, but a small, intrepid hope pinned him to the spot.

'Cliff?' Wanda seemed to be considering him, and his heart bucked beneath his best shirt. 'How could I love someone like Cliff, when, you know …'

'I do know, love.'

Cliff imagined the casual mime of his stigmata. He barged past dancers and carried his puckered face – and, yes, his anger – out into the night.

Beyond the hatch, Doris said, 'Yes, Cliff *is* a bit serious for you. All that reading!'

'Cliff makes me feel stupid, Boss. He's a catch, God, such a kind boy, so easy-going, but he's deep and I prefer my men shallow.' Through the hatch Wanda caught sight of Mr Bigtime. 'Uh oh,' she said to Doris. 'Trust him to dance with the prettiest girl here the minute my back's turned!'

Doris didn't find it funny; she liked her men gallant. 'Go on,' she said, taking a dirty cup out of Wanda's hand. 'Go and stake your claim.'

As Wanda passed him, Beacham slammed down his glass and shoved his way through the crowd. Nanny looked after him, her face a curious mixture of fear and relief.

Only Agnes had witnessed their low-toned tiff, the sort of hissing words unhappy families exchange in public. Agnes was wondering what had aggravated Beacham when someone pushed her out of the way.

The culprit was Stan. 'Oi!' Agnes pushed him back as he made for the door. He wiped his mouth as if about to fall on prey. Full of grievance, Stan always fermented and fizzed after a night on the beer. Agnes considered following – boxing was a grand spectator sport – but it was the last dance, and she grabbed Alec, spinning him like an aristocratic scarecrow.

Mr Bigtime's voice in Peggy's ear was fluid, persuasive, like a radio announcer. She found herself telling him of her ambition to join the ATS the moment she was old enough; he was a superior sort of chap, and when he said, 'Bravo! You're perfect for the Auxiliary Territorial Service,' she felt a surge of patriotic pride.

'May I cut in,' said that upper-crust girl from Brookfield. Wanda took hold of Peggy's dance partner with a firmness that brooked no argument.

Bravo, echoed Peggy, who got the message. She slipped out of hold, and a whoop from outside turned her head like a gundog: her brother's whoop. She would rout Billy and take him home.

Outside, Peggy felt her way through the blackout. She heard some scuffling, much smooching. *Best not investigate the shadows too hard.* 'Billy?' she called. 'John?' but came across two much older boys.

Kos and Alec turned flushed faces towards her, chests puffed out like pigeons.

'Don't mind me!' said Peggy, hurrying on.

When she had gone, Kos said, 'You have no right to ask that of me.'

'No right? Pamela's my *wife*, man.'

'That's just a title. Do you appreciate her?' Kos paused. 'Are you faithful?'

So she told him. The sharing of secrets was worse than the lovemaking he couldn't help imagining. 'That's somewhat vile of you, Kos, bringing that up. Especially as you're an adulterer yourself.'

'I am a man in love. Unlike you, I am not afraid to say so.'

What else has Pamela said? Just because Alec wasn't some troubadour, scattering rose petals and whatnot. 'I'll ask you again. Do the decent thing and leave this place.'

'The decent thing is whatever binds me to Pamela. It would not be decent to desert her. I have nothing left but Pamela. You have your house and your land and your position, and they mean more to you than your wife.'

'I should strike you for that.'

'Go ahead.'

The swine's grinning at me! An Englishman would know the script and this scene would be done and dusted by now.

'Pamela,' said Kos, 'is my reason.'

'What does that mean?' Alec was infuriated with this poetic brick wall of a chap.

Kos shrugged. 'She's my reason for this. Everything. Living.'

'Do write that on scented notepaper, but here, man to man, I'm telling you that Pamela's mine and this has to stop.'

'She's no bone for dogs to snarl over. Decent thing? The decent thing is to love your wife so no other man could possibly come between you. I've lived a decent life and I've lost everything. Yours is not the only ancient name, Pargetter. I pledge my life to destroying the Nazi threat, and you? I won't be told what to do by, what's that English phrase? A stuffed shirt?' When he turned away the dismissiveness of the move struck Alec like a fist. 'May the best man win, Alec.'

Peggy was back. Her face was white. She took Alec by the lapels. 'He's hurt! Help him!'

She led them to Archie, laid out like a fish on a slab, head angled awkwardly against a drainpipe. In the dark, the blood on his face looked like paint.

SPRING

1942

So each had a private little sun for her soul
to bask in.

THOMAS HARDY
Tess of the D'Urbervilles

MARCH

Brookfield was as busy as a hive. Calves were arriving, grunted out onto straw. One turned up dead, and Wanda had cried over it. Doris gave the girl a hanky and set off to Woodbine Cottage.

'How's the patient?' she asked Blanche when the front door opened.

'I'm fine. Oh, you mean Archie?' Long accustomed to being nursed, Blanche was a poor caregiver. 'Take him up this cup of tea. Save me a trip.'

Doris sat gingerly on Archie's bed. Or Jane's bed. She had never before set foot in Jane's bedroom; strange that such an intensely private woman should be on everyone's lips as they feverishly decoded her will.

The vicar's wallet means the vicar'll get all the dosh!

Pamela's hoop means we're going round in circles!

Bob's spade means we must keep digging for meaning!

Archie sat up in his striped pyjamas and balanced the cup and saucer on a pile of magazines.

'You're looking better,' said Doris. His nose had a new kink: went east where it used to go west. The bruising around his eyes had faded to yellow, like the brush of pollen from a lily. 'Blanche looking after you?'

'She does her best.' Blanche couldn't boil a potato or make a bed, but she sat with him and smoked and told him tales of Ambridge as if it was a metropolis full of intrigue and lust, so on balance she was the kind of nurse Archie preferred.

'Dan said to tell you that he and Alec are on it, they'll find whoever did this to you.'

'That's nice,' said Archie.

They both knew there was no thirst for justice. An unvoiced, implied suggestion hung in the mote-filled air. 'Archie *is* outrageous,' someone would venture, then someone else would agree he could be 'rather provocative'. Perhaps, went the train of thought, he approached the wrong man and rubbed him up the wrong way.

Perhaps, he 'asked for it'.

Doris saw the beating of a young man as nothing more and nothing less than a crime. She wasn't the only visitor to make a regular pilgrimage up Woodbine's staircase. Mrs Endicott brought fresh bread and many, many tips for restoring his health; staying out of draughts seemed crucial. Nance had just left, and Agnes changed the sheets when the tea spillages and cigarette ash got too much for her to tolerate.

The bar of chocolate Frank had given Doris to pass on was disrobed and shared over the coverlet.

So there was sympathy, but not the outcry Doris would expect if, say, her Jack had been jumped.

'It'd be a lot easier to find the lowlife if your memory came back.' Doris looked sideways at Archie. 'Nothing?'

'It's all a blank.'

'Some say Stan Horrobin's a likely suspect.'

'Like I say . . .' Archie spread his hands, with the kind of frank gaze that always indicated a lie.

Blanche joined them. 'Chocolate! You'll spoil him, Doris.'

Archie stuck out his tongue at his employer. The anarchy at Woodbine amused Doris, but she was glad to leave it.

As Blanche directed Doris to the coat she had thrown on a sofa, she appropriated Connie's line. 'It's all right for you, Doris.'

'Is it?' Doris had been up all night holding a lantern over their best cow, the one who'd given them a dead calf.

'Family around you, secure home.' Blanche looked at the ceiling, melodramatic.

My secure home almost fell down a pit. Her family was missing its crown jewel; Doris didn't know where Jack was. *If* Jack was. 'Count your blessings, Blanche.' She smelled scent on the silk of Blanche's dress, and the kid shoes were free of mud. The ring on Blanche's finger would build a new cowshed *and* carpet Brookfield's bedrooms. Yet, in the face of losing her home Blanche remained inert and sybaritic.

'Toodle-oo,' called Blanche before slamming the front door behind Doris.

* * *

The year was a hill: Ambridge ran down it like a child.

The warmth, slow to appear, gathered pace. There was a shift, a change abroad. A chiffchaff darted past Lorna as she crossed the lawn behind Arkwright Hall. The bird had her unremarkable colouring, and her quickness of mind.

Unlike Lorna, it went after what it wanted, plucking newly hatched insects out of the air.

Snatch. Snatch. Snatch.

Since the night of the dance, Cliff had been a dark cloud, hovering damply over the hall, ready to rain on one and all. Was he ashamed? Was he angry? Was it common or garden self-pity?

He gave Lorna no confidence to say what was on her mind. But she determined to say it; *It's true, after all!* She turned on her heel; she must find him; this courage wouldn't last long.

Snatch. Snatch. Snatch. The chiffchaff disappeared.

Nance was glad that men didn't notice the little things the way women did.

Dolly'd be onto me in a flash. The men simply told her, 'He's over at the pump, washing up,' when she said she had a message from the office for Ted Wrigley.

His boiler suit peeled halfway down, his chest bare, Ted had stuck his head under the pump.

'Hello, stranger,' said Nance.

He jerked up, showering her with water. Her laughter and her 'Mind out!' got him through his open-mouthed surprise.

'How do.' Ted grabbed a towel, a stiff one the men all shared, one Nance wouldn't touch with a bargepole.

'You changed shifts,' she said.

'I do nights now.' Ted raised an eyebrow. *And?* it asked.

'So, well, I miss your sister's baking.'

Ted laughed. He was so easy. No sulking. No mystery. 'Walk me out?' He pulled his boiler suit up and eased his arms into the sleeves of a wool jacket. It had been smart once, now it was just a work jacket. It smelled dense but good, like a tree might smell if it worked for a living.

Nance saw him to the main gate. She turned and they were a hair's breadth too close. His hand brushed hers.

Every hair on Nance's body stood to attention. She was a bell that had been rung. She hurried away without a farewell, not to examine her reaction but to ignore it.

'They said I'd find you here.' Lorna had climbed to a sloping attic classroom.

'They were right.' The cloud was lifting, but Cliff was not his usual self. He was aslant, like the eaves of the room. Off-kilter. He met her eyes in the mirror over the small, servants' grate; the house bore many relics of its pre-war civilian life. Marble fireplaces. Framed hunting scenes.

'Admiring yourself?' she asked.

'Hardly.' Cliff looked down at the books lined up on the mantelpiece.

'You should.' Lorna was a chiffchaff. 'You are beautiful.' She knew this in the same way she knew that she was not beautiful. 'But you don't seem to know it, so I thought you needed telling.'

He had a book in his hands. *Tess of the D'Urbervilles*. The lettering made no sense; he suddenly couldn't read. *'What?'* he said.

'You can tell everything about people from their eyes. And yours is lovely. I . . .' The chiffchaff faltered. 'I love to look at it.'

She left the room. Like a page turning, she had been there and then she was not.

Cliff threw *Tess* – his beloved *Tess!* – across the room. Walked over it splayed on the floorboards, turned the collar of his jacket up as far as it would reach and raced downstairs.

Battle lines were drawn.

Connie on one side of the kitchen, Stan on the other. Maisie and Bert under the table. Vic out killing something. Cliff face down on his bed.

The cuckoos in the nest, the Perkins boys, crouched outside, beneath an open window.

Connie both cowered and attacked, forward and back. 'Couldn't help yourself, could ya, Stan?' She dodged a swiped fist. 'Making a show of us at the dance. They all know it was you what done Archie!'

A crash. A curse.

'Let's get away,' whispered John. There was a green-grey track from his nose to his mouth that Peggy would have wiped away – hard – with a wetted handkerchief.

'We could go to Luca.' Generally the word was the deed with the older brother, but Billy didn't move.

'He'll be worried about us. He loves us like we're his,' said John.

'Yeah, he loves us,' said Billy, 'like Dad loves us.' He had joined John at the church of Luca; with so little to believe in, the Italian hulk of a chap made a handy depository for hopes and fears.

They still didn't move.

'He expects us to bring a bike,' said John, his voice tattered. 'But where we gonna get a bike, Billy?'

Luca's expectations, so innocent and wholesome, weighed on them.

'Clothes are easier.' Billy eyed Stan's waistcoat flapping on the line.

It was Stan's only fancy piece of clothing; he would hook his fingers in the waistcoat's pockets as if making a speech. They could whip it down in a jiffy and spirit it away to Quartershot.

There would be consequences. Not for them. For Connie. They knew they couldn't do that to her. They might as well punch her themselves.

There was nice gear in Cliff's room. An Aran jumper and a decent coat, folded up all dainty like.

But they couldn't steal from Cliff. He was quiet, like a still afternoon in the constant typhoons of Broom Corner.

The boys were not cut out to be felons.

'Luca will understand,' said Billy.

'He won't,' said John, and keenly felt his own inadequacy.

* * *

Doing her rounds on sore feet, Doris was as reliable as one of Mussolini's trains.

Like those trains, she was also in need of a service, and would benefit from being kept quietly in a shed for a while.

She was not expected at Furnivall Manor. The peacock on the lawn, a rococo detail on the damp March day, didn't deign to greet her. Doris was hoping to catch the ladies of the house alone while Beacham was off playing soldiers with Dan and the rest of them. Words might flow more freely.

She liked nothing about the house. Not the capricious owners nor the tense spider's web of relations below stairs. She suspected a pincer movement, an alliance of bullies with Nanny playing Kiev to the other pair's Axis forces.

Children needed to know what was expected of them, and who was in charge. Lard all that with love – the unconditional kind Doris mined effortlessly in her own heart – and you'd be fine. Matters had got out of hand at Furnivall Manor: Irene's belligerence might provoke Beacham, and neither female was safe around him.

'Oh.' Nanny was taken aback at the sight of Doris, but too polite to protest when Doris passed her and headed for the stairs.

'Part of the job, these visits,' said Doris. 'Up here, yes?'

'Irene's napping, though! She hates if I—'

'Irene hates a great many things, it seems. Let's be firm, Nanny, eh?' Doris's hand was on the brass knob of the grand door to Irene's room. 'This is locked.' She frowned at Nanny.

'She does that,' sighed Nanny, and took out a clutch of keys.

'Don't tell me you allow the girl a key?' Doris imagined

308

her Christine having such leeway; *I'd never get her to Sunday school.*

'She has her little ways. I don't like to go against her.' Nanny avoided Doris's eye and fiddled with the keys.

Irene lay on the floor, beside a fussily made bed piled high with embroidered bedspreads and cloud-like pillows.

'What're you doing down there?' asked Doris.

'She prefers it. Don't you, dear?' Nanny stood near the bed, but not too near.

'It's not good for her to lie on floorboards.' Doris wasn't entirely clear why this was so, but she was nonetheless certain about it. 'Don't you like your bed, Irene?'

'It's not *my* bed,' said Irene. She was monotone, unvarnished. 'My bed's at home.'

'And you'll sleep in it again, but for now you must do as Nanny tells you.'

'Her?'

Nanny's smile was so craven it was grotesque.

Over some seed cake, Nanny laid out her manifesto. 'The bairn's been starved, Doris, *starved* of love. She doesn't know how to accept it. It takes patience but I'm curing her.'

'Irene's not sick. Her family probably have their own way of doing things.'

'Please don't send her back.' Nanny put down her cake.

'She'll have to go home eventually. Some children are already heading back to London. If the family request it we have no choice.'

'Believe me,' said Nanny. 'Her family won't request it.'

'Just remember that in the end children belong with their parents.'

Nanny smoothed Doris's coat before handing it to her. 'Even if the parents are bad people?' she said, and buttoned Doris into her coat as if she was a toddler.

Morgan tried; Doris did her best; now it was Lorna's turn to put her shoulder to the wheel.

All three of them communed gravely about Cliff's absence from Arkwright Hall. They agreed it was a crisis of confidence, a stumble in his struggle to live with his damaged face.

Only Lorna knew she had chased him out of the school with her eulogy to that very face. The face she missed. The face that held worlds for her. The one she could never hope to touch because Cliff's love had landed elsewhere, and really, what attractions could a Lorna boast beside a Wanda? A chiffchaff was nothing beside a bird of paradise.

There had been no plan when she spoke up. She'd been taken in by Brontë and Hardy and the other poets who had long misled her about love. Lorna should have paid closer attention to the tragedy that peppered their tales.

The turn-off for Broom Corner was pretty, with clumps of wood anemones turning their faces to her. The house changed the mood, sunk in its hollow, a dead car rusting out front.

Please don"t let Stan be at home. His fingerprints were all over poor Archie. When challenged Stan simply smirked that

Archie 'had it coming'. Nothing could be proved, however, and Stan remained cockily at large.

Recognizing Lorna, Stacey's welcome was fulsome. Her barking brought out Connie. 'Come to persuade him back, have you? Good luck with that.' She sat Lorna down and told her it was always going to end up this way. 'I told him, I did, I says don't set yourself up for them to throw stones at. Bad enough being a Horrobin without having a busted face.'

'I thought if Cliff knew how much we need him he might—'

'And me? Don't I need him?' said Connie, as Cliff bowled into the kitchen, Maisie on his back and Bert beating a tune on an old feed tin.

He saw Lorna and his face closed. All movement, swift and strict, he took her out to the front of the house. He wheeled on her when they reached the gate. 'What'd you come here for?'

Lorna began to burp out her reasons.

He didn't listen. He said, 'Nobody comes here, this is private.'

'How else can I let you know the children miss you? You're part of their day and you just dropped out of view. There's enough of that in a war without you doing it as well.' *You dropped out of my view, too.* Lorna knew Cliff wouldn't mention her outburst about his beauty; unsure whether to be relieved or insulted, she decided to be neither. *Shush, Emily Brontë; I'm not listening anymore.*

'Arkwright Hall was a mistake. I don't fit in.'

'If I can be honest, Cliff, you don't really fit in *here*.'

He chewed on that for a moment. 'I know,' he said at last,

311

miserable, a square peg in a grotty round hole. His real eye, the window to Cliff's soul, was as glassy as the other one. He was ashamed of his home and he loved his home; these truths ran on parallel tracks. 'I can't escape.' There was quicksand around the derelict car.

'Cliff, you're shirking. Other teachers have to fill in for you. The children are falling behind with their reading. There isn't time for Hardy-style introspection, so I'll see you tomorrow, nine sharp, yes?'

After Lorna left, with Cliff's reluctant 'Okay' safe in her handbag, Connie said, as she stretched three rashers of bacon to feed her horde, 'Nice girl.'

'Too nice for me.' Cliff turned his mother, put his hands on her shoulders. She was so small, like a brittle skeleton he might find under a nest. 'If I earn, if I save, would you let me set you up somewhere without *him*?'

Connie couldn't even laugh at such madness. 'You and your ideas,' she said.

'Not going to church?' Archie was shocked. 'Everyone'll notice, Blanche.'

'Couldn't give two hoots.'

Archie gave two hoots. Literally. 'Too-whit, too-whoo!' He was better, all healed. On the outside, at least. Fit for purpose, with a carnation in his buttonhole. 'You're on the fast track to hell, doll.'

'You're not going to church either.'

'But I'm an incomer and a nancy boy to boot. My accommodation in hell is already booked.'

A sheaf of papers sat on the red chenille tablecloth. Some keen solicitor, years ago, had typed an inventory of Woodbine's contents. Blanche put a red tick beside what belonged to Jane. Walnut dressing table: tick. Pair of late-Victorian lustre vases: tick. There was a torrent of red ticks; as relatives shuffled off this mortal coil they all left their chattels to Jane.

'*These* are mine.' Blanche brandished a list. Fox fur coat. Silver brush and mirror set. 'One page for all my impedimenta.'

'Lucky you. I can fit everything I own in one bag.'

'Hold on ...' Blanche took up the reading glasses she was too vain to wear. 'Ooh.' She ran a finger down the lists. 'That's interesting.'

'I assume by your tone I'm expected to ask what's interesting?'

'My aunt's jewellery box. It's not mentioned.'

'The aunt who took you to the States?' Archie perked up. He thought of America as the land of opportunity: huge steaks and huge men.

'If it's not on the list that means Alec is unaware of it. Which makes it *mine*.' Blanche threw down the glasses. 'Where did I last see it? Where *is* it?'

Archie, who came from a home where a box full of jewellery would never be mislaid, helped her search. 'Hey hey! Slow down.'

The drawers in the handsome dresser were on the floor.

Fish knives were tipped out. Soon the linen cupboard was ransacked, quilts and pillow slips underfoot. Blanche marauded through Woodbine Cottage like a menopausal Viking.

'You can't miss it. Huge. Heart-shaped. Pink velvet.' Blanche pulled down the ladder to the attic. 'Inside is a full parure.'

'A par-*what*?'

'You know, a set. Necklace, earrings, brooch, bracelet and a diadem. That's like a tiara,' she said when Archie looked blank. 'All emeralds. Green stones.'

'I do know what a soddin' emerald is.' Archie pulled her away from the creaky ladder. 'Here. Let me. You'll do yourself a mischief.'

She slapped him away to clamber upwards like a monkey. 'If I can get my hands on that box, Archie, I can bugger off with it and forget this stupid house.'

His foot steadying the ladder, Archie said, 'It's not just a house.' He loved Woodbine. It was warm and old and fine. 'It's your home, Blanchie.'

From the attic she shrieked, 'Where is it?' Her feet made prints in the dust. She was flagging. She opened crates, pushed aside piles of fabric.

Jane had kept everything from their shared childhood. Dolls with psychotic expressions. Books of nursery rhymes. 'Goosey bloody gander,' murmured Blanche.

The box wasn't there. Her hand found a teddy bear.

'Blaze.' Blanche put him to her cheek. The threadbare

velveteen unlocked a hoard of memory that even anti-nostalgia Blanche couldn't ignore.

A childish bed. She is snuggled deep in it, set against a dam of pillows. 'Here,' says Jane. A tiny Jane with ringlets. 'Take my best friend, Blaze. He'll help you get better.' Blaze's button eyes don't register any chagrin at being sacrificed.

Little fool, thought present-day Blanche, unimpressed by the selflessness.

But then the scene changes. Blaze's stare remains the same, but the girls change places. It's Jane who is droopy in the bed – *You had the mumps!* remembered Blanche – and young Blabs stands beside her. She holds out Blaze. 'Here, take my best friend, Blaze,' says little Blanche. 'He'll help you get better.'

Me, thought Blanche, astounded. *I was the selfless one that day.*

Next door to Woodbine Cottage, in The Bull, the gentlemen talked of this and that. And of the heron.

'He were here again.' Walter was thrilled, as if a film star had dropped by. 'Stood there, all folded up. I held me breath until he took off.'

'Can you eat heron?' asked Stan from his corner.

'You what?' Mick Lister put down his glass with a clunk.

'Never mind him,' said Bob. 'Just Stan being Stan.'

'Herons are *special*,' said Walter, reprovingly. 'They're priceless.'

'Priceless?' Stan livened up. 'When people say that they don't mean it don't have a price, they mean it costs a fortune.'

'Herons don't cost a penny,' snapped Mick. 'You can't sell 'em.'

'You can buy and sell *anything*,' said Stan.

Pamela was doing what she was put on Earth to do. Telling other people what to do and how to do it.

The man up the ladder had been clearing Lower Loxley gutters since before she was born. This didn't stop Pamela shouting up, shading her eyes from the sun, 'Are you quite sure you removed that dead nest?'

'Quite sure, ma'am.'

The sun was insistent. Summer cleared its throat in the wings. Pamela had always been more of a winter gal: stockings and coats and heavy fabrics. Now she inhabited her body differently as she wandered the woods with Kos. She grew and rippled like the ferns they passed, and the sun fell on her face like a blessing. A pagan one, not one from Henry's stuffy speeches.

'Morning!' she carolled as she passed chaps in the hall. Pamela had asked neither Alec nor Kos about the exchange at the dance. It was between them, she decided.

Alec's jealousy was intriguing. Her marriage was, to the casual eye, dead. As the proverbial dodo. Just because Pamela could state this truth so flatly didn't mean she had always been so accepting of it. The Pamela of one year ago was twisted, cramped, unable to drown out the hoof-beat of anxiety. Rejection – she got used to it. Loneliness – ditto.

Why did Alec approach Kos and not me? That irritated her. Pamela was easily irritated; she was irritated by how easily irritated she was. But Alec seeking out Kos was a major bugbear. She was capable of running her own life, infidelity and all. Kos was not the boss of her any more than Alec was.

The irony of it. After some bumpy terrain when Alec first found out, he and Pamela were getting along better since she found Kos. There was a lightness to their interactions: *I no longer need him to prove anything to me.* She could accept the rents in the fabric of their marriage without rancour.

He's making an effort. It had taken an affair to get Alec to discuss the events of the war with her. He accompanied her when she went to Ambridge; that morning she had made him howl with laughter outside the shop. She knew their rapport was fed by a bubbling stream of jealousy; she had stood waist-deep in that stream and she felt for him now.

Suddenly, Kos.

Like a conjuror's trick, thoughts of Alec vanished. Everything was Kos, and the hand he reached out to her.

She slapped it away. 'Someone will see!'

They sat apart at the dining room table, their feet touching beneath it. Kos had the newspaper. Dodgy and Terence sat with them. A silver coffee pot stood on a lace mat.

'A storm has burst over Germany.' Kos's eyes were on the newsprint and his foot nudged Pamela's shoe.

'Essen's getting it pretty bad.' Dodgy couldn't quite revel in the enemy's decimation. 'Carpet bombing ... not how you win a war.'

'The Yanks coming on board has changed everything.' Terence was chipper, caffeinated. He splayed out his fingers. 'If this stupid hand of mine would heal I'd be up in the air over Essen right now.'

'Soon, dear boy, soon.' Dodgy didn't comment when Kos said he couldn't wait to 'get up there'. They all knew the blackbird was condemned to hop along the ground for evermore. 'Kos, what d'you make of the latest titbits from Alec's MP chum? That wild scheme to send servicemen into the Warsaw ghetto with faked Jewish identity papers.' They had mulled over the Top Secret plan with their brandies of the night before, some of them incredulous that such a gambit would ever be sanctioned. To Pamela, Dodgy said, 'You were in bed, dear lady, but I can tell you it's either the bravest or the most preposterous thing I ever heard. Inevitably, the fellows get rounded up by the Nazis and sent to one of those contemptible camps.'

'It's *brilliant*.' Kos sat forward. 'They will infiltrate, set up an underground in the camps that can supply us with intelligence about what really goes on in there.'

'Sounds like a film script,' said Pamela.

'War always does.' Kos's shoe pressed Pamela's ankle and – hey presto! – a new erogenous zone.

'Saw young Archie on The Green.' Dodgy reached for more coffee. The only good coffee, he frequently said, he had ever tasted in England. 'Nose busted. Cowardly, jumping a man in the dark like that.'

'He asked for it.' Terence was contemptuous. 'Mincing around the dance like a girl. Flirting. With *chaps*.'

'Not with me!' said Dodgy, amiably. 'Hardly merits a duffing up.'

'There are real enemies,' murmured Kos, 'without creating ones close to home.'

Terence said nothing more; Kos had status among the blue uniforms.

Nance took the same route home every day. Today she was on foot, her bike upside down in Walter Gabriel's shed awaiting a diagnosis, and she took a more circuitous route.

Ted was with her.

They walked through the haze of spring hedgerows, their path trimmed with the greens and yellows and tentative mauves of the season. All was potential, promise. Except for Nance, who was locked-in and parched, like Woodbine Cottage's once lush garden that had set the village a-clucking.

'So where's this mate of yours live?' she asked. They kept a good couple of feet apart. She held wood sorrel in her hands. Ted picked it for her, thinking it was clover. The leaves were similar, but not the same. 'This mate you're visiting?'

'Um, over on, err, something lane.' Ted gave in and laughed. A rueful *ha-ha*. 'I make a terrible liar, Nance. There is no mate. I'm just, I just wanted to walk with you.'

She was so, so pleased. And so frightened. Nance was not a transgressor; she found no attraction in the sickly sweet, the stolen; she liked plain materials and neat rugs.

And yet.

Ted stopped. The air around him throbbed. He pulled her towards him. He was vigorous, impatient.

Nance let him.

Honest in all things, there was no point lying to herself about her fantasies of this moment.

His mouth on hers was different to the fantasy. Ted smelled of the cheap Spanish Shawl cigarettes he smoked. Nance was surprised when he walked her backwards, like a doll, off the road and along a track.

'Ted,' she said. Not *No*. She didn't say that. Because he was taller and wider than she was, and somehow that ignited her.

She kissed him with all the passion corked up inside her since her wedding night. They stumbled and turned and her back was against a shabby barn.

Ted leaned into her, over her.

Nance was a bottle of pop, shaken for over a year, that would fizz all over the countryside.

Within the activity there was time to shape whole thoughts. Within the pressing of hands on flesh. The writhing. The unleashed physicality that took hold of her. *How is a modest man such a brilliant kisser?* she thought. *He's had practice.*

Ted put a hand over her breast. Her coat was undone – how? She froze.

Ted said, 'Nance, oh, Nance.'

She allowed. Permitted. Loved it.

Nance became bold. Explored. Avid to know what all the fuss was about, she moved her hand downwards. 'Ooh, Ted.' She was horrified, aroused.

Crabwise they moved to the barn door. Ted held him to her as he kicked it shut behind them. They were invisible now, in the dark. Just form. Soft and hard and insistent.

He bent and Nance bent beneath him because she was part of him, some odd amoeba. They were on the floor.

And Nance rebelled.

She was a married woman. She could not have sexual intercourse on a barn floor with a man who was not her husband. She pushed at Ted, mildly at first, then sharply because he was still in that haze from which she had recovered.

He knelt and watched as she settled her coat, did up her trousers with clumsy speed. He jumped up. 'Nance, come on, no, girl, please!'

She jumped away from him as if a puppeteer had yanked her strings.

Something in her face sobered him. He retreated, held out both hands as if to keep her at bay. 'I wouldn't force you, Nance.'

'I know that.' She tugged straw out of her fringe. 'If things were different, Ted ...'

She ran and he ran after her, but only as far as the road. He sat, then, in the dirt, and looked at nothing for a long while.

The mirror was two centuries old if it was a day.

It had reflected much and that evening it gave Alec his pale face and the Home Guard cap that would *not* sit right.

'There.' Pamela came up behind him and with one tweak fixed the problem.

She smiled at him in the pitted glass. Her eyes changed when Alec said, 'If I can see that bastard's foot against yours under the table, surely others can, too. Our son's at home. What if Gerald gets wind of you and this pilot?' As his wife's eyes hardened to agates he said, 'Or don't you care?'

She turned but he was fast and kept pace with her as she stalked – clack-clack-clack over the stone floor – away from him.

Hero followed them both at a respectful distance.

'Do *not* ignore me, Pamela.' The suppressed anger that made his moustache quiver was not entirely just; Alec knew that. He appreciated Pamela's discretion, her delicacy in keeping evidence of the affair from him. All the more admirable because she wasn't of his class; among Alec's peers there was insouciance about such matters. Stepfamilies abounded. Mistresses were squirrelled away in Mayfair apartments. No need to *talk* about the whole business. It was Alec who was behaving like a shopkeeper, as his father would have put it.

Pamela faced him, chin up. 'Out of interest, when were you going to tell me?'

'Tell you what?' Alec was brought up short. *She does this to me all the time.* And with such ease. 'Don't change the subject.' He looked about him; all walls have ears, but Lower Loxley's walls were particularly infested.

'About the private investigator. The search for your Irish girl. You changed your mind and were going to leave me for her, weren't you? But she jumped ship before you could do it.' Pamela paused. A couple of beats, as exquisitely timed as

322

anything Mozart had ever composed. 'And your little daughter? Hmm? When were you going to tell me about her?'

She knew he'd be speechless, so she left him there. With his dog.

Nance would never remember running home. She left the barn and was suddenly in her own porch as if whisked there by magic carpet.

Out of breath – *I may never catch my breath again!* – she was wound up, thwarted. Something had been awoken and denied, all in the space of a few minutes.

Still in her coat, she marched to the kitchen.

Genial at the stove, Magsy turned, ladle in hand.

'Magsy, please go home,' said Nance.

Magsy closed her eyes briefly, laid down the ladle, and left the house by the back door, taking her hat and coat from a hook.

Bewildered – *What? No resistance?* – Nance recovered and moved on. She needed something, needed it with a deep-in-the-woods primal desire. It was only just out of her reach. She could ask. It was her due.

She stood at the closed door to her husband's surgery. She undid the buttons on her blouse. She knocked.

'Get out,' said Gerald. He was balled up on his bed like knotted yarn. Knees to chin. Eyes squeezed shut. A child's attitude, but Gerald was no child.

He's no man, either. Alec, at the end of the bed, saw a creature in transition. Soon old enough to fight, but not sensible enough

CATHERINE MILLER

to be sent to the shop on an errand. He was burly, Gerald, big-nosed. These should have been his last months at school, he should be among his peers, not haunting the house like a boorish ghost. The masters had tacitly given up on him, sent him home to vegetate. 'A scandal like this, stealing a fellow's watch, it can follow a man all through his life.' Alec fancied he heard the whirr of ancestors rotating in the Pargetter tomb. 'We must deal with it, son. Admit it, Gerald. You stole that watch.'

'How dare you!' Gerald uncoiled and sprang up. A growth spurt meant he was eye to eye with Alec. His father's appearance in his room, his bolthole, confounded him. The old man's wrath generally had a warmed-over quality to it, none of this melodrama. Bursting in, reading the riot act? *Simply not cricket.* 'Other fathers believe their sons.'

'Other fathers don't have to read your school reports.' Alec struck the bedstead. He hurt his hand but he didn't wince. Gerald was a handy vessel for his indignation, for the moralizing that Pamela simply refused to accept from him. 'You've lied about fighting, about being caught off school grounds, and as for that business with the French mistress ... Why *should* I believe you, Gerald?'

'And why should I believe you, Father? We both know you lied to Mother.'

The silence seemed to mark an agreement that, yes, Gerald had gone too far. He took off, like a partridge breaking cover.

'Don't you run from me, boy!' Alec winced as he gave chase. *I sound like my father.* He would never beat Gerald, never lock him in the stables to teach him a lesson. Instead Alec wanted – and he only realized this as he stumbled down the stairs – to hold Gerald and somehow make him a little boy again, uncomplicated, *clean*.

He didn't want his son to truly know him. He didn't want to see disappointment in the boy's eyes.

'There are things I could tell you that might change the way you see your mother!' said Alec, and almost careered into a maid.

She put her head down, her demeanour appeasing him, letting him know that yes, of course, she owned a pair of ears but they were switched off and she hadn't heard a thing, honest.

'Like what?' Gerald paused on the bottom stair.

Alec wouldn't say it. He was disgusted by the Alec of a few seconds earlier who had been ready to disparage Pamela to her son.

'I hate you!' roared Gerald, his histrionic exit marred by his tripping over something small on the back step. He pelted through the yard, off to hate some more and possibly cry.

Alec sighed and stooped and picked up the stone his son had kicked to one side.

Not a stone, on closer inspection. A piece of shrapnel, shaped like a star.

When Morgan heard the knock he assumed dinner was ready.

He looked up and saw his wife at the surgery door. She was naked.

'I want to be your wife, Morgan,' she said.

He held his pen above his blotter. He blinked.

'I'm a woman, not a doll.' Nance kept her hands by her side.

She did not cover any part of herself. She trembled, though. 'There's no need to be careful of me.'

Morgan spoke so fast it bordered on gibberish. His pen remained aloft. 'But you're so young, my dear, and I'm so old, and there's been so much between us we didn't expect.'

She was at his side. She stooped and kissed him. Her body seemed to give off a powder, a pearly dust that made the fusty room sparkle.

'There,' she said.

His moustache was a feather bed, good to sink into. His breath smelled of mint.

Mesmerized by her flesh, Morgan whispered, 'You're laughing?'

'Your moustache is tickly.'

She kissed him again. She moved her mouth, the way Ted had.

Her daring excited him, that was clear. After a lifetime of blushing and staring at her feet, Nance took charge.

She left him at his desk, and looked over her shoulder as he almost toppled his chair in his haste to follow.

Nance had never felt the wooden stairs beneath bare feet before. She sped up, with a happy shriek, her husband right behind her.

Wizbang snuffled his way to the fence first. He loved the smells of Quartershot Camp.

'Hey, boys.' Luca looked past John and Billy. 'Where's my bike?'

They said nothing. They had failed him.

'Ah, boys.' Luca's sigh was long and loud but not mean, which made it worse. 'You let me down. I rely.'

'It's tough,' mewed John. 'We're only kids.'

'Only?' Luca waggled his finger. 'Never! You are British gentlemen. You are heroes.'

John didn't feel like a hero. He had a frog in his pocket and lice in his hair. 'Sorry,' he mumbled into his scarf.

'I cannot scold my good brave boys,' said Luca.

'Do you ever give Bruno and Vittorio a ticking off?' asked Billy.

'I teach them with love, only love.' Luca's big face was soft.

John leaned against the wire. He wished Luca could cuddle him, like their dad used to. Lady hugs were great, nothing wrong with a nice lady hug, like Peggy gave if she was in the right mood, but oh, a dad hug! Tight and sudden, lifting you off your feet.

John was crying. He rubbed his eyes. *How did that happen?* His voice was clotted when he said, 'I promise promise promise we'll get you a bike.'

Luca put a finger through the wire and tickled the scarf, the one Mum knitted. 'I trust you, little John.'

March comes in like a lion and goes out like a lamb; the moment shimmers.

Bob clings to sleep, despite the noise coming from beneath his bedroom window. He is deep in a dream, talking to

CATHERINE MILLER

a living Jimmy, but a muttered curse from outside breaks through and the spell is broken. The noise – something being dragged? – intensifies but Bob can't care. He puts his pillow over his head and wills himself back to the dream. *There is Jimmy!* But the boy's digging his own grave in hot, foreign earth and has no time for his father.

Gerald, in pyjamas, shins down a tree. He has found, at last, the well he remembers from childhood. He clears away the greedy, clawing shrub that has grown over it, and produces a gold orb from his pocket. He lets go and is rewarded with a wet sound when the watch hits the thick, dirty water at the bottom of the well.

Morgan and Nance are asleep. They are the wrong way up in the bed. The covers are rucked up around them, and Morgan still wears one sock.

Hair in curlers, Magsy sits in her kitchen. Her tea has gone cold. She knew this day would come. *I am redundant*, she thinks.

The magic window on the landing is dark. Pamela, heart jitterbugging, stands in her gauzy nightdress and concentrates on the glass panes. Is it her need that makes the window jump to life as a candle is lit in the aptly named folly? She flies out into the darkness.

328

APRIL

The birds were up before Nance.

They threw their song from throat to throat, an invitation. She heard a wren. A collared dove answered from the misty garden. Then song thrushes and greenfinches, more than Nance could identify.

Throughout the country, from farm to farm, town to town, the nation was sewn together with birdsong.

Sitting on the deep bedroom windowsill, wrapped in Morgan's shirt, Nance was happy.

Over at The Bull, Bob ignored the birds and scratched his head as he surveyed the cause of last night's commotion.

'What the . . .' He had been trained out of swearing by his wife so he left the phrase unfinished. Who, he wondered, would get up in the middle of the night to creep to the pub and *plant begonias*?

His tubs, made from old barrels, had been his pride and joy before the war. Now, with scant pride and joy hard to find,

Bob turned his back on the flurry of pink. *Good luck to 'em*, he thought. He had no time to water or tend. Let the papery, intense blooms fend for themselves.

Mrs Endicott was sharing her thoughts.

There were those in the queue who would rather she paid up and let Frank get on, but a lifetime spent in Ambridge gave Mrs E certain privileges. One of these was to ramble at length without being prodded with an umbrella, as Agnes longed to do.

'One wonders,' she said, 'where we *are*.'

'You're in Ambridge,' said Susan Grundy, puzzled by the question.

'No, my dear, where we are in the war. When one reads about the Great War one knows whether it's nearly the end or slap bang in the middle. But here we are, our third Easter at war, and are we nearly done? Or, heavens above, do we have ten more years of this?'

'Can't last ten years.' Doris was positive, with nothing to back it up.

Frances said, 'God would never allow it.'

'God,' said Agnes, 'allows all sorts.'

'I know a *little* more about our saviour than you,' said Frances. 'He has a plan.'

'You're married to the vicar, not God.' Agnes's mood was rarely sunny and it was not improved by having to stand in line for two measly ounces of butter. 'The war'll be over by Christmas.'

'Which Christmas?' Susan's question was innocent but it struck a chord.

Agnes said, 'Frances, happen you'll own Woodbine Cottage by Christmas.'

'I haven't given Jane's will a thought in weeks,' said Frances.

Nobody believed her. Frank said mildly, 'Let's hope Blanche gets her due.'

'In that case,' said Agnes, 'Blanche'll get nothing.'

'Anything else, Mrs Endicott?' Frank would not be drawn into gossip. Having been its victim he knew how sharp its talons could be.

That lady had more thoughts to share. 'I have a theory,' she said. 'About the will. The first personal item was a child's toy, the second a wallet. So, the child has grown up, entered the world. Next, a spade to dig the foundations of their home.'

'The story of a life,' said Agnes, until now wedded to her Pargetter hypothesis. 'With two more instalments, it's a long life, too.'

'A mature person. Someone like myself,' said Mrs Endicott very, very, *very* casually.

'I'm not mature,' said Susan, dismayed.

'I am,' said a voice, and they all turned to see Nanny.

'You don't count.' Frances was blunt. 'You didn't know Jane.'

'Whereas *I*,' said Mrs Endicott, finally gathering her bag, 'knew the dear lady from before I married. Good day!'

As the bell above the door gave a *ding!*, Doris said, 'Wasn't Mrs Endicott's maiden name Baxter-Lowndes-Ridley?'

331

'She was *triple*-barrelled?' The antics of the upper classes never ceased to astonish Agnes. She caught on. 'B, L, R!'

Another horse entered the race. A slow and stately one, to be sure, but the ladies knew their Aesop's fables and didn't rule out this nag.

Magsy was next in line. 'Jane *was* fond of Mrs Endicott.' She slid her list across to Frank.

'I've kept you a packet of mustard, Miss Furneaux.' Frank stooped below the counter. 'For Morgan's gammon.'

'No, thank you. Morgan's meals are nothing to do with me anymore.'

Looks were exchanged. A troubled one, if you were Doris; a rabid one, if you were Frances. Magsy left, her cheeks hot, withstanding the hundred and one unasked questions. She dropped her purse just outside the door, and Nanny stepped out to help her round up the rolling coins.

Agnes forestalled Frances's attempt to genteelly queue-jump. 'My turn! Frank, *please* tell me you have Lux in?'

'I do.' Frank called to Irene, loitering by the soap flakes. 'Little girl! Kindly hand me the packet that says *Lux* in big letters.'

Irene stared at him but didn't move.

Doris said, 'It's right behind you, dear.'

'My eyes have gone funny,' said Irene. 'I can't see it.'

Frances, whose attitude towards children was Victorian – they should do as they're told, and quietly – said, 'A liar, to boot!'

Back from her errand of mercy, Nanny stopped dead on

the doormat. 'She does have bad eyes,' she said, forlorn, unconvincing.

Agnes grabbed the Lux herself. 'Cheeky piece,' she said.

Doris had questions – gentle ones, disturbing ones – about why Nanny would sanction such untruths but before she could ask them, the shop was invaded by a tall man, high and wide and shouting.

'Three weeks!' Kos slammed his fist on the counter, and the women jumped as one. 'I ordered shoelaces *three weeks ago!*'

Such fury over shoelaces was comic, but nobody laughed. Kos was transfigured, an avenging angel with bloodshot eyes. 'Answer me!' he bellowed.

Speechless, Frank dropped the Lux.

Later, as Agnes unpacked her paltry shopping, she said, 'And then, Denholm, who'd you think rushed in? Only Pamela! She was all smiles, says "Ooh, Squadron Leader, let's leave the ladies to their chit chat," but he had none of it, he goes, "I don't like waiting" and I thought any moment now he's going to boff old Frank on the nose. Then Pamela says, still sweet, "Let's get back to Lower Loxley" like she's making a child behave in church, and this Kos, he sinks, like a balloon after a party, and rushes out, all embarrassed like.'

'Hmm,' said Denholm.

'So, Denholm, quite a morning! Is Mrs Endicott going to inherit Woodbine? Is that evacuee possessed by Satan?' Agnes handled the taped-together packet of Lux with care. 'Is the airman a raving lunatic? Was it him what bashed poor

Archie, not Stan? And what on *Earth* is Pamela Pargetter doing high-stepping around Ambridge with him? Eh?'

'Yes,' said Denholm. Then, panicking, 'Or do I mean, no, dear?'

'Can't we take a day off?' whined Archie.

He wore a floral apron and he wore it well, but he drooped beneath it. 'We've searched *everywhere*, Blanche. That dratted jewellery box isn't in this house.'

'It's here somewhere, I know it,' said Blanche, thinking *It's mine!* So little belonged to her, not the pans in the kitchen nor the insipid embroidery of gambolling lambs over her bed. 'Keep looking.'

'I'll *buy* you earrings, doll.' Archie replaced the silver cutlery in a green-felted tray. Blanche had taken to investigating ever-smaller nooks and crannies in her desperation.

'Ha!' The winking emeralds were beyond Archie's pocket. They were Blanche's insurance policy. The latest theory about the will had reached her ears: Emmaline Endicott, Baxter-Lowndes-Ridley as was. She recalled Mrs E visiting with soup and sympathy when Jane was laid low with her heart, happy to sit and listen to Jane as if she was fascinating. *Which,* thought Blanche, *Jane most definitely was not.*

At the window, Archie put down the cutlery tray and pulled the blackout blind. Night was settling in; no ladies were about; it was the hour when menfolk tramped to The Bull. To sink a few pints.

And break a nose or two. Archie lived under curfew. He was fair game, that had been proven. Earlier, he had almost bumped into the vengeful citizen who taught him a lesson at the dance, but turned into the cottage just in time.

Their contract, made in blood, was unbreakable. Archie would never squeal; the man would never confess.

With the blind down, he was safe. For now.

'Archie,' said Blanche, wound about herself in a dining room chair, her ironing board figure in knots. 'You've guessed Jane killed herself, haven't you?'

He hadn't. 'Jane? No! That's so sad.' His eyes filled with tears. Archie was made of tender stuff. 'Poor lady.'

'Don't you want to know why?'

'Okay, I'll bite. Why?' Archie, a trawler of his own soul, knew there couldn't be just one reason for such an act.

'Me.'

'You?'

'My ... well, the way I am. The way I was to Jane.'

'You can't make someone commit suicide. Jane probably just—'

'She left a note.' Blanche drummed her fingers on the dining table. 'Me, Archie. All me.'

He switched on a lamp, and the room turned peachy. Blanche still looked haggard. 'Sounds to me like you'd do things different if you had your time over again. You've got me now, doll. I'll keep you on the straight and narrow. Don't be so hard on yourself.'

Blanche wanted to laugh. *The silly boy thinks I'm a good person.*

'Time to get some dinner inside you.' Archie was off to the kitchen. 'It's meatballs à la Archie, made to my secret recipe and containing not one speck of flippin' meat.'

The gammon steak on Morgan's warmed plate was the result of intense bartering between Nance and a butcher's wife in the mill's packing department.

Nance, elbows on the table, watched her husband as he ate. 'Well?'

'Delicious.' Morgan kissed his fingers.

'As nice as Magsy's?'

'Better.'

They talked like this, now. Morgan heard her sing about the house, and she heard him *pom-pom-pom* his way through his beloved Gilbert and Sullivan.

The pantry was rearranged. The wedding present dinner service was used every night. She had switched some paintings around. Homeleigh was Nance's territory. She was no longer a guest.

And yet, Magsy was still at the table with them, the ghostly lack of her eloquent. Each day they wondered should they pay her a visit. Together? Singly? Each day they were struck anew at how she left without comment, and sank without trace.

'Good news,' said Morgan, 'about Cliff returning to Arkwright Hall.'

'Very,' said Nance. They were yoked together in all things. His work. Her work. Bed.

'Is there any mustard,' he asked, 'to go with my delightful gammon?'

Stricken, Nance had to confess there wasn't.

'No matter,' said Morgan, who had hoped to defuse some of the overcooked meat's fearsome saltiness.

The wood was awash with bluebells, all of them stealing a march on the green canopy that summer would soon close over them.

Billy and John paddled through the blue, true secret agents, smuggling contraband.

Billy couldn't quite manage the bike. It wheeled away from him like a frisky pony. Bringing up the rear, John wondered what sentence an Ambridge judge and jury might impose for bike theft. The lack of their reputation – such as it was – would be worse than any punishment.

They were early, and Wizbang barked in cheerful recognition when he saw Luca beyond the diamond shapes of the fence.

Luca's face was sooty with annoyance. 'Don't bring dog again!'

The boys looked at Wizbang. They were a trio. 'But,' said John.

'Do you do what your papa tells you?'

'Well, yeah,' said Billy.

'Good. So do not bring dog.'

The surprise was spoiled. Typical grown-up meanness! Billy wiped his snotty nose. 'Look, Luca, over there.'

Luca looked to a hawthorn. He knew the spiky shrub as *biancospino*. Handlebars peeked out like antlers.

Luca blew the boys a kiss. 'British gentlemen! Clever soldiers!'

The boys wriggled. John could burst; he buried his face in his stripey scarf.

'I know you can do this, I trust my boys.' Luca spent praise like a sailor on shore leave. 'My boys are the best.'

His plan had been refined. Billy and John listened with the sort of application they never brought to lessons. 'On the day, leave bicycle at front of camp. You will see guard hut. Behind hut, please, after last patrol at two o'clock in morning.'

Billy nodded. Any excuse to hop out of bed and do something lawless. 'Did you get a map?'

'I risk life, but yes.'

John shivered at the thought of Luca risking his life. Luca's life was all bound up with his dad's life. They were twins.

'Next you bring me knife.'

'Knife?' John had been schooled all his life to stay away from knives. The way his mum went on you'd think they could leap out of drawers to get at him. 'What for?'

Luca made a sawing motion. 'To cut fence.'

That satisfied Billy but John said, 'You're getting out under a lorry. You don't need to cut no fence.'

'A good soldier,' said Luca, 'always has plan B.'

The garden was never out of Blanche's eyeline.

Every window in Woodbine gave out onto greenery.

Jane had planned it that way. It was as if the garden tapped on Blanche's shoulder, nagging, whining, complaining of her neglect.

Perhaps I should listen to nature, as Jane suggested. She had not once followed her sister's advice in life, but Blanche manhandled the back door open, fighting against the wisteria which had gone on the rampage, unchecked, unmanaged.

Within five minutes she was back indoors, uncorking the sherry. Her nails were caked with soil, there was a caterpillar in her hair. 'I've listened to nature,' she informed Archie, 'and it talks nonsense. Which are the weeds? One of those bushes literally attacked me.'

She was as unversed in plants as she was in people.

Far from the house, Pamela and Kos were still on Pargetter land. They tramped away from the manicured gardens, until they were silhouetted on a distant ridge, pipistrelles swooping, dainty and eerie, about them.

Pamela was not imaginative; she did not feel as if she was treading on Alec's soft parts as she trod on his land. She did not feel his heart underfoot, so she hooked her arms around Kos's waist as he put his around her shoulders. They staggered and laughed and kissed. Carefree, like lovers, which they were; like young people, which they were not.

The eagle ring sat on her finger only during these walks. The power it gave her, to explode a smile on Kos's taciturn face, excited Pamela. It wasn't a wedding ring; it was better than that.

Because Pamela was a warrior beneath her couture, she brought up the forbidden topic. 'Darling, accept it. You'll never fly in combat again.' She was ready when he tried to pull away. She was thin but strong. He gave in. They remained glued together. 'You're a man of courage, so face it. Find a way to be part of the fight, but from behind a desk.'

Kos snarled like a dog.

'Use me. I can pull strings.' Sweet old Magsy might be a bore but her MP brother ran a discreet black market in favours.

The timing of Pamela's sermon was no accident. Out there on the ridge there was no furniture to smash, no mirrors to break. Such outbursts were more frequent now. She had been forced to show her hand in the village shop, witnessed by Ambridge's most organized and diligent gossips.

The triggers could be tiny; the sort of banal setback people contended with every day. Or it might be mention of the war. Kos was a machine, tooled to avenge.

And all the while, his scar, his tribal mark, flashed his pain to the world.

'Keep calm, keep with me.' Pamela was cool and sharp, grounding him.

'I am not built,' said Kos, 'to push pins into a map.'

'If you fly you'll put the other men in danger.'

'Then I go alone.'

'There's no place for a lone wolf, Kos. You're part of a huge apparatus.' Pamela was steady, measured. She never lifted the corner of her fear, even when he ransacked his room, a loose cannon. *But he scares me.* He was big and she was slight, despite being fashioned from steel. When anger claimed him, Kos didn't see her. *I become a shadow.* She could be collateral damage during one of his eruptions.

Pamela didn't blame Kos, nor did she feel swindled that she had never known him whole and serene. She turned the anguish to determination: *I'll help him.*

Helping Kos meant thwarting him.

He asked, his face near hers, 'Have you told the chaps?'

'About what?'

'The headaches, the blurred vision, the violence.'

'It's hardly that,' said Pamela, although it was entirely that. 'I haven't breathed a word, my darling.' *No need: they see it for themselves.*

'I can't be LMF.'

Lack of moral fibre: the label that grounded airmen for life.

'You have more moral fibre than any man I've ever met.'

He pulled roughly away. His eyes were lava. 'Yet you chain me to your side.'

'No.' Pamela was an exclamation mark. 'Do *not* accuse me of that.' She lifted a finger as he opened his mouth to speak. He was primed to let rip, to become the other Kos. 'Stop. I will not tolerate being ill-used. Take a moment and don't speak until you can discuss this with restraint.'

His chest moved. His fists clenched and unclenched. Then his face collapsed and Kos put his hands to his head. His big head, stuffed so full of death and pain. Actual pain, not just the existential ache they all felt every day of the war.

'Oh, my love,' said Pamela.

With great effort, Kos swallowed, and was right again. Tall. Straight.

They swayed and drew something from each other. For Pamela it was the deep, unusual satisfaction of mattering; Alec would replace her with Hero without a blink. Her common sense and experience held no currency for her husband.

'Look!' Kos pointed at two hares, boxing wildly, out in the open. 'They compete for a mate.'

'Typical men.'

'But one is a female. She's fighting the males to discover who's strong enough to be her sexual partner.'

He raised an eyebrow at her, and Pamela laughed so loudly that the hares ran off.

The birds, courting and building nests in trees not quite in full leaf, didn't notice Doris, but she noticed them as she made for the village hall, and the fourth will reading.

The birds' industry soothed Doris when she cowered from headlines of Japan causing havoc in Burma, or those twenty-four thousand US troops, all of them sick and starving, trapped on the Bataan Peninsula.

And Jack out there, her lad, just a ping-pong ball in a gale. He was a poor correspondent but she wrote to him weekly, painting a sunny picture of Brookfield. She rather envied the fictional Doris who gathered wildflowers and savoured sunsets over the paddock.

Doris joined the stream of villagers heading, like lemmings, for the hall. Connie and Stan approached from the north, and Mrs Endicott slowed the vicar down by taking his arm.

Beside Doris, Wanda was quiet. Doris handled her with tongs; if somebody is that much younger than you, yet knows about, *ooh*, *opera*, and has dined at the Café de Paris there's no point pretending you can be friends. 'Missing your bike, I daresay.'

'You bet.'

The theft of Wanda's bike had been bemoaned in Henry's Sunday sermon – 'How times have changed!' – with more condemnation than Archie's attack. Doris asked, 'Did you get through to your ma?'

'Not yet, Boss. Frances said I'm welcome to use the vicarage phone again later.'

Bath was catching it. Bombs rained down on the mellow stone of Wanda's home city. Doris wasn't the type to offer saccharine comfort. 'Where's your father stationed?'

'Gibraltar. HMS *Penelope*.'

'Not HMS Pepperpot?' The ship, better known by its nickname, was strafed endlessly by enemy aircraft. 'You kept that quiet,' she said. *There's depth to Wanda.*

Wanda didn't speak. She was hostage to her fears. So Doris chattered instead, enfolding her in a blanket of soft, domestic, anodyne news.

'Here comes Nanny and little Irene. Did I tell you about the to-do in the shop when Irene cheeked Frank and wouldn't hand over the Lux?' The telling of that got them to the hall.

'It's obvious, surely?' said Wanda. 'Poor kid can't read. That's why she pretended she couldn't see the Lux.'

'No, no, Irene's a champion reader. It was pure devilment on her part.' Doris noticed the shine on Irene's plaits as they took their seats a couple of rows behind her.

'Bet you a guinea Irene can't read but is too embarrassed to admit it.'

Arthur Sweet complained to one and all. 'I can't keep up with this riddle of the will. What's the letters so far?'

'B, L, A,' said someone.

'No! B, L, *R*!' said someone else.

The azalea/rhododendron war raged; fewer casualties than the real one, but with zealots on both sides.

'If today's plant begins with "B",' said Agnes, as if they were playing bingo, 'that makes it B, L, A, B. Surely that'll mean Blabs, or Blanche, gets Woodbine.'

'Take heart, Blanche,' said Morgan as the lady took her seat on the front row. 'We may well get a "B" today.'

'Which will also,' said Blanche, 'be good news for the Pargetters. Remember, Blessed Light Reveals Bountiful Hope.'

'Are we all here?' Ignoring Blanche, Alec raised his voice from the stage. 'Good. We can begin.'

Swivelling in her seat, Agnes whispered to Doris, 'If today's letter is "I", that almost spells "Blair" The Horrobins'll be in clover.'

'Agnes!' said Doris. 'Alec called out your name.'

'Eh? Me?' Agnes sprinted to the stage where Alec held out something small and sparkling.

She took it. Held it up to the light. 'One earring?' said Agnes. '*One?*'

'What a horrid snub.' Mrs Endicott was appalled.

'From beyond the grave,' said Frances, in a sepulchral tone.

Denholm sank in his seat, lest he be called upon to defend his wife's honour. That was not his forte.

'You sure that's all?' Agnes looked to blame Alec.

'Quite sure.'

Pamela saw new lines on his face. *This war is ageing us all like prime ministers.*

Wondering aloud, Mrs Endicott asked if the single earring was a promise, a placeholder. 'Will dear Agnes inherit the other earring along with the cottage?'

'Wait, Agnes,' said Alec, as she turned away. 'Your plant.' Walter lifted the cloth.

The village, as one, leaned forward to see a tub of massed, jolly, scorching red flowers, the simple shapes a child might draw.

'A busy lizzie,' said Walter.

The murmur travelled the room like a virus. 'It's a "B"!'

'Blabs!' yelled Susan Grundy.

'Or Mr Alec!' said a Lower Loxley tenant. 'Blessed light reveals whatnot!'

As Agnes descended the steps, busy lizzie in her arms, Blanche said, 'Do enjoy your one earring, dear.'

Archie nudged his employer. 'Could it be from your missing jewellery box?'

'No, looks like a cheap little opal.'

The inheritance was officially out of Stan Blair Horrobin's reach. Shoving, pushing, he bulldozed his way out. All the Horrobins hung their heads at the prospect of the next few hours with their paterfamilias.

'Hang on, Stan,' called Susan. 'My nan used to grow busy lizzies but she called them impatiens.'

The letter 'I' seemed to hover over the audience, shiny and showing off.

'Impatiens?' Stan stopped so suddenly his little Maisie bashed into the back of his legs. 'B plus L plus A plus I!' He punched the air. 'Blair! We're gonna be rich, kids.'

The reverend was unsettled. 'We don't know that yet.' He hoped Blanche would inherit, not least because the first port of call for the genteel homeless was the vicarage.

'Perhaps one day,' said Mrs Endicott, as the crowd dispersed, 'they'll produce a Hollywood film of this. I can see Michael Redgrave playing Alec.'

When Morgan suggested Bette Davis for Blanche all agreed that couldn't be bettered; he was cheerful; the new plant ruled him out of the running to inherit and that was the way Morgan wanted it.

Odious when unhappy, Stan was worse when jubilant. 'About time,' he said to Agnes, out in the sunshine, 'one of us got a leg up the ladder.'

'You and me, Stan Horrobin, are not *us*.' The earring stabbed Agnes's palm.

Alec was last out. Pamela saw his surprise at seeing her loiter, waiting for him.

Home Fires at Ambridge

Home Fires at Ambridge

The rules were simple: they must not embarrass Alec. Kos had gone on ahead. In public, Pamela fulfilled all her wifely duties. Duties which were all the more stringent for not being written down.

She took his arm. 'You did well in there. These will readings are tricky. Very volatile situation, and the village looks to you and your kind for a steady hand. You supplied exactly that.'

'I hope so. I feel horribly underutilized. My battlefield's the village hall. Doesn't sit right with me.'

'We can only do what's asked of us. Duty is duty.' They were in step as they crossed The Green. 'You're a man of honour.'

Grateful, Alec touched her hand, and his fingers grazed the eagle on her finger.

Pamela slipped it off and stowed it in her pocket. 'Forgive me,' she said.

'I do,' he said.

She put her arm back through his, and they passed an elderly couple, who expected and received gracious nods from Mr and Mrs Pargetter.

'I know now,' said Pamela, when they walked on, 'that you *didn't* choose to stay in our marriage. I know you would have left if you could. But you honoured it, like you're honouring your duty to Jane.'

'That was then.' Alec pulled his arm tight against his side. It brought Pamela closer. 'I feel differently now.' He hesitated. 'About you, Pamela.'

347

It was a cue. Pamela said nothing.

'It's devastating,' said Alec, 'to discover that a child one knew only vaguely is one's own child. It's one thing to lose a . . .'

'Use the proper word, Alec. I won't break.'

'To lose a lover.' Alec's lip sweated beneath his moustache. 'I could cope with that. It finds its level. But to know there exists a little girl, your little girl, and she has no protector . . .'

'Why are we discussing this?'

'So I can explain about that private detective. It was to find my daughter.'

'Your daughter,' repeated Pamela. She was contemplative. No sharpness now.

They left the village, following a lane that led from Ambridge to Lower Loxley like an artery.

'Bit of a trek, but I can do with the exercise,' said Pamela. She slid her eyes towards Alec. 'These lanes must be fun on your motorbike.'

He buttoned down a smile. 'But you know, dear wife, I own no such thing. You have forbidden it and therefore it can't exist.'

'Poor thing,' said Pamela. 'Condemned to hide in some distant stable. I do hope you toss it a carrot now and again.'

'You should come out on it sometime.'

Does he know I went up in Kos's plane? 'Hardly my style.'

Lower Loxley grew as they approached it. The terrain turned civilized. On the terrace the men – *their* men – loafed in groups, cigarette smoke rising above them.

A little apart stood Kos.

They both spotted him at the same moment. Alec tried to withdraw his arm, but Pamela kept her hand through it. They took the steps together.

Kos's face was dark, like a storm, as they passed him.

He must surely know I'll go to him later, thought Pamela. Respect took many forms; Alec wouldn't hear her steal out of the house.

'Duck tonight,' said Pamela as she relinquished Alec on the upper landing. 'Your favourite.'

Alone in his room, Alec pulled off his tie. He was altered, a little breathless. It took a second for him to register Hero at his side.

'Hello, boy.' He fondled the dog's snout the way Hero liked him to.

Alec feared he was 'coming over funny' as his old nurse-maid would say. *Or is this what hope feels like?*

He went from mirror to wardrobe to window. Warmed – and agitated – by the green shoot of rapport with Pamela. It was so long since they were kind to one another.

Hope was strong stuff, to be handled with caution. 'Old Pamela's not so bad,' he told Hero. 'Not so bad at all.'

Doris stirred brown food in a black pot.

Her mind snagged on a nail. Stuck. Not on the new calves she'd watched taking their first steps, nor the sacks of seed potatoes she'd upended into the hopper.

It was Irene she thought of as she stirred, her wooden

spoon making circles in the stew as the family gathered from all points of the compass, lured to the kitchen by the rich, storied aroma.

'So ... Nanny likes to boast that she and Irene read the Bible together,' said Doris thoughtfully.

'Not this again, love.' Dan pulled a shirt from a pile of ironing that smelled like morning. Pink, clean, he was fresh from his pre-dinner scrub. 'You're the billeting manager, not mother hen. I'm more concerned about this one, here.' He jerked a thumb.

Wanda was asleep at the table, head on her arms.

'What? Nothing.' Wanda jerked upright. She had been pressing primroses with Christine when she flopped, mid-press.

'This week's been too much for her,' said Doris. Wanda had been lent out to Valley Farm. 'Until you get another bike, your work's here, got that, Wanda?'

'Yes, Boss. They offered me a lift back, but I missed it.'

'They should've made sure.' Small bits of love, floating around, it all added up; *we have to take care of one another*. If there were no mother hens clucking about, where would it all end?

'Christine, want to write the address for me?' Wanda slid tiny yellow flowers wrapped in damp blotting paper into an envelope. 'My mum loves primroses.'

The flowers were an act of faith that Wanda's mother would be there to receive them. Bath was still being pummelled. Nobody picked up the phone in Wanda's house.

350

'Why,' asked Wanda, 'can't Nanny be frank about Irene not being able to read? She should send her to Arkwright Hall so the child can learn. Nanny's holding her back. But why?'

'Irene might be teased about it. Children can be cruel,' said Doris.

'Flipping cheek!' said Christine.

'Don't say flipping,' said Doris.

'You mean, Nanny's *protecting* Irene by lying that she can read?' said Wanda. 'A woman who tells everyone children are her life?'

Christine was righteous. 'A lie is a lie is a lie.'

'All right, Saint Christine, lay the table,' said Doris. She was conscious of how humble the cloth was, how plain the crockery. Doris imagined Wanda's home to be a wonderland of quality goods. *If it's still standing.* She determined to give the girl the biggest portion of stew.

A jug of milk was put on the table. Wanda fetched glasses. Christine kicked Phil as he took his seat and said, 'Why doesn't *he* ever help?'

'I'm a boy,' he said. 'In case you didn't notice.'

'Manners,' said Doris, absentmindedly. She couldn't find the salt. Who had moved the salt? What fiend would be capable of such an outrage? 'I mean, now that we know Beacham's been in prison . . .' Furnivall Manor was still on her mind.

'What was his crime?' Wanda was no longer drowsy. She was engaged.

'Not sure.'

'Violence.' Wanda *was* sure. 'That man's angry.' She stood

and stared into the middle distance as chairs were pulled out and milk poured.

'Sit, Wanda, love,' said Dan.

Wanda didn't sit. 'Boss,' she said, slowly. 'If Irene can't read she can't write, correct?'

'Well, yes.'

'So, how did she write that offensive bidding prayer?'

Wanda and Doris regarded each other.

Doris tore off her apron, pushed at Dan. 'Up, you. We're going to Furnivall Manor.' To Wanda she said, 'How did I not spot that? Someone else wrote that prayer to make Irene look bad.'

'Someone,' said Wanda, 'who wants Irene out of the house.'

'Someone,' said Doris, 'with a criminal record.'

'Ooh,' said Christine.

'Dan!' Her husband's hesitancy frustrated Doris. 'Come on, we've got to get Irene out of there before that swine hurts her.'

'If you want my opinion,' began Dan.

'We don't,' said Doris, just as the door flew open.

A farmhand from a neighbour's smallholding said, without preamble, 'Mister, you're to come. We're losing a cow.'

Proud of his reputation as 'next best thing to't veterinary', Dan went out after him.

Doris didn't complain. Cows represented investment, time, *pride*. She wrapped the men a hunk of bread and dripping.

'He's taking the truck,' said Wanda, alarmed.

Unhappy, reluctant to say it, Doris said, 'Irene'll have to wait until tomorrow, love.'

'Or will she?'

Two beams of light travelled across the kitchen wall. Wanda pushed aside the gingham curtain. An engine dwindled.

In the driver's seat, Mr Bigtime was cheesed off. He had flowers, he had a box of chocolates, and he had big plans to take Wanda somewhere remote. He did not want to transport her matronly, be-hatted landlady cross-country through a blackout on a wild goose chase.

'In that case,' said Wanda, handing the chocolates and flowers to a delighted Christine, 'we have no choice but to commandeer this vehicle. Get in, Boss.'

Doris got in.

The apron Agnes wore was nothing like the one she used to wear in service at Woodbine Cottage. That had been starched and itchy; this one was striped and loud, with a Latina ruffle at the collar.

Working by moonlight, she re-potted her new busy lizzie – or was it an impatiens? – in the greenhouse she had reorganized, clearing away all the dusty dead things Denholm's mother had left behind.

The busy lizzie's leaves were pleasing, dark green with an elegant point. She took great care, folding in compost she had made herself from grass cuttings and vegetable peelings. She patted down the earth around the stalk. She wiped the pot.

The inherited earring, a milky opal button, sat in one ear. In the other ear she wore its partner, stolen from Jane's bedroom many years earlier.

Who could wear one earring? Agnes had snatched it to deprive Jane of it. Bitterness. Envy. They both had their part to play in Agnes's part-time career as Lady Thief.

You knew I took it, Miss Jane. Agnes looked about for the best spot for the busy lizzie. The impatiens. Whatever it was.

You knew, Miss Jane, yet you didn't sack me.

The police might have been called. Agnes would have never lived it down.

She slapped her hands together. Rich, brown dirt flew off them. Did the legacy mean she was forgiven? *Or is Miss Jane punishing me in her mild way?*

A plaintive cry from inside the house. Denholm was up on his hind legs and conjecturing about dinner.

'Hold your horses!' called Agnes. She looked out at the garden and remembered.

She had always known of Miss Jane's romantic ambitions for Denholm. Jane had daydreamed the doddery bachelor into a Prince Charming, hope beating in her desiccated breast that he would ask for her hand.

Prince Charming didn't notice Jane or her hopes. He noticed very little. When Denholm did propose, it was to Jane's maid. He still assumed the proposal was his idea, when in fact it had been the zenith of a pyramid of carefully plotted glances and lures and nudges. There had been an expertly timed kiss outside The Bull that almost blew the top of his head off.

I stole you, too, Denholm, thought Agnes.

*

354

Mr Bigtime turned out to be Mr Smalltime.

He refused to drive any further than the gates of Furnivall Manor. He asked Wanda how would it look if it got into the press, him, a titan of business, embroiled in provincial ballyhoo?

'How will it look,' asked Doris, getting out of the low-slung car with some difficulty, 'if me and Wanda get murdered and the titan of business didn't lift a finger?'

'Have this back.' Wanda threw the fine gold bracelet that now felt like a handcuff onto the passenger seat.

He sped off then, but not before Wanda thumped the car's gleaming bonnet. Her face was full; they would never mention the cowardly Mr Bigtime again.

Doris led the charge in her wider-fit shoes, handbag over her arm. An obsidian block in the darkness, the manor revealed itself as a lack, not a presence. A house-shaped hole cut into the night.

'We don't leave until we have answers,' said Doris.

'Too damn right,' said Wanda. She added, 'Sorry, Boss.' Doris hated to hear women curse.

When Doris made to knock at the servants' entrance, Wanda simply pushed the door and strode in. 'Hello!' she called, loud, confident, not to be ignored.

Beacham appeared in the gloom. 'Bit late for visitors,' he said.

'I'm here on official business,' said Doris, her handbag in front of her like a shield.

'Official snooping business.'

Wanda said, 'She has every right.' She stood like a bucca-neer, hands on her hips, legs apart.

'Who the hell are you?'

'She's with me,' said Doris. 'I want to see Nanny and I want to see Irene.' She stared Beacham down. 'Now.' She added 'Please' because even storming soldiers should be polite.

'Now look,' began Beacham, as Wanda let out an exasper-ated 'For heaven's sake' and barged past him, calling 'Nanny! Irene!' as she went.

Doris followed, blood rushing in her ears. This was tres-pass, surely? Beacham ran backwards, hands out, trying to contain them like a snapping sheep dog, but they were on the black and white floor of the soaring hall in seconds.

'Get out!' he shouted. He ran up to Doris, stopping short of her, as if her mackintosh was a moat. 'Before something happens,' he said.

Thin and straight as a pencil, Nanny shot down the stairs. Her hands kneaded one another, her face all concern. 'Irene's in bed.' A battle seemed to go on in her face for control of her expression. 'What's gannin' on, Doris?'

'I need to see Irene.' Doris endeavoured to smuggle her suspicions past Beacham to Nanny. *I'm here for* you! she wanted to say.

'Is her room up here?' Wanda was already halfway up the carved stairs.

'Please don't!' called Nanny.

Doris whispered in her ear, 'It's all right, we know what's going on,' and bustled up after Wanda.

Beacham stayed down in the hall. 'I wouldn't,' he said, 'if I were you.'

Nanny was shaking. 'I told you, Irene locks herself in.'

'We both know that's not true.' Doris saw terror announce itself on Nanny's features – a real emotion at last. 'I promise you, this ends tonight.'

Even as she said it, Doris felt the folly of pitting herself physically against Beacham. She felt his animosity climb the stairs behind her, grab at her ankles. The long corridor was dead, dusty, the old house's ornate details obscure in the moonlight, and full of menace.

'This is the only one that's locked.' Wanda had tried all the doorknobs. 'Irene!'

Nothing from within.

'The lass causes havoc,' said Nanny, her face in deep shadow, 'if she's allowed to roam.'

'We know about Beacham,' whispered Doris. 'You don't have to cover for him anymore.' As if she had summoned him, Beacham appeared at the far end of the dark hallway.

His outline grew as he came closer. Unhurried. Sure of his prey.

'You stop right there, you,' said Doris. That tone worked with children and farmhands, but not with Beacham.

Wanda stepped in front of Doris just as Beacham raised his hand.

Doris didn't flinch. 'Don't you touch my Wanda!' she shouted.

Beacham held up a key. He unlocked the door, and stepped back. 'Enjoy yourselves,' he said.

'Oh, lad.' Nanny sank to her knees, face in hands. 'What've you done?'

The door squeaked open on old hinges and the room revealed itself in silvered shapes, bit by bit. An empty bed. A hanging figure dangling by the window, its red flash of hair like a struck match.

'Irene!' Doris was at the child's legs, hoisting them. She felt helpless, a speck in the universe, like she had felt holding her mother's hand the night she lost her. 'Wanda! Quick!'

But Wanda didn't help. She pointed to a corner. 'She's here, Doris!'

Doris sprang away from the hanging legs. They were not human. It was Sukie the doll who hung there.

Irene crouched, barefoot, in a long white nightdress. No emotion. No nothing. 'Help me,' she said. She said it without inflection, no rise and fall. She said it as if she didn't expect to be heard.

Wanda held out her hands and hoisted Irene to her feet.

Doris bent over her, all the while tracking Beacham, who filled the room like a bad smell and had gone to Nanny.

'Don't you lay a hand on that woman,' said Doris. She and Wanda manouevred Irene from the room. She held out a hand to Nanny. 'Come with us. You're safe now.'

The expression on Nanny's face, caught perfectly by the moon stepping out from behind a cloud, was not what Doris expected.

Beacham said, 'You think you know it all, Doris Archer, but you never really listen. When I said she was peculiar I didn't mean the girl. I meant my wife.'

'What wife?' Doris was unnerved.

'Bairns are my life,' said Nanny. 'You've been a bad, bad girl, haven't you, little one?' Sorrowful. Resolved.

Irene shrank behind Wanda, trying to diminish herself.

But Nanny wasn't talking to Irene. 'Bad little Doris,' she said.

Beacham moved then, making good on the menace he promised. He held onto Nanny, hard and fast like a policeman. 'Get the girl away from here,' he said.

They didn't need to be asked twice.

MAY

Pamela watched the women, a herd of them, approach the steps. She waved from the French window. She would be erect, correct; *I must not let them see how I feel.*

The ladies waved back. Magsy and Mrs Endicott lagged behind, heads bobbing as they fulminated – in ladylike fashion – about the lack of justice for that nice Archie.

'I had a cousin who was, well, like Archie,' said Mrs Endicott. 'Invaluable at debutante balls. One could trust him with the girls, you see; no hanky-panky.'

'To think Stan got clean away with it. I'd happily swap Stan for a coachload of *homosexuals.*' Magsy considered herself awfully modern for using the term. 'It's a disgrace.'

'God pays debts without money.' Mrs Endicott resurrected a saying from her youth.

'Hmm. Sometimes the Almighty might need a little help.'

Pamela clapped from the house, hurrying them along. She knew the committee would be hard to manage today, all of them keen to gabble about Jane's will. The last reading, only a month away, would solve the riddle and see Woodbine Cottage handed to Blanche, or to Stan, or to Mrs Endicott, or – heaven forfend – the Pargetters. Or maybe some other Ambridgian would come up on the rails to claim the prize.

I don't care. Pamela cared about nothing except hearing Kos's voice, seeing the candle burn in the window. He was gone, disappeared, without a word to her.

'Welcome, ladies!' They were on the terrace now.

Where is he? she thought. It was foolish to imagine that a man like Kos would share his every move. Pamela knew he held a wilderness of feeling and experience she couldn't be party to.

It hurt, though, to be locked out.

'Yes, Mrs Endicott, a perfect day, as you say!' Pamela stood back to let them in.

He's trying to find a back door into flying. Kos would not rest. He was driven. She adored him for that; she feared what it meant for them.

'What's that?' Pamela made Mrs Endicott repeat herself.

'I said, don't be fooled by sunshine, my dear Pamela. My parlour maid was once hospitalized after a reckless donkey ride on Paignton beach.'

AMBRIDGE WOMEN'S COMMITTEE
MEETING MINUTES

Date: 1st May, 1942
At: Lower Loxley
Chairwoman: Pamela Pargetter
Present: Frances Bissett, Emmaline
Endicott, Blanche Gilpin, Agnes Kaye,
Connie Horrobin, Susan Grundy.
Absent: Doris Archer
Minutes: Frances Bissett

1. Pamela asked 'Where is Doris? She is
always here she is our Rock of Gibraltar.'
Wanda said 'You can ask her yourself
when you see her' which I myself thought
quite pert.

2. Pamela said we must come up with a
theme for the village pageant in July.
Wanda suggested Lady Godiva. Mrs E *laughed*.
Connie put herself forward for role
of Lady G.

3. Mrs E suggested The Garden of Eden
and Blanche said 'Are you getting at me
about Woodbine's garden?' and Mrs E said
'No dear I am not but it is sad to see
poor Jane's flowers so neglected' and

Blanche said 'Don't call her poor Jane' and left the meeting just like that.

4. Pamela said it was Blanche's prerogative to come and go as she pleased and could we please get on.

5. I myself asked Pamela if she was quite well as she seemed downcast and she said 'Thank you for your kind concern dear Frances but I am tiptop.'

6. Mrs E asked for a glass of water and almost swooned in the heat. But not quite.

7. Pamela asked for a volunteer for the church flower-arranging rota. Pamela volunteered Susan. Agnes said 'She is just a kid she does not know her sweet peas from her phlox' and Pamela said could we please get on.

8. I myself showed the committee a bottomless barrel I had myself found and suggested it might make a charming and witty flower container for St Stephen's. There was not much interest but Mrs E said she would 'see what she could do' and offered to take it home with her.

9. Mrs E said 'If somebody with a big brain would just examine the clues in poor I mean dear Jane's will I am sure they

would discover that Woodbine will go to
Borchester Cats' Home.'

   10. Agnes said 'No it will go
to Blanche.'

   11. Connie said 'The clues will
spell Blair. Me and my Stan will be on
easy street.'

   12. Agnes said 'If the police don't do
him for beating up our lovely Archie' and
Connie said 'Do you want a fight' and
Pamela said 'Please ladies.'

   13. A man passed the window and we all
looked because Pamela looked and Magsy
said 'Oh it's that nice Polish gent'
and Pamela said 'Oh is it' and then she
interrupted me myself halfway through a
sentence and said 'Why don't we call it a
day ladies?'

As the committee dispersed, Doris was at her own kitchen table with her own husband, and very glad she was of them both.

'So,' she said, tapping the table for emphasis, 'they're wed, those two.'

'Beacham and Nanny? Why lie?' Dan's kind, tired face spoke of a sleepless night.

If he keeps interrupting I'll never burp out this story, thought Doris. 'Because of his criminal record. Had to cover their tracks. Employers might recognize their real names – Michael and Edna Styles – from a kidnapping case, years ago.'

Beacham had gone into detail about their past, clearly relieved to unburden himself. Doris and Constable Jenkins had been hammered into their seats by a tale which had come out fast and perfect, as if rehearsed many times.

'They never had children, you see. Beacham knew Nanny – I keep using their fake names! – couldn't cope with having a family. She's always been a little off, he said, *different*.' Doris crawled along the story like an ant on a crack in the pavement; it felt so much bigger than her. 'They were in service, cushy jobs by all accounts, big house in Edinburgh. Nanny got sick, took to her bed, in an unused room so as not to disturb her hubby. Meanwhile the papers were full of a baby took, pram and all, from outside an ironmongers. Beacham guessed, of course. He broke down the door, found the little scrap in there with Nanny. Emaciated, but clean and dressed up. Dying, really, although the poor cherub recovered.'

'Beacham took the blame?'

'Exactly. Said he did it. Endured a big trial, went to jail. Came out five years later and he and Nanny, or Edna, took on new names, became brother and sister, and went back into service.'

The Brookfield cockerel looked in at the back door. Glen flopped onto the mat. Life went on as the peculiar tale spread out over Doris's scrubbed table.

'He insisted on one rule. They never take a position in a

house with children. The new folk at Furnivall Manor, they're elderly, apparently, all their family grown up. Quite infirm.'

'So why did they ask you for an evacuee, love?'

Doris sighed. 'They didn't. Those letters weren't from the owner.'

'Oh Lord, they were from *her*? This Edna?'

'Yes.' Inquisitive Doris with her high standards and her attention to detail had delivered Irene into the embrace of a disturbed, deluded woman. 'Nanny should've been *helped*, Dan, but her husband couldn't bear to think of strangers looking after her, locking her up. He meant well.'

'Hmm. Fella should've spoken up when he saw little Irene getting maltreated.'

That was undeniable. The hand-sewn frocks disguised a famished body. 'She didn't want Irene to grow, or change, so she barely fed her. Treated her like a dolly, and treated her dolly like a naughty child.' Sukie, the little girl's double, had been punished. Locked up. Hanged. 'She never laid a hand on Irene, just smothered her with attention. Tried to make Irene call her "Mummy" and disciplined Sukie when Irene refused.'

'The kid has guts.'

'She does.' The kid was upstairs, sharing a bed with Christine, neither of them charmed by the arrangement. 'The stealing – that was lies. The bad behaviour, the locking herself in, all made up by Nanny so we'd give Irene a wide berth. Irene's natural haughtiness and her tendency to lash out at the likes of Maisie Horrobin backed up Nanny's story. But all along they were play-acting day in, day out, a fantasy of perfect family life in an empty, remote house. Nanny dominated Irene. Didn't break her, I hope, but the child couldn't see past her and was too frightened to speak up.'

Doris hesitated. 'Irene tried to tell me, Dan. And I didn't listen. No, no, she *did*.' She knew he would try to play it down. 'The sleeping on the floor. The silence. The stares. She was asking for help without words. And I ignored her.'

'Love, you can't take responsibility for everyone.'

'I didn't listen, Dan. Not even to Beacham, when he turned up at Lower Loxley and begged me to take Irene off his hands.'

'Beggars belief how a scrawny little piece like Nanny had that big lunk of a man under her thumb.'

'There's more than one way to skin a rabbit, Dan. She had him frightened of what she could do, of losing her again. He's broken, too, in a way that fits perfectly with her jagged edges.'

'I should've been there, love.' Dan looked miserable. 'Shouldn't have left it to you and young Wanda.'

'How were you to know?' And besides, Wanda was as staunch a wingman as Doris could want. For all the differences of birth and education, the women were alike in all that mattered. They had done this thing together, then put Irene to bed together.

And then they'd cried together.

Pamela knew the drill. She must walk the ladies as far as the edge of the terrace and take a civil leave of them. 'No,' she told Connie, with as much graciousness as she could muster, 'there's no payment for attending committee meetings.'

'What a racket!' Connie said loudly she'd been 'taken for a ride' and would not be back.

'Marvellous,' murmured Pamela, not listening, scanning the chaps on the terrace for Kos. 'Bye bye now,' she said to nobody in particular as she spotted him, bending to shake Terence's hand.

She wanted to leap on him – Pamela had never leapt on anyone – but she made her way across the sun-warmed flagstones with careful casualness. She wouldn't waste her breath asking where he had been; he would be uncommunicative, like all men when women asked them the important questions.

The heron was back.

Mrs Endicott saw it first, and put her hand on Magsy's arm, just as the lady tripped over something in the grass.

'What's this?' Magsy looked down at a pair of trousers. Then she gasped as she took in the bird.

The heron was an ethereal being. Too exotic for Borsetshire.

'It's like an angel,' breathed Mrs Endicott. She held the rotting barrel so beloved of Frances Bissett to her chest, and tears stood, starry, in her eyes. She jumped when Magsy poked her, and followed her friend's line of sight.

'Now, *that*, my dear, is no angel.'

They watched as Stan, trouser-less, waded stealthily across the pond.

'What's he up to?' Mrs Endicott rarely got cross. She was cross now, however; the juxtaposition of exquisite nature and mendacious humanity was too much for her. 'Is Stan planning to trap our heron?'

'And eat it!' Magsy clutched her pearls. 'Or perhaps he imagines he can sell it!'

Stan stretched out his arms. The heron stood, unwitting and impassive, within reach.

Mrs Endicott clapped her hands. Once. Loudly. The heron beat his wide wings and took off.

Stan raised his fist. 'You interfering old—'

The ladies didn't hear whatever title he gave them. Mrs Endicott squeaked, 'Run, dear!' and Magsy did just that, stooping first to sweep up Stan's trousers.

They waddled and laughed and needed two sherries apiece to regain their equilibrium. 'Ooh!' said Mrs Endicott, eyes wide. 'I dropped dear Frances's barrel!' And they both laughed some more.

It was dark in the pantry.

Blanche took down each box, each jar, and her lacquered nails scrabbled at the back of each shelf. The heart-shaped box was somewhere in Woodbine Cottage; in dreams she felt its moulded velvet against her hand. It was ticket, passport, escape hatch. It would allow her to snatch something back from Jane's funeral pyre, a conflagration that threatened to burn Blanche to the ground.

Up on a high shelf sat a large metal container easily big

enough to contain the pink box. On tiptoes, on a stool, Blanche had her fingertips on it when there was a rap at her door.

'Blast you, whoever you are.' Blanche got down, opened the door and said, 'Yes, what?' to the young woman on her step.

Petite, bonny, the visitor said, 'I'm Monica.'

'I'm very glad for you.' Blanche shrugged, cross, before remembering. 'Monica Jackson? Archie's Monica?' She took in the feared sister. A small woman, in a dress that matched her hat that matched her handbag. *She's shaking.* Nerves? Fury? 'Archie's gone away. Didn't say where.' Blanche loved to lie; lying to protect Archie was even more fun.

'No, no, I'm here.' Archie came up behind Monica with a basket on his arm. 'Hiya, Mon.' He gave the basket to Blanche. 'I'll take it from here.'

In the pantry, the container was found to hold only a family of affronted weevils.

In gumboots, with a pail and a wide brush, Doris cleaned the cows' winter quarters.

The farm cycle of dirt and cleanliness never rested, like its companions life and death, work and growth. From her perch on the wheel of life, Doris had a grand view, but no time to savour it.

Brookfield was solid; she did her best to believe in its durability. Worry gnawed like lingering sickness; money worries were the most pernicious of all. It felt shallow – *It's only money!* – but the grubby stuff underpinned her life in a way unthinkable just a few years ago. Doris feared debt. She feared the breach of the sacramental contract that bound her and Dan to the farm.

That morning, over his second breakfast of a post-dawn slice of bread Doris had made herself – never quite as good as her mother's – Dan had said he didn't like the look of one of the cows. When pressed by his wife, who was feeding six people and trying not to trip over Mother Cat and keeping an eye on a pig's head boiling on the stove, all he could offer was that the animal had a 'funny look in its eye'.

'The cows are *fine*,' she had said, but now she reconsidered. Dan was a nonchalant man. He understated. They could not afford sickness in the herd.

Walter blocked the sunlight. A good worker, happy to help out a neighbour, he was handy to have around, even if he did keep holding her up, as he did right now.

'Hear that cuckoo, Doris? Remember the rhyme? In April come he will. In May he sings all day. In June he changes his tune. In July away he will fly. And in August go he must!'

'Very nice.' Doris dragged the stern broom across the sopping floor. What if, in August, go *she* must? They had all heard of farms collapsing with the same suddenness as the yard yawned open this time last year. 'If you've finished, Walter, Wanda might welcome your help hoeing out the thistles.'

A shriek from the house. Irene had found her voice, and it was a loud voice. She and Christine bickered, even though Doris had had a word with her daughter about her Christian duty to share her bed and her books and the affections of Mother Cat. The girls were not natural playmates.

Doris knew how saplings could be stunted by lack of sunlight, so now, shamed by her readiness to believe Nanny's sleight of hand, she bestowed the sunlight of attention on Irene. The top of the milk. The crispiest rasher.

Only those who knew Monica Jackson well would know she had been crying.

Escorting her to the bus stop, Archie knew her very well indeed, and he was the one who had made her cry.

The tubs outside The Bull cried out for compliments in their showy pink regalia. 'Lovely display, Bob,' said Archie.

'Nowt to do with me.' Bob was rolling a barrel past the flowers. 'Some crazy bugger waters them at night.'

'You don't say!' Archie hustled Monica past the inn, and whispered, 'Please don't cry, love.'

He told her, back in Blanche's parlour, that he couldn't apologize for who he was. Archie was gentle about it; explained it would be like asking a cat to apologize for being a cat. 'It can't help being a cat and there's nothing wrong with being a cat.' He chose cats because Monica loved their moggy, even when it tore her nylons.

Monica had cried more when Archie told her there was no way he'd come home to live under his father's roof. 'I wouldn't expect you to live your life in disguise, Mon.'

She had conceded, with a voice dredged from her depths, that she couldn't expect that of Archie, either.

So many tears. Archie had listened to her, but had not held her, nor promised to make it up to her. He had given Monica false hope in the past; it was, they both knew, the cruellest path he could take.

They were almost at the bus stop. 'Only five minutes to wait. If it's on time. Which'd be a miracle.'

They laughed unconvincingly together. Monica blew her nose. They stood in ashes; whatever they had been was razed to the ground.

Archie felt her carnivorous gaze on him. She was setting his face in her memory. Her own face was lovely to him, composed and pretty, with the natural neatness of an animal.

Then Archie saw him.

Since the St Valentine's Day dance Archie had become adept at nipping across the road or backing into a doorway when he encountered him. Or even just some man who looked vaguely like him.

Unable to desert Monica, Archie was on a collision course with his attacker.

I won't be able to take it if he knocks me down in front of Monica.

Archie's whole body remembered hitting the ground, spitting blood. He couldn't hear what Monica was saying because of the white noise in his ears.

Eyes down. Archie must *not* witness the thwarted masculinity in the chap's eye, because that was what got him punched back in February.

They drew level with one another. *He didn't recognize me*, thought Archie.

Ted sauntered past, hands in his pockets.

*

The chaps' drawing room reminded Pamela of the wood where she walked with Kos. The dark furniture of the trees resting on the colourful carpet of wildflowers.

Terence took a martini from her and spoke over her head. 'Where'd you get to the past couple of days, Kos old boy? We needed a warm body to play doubles.'

'I was not here,' said Kos.

'Well, we know *that*,' laughed Terence.

When Kos refused a martini, Terence called, 'Are you mad?' after him as he left the room. Terence worshipped Pamela's way with gin and vermouth, not to mention her sophisticated appreciation for ice. 'Evening,' he said to his buddies in the corner, strolling over to rubberneck at their card game.

Dodgy said, his teeth clenched around a cigar and a spectacularly bad hand of cards in his grasp, 'Bet you Kos was down in London, trying to get himself OK-ed for flight.'

'Someone needs to tell him,' said Terence, 'that the outcome of the war doesn't rest entirely on his shoulders.'

'Isn't that rather marvellous, though?' Pamela was languid. 'Surely nobody would fight if they didn't feel that way?'

Alec looked up from his cards. 'I don't pretend I matter in this mad mosaic.' He put down a queen of hearts. 'But we must all do our bit.'

'Our bit,' drawled Pamela. 'Your bit. My bit. What do all these bits add up to?' She smiled at Alec as she said it; their rapprochement, so unexpected, should be nurtured. She knew he felt second-rate bumbling along with the Home

Guard. She knew he longed to escape into war, like Kos. 'Although, darling, you do a highly commendable bit, I must say.'

'Hear, hear, sir,' said Terence, who had been informed that he must convalesce another month at Lower Loxley, and was vastly relieved that his own bit consisted of playing tennis and getting sozzled on Pamela's martinis.

'You know how women are,' said Archie. He and Blanche were discussing Monica.

'No, I don't, not really.'

They sat, elbows on the table, in the debris of dinner. It had been delicious, wrought from a tiny cut of meat Archie described as 'Arse-end of pork'.

'She's changed.' Archie's quiff stood at half-mast. 'Her points are all filed down. She's *nice*. Monica hasn't been nice for years.'

He had already admitted his fib to Blanche, who had been *thrilled* to hear that Monica was not Archie's sister but his wife. 'Second case of it in the village,' she had said. 'It's like buses; you wait for one counterfeit sibling to turn up, and two come along at once.'

He'd told her everything. How he'd married Monica within a month of meeting her in a desperate attempt to 'cure' himself. 'I was dishonest, simple as that, doll. I made her happy, but it wasn't real. So, on our first wedding anniversary, I came clean. It wasn't pretty.'

Monica had spat venom. Orated like a member of the

House of Lords at their kitchen table about how Archie 'revolted' her, how 'unnatural' he was. She took his father the news on greased soles, and he hit Archie so hard he walloped any dewy-eyed belief in family life right out of the boy. That night scarred him in more ways than one.

'I didn't run out on her.' Archie stressed that point more than once. 'I told Monica she could have a divorce, start again with some man who'd love her like she deserves to be loved. As she put it, someone normal.'

'Normal?' Blanche wrinkled her nose at the very idea.

'I love you, you bonkers old broad,' said Archie.

Nobody had ever told Blanche they loved her. Not even little Blabs had heard those words. It felt like sugar on her tongue. It felt alien.

'She went to kiss me as the bus came.'

'Yikes.'

'Yikes indeed. I pulled away.' *Rudely*. Archie wished he'd let Monica touch him. He knew how it felt to crave softness and have it denied.

'Quite right, too. Good old Monica wasn't in the mood for kissing when she squealed to your father. When she called you vile names.'

'She still won't divorce me.' Archie groaned. 'Says she'll wait for me. Like I'm getting over a cold.'

'The silly piece loves you.'

'Monica's not a silly piece, Blanchie. She's a woman, and I'm her husband. I'm not sure that she really does love me. It's more about reputation.' Archie had seen up close how vital respectability was to his family. They valued it over honesty or kindness; they drew blood over it.

Most of the family news Monica brought was already forgotten. An aunt had a baby, a great-uncle died, him next door had been fined for breaking blackout.

It was the news about his little brother that would keep Archie up all night.

'Why'd our Tony join up?' Archie asked Blanche. 'Why'd they take him? He's obviously underage.'

'They're desperate,' said Blanche, who knew how they felt.

'And here I sit, warm and snug.'

'You're *getting away with it*, darling! Enjoy it.'

That was the trouble; all of a sudden Archie couldn't.

There were those who said they had witnessed it. Arthur Sweet was adamant he had stood back to let it pass. Those who were indoors and missed this Halley's comet of an event kicked themselves.

'I saw 'im, all right,' said Arthur, smug. 'Stan Horrobin passed me, large as life, holding a barrel around his middle, his two skinny wet legs sticking out like knitting needles and his face like a slapped bum.'

The vicar would hate to hear it said, but there were two places of worship in Ambridge, and on Sundays many paid homage to both.

From St Stephen's to The Bull, they trod a well-worn path, like cattle strolling home from pasture.

Talk was much the same in the church porch as the low-beamed inn.

'Reverend,' said Magsy, 'we're all praying that the bleeding heart and the lady orchid and the azalea and the busy lizzie point to spelling out "Blabs".'

'Of course, dear lady.' Henry liked saying 'dear lady': it hit, he felt, all the right Man of God notes. 'We must implore the Almighty to send us an "S" at the fifth will reading.'

Meanwhile at The Bull, Stan stood as straight as he was able to after four pints and crowed. 'Admit it, good people of Ambridge! I'm the favourite. If you think an azalea's really a rhododendron and switch to Latin for impatiens, I'll soon be snug as a bug in a rug at Woodbine Cottage.'

'I still fancy Alec,' said Dan. 'That motto of his.'

'Blessed light reveals bountiful hope,' intoned the men together, much as they had recently said their prayers in church.

'Alec'll sell and give the proceeds to charity, you just watch.' Dan had great faith in his friend.

'Not him,' said Stan, slouching out, beer on his chin. 'Them toffs, they don't get rich by giving away their cash.'

Bob wondered out loud what Stan would do with such a windfall.

Mick Lister said, 'Drink hisself to death,' and there was some bountiful hope in his voice.

* * *

May is nature's Christmas morning, arms laden with gifts. The sap, the buds, the scent, the beetles so busy.

Cliff felt in tune with it all as he walked, tall and strong and *well*, to Arkwright Hall. He saw the metallic damselflies hover like air aces. He bit into an apple and its crunch was music.

Since he went back to work, Cliff had found new treasure at the hall. He had clicked into place, as if he was machine-made to fit in with the school, with the children. He was on a journey with them, and they made a little progress every day. The path would lead them to the company of books, to *Wuthering Heights*, to Hardy, to poems and adventure and solace.

He mattered.

Cliff was almost at the crossroads. If he timed it right he might bump into Lorna.

Lorna was part of the May, his May. Could it be true that she had become beautiful? That was daft; Lorna hadn't changed. *I just wasn't looking closely enough before.*

When Lorna looked at him, Cliff felt she saw him. The real Cliff, the one behind the flayed face. Her gaze was magical; it perfected him.

If only it could give him the courage he still lacked. The real Cliff was cowardly; he could never speak up and tell Lorna how he felt when he turned his good eye upon her and she opened out like a summer morning.

Doris and Dan stood over the little mess in their top field. It should have been a calf, but now it was something else. It had stopped growing, left its mother early. The unhappy cow stood to one side, head hanging.

Doris said, 'I sent Phil for the vet.'

They knew what the vet would say. The trouble had begun long before today.

'We should check for more misbirths in the grass, love. They'll infect the pasture, and the herd.'

Disease travelled fast. Especially this one, which, super-stitiously, they didn't name. Nothing was certain until the veterinary arrived with his bag of tricks.

A shout from Wanda in the corner of the field, where an oak stood guard. 'Another one here, Boss!'

If they were right – *And we are right*, thought Doris – Brookfield would be decimated. The time and love spent on the bloodline wouldn't matter one jot.

Brucellosis.

Always whispered, and always about other farms. Doris recalled shaking her head, saying, 'Those poor people.'

Paying for the treatment would mow them down like machine gun fire.

The thought of weapons always led her to Jack.

'And another one!' yelled Wanda.

Doris thought of Jack. She thought of debt. And she fondled the sad cow's ear.

'Tonight's the night!' Billy used the expression he'd read in comics. 'It's now or never!' That was another one. He tingled all over. He couldn't separate the excitement from the terror and didn't want to. He liked them both.

Still light when they set off for Quartershot Camp, the day had turned its back by the time they crossed into the wood. Above them the trees rustled and beneath them the soil murmured, the way it could if you bothered to listen. If you were small and already near the ground, like John.

He tied his scarf tighter. 'We do Lower Loxley first, remember,' he said.

'Get back!' Billy yanked him into cover.

The tramp of feet made them crouch. They watched that what's-his-name, the posh one, lead his Home Guard blokes past. One of them wore a Fair Isle instead of battledress.

'Coast's clear.' Billy heaved the sack over his shoulder, full of self-importance, as befitted the leader of a prison break.

By the time they reached Lower Loxley it was pitch black. They crouched again when Pamela appeared at a little round window, her face all moody.

That night's offering was a particularly fine one. John found it hard to part with.

Billy snatched it and laid it on the step, like the other tokens they'd left for Pamela. 'S'only a silly picture of a dog.'

John begged to differ; he felt it to be a particularly fine picture of an unusually nice dog. He had cut it out of the newspaper Connie balled up for the fire. 'D'you think these presents will ever make up for the ten bob we took?'

'Yeah, 'course.' Billy pulled him away. There was work to do.

*

Pamela thought the chaps' drawing room was empty as she fussed with the curtains, but Dodgy spoke from a wing chair.

'The days'll be longer soon, Pamela, after next month's solstice.'

'Backgammon, Dodgy?'

'Ra-*ther*!'

She went in search of the board, but in the hall she grabbed her coat and abandoned the mission. Dodgy was two drinks in and would forget about backgammon. And after all, 'Tonight's the night,' she said to herself as she tore to the back of the house.

A little way down from the mill gates stood Nance, shifting from foot to foot. It was wrong, what she was about to do, but she had agreed to it and so must see it through.

'Evening,' said Ted.

'Oh, flipping hell, Ted, didn't see you there.' The night delivered him with no warning.

'Bit nippy.'

'Not really.'

Down the road, two thin beams of light appeared.

'We never talk no more,' said Ted. 'I miss you, girl.'

'You ignore me, Ted!' Nance could have laughed at the injustice.

'They all know, so it's a bit, well, humiliating.'

'They all know what?' Nance gawped. 'You never told them about the barn?'

"'Course I bleedin' didn't.' Ted switched from shamefaced to nasty as if Nance had pressed a lever. 'Why would I tell folk you made a fool of me?'

The beams of light grew more intense, white slits in the dark.

'I didn't mean to,' said Nance. She wanted forgiveness. She knew she wouldn't receive it. 'It was a mistake, Ted.'

'Thank you *very* much.' Ted nodded at the car which waited, purring, with slitted hoods over the headlights. 'Better run along. Your old man's waiting.' He stressed *old*.

'Yes, my husband's waiting,' said Nance. She ran to the car.

'That chap need a lift?' asked Morgan. He rarely used the car for non-professional outings, but had made an exception for that night's late shift. Nance, with her ever-springy conscience, had felt guilty as she waited, like a black marketeer, for her ride home.

'He prefers to walk,' said Nance. They passed Ted with a cheerful note from the horn.

Nance leaned towards Morgan, as she always did. A pot pie awaited them at home. He would compliment it, as usual, and then, unasked, correct her efforts with the crossword, as usual. They might 'do it' later – she still found it hard to use the proper term – and he'd snore afterwards and she would lie there and think what a great man Morgan was for his age.

For any age.

*

The vet had a great deal to say, but Doris heard only the one word.

Brucellosis.

Luca waited, his exuberant hair hidden by a knitted hat, his hands together as if praying.

'What's that?' Billy pointed to the black armband over Luca's sleeve. 'Never seen that before.'

'Nothing.' Luca rolled it down and it dropped to the mud. 'You have it?'

They understood his question. They understood the lack of levity. *Tonight's the night.*

Reverently, Billy handed over the knife that, until one hour earlier, had lived in Stan's workshop.

No work went on in Stan's workshop, but it was a forbidden and protected place. There would be repercussions. The boys would confess, take the beating that would otherwise fall to Connie.

It was, they agreed, worth it.

'Got your outfit on?' said John.

'Yes. When I jump off lorry I take off camp clothes and underneath I am different.' They had brought the spoils of many Ambridge washing lines; Luca would leg it in the vicar's trousers. 'Do you know how to say goodbye in Italian?' Luca looked over his shoulder. Eleventh hour nerves.

'Nah!' laughed Billy.

'Arrivederci.'

Billy gave it a whirl, but John wouldn't say it. He unwound

his scarf. 'This is for you, Luca. Me mum made it.' It was more precious than myrrh.

Luca dragged it through the fence. He coiled it round his neck without a word. He turned away.

'Arrivathingy!' called John.

Luca waved, just once, but didn't turn around.

'He don't want to see us sad,' said Billy. He sounded unsure.

John stared after him. His neck felt cold where the scarf had sat.

Stooping, Billy used a stick to drag the black armband towards him through the fence. He wound it round his head. He saw something else in the dirt and panicked. 'Luca!' He didn't dare shout too loud, and their friend didn't reappear. He retrieved the photograph of Bruno and Vittorio with their granddad.

It was almost more than John could bear. It was sinking in that he had lost Luca, yet no puff of green smoke had delivered his dad. And now Luca was escaping without his precious photograph. 'Luca'll be so upset,' he whispered. 'He loves his boys.'

Lorna wasn't getting much in the way of conversation from Cliff, so she resorted to Stacey as they skirted the woods.

'Your master's very good to walk me home, isn't he, Stacey? And after helping me move the furniture, too. Quite the Sir Galahad.'

'Couldn't expect you to lug all those desks on your own.' Sir Galahad was gruff.

'This is me,' she said at a fork in the road. Smoke curled from the house in the trees.

'Lorna,' said Cliff, in a leading manner, so that both girl and dog turned expectant faces to him.

Lorna's glasses reflected the moon. He couldn't read her eyes. 'Yes?' She frowned. 'Cliff?'

'Don't frown,' he said. 'It's nothing bad. I just have something to say.' Cliff swallowed. 'It sounds ... Look, I'm no Hardy, Lorna, and I'm certainly not Emily Brontë.'

She kept frowning. 'Spit it out, Cliff,' she said.

'I'm never bored when I'm with you. Not for one second.'

She smiled, then. She was giddy, like a baby shown a bauble.

That worked wonders on Cliff's confidence. 'I think you're lovely. Like, *so* lovely, like your eyes are great, and your teeth, they're so *little*.'

Lorna threw back her head and laughed.

Stacey danced on the spot. She liked how this was going. Felt like they might break into a run.

'I'd love to kiss you.' Cliff rammed his hands into his pockets. 'But I can't ask that of you.' He pursed his lips. They had shut up shop. The window of confidence slammed shut.

'What if *I* kiss *you*?' said Lorna.

She put her hands on his shoulders and stood on tiptoe. Their mouths had not quite met when she whispered, 'I've never kissed a boy before.' Lorna put her lips to his skin, to the tortured flesh around his mouth. She travelled tenderly, taking her time, all over his face, sanctifying all she touched.

When she got back to his lips, Cliff's arms sprang around her and he pressed his mouth to hers.

They swayed. It was all a bit messy.

'We need to practise,' said Lorna, in a soft, secret voice she hadn't known she owned. 'If that's all right with you, Heathcliff.'

'Fine with me, Cathy,' he said, and Cliff bent his head into the next kiss, a move he'd seen in the movies.

It worked. It *really* worked.

'Yuk!' said the night.

The lovers sprang apart.

Billy said it again. 'Yuk! What's *wrong* with you, Cliff?'

John averted his eyes. He would not be party to Cliff's shame. Kissing a girl. And Miss from school, at that.

'Nothing's wrong with me!' Cliff's bad side was towards them. It smouldered where Lorna had kissed it. His good eye was on Lorna and never wanted to leave her.

She walked away backwards, dropping his hand at the last possible moment. 'See you tomorrow,' she said.

'It gets worse,' said Billy. 'Look at their stupid faces.'

After Lorna turned off the track, Cliff fell into step with the boys. He was jaunty; Stacey was still hopeful about that run, and hopped about their legs. 'Where's your scarf, John? You haven't taken it off since you got it.'

'Lost it,' mumbled John.

'That's a shame.' Cliff knew the scarf's provenance. 'What's this?' He took the piece of paper from Billy's hand.

'Hey, that's mine,' said Billy.

Cliff studied the image. Smiled. 'What're you two doing with a clipping of Mussolini and his children?'

'No, that's ...' Billy couldn't reveal who it really was; tomorrow morning Luca's escape would be front page news up and down the land.

But John knew it wasn't a proper photograph. He had always known it was cut out from a newspaper and had never questioned it because the answer might spoil everything.

John couldn't pin down the moment when his belief had faltered.

Cliff gave it back. 'Not turning into little fascists, I hope?'

Billy pulled the black armband from his head and chucked it into the dark.

'You can say I told you so if you like.' Doris was mucky and worn out. They'd found and cleared up three separate little heaps of misfired life in the fields. She tipped milk into a saucepan to scald; the simple, gorgeous white stuff was suspect now, and must be boiled before use. 'You were onto this weeks ago, Dan, and I ignored you.'

'What good would saying I told you so do?'

'What now, Dan?'

Light-hearted, never-go-looking-for-trouble Dan said, 'Only wish I knew, love.'

Pamela stood at the foot of the steps that would take her to the room high in the folly.

The beaded bag hanging off her shoulder glistened in the

deep shadow. She could hear a conversation above her. Kos was not alone; one of the new intake of crocked pilots was with him. A Scot, vanilla-skinned and keen as mustard.

'That's a daring plan, Kos,' he was saying. 'And doomed, but you know that. Why sacrifice yourself like this? Those damn death camps are beyond our reach now, but we'll have a day of reckoning when the war's over.'

And then, the oddest noise. *Bip!* Short, exclamatory: both men laughed at it, and then they parted, like men did, with hearty back slaps.

Tonight's the night.

Pamela stepped back to let the visitor pass, then flew up the stairs. She caught her breath. A ghost stood in the candlelight. 'Mavis!' she said to the little Pekinese. She began to cry. Her nose ran.

'Darling, I want to make you happy, not tearful!' Kos thrust the dog at her. 'Not Mavis, no, this is Minko.' The dog was a little lion, flat-faced, paddling in mid-air. 'She's yours.'

'Minko.' Pamela took the dog, allowing it to lick away her salty tears and do irreparable damage to her careful maquillage.

'You like her?'

'I adore her.'

'Minko was my secret mission.' Kos kissed Pamela over the dog's domed head. 'I wasn't on war business. I was on Pekinese business.'

'Much more important than the silly old war!'

'When we are apart,' said Kos, who had stopped laughing, 'hold her, and think of me.'

'Are you going somewhere?' Pamela let the dog down. It let out a peremptory bark – *Bip!* – and tottered off self-importantly in its fur crinoline.

'One never knows.'

A mistress of deflection, Pamela recognized Kos's vague answer as a refusal to share. 'If you do plan to leave Lower Loxley, it won't be for anything official. They want you to stay put for the foreseeable future.'

'The RAF doesn't run my life.' Kos drew his finger down the satin bodice of her evening dress. 'That colour makes you look like a column of smoke.'

'It's just grey.'

'Ah.' Kos dropped his finger. Studied her. 'You have something to say. Something difficult.'

In her marriage Pamela had always been background music; it was strange to be heard so clearly. 'We have fun, don't we?' she asked. Bright. Controlled. And somehow nasty, which was not how she meant it. 'It's been the most enormous fun, but this moment had to come. This moment was wrapped up in the moment we began. Kos, you know we must part.'

She leaned back, as if falling. Pamela had planned to be in charge of herself and the conversation, to be warm but controlled, to let him know that she would never forget him, but to warn him that she was not to be persuaded.

All useless, she saw that now. She felt as if she had been pushed out of a plane. And slit her own throat beforehand.

'I love you,' said Kos, calmly. 'That matters, surely.'

'You don't love me.' Pamela was a knife, and she plunged into the middle of him. Yet they both stood, tall and cool, as their wounds gaped. 'And, Kos, I don't love you.'

A white lie, nothing more.

Pamela opened the glittering bag. 'Here. I felt these should return to you.'

'You insult me.' Kos accepted the folded letters with his mouth turned down. 'You can't have your letters back.'

'I only wrote you one.'

They both remembered what it said. *I am yours.* Kos looked into her eyes, pleading with her. He said, 'Yes, it's all been very one-sided.'

Oh God it hasn't, thought Pamela. She wanted to touch his scar. She wanted to heal it. She wanted to bar the door and live in that room with him. 'It's been ... lovely,' she said.

'Don't worry, I'll burn your note. There'll be no evidence for your husband to find.' Kos's English was bitterly perfect. 'I beg you, do not offer me my ring.'

It sat in her bag, waiting its turn. 'Be sensible, Kos. It's an heirloom.'

'It was given with sincerity. Melt it down for the war effort if it's too inflammatory to keep. Throw it away. I don't care.'

'You said it keeps you safe.'

'I am not superstitious.'

Pamela said, so quickly it sounded like nonsense, 'I choose duty and family. Because I have to. It's the way I'm made. You'll forget me.' *Please, please don't forget me!* 'What will you do?'

'I've found a way to serve Poland. I was about to tell you about it. Minko was to keep you company until I came back.' He looked down at the foolish dog. 'Now she's my parting gift.'

This plan will be just more delusion. And no longer her business. Pamela held out her hand. Kos stared as if he had never seen a hand before, and then shook it, once, firmly. 'Goodbye,' she said.

'Goodbye,' he said.

And because nothing intervened, no act of God, Pamela left the folly with Minko in her arms, and paused a few feet away to vomit in the dark.

She went in the back way to the house; Alec came in through the front; they met in the middle. He was folding up his Home Guard cap and she was feeling the contours of the eagle ring through the bag.

'I could murder a drink.' Alec registered Minko. 'Ah. Another Peke. Jolly, um, good.'

Behind him, Hero quailed.

'It's over,' said Pamela.

'Good,' said Alec. Then, 'Thank you.'

'Don't thank me. It should never have happened.'

'Well, that's . . . thank you, anyway.' Alec was shorn of attitude. He looked younger. Relieved and irresolute.

'I do understand you a little better now,' said Pamela. 'One good side effect, I suppose.'

'You've been crying.'

'I most certainly have *not*.'

He smiled, something released by her reaction. 'It's not a crime, darling.' He moved to her, his arms out.

'No.' Pamela stepped back. 'I have to ...' She turned away, but held her hand out behind her back, and when he took it, she squeezed. Her eyes on the wooden plaque – *Ostenditur spes alma lux beatissima* – she said, 'I want to try.'

'Yes.' Alec looked at the back of her neat head. 'Me too. Anything.' His enthusiasm surprised him. He assumed enthusiasm to be a thing of the past. Like bananas.

'For a while,' said Pamela, 'let's try commitment, no love affairs, a little kindness?'

'Yes.'

She rushed to the stairs. Alec didn't know if she heard him say, 'And maybe a little sacredness?'

She faltered on the stairs, as if struck, but he knew better than to offer help. She was suffering. She was letting go of love. Letting go of the rope and feeling it hurtle down a well.

Pamela has never felt that strongly about me. With years of practice under his belt, Alec was able to angle that fact so that it seemed like a good thing; when he inevitably went to war, and just as inevitably died there, it wouldn't cause great sorrow. He wouldn't leave much of a gap. Pamela and Gerald would mourn, and move on.

It's better that way. Alec was raised to avoid causing offence.

'Would you,' asked Pamela from the stairs, 'be so kind as to offer my regrets to the chaps, but I have the most awful head and really must lie down.'

She met herself in the dressing table mirror. The satin of

her dress was flecked with spittle. Her face was a hatchet inherited from her mother. She pushed cold cream over her features.

Pamela was glad to have finished it, even though she may have finished herself along with it. She could regress, now, to the real Pamela, the core Pamela, not the soft and lovely thing Kos described when he made love to her.

She needed bonds. Formal promises. She wanted to owe Alec fidelity; her recklessness terrified her. In all of this, Pamela was as hard on herself as she was on others.

There was relief, along with pain, in muting the colours of her life.

SUMMER

1942

My eyes were dazed by you for a little, and
that was all.

THOMAS HARDY
Tess of the D'Urbervilles

JUNE

Sheep must be sheared; hay must be made. The year turned so relentlessly that Doris suspected she might meet her old self coming back along it.

The sheep knew nothing of disease, or debt, or war. They didn't know that the farm, gentle magnificent Brookfield, had the air of a plague pit. Since the vet told Doris that brucellosis could leap from animal to human, she had taken to peering very closely at 'her' people. Now it was Wanda she studied, as Doris stood, arms folded, in the middle of the yard and the girl looped around her on her new bike.

'This is *heaven!*'

'Can't have you traipsing about the place morning, noon and night,' said Doris. 'Can't have you stranded.'

'You are so, *so*, kind.' Wanda pedalled harder. Glen chased her. Dan applauded from the kitchen window.

The bike was third-hand, but even third-hand bicycles made a difference to Doris's pile of pennies. Deep into emergency funds, with medicine swimming through the herd, the farm demanded more and more, like a blackmailer. 'That saddle's sideways,' said Doris, as Wanda braked with maximum drama.

'It's perfect.' Wanda left the bike on its side and stood awkwardly in front of Doris.

'Here now! Tears?' said Doris.

'I know how things are with the farm.' Wanda was choked with feeling. 'This bike is so generous.'

'Take good care of it, love.' Doris felt they understood each other, which was a right royal turn-up for the books. When Doris disapproved of Wanda's 'modern' habits it had been her only way of worrying about the girl. *No need*, thought Doris now. Wanda was as solid a young woman as she had ever met, trousers or no trousers.

Wanda remounted her lifesaver bike. The phone had rung in an empty house all those times she trudged to the vicarage to call her family. Mother, Grandmother, the dachschunds, all had decamped to a Civil Defence Centre. They were home now; her mother lamented, 'When will this war end so we can drag you back to civilization, Wanda?'

Off along the track, swifts wheeling above her, and the soft conversation of cows on the breeze, Wanda thought, *I'm at the centre of life right here, Ma!*

Doris called after her, shading her eyes to watch her dwindle into the shimmer. 'Don't go breaking any hearts today, y'hear?'

* * *

Almost, but not quite, late for the service, Billy followed his little brother into St Stephen's.

It was rare that John took the lead. Billy would happily dive into murky woodland or echoing caves, but the smell of polish and the snooty expressions of the plaster bishops made him wary of the church.

'Stay right there!' Frances stopped them both in their tracks. 'Look!' She pointed at the mud they'd brought in on their boots. 'On my lovely clean floor! Out! Wipe!'

John, already fearful of divine censure for his many and varied new sins, began to cry.

'Oh. Oh no.' For Frances, children were like the poor; necessary, but a mystery to her.

'Suffer the little children,' said the vicar, descending from the altar to take John's hand. 'To come unto me.'

'Vicar,' whispered John, when he'd recovered a little. 'D'you reckon my dad might be in Italy right now?'

'I highly doubt that, John. Don't worry about him. The Lord has his eye on us all.'

John shrank into a pew; that was what he was afraid of. *Jesus knows about the stealing.*

The congregation coughed out 'All Things Bright and Beautiful', Mrs Endicott bringing none of her St Valentine's Day brio to the serious matter of the organ. Archie turned the pages of the sheet music for her, dapper in a bow tie, with his hair greased.

Morgan and Nance were in their usual spot. Magsy had taken to sitting at the back. Frank, too, had changed his habits, and was among the Home Guard, who brought a whiff of tobacco to the more ecclesiastical scents.

Connie slumped beside Cliff, her head on his shoulder, new bruises opening out and changing colour on her gaunt face like a macabre sunset.

Cliff patted his mother's hand, and sang along, but throughout the service he watched the back of a brunette head. He enjoyed how Lorna's parting zigzagged at the back, how she hoicked up one shoulder when bored with Henry's homily. The blondish waterfall of Wanda's hair did not distract; Heathcliff had found his Cathy.

The Perkins boys did not attend to the vicar's rhetoric on loving one's neighbour as oneself – 'Even if that neighbour should inherit a sizeable legacy you may consider to be yours by right' – and they muttered together about their fallen idol.

'We've gotta confess before Luca gets to London,' said John. 'What if he stabs Churchill with Stan's knife?'

'You know everything gets worse if you tell an adult.'

There was no arguing with that. 'Jesus'd want us to tell.'

Billy didn't care what Jesus did or did not want. 'Who you more scared of? Jesus or the police?'

John wasn't scared of Jesus at all. He was scared of Jesus's opinion, of Jesus tutting at his behaviour, at his mum finding out he stole a whole bleedin' bicycle. And a weapon. The knife slashed through John's dreams most nights. All for a man who lied to them about having sons. There was no Bruno, no Vittorio on hand to help Dad. He whispered, 'We done bad things, Billy.'

400

Billy agreed, but he said, 'No we never, shut your face,' and Agnes turned round to narrow her eyes at them.

Outside, Henry shook hands, bowing over the older ladies, agreeing that yes, the final reading of poor Jane's will would answer all their questions. As he let Connie pass, with no comment or sympathy for her battered face, he said, 'I like to think Jane's looking down approvingly on me, as I shepherd my little flock.'

The next in line was a stooped woman. Dorothy Hughes's mother was old before her time. 'Lovely service, Reverend,' she said.

'That's what I heard,' said Mrs Endicott, to the shop at large. 'Coal. They're nationalizing coal.'

Connie perked up. 'Does that mean it'll be free?'

From the end of the queue, Agnes twiddled her opal earring and said, 'Nothing's free.'

'Unless,' said Connie, 'you nick it.'

Agnes took down her hand.

Using her own coupons, Magsy bought a small loaf and 'one nice egg, please'. Lowering her voice, as the others provided cover with their hearsay and scandal, she said to Frank, 'Am I correct to think you are no longer invited to Homeleigh to dine with your daughter and Morgan?'

His dirty linen never aired in public, Frank concentrated hard on placing the egg in Magsy's shopping bag.

'I, too, find myself excluded,' said Magsy. 'Why not

unite in our ostracism and enjoy a quiet dinner at my own home?'

Frank would gladly have swapped places with one of our brave boys toe to toe with the Hun. 'Um, well, I, hmm,' he said.

'Excellent.' Magsy took that for a firm *Yes*. 'I find I don't cook so well when I have nobody to cook for.'

Feeling a little faint, Frank rallied to join in with the dissection of the Battle of Midway. 'Big win for the Allies!' he said, finding a reel of black darning thread for Connie. 'Showed the Japanese what for.'

'Perhaps,' said Alec, making the ladies turn to the new arrival. 'But the news from Gazala is very bad, Frank. Very.'

'Gazala?' Mrs Endicott waited patiently for her soap. 'Is that the new tearoom in Felpersham?'

'Not quite,' smiled Alec. He had learned in his youth how to correct a lady. 'It's in Libya, west of Tobruk.' He hurried on before Mrs E could enquire if Tobruk was one of his dogs. 'That chap Rommel is quite the strategist.'

'Never mind all that, *Alec*.' Since lunching at Lower Loxley Agnes used his first name liberally, and always with a touch of italic. She was keen to get to the nitty-gritty. 'Go on. Let the big hairy cat out of the bag. Who'll get the cottage when you read out the last part of the will?'

Every ear pricked. Frank's pen paused over his ledger.

'I have no idea. Frank, I'll come back later,' said Alec.

'He knows, all right,' said Agnes, when Alec had marched smartly away, for all the world as if he was in uniform. 'One thing's for sure; it's not Blanche. Jane would never set us all on tenterhooks just to leave it to her sister in the end.'

Connie's laugh whistled through her missing tooth. 'The plants are a red herring. It's the bequests Jane handed out that matter.'

'How would you know?' The double-edged message of her own bequest made Agnes all the more acidic.

'I know as much as you do!' Connie reared up. 'Which is to say, nothing at all. Your new friend, *Alec*, won't confide in someone who was a maid this time last year.'

'Ladies, ladies!' Frank prepared to duck behind the counter.

'Don't worry,' said Agnes, nose high. 'I won't lower myself to Connie Horrobin's level.'

'Not that big a reach,' said Connie.

Inserting her plump self between the sparring women, Mrs Endicott said, 'What if Jane was secretly, passionately in love with a gentleman of the district? He may be the beneficiary. Wills often contain the unexpected.'

Not my Denholm's will, thought Agnes, who had written it herself.

Frank, keen to move on from the controversial, handed Magsy her change and said, 'Almost the summer solstice! Something to be celebrated, surely?'

From the threshold, Doris said, 'Pardon me if I don't do a somersault, Frank.' To the Perkins boys, loitering with intent in the sun, she said, 'Hang about, lads, and I'll bring you out something nice.' There was wild garlic tucked into her handbag, plucked on the way, a penny wise addition to that evening's meal. Doris cut corners where she could, and tried not to dwell on what would happen when those corners met in the middle.

Connie said, 'Happen *you'll* get the cottage, Doris. Jane'd trust you to look after it.'

'Lord, no, it's not coming my way.' Doris squashed that idea, even though she had already totted up what Woodbine's contents might fetch at auction. She had rapped her own knuckles for such a lapse. 'The initials of the plants, the wallet, the spade, the whatsits, they all mean nothing to me. Anyway, keep your voices down. Archie's coming over The Green and it wouldn't do for him to overhear all this.' She winked at John, expectant on the step. 'Heard you had some barley sugars in, Frank?'

She heard John gasp – 'Coo!' – as she ferreted out her coupons.

Mrs Endicott waved her own ration book. 'The little ones are welcome to my sweet ration, Doris.'

'Bless your heart,' said Doris. Mrs E's sweet tooth was infamous. 'Can I leave my list, Frank? I have to get back to Brookfield. I had two of them Italian prisoners from Quartershot booked, but since that one's escape they've lost all their perks. Shame.'

'He won't get far, the silly beggar,' said Connie.

Billy and John looked at each other.

Frank said, 'Probably get shot in the blackout.'

John sank suddenly to the step.

Doris held the wrapped sweets out to the boys. 'Such a pity

the other prisoners have to suffer.' The barley sugars gleamed like copper. 'He was a fascist, they say.'

Frank nodded. 'Troublemaker, I heard. Bullied his camp-mates, trying to drum up support for Mussolini. They had no taste for it, apparently. The guards had to intervene when his own countrymen turned on him.'

'What *is* a fascist?' asked Billy.

Doris wasn't entirely sure, beyond one hard fact. 'Like the Nazis,' she said.

John threw up. He was empty when he finished, and on the floor.

The women cleaned him up, and held him, and another barley sugar was sourced – the last one in Borsetshire – and they pleaded with the poor little chap to stop sobbing.

Archie arrived and bent down to ruffle John's hair. He waited, eyes averted, for Ted Wrigley to pass by.

But Ted didn't stop. He stood a little way off from the shop. Waiting.

Archie straightened up, and took off. Sometimes, you just had to run.

Alec found the picture in his pocket, where he had stuffed it after finding it by Lower Loxley's back door.

He straightened it out. 'Damn nice photograph of a fine dog,' he said to Pamela. She was at her desk; he was, as his wife was wont to call it, 'hanging around'. He did a lot of that. 'Isn't it? A really nice dog.'

Pamela had no interest in the dog, nice or otherwise.

'Goodness knows who's leaving these tokens. The one before this was a tiny skull. A bird's, Terence thought. Sinister but somehow lovely.'

Much like you, thought Alec. He looked at her more these days, and found more to like each time. He had spent years filing his wife under Not My Type, but now he noticed her frosted complexion, her clever eyes, her natural elegance.

He didn't dwell on why he had married a woman who was Not His Type; a man could only dwell on so much at any given time.

He had assumed Pamela's good-egg move of ending the affair to be a cure-all. Foolish, really, to imagine they would fall into step immediately. *Especially as we've always been poor dance partners.* He trod on her toes, he knew that, but she was so stiff in his hold.

He hoped she noticed how hard he was trying. Alec wanted to repair, and to build. He wouldn't blink this time. He would keep his eye on the marital ball.

Pamela swivelled in her chair. 'Shall we take the gig out, one day soon?' She was, he saw, tentative beneath the veneer of self-assurance. 'A picnic, maybe?' She was not bright when she suggested this. She was trying, too.

'We could go as far as Netherbourne.'

'Splendid,' said Pamela. 'Oh, Alec, do look at Hero.'

Only the dog's nose was visible. He skulked behind a sofa.

'Honestly, boy!' said Alec. 'This is most unmanly.'

Minko was on patrol. Noisy, bad-tempered and irretrievably thick, the Peke was impossible to train; they found whiffy evidence of her presence on floorboards and cushions and Alec's monogrammed slippers.

'You never let her out of your sight,' said Alec, as Pamela brought the hideous furball onto her lap. He patted the dog's rounded head. 'Her fur's damp,' he said, puzzled.

Minko, although dim, was discreet and would not reveal how Pamela had held her to her breast and sobbed into her coat.

Offhand, scratching Minko's ears, Alec said, 'I heard old Kos took off in the night. A car spirited him away. Nobody knows a thing. Official, they think. Secret.'

'Really?' Pamela returned to the letter she was writing.

'I'll leave you to it.' Alec backed out.

Pamela bent over her dog.

Archie ran.

Ted caught up.

Longer legs, you see.

Ted put hands on Archie, looked about and saw the coast was clear, and bundled him to the back of the village hall. Near the spot where they'd parted on St Valentine's night.

Archie leaned against the brick. He said nothing; he had learned that anything he said would make matters worse. He closed his eyes and braced himself for the feel of knuckle.

He opened one eye. Then the other.

Ted stood a few feet away. Breathing hard. Head down, like a vulture hanging over a cadaver.

'Well, get on with it,' said Archie. 'Hit me.'

'I'm sorry, all right?' Ted raised his voice. 'Sorry!'

Archie rebuttoned his shirt. 'For what? Just so I know.'

'You know for what.' Ted rolled his eyes when Archie shrugged. 'For hitting you, like.'

'And kicking me? Are you also sorry for kicking me in the stomach while I lay on the ground?'

'Pack it in,' said Ted. 'I told you. I'm sorry.'

'D'you know what'd be nicer than an apology?' Archie patted his hair; not too much harm done. 'Not to hit me in the first place.'

The dismal procession through the village brought them all from their houses.

Blanche and Archie stood outside Woodbine Cottage. Bob was by The Bull's begonias. Frank abandoned his counter.

There was silence until Agnes yelled, 'Fascist scum!' and threw a withered apple.

It struck Luca on his shoulder but he didn't register the blow. Alec sent Agnes a look of reproof as No. 9 Platoon led their prisoner towards the village hall.

They could have done with Beacham in the restraining of Luca, but they had managed. Dan had quite a tale to tell Doris later, of how they came across the sleeping escapee in a pig sty. The man had roamed in circles, following the torn and erroneous map they found in his pocket. Chas Westenra carried Wanda's stolen bicycle, useless now, with a bent wheel.

'Boys.' Alec tipped his hat at Billy and John, standing like skittles on the edge of The Green.

Billy put his hand over John's eyes, but he was too late. His brother had already seen Luca's vacant eyes, his forlorn shoulders. There was no recognition for them in his face.

John ran, crazily, towards the pond. Billy stayed and watched Luca until the men locked the village hall doors behind them.

He was just a man. He was nothing like their dad; *Dad wouldn't lie to a kid*. The humiliation of capture, its hopelessness – maybe he shared that with their father.

A thought burned. *What if Luca tells on us?*

He and John would be the worst thing of all. They would be traitors.

Four days until the final will reading, but Doris let others scratch their heads over it.

She had plenty to occupy her as she stood in the barn and looked at the tarpaulin laid over the humped bulk of a dead cow.

Funny, that switch, from alive to not. The animal had clung to life. Kicked in the leaving of it.

Milk production was down. The cows were stoic, and so was Doris, but she feared she might have reached her last few dregs of endurance.

The farm could fail. They could become a statistic. With a stroke of a solicitor's pen Brookfield would fall, like Rome, like Ancient Greece, like that dairy past Ten Elms Rise. History would close over them, and she and Dan and Jack and Phil and Chris would ... *what?*

Wanda came in from the yard. 'I know what's troubling you,' she said. 'It's wrong, plain wrong. The world's gone topsy-turvy.'

Doris was disappointed in herself; she tried so hard to keep the money debacle away from the labourers, from the kids, from Wanda. 'It's nothing,' she said.

'No, it's a shame, a blot on the justice system,' said Wanda. When Doris looked dumb, she said, 'Edna and Michael Styles. Nanny and Beacham. You don't know?'

Doris didn't know.

'Nanny made bail. And then they both absconded.' Wanda was sorry, then, for shocking Doris. 'Come inside, Boss. I'll put the kettle on. Let someone look after you for a change.'

With the solstice approaching, the land was more juicy by the day, erupting beneath Alec's feet as he walked his land. Summer England was a lush place, fragrant and ripening.

Surely he could fight the war here, if that was what life demanded of him? Duty was duty, after all, just as Pamela said. Alec looked back at his old self of a month ago with something akin to embarrassment. All that striving, and chafing at his bonds. All that *What about me?* One doesn't get to choose one's duty; one just does it. The warriors would need a nation to come home to; Alec must steward that nation and from now on he resolved to put his back into the job.

Pamela had told him 'Well done' for reeling in Luca Scuderi, the fleeing fascist. The story had amused her – a pig sty, a scuffle, young Chas Westenra's nifty way with a hurled bucket. She had meant her congratulations, however, and she would sit, impeccable, in the front row when Alec opened the last dratted envelope at the final will reading.

She chose to stay with me, he thought, and allowed himself a 'Well done' for that, too. Kos was quite a fellow. The sort of rival no man wants. Even his absence had presence; the whole house speculated on where he might have gone. Up in the air. To enemy territory. Smuggled into his homeland's resistance. *But Pamela chose me.*

Such a vote of confidence after the way he had let her down was meaningful. Alec had been searching for meaning, for something holy. Maybe it had been sitting in his own drawing room all these years. 'I will deserve her,' he told the birds and the sky and the treeline. It was a vow. His wife was slowly, and with trepidation, opening up, turning to him. He took note.

In step at last, the Pargetters of Lower Loxley would be formidable.

A little late, peace broke out between Christine and Irene, as they sat on the glossy green bench at Hollerton Junction. Christine's *Encyclopaedia of Flowers* lay open across their laps.

Doris paced, watching the horizon for the train. Like the poorly cows, the farm had become a delicate dependent; Doris didn't quite trust anyone – even her Dan – to notice its little ways like she did.

The girls tested each other on flower names. They were very competitive; Doris kept an eye.

'Daisy,' said Christine.

'Bellis perennis,' said Irene. Then, 'Snowdrop?'

A pause. Some silent jubilation from Irene, before Christine gasped out, 'Galanthus nivalis!'

'Five–three to me,' said Irene.

It was all the more extraordinary, this feat of memory, when Doris recalled that Irene couldn't read. Christine had patiently recited the flower names, over and over, until the words were stuck in both their heads.

When the train took shape in the distance, the score was six all.

'It's a draw, Mum,' said Christine.

'Lovely,' said Doris. She was not attending. Because Doris knew who would inherit Woodbine Cottage.

The answer to Ambridge's riddle had leapt out at her, clear, obvious, cruel. There would be trouble, terrible trouble, come Friday.

The train arrived, with all its man-made clamour, in the thick stillness of the summer day.

One of the carriages delivered Peggy. She had a distracted smile for Doris, but no greeting, no asking after Jack. Speeding, intent, she was gone, before Doris could hail her.

Doris settled Irene into a seat. Checked her ticket. Checked the label she'd tied through the handle of the little suitcase. 'You remember where to change? You know to ask the guard if you're confused?' *As if,* thought Doris, *Irene would be confused.* She retied the bow on her left plait. 'All set, love.'

'Keep me,' said Irene. Her eyes had brightened at Brookfield. All it took was decent meals and decent people.

'Oh, now, don't you go upsetting yourself.' Doris's big blunt face creased.

'They don't love me at home,' said Irene. 'Keep me, Doris!'

Doors slammed along the train. A whistle blew. Somebody shouted.

'Irene, dear, it's the rules, I can't ...' Doris backed out. 'Be brave!' she called as the train began to move, heavy and lumbering, like a waking giant.

'Oi!' Christine pitched the *Encyclopaedia of Flowers* through the open window. 'That's for you!'

'You love that book,' said Doris.

Christine was violent with feeling. She pressed her face against Doris's chest and cried there. 'I hate the war,' she said, with all the passion a nine-year-old could muster.

That is to say, a lot.

Three days to go until the final will reading.

The thought landed, dull and unwelcome like a bill on the doormat. When the big moment came, when poor Jane had her post-mortem revenge, Blanche would run mad. *I'll caper across The Green. I'll kiss the vicar. I'll push the Women's Committee into the pond and set fire to the village hall.*

She owed the villagers nothing, those ghouls who watched her life like they were in the cheap seats at the Odeon.

It had begun to spit rain. The summer was not as scorching as the previous one, when Spitfires and Hurricanes had a bland, blue sky to frolic in. Blanche heard Archie scrape mud off his shoes at the door.

'In here, Arch!' she called. 'Let's have one last push and find this blessed jewellery box, so I can spirit us away for a few nights at The Ritz when they evict us from this dump.'

Archie was so serious he looked like a different person.

'What is it?' Blanche snapped. She had a presentiment. 'Well?'

'I've joined up, doll,' said Archie.

For such a sprat, John could *run*.

Connie tried to catch him as he flashed past.

On the far side of a table piled high with furry carcasses, some of them half-skinned, Peggy had a tight grip on Billy.

'I don't believe you!' John shrieked as he tripped over Wizbang. 'That's not my dad. You're lying. It's a mistake.'

In the one, godforsaken easy chair, Stan battled both a hangover and the knowledge that the next instalment on their loan was due. 'Shut that kid up, or I'll do it for you!'

Peggy could cry – it sometimes helped – but she was on duty as Big Sister; so much of the war was women's work. 'Come here, John.' Her brother crept towards her. 'And listen.'

*

'You fool,' said Blanche. 'You fool, Archie, you stupid fool.' She banged the table. 'Joined up? But you said . . .' Archie was leaving her; that's all the news meant to Blanche. 'Go then.' She waved a hand as if the war raged out on The Green. 'Get yourself blown to bits. See if I care.'

'Be nice, you daft old moo.' Archie, never one for boundaries, stepped over Blanche's and put his arms around her. 'Give in, and just be bloomin' *nice*, for once.'

It smelled good in the nest of Archie's arms. Cologne and the pomade he used on his hair. Blanche's arms disobeyed her and clung to him. 'Don't get killed, Archie,' she whispered. 'Please.'

'I won't get killed, I'm not that sort of person. I'll go, and I'll come back, just you see.'

As Blanche thawed, flopped on a dining chair, he told her how he wrote to the powers that be and told them his homosexuality was cured. 'Poor bastards are so desperate they pretended to believe me.'

'But you had an exemption.' Blanche, a lover of the crooked path, the wiggly way, was stumped by his principles. 'Why the change of heart?' She was trying to hate him for the stupidity of it all.

'It was Monica. Well, not *her*, but what she told me. How can I stand by and let my little brother lie about his age and go to sea so I can play house with you? Turns out,' he laughed, 'I'm butch!'

'Well, I never expected *you* to let me down.' Blanche was bone-white, bleached. 'You needn't expect a pay packet when you're walking out on me like this.'

'Couldn't give a stuff. Spend it on scent.'

She laughed. 'Don't go,' she said.

'I have to,' he said.

Peggy put her hand on John's head and turned him, physically, to look at the small, two inch by two inch, black and white image.

'I took this especially,' she said. 'To prove to you that Dad's home, safe and sound. That's our backyard, look. The bin. The trellis. See?'

John allowed himself to look. The man's face swam into focus. He was very thin, but he could be nobody else. It was his father, with his funny upside-down Vs for eyebrows. 'Daddy,' he said.

'Daddy,' repeated Peggy, and she held both boys tight. Distance brought her brothers closer. Before the war Peggy had never grasped that children had interior lives; she'd assumed they ate and played and fell asleep like puppies.

She had known John would doubt her good news; he was a little pessimist. That's why she borrowed next door's camera – so *up* themselves, next door: typical of them to have a camera – and raced to Nowheresville to show him the evidence.

John said, urgently, to Billy, 'This photograph's real, though, innit? Not like *his* photograph?'

'His who?' Peggy didn't like secrets. Well, not when other people had them ... her own secrets were necessary. Like how changed she found her father, how brittle and sad.

Like how often she thought of Jack Archer. *Of all people*. That round-faced little no-mark who had flirted himself inside out before tootling off in a tank. 'Who?' She prodded Billy.

He said, 'Some madman we met in the woods.'

'This pair,' said Connie. 'Always making up stories. They do keep me entertained.'

'Hmm.' The boys knew what Peggy meant by that noise in her throat. She meant she would get to the bottom of it. For now, Peggy laughed along with Connie, because the little blighters *were* entertaining. 'Here, Johnny, where's the scarf Mum made you? You swore you were going to wear it all through summer.'

'He lost it,' said Billy, before any God-fearing confession might be made about Luca.

Peggy tutted. 'Careless boy! Mum spent ages knitting that.'

Connie put her hand on his shoulder. 'That's not like you, John,' she said.

But John knew it was just like him. The new, bad John who lied and stole.

Nance pushed a stray hair up into her headscarf. 'So that's all right with you?' she doublechecked as the gaffer wrote on his clipboard. 'I can swap tomorrow's shift?' She *had* to attend the fifth will reading, the eerie highlight of Ambridge's summer. A glittering and ambiguous landmark just before the solstice.

'I said yes, didn't I?' The gaffer yelled 'Break!' and the

forklifts stopped and the pallets were lowered and the men jumped down, heavy-footed, lusting for tea.

'Thanks ever so.' Nance was in a sea of men. They surged past and around her, and she heard one of them say, in that specific, mocking voice always used to fling a sexual comment, 'Cracking arse you've got there, girl!'

She coloured. Put her head down. Such remarks were rare now; the men accepted her as a hard worker, and a good sort. But it did happen, and when it did she was without her protector.

Ted would've stood up for me.

She looked up and saw who had spoken. It was Ted.

Stan hammered at the door of The Bull. 'It's shut,' he said, when Platoon No. 9 broke step and moseyed over, hope in their hearts for beer and badinage.

'Never,' said Dan. The Bull's door being barred to Ambridge was unthinkable, like seeing His Majesty in the nuddy.

'He's right,' said Chas Westenra, rattling the handle.

A shout from the yard chilled their blood. 'We're shut!'

The men hurried around the side of the inn, to where Bob stood in a crater. He was digging ferociously, like one of Stan's terriers in pursuit of a ferret. He grunted and sweated, and his spade – Jane's spade – hit something hard. Cold-shouldering the spectators, he leaned down and dragged something out of the ground.

Something with bars. It was a metal bedhead. Dan jumped down into the hole and ignored Bob's grunt of, 'Get out, Dan.'

'Accept some help, man.' Dan brushed soil off the head-board. Other, smaller, treasures lay around, all pushed up like a litter of pups from The Bull's yard.

The men set to laying them out while Bob dug deeper.

A bedspread, mouldy now. A boot. Books.

It was a herculean task. The ache and effort reminded Bob of the night he buried it all. Everything of Jimmy's had gone into the ground. It was a grave; his son had no plot in the church-yard; Jimmy's life had been sunk into the dirt of The Bull.

Another clang as the spade found something.

Bob retrieved the swimming trophy. He held it, and swayed. The men darted forward, but he didn't need them. Bob stood straight again.

He stared up at Jane's window in Woodbine Cottage. She had a clear view of him that night, if he'd but known it.

She couldn't sleep, just like me, poor lass.

Minko had been told, most firmly, not to follow Pamela to the attic. Minko ignored this order, as she ignored all orders. Minko went her own sweet way in all things.

Her paws scattered polka dots in the dust. So much aban-doned treasure up in Lower Loxley's eaves. It held little meaning for Pamela; she was about to add to the bounty.

The day before the conclusive will reading felt like the right time to put away Jane's hoop and stick. Pamela won-dered if the other beneficiaries' lives had been touched by their bequests. The hoop had sent her running along the road to the airfield.

To Kos.

She laid it carefully in a corner, like a wreath. Perhaps some twentieth-century Pargetter would come in search of old-fashioned tat for a jumble sale, and see the hoop and stick, and consider them quaint.

'Minko! Heel!' she said, aware how pointless that was. The dog darted in front of her, and then carried on, down the winding spine of the house's stairway. It waited, panting, on the turning where the round window painted a circle of moonlight on the floor.

Pamela stopped on the stair that gave the best view out of the window. She was surprised she hadn't worn a dint in the wood there. The window was a blank circle. No light in the folly.

She tried to be glad about that, to recognize the rightness of it. She heard Alec laugh in the drawing room, and descended to join him and the chaps.

It was noted, when Frank dropped into The Bull, that he was 'all spiffed up'. A suit. A tie. *Eyebrows trimmed*.

'Where you off to?' asked Dan, checking his watch. Thanks to the episode out in the yard, his half-hour with his Home Guard pals had stretched somewhat. Doris would give him the silent treatment when he got home. He pulled a fresh pint towards him; Dan was not the sort to drown his sorrows, but now that ruin tapped on his shoulder, only Bob's good brown stuff could muffle its constant whining.

'Just off to my Nance's,' said Frank. 'For dinner.' Nobody

behaved as if this was unusual, and Frank was grateful. He hugged the miracle to himself, wondering if he had gone too far by putting on the suit last worn on Nance and Morgan's wedding day.

'It must make you proud,' said Dan, 'when your child grows up, and then *they* feed *you.*' He turned, stricken, to the bar. 'Sorry, Bob, sorry, didn't think.'

The men were silent. Dan had broken the rule. None of them had mentioned Jimmy's name as they helped Bob mine the boy's belongings from the ground.

'Let me pay up,' said Dan. 'I'll be off.'

'It's on me, Dan,' said Bob. 'Who'll have a little something with us?'

Stan slammed down his glass. 'Decent of you, Bob,' he said. The other men were reticent.

'You sure?' Dan was suspicious of his reprieve.

'We could all do with a drop of the good stuff.' Bob poured a tot for each of them from the hallowed bottle. 'Hold on, hold on,' he said, as the glasses were taken up. He scrabbled beneath the counter. 'There,' he said, and propped up Mrs Endicott's incompetent, loving portrait of Jimmy. He raised his glass to it.

'To my Jimmy,' he said.

The men echoed him. They gulped down the whisky, and let out loud sighs of satisfaction.

'S'cuse me,' said Bob. 'I'll just fetch a clean cloth.'

'A *what*?' Stan didn't come to The Bull for housewifely standards.

'Shush, Stan,' said Dan.

Bob went to the scullery and leaned against the uneven, whitewashed wall. He thought of Jimmy. It hurt. He didn't break. He thought of Jane's spade, of the ruined backyard, of the hot and dusty earth where Jimmy had fallen. It all hurt. But none of it broke him.

He picked up a cloth and went back to the bar.

Magsy was already at the table when Frank arrived at Homeleigh. She, too, had dressed for the occasion, all in purple, with frills upon frills and ruffles upon ruffles, her stiff grey hair teased upwards into an ice-cream confection.

'That's a grand table,' said Frank. He was nervous, on best behaviour.

'Isn't it just?' Magsy was hearty in her praise, even though she disapproved of the best napkins on a weeknight, and would have put one large flower arrangement in the centre instead of two modest bowls of roses among the cruets.

Frank tucked his napkin into his collar.

Magsy overlooked the gaucheness. She was prepared to find everything to her taste. She was, like Frank, relieved beyond measure to be back inside Morgan's home.

Backing in with a large platter, Nance had to blink as she watched her husband take note of Frank's napkin, and then tuck his own into his collar; kindness towards her father was one surefire way to Nance's heart.

'Here, let me help.' Magsy pushed back her chair.

'Sit, Magsy dear,' said Morgan, perhaps half a beat too hastily.

'You're my guest, Magsy,' said Nance. 'Let me spoil you.'

A moment of understanding, then, such as had never happened between the women. Magsy would not offer to help again.

'What's on the menu?' asked Frank, as the silver tray was set down. 'I've missed your cooking, Nance.'

'Breaded veal,' said Nance.

Wiener schnitzel, thought Frank. He was fearful for a second, suspicious of some prank. Then he read his daughter's face. 'Delicious,' he said.

'Just wait until you see dessert,' said Morgan. 'Your favourite, Magsy. An enormous apple pie, with such fancy lattice pastry.'

'Best of British!' smiled Magsy.

Apfel strudel, thought Frank.

Beneath the table, as their guests cut into the (slightly dry) veal, Nance and Morgan held hands like teenagers.

No need to tell their guests about the baby just yet.

The letter in Peggy's hand ran to three pages. She had written about her brothers, her job, her dad who had secured a job on the railways which might be too much for his altered, fragile health. Her correspondence with Jack Archer was generally concise, the result of duty – she felt grateful to all the men who went to fight – and Peggy didn't know why she had felt the need to share real feelings and real opinions with the cocky upstart; she was sure she would come to regret her postscript.

P. S. Who knows, maybe we'll have that date you keep asking for when you're home on leave?!

Tottenham Court Road heaved with khaki. Peggy stood out in her floral cotton. Making her way to the postbox, she passed Lyons' Corner House with barely a look, the way she might pass an ex-beau. Her last guinea had been handed over to her parents; even the 1/6 three-course option was beyond her.

She saw him, then. He said it the same moment she did.

'Fancy meeting you here!'

They both laughed. He was out of context in town. Ambridge and London were separate universes.

'Seems like fate.' He motioned to the restaurant. 'Can I stand you a little something? You must be hungry, *everyone's* hungry these days.'

Peggy put her head on one side. 'Aren't you spoken for?'

'Sadly, not anymore.' Mr Bigtime held out a gloved hand. He took the letter. 'I'll post that for you, but only once we've tried the table d'hôte.'

Peggy allowed herself to be steered into the welcoming glamour of the Corner House.

Walter enjoyed the soft feel of midnight, the watering can bumping against his shin as he crept around The Bull.

He stopped dead.

Each night at this hour he left little Nelson asleep in the

424

cottage and assiduously watered the begonias he had planted. That night, someone had got there before him.

Bob!

Walter backed away. The flowers were Bob's business now.

If you were a bird – say, a falcon, or maybe a more humble blackbird – and you flew over Ambridge at midday on Friday nineteenth of June 1942, you would see a pattern both definite and shifting. The jade triangle of The Green and the rigid rectangle of the village hall, and several black dots on the move.

The bird wouldn't know it was a year since one of their number had died, but each little black dot knew it. Some of them nursed hopes of being richer by the day's end, of heading into the summer solstice with a cottage added to their worldly goods.

One of the black dots – if you swooped down you would see it was Blanche – worried she would end the day homeless.

Inside the hall, the chairs were soon filled. Men leaned gallantly against the walls.

Not all the men: Stan sat on one chair and put his feet on another, until Magsy imperiously tapped his boot. Down came his feet and Magsy ostentatiously wiped the seat with her handkerchief.

Connie had little Maisie on her lap. She crossed her fingers for Walter to reveal a rose or some ruby chard, or raspberries. That's all they needed for the full set. That's all they needed to spell out 'Blair', Stan's middle name, and make their fortune.

The Horrobins' ship would finally come in, capsizing all the other little tugboats as it did so.

Mrs Endicott had brought her knitting; Wanda complimented her neat stitches. Mrs Endicott was hurt that Doris didn't join in with this eulogy but Doris was busy watching Blanche, and wondering how she would react to the decisive final act of Jane's theatricals.

The leading lady was in satin, carefully inappropriate. Shoes to match. A red feather in her hair. A little crooked, this feather; Archie wasn't around to fix it.

She didn't miss him. She would miss him tomorrow, Blanche decided, or maybe next week. It had been a grave mistake to allow Archie in; life was so simple before he came; not needing anyone was the key to peace of mind. And now the house felt quiet without his singing and his jokes and his superb way with an insult. The feather shivered as Blanche fidgeted.

At her shoulder, the vicar bent down to say, 'All will be well, dear, whatever the outcome.'

'Easy for you to say,' said Blanche. 'Even with those dentures.'

Frances was unctuous. 'What cannot be cured must be endured.'

Blanche laughed in her face.

In his unsought place in the spotlight, Alec caught Pamela's attention, and beckoned her up to the stage. As he took her to one side, every pair of eyes watched them.

Pamela held up crossed fingers. 'Here's hoping it's not a hollyhock.' An H would round off their family crest; the

Blessed Light would reveal, not Bountiful Hope, but Terrible Gossip. She saw a peculiar light in his face and, suddenly fearful, she lowered her voice to say, 'What is it?'

Pamela's expression didn't change when Alec told her he had been called up. 'When do you go?'

'Eight days' time.'

'I see.'

Back in her seat Pamela didn't hear her husband read out the much-anticipated final section of Jane's will. She missed the familiar appeal to 'listen'. *So. He's going . . .* Irony generally amused Pamela, but this twist was too dry even for her urbane tastes.

Standing behind Alec, Walter Gabriel drew himself to his full height as the moment of revelation approached. He wore his best – his least worst – jacket for the occasion.

Dead Jane spoke for the last time. 'My final bequest is unusual.'

Agnes grasped Denholm's arm, and he woke up.

Connie had a coughing fit.

Mrs Endicott dropped a stitch.

Doris sat very still.

Pamela didn't hear Alec carry on in an impersonal drone. 'The personal item and the plant are to be shared between two individuals. They can confer and decide who keeps what. The final two beneficiaries are my dear sister Blanche Gilpin and Mrs Doris Archer.'

Blanche leapt to her feet, while heads swivelled to Doris, who remained in her chair.

'Show me the plant!' shrieked Blanche.

Walter whisked away the sacking.

'What *is* that?' Blanche couldn't identify the simple, elegant herb.

'It's sage, missus!' said Walter.

'S!' Blanched punched the air. 'The house is mine!'

There was pandemonium. Cheers, one muted boo. Morgan said he had always known Blanche would get the cottage and Nance permitted him this fib. Agnes pouted. Dan clapped and called, 'Quite right too!'

'Fix!' yelled Stan.

'Those poor pussies,' said Mrs Endicott. 'The Cats' Home got nothing in the end.'

Already on the stage, Blanche flapped her hand at Doris. 'Come *on*.'

Slowly, Doris ascended. She ignored the little cheer provoked by her be-scarved head rising above the audience.

'As I said.' Alec raised his hand and the villagers quietened down. 'Doris and Blanche can decide between themselves who receives the sage and who receives the personal item.'

'Who cares?' Blanche gurned. 'I keep Woodbine, so who cares about a stupid plant and whatever tat you're hiding in that desk?'

'Jane wrote one last note.' Alec returned to the stiff writing paper. 'I send a final, heartfelt message about the healing properties of sage, or salvia, as Walter and I call it. Blanche and Doris – choose with care!'

Alec opened the drawer and took out a heart-shaped box covered in pink velvet.

Blanche snatched it. Held it to her heaving chest.

'Miss Gilpin, no,' said Alec. 'Your sister was clear. This must be a joint decision between you and Doris Archer.'

'Doris, this is family jewellery. Surely you wouldn't take it from me?'

Dan knew what his wife would say. He also knew that selling a few shiny what-nots might save the farm. *Their* legacy. But he applauded with the others when Doris said, 'This decision is yours to make, Blanche. Do keep it, if that's what you want.'

As Doris accepted the sage, Blanche pulled at the catch of her box. It opened.

Within, loose in one of the niches that should have contained a tiara and a ring and earrings and a necklace, lay one small brooch. Instead of massed emeralds, Blanche saw delicate enamel work in the shape of tiny blue flowers, dotted in their centres with yellow.

Over her shoulder, Walter said, 'Them's forget-me-nots.'

'How poignant,' said Mrs Endicott.

'We will forget her not,' intoned Magsy.

Blanche threw the brooch overarm. 'Damn you and your tricks, Jane. Where are my emeralds?'

The brooch struck little John in the face. There was tutting and fussing and Alec felt the mood shift.

Belligerent little Agnes said what they were all thinking. 'You got your cottage, didn't you, you ungrateful wretch!'

Alec said, 'It seems as if our business is done at last. Let's all file out quietly and—'

'Hold on a minute.' Walter's burr cut through, halting the cracking of arthritic knees and scrape of folding chairs. His fingers were sunk into the sage pot. 'There's a bit of cardboard poking out of the soil.'

Doris, hasty, said, 'No, Walter, leave it.'

He pulled at a leather lace, and out came a pouch, covered in dirt.

All were rapt.

Especially Blanche, who dropped the velvet box as Walter opened the pouch and produced a key. Blanche recognized the key. She didn't have to read the crumpled cardboard tag that read 'Woodbine Cottage'.

'She was a clever old dame, my Miss Jane!' Walter was intoxicated by the secrets that opened their doors to him, speedily, one after the other, as he brandished the key. 'She knew Blanche couldn't resist jewellery! We should've been looking at the Latin names all along.' He reeled off the list on his fingers. 'The bleeding heart is also dicentra, your lady orchid is orchid purperea. Latin for azalea is rhododendron, and everyone knows a busy lizzie is an impatiens.'

'And sage,' whispered Doris, over the head of her leafy prize, 'is salvia.'

'And what does all that spell?' Walter threw his hat in the air.

'Doris!' shouted the crowd, as one.

The village hall had never witnessed such scenes. The stage was overrun, with Doris the epicentre of a round of 'Hip hip hooray!' Her back was slapped, her hand shaken, and a cloud of astonishment rose and burst above them all.

She was buffeted, staggering, clinging onto the pot, mud on her good dress. She had seen the truth in Christine's *Encyclopaedia of Flowers*. Known the poisoned chalice was coming her way. She smelled the woody herb. She smelled an eleventh-hour reprieve. She smelled salvation.

Salvia.

Wanda leaned in close. 'Your money worries are over, Boss.'

At the edge of the whirlwind, Blanche drooped, shell-shocked. She was in hell, a hell she chose. *I forced Doris to take the sage*, she thought. If she had relinquished the box that key would be in her hand and nobody would care about the first letters of stupid plants, about their Latin names. Her mind struggled and leapt like a rabbit in one of Stan's traps.

Dan was there, suddenly. He took Blanche's arm. 'Let's get you out of here, love,' he said.

She turned blindly away, hating him, only to find herself in the embrace of Mrs Endicott.

'A dreadful shock, Blanche. You have a home with me as long as you need it.'

'I don't *want* a home with you.' Blanche shoved past her, slapping away other hands that reached out to her, other neighbours willing (if perhaps not madly eager) to offer shelter. She didn't hear their good wishes; Blanche's ears heard only the mutters of, 'Well, she was too greedy to let Doris have the box,' and 'Been asking for this her whole life, she has.'

Blanche fled. She needed Archie, his humour, his love. But the house would be empty. And the house belonged to Doris Archer.

'Should I, dear?' the vicar asked his wife as Blanche ran.

'Don't you dare offer that woman a bed in my house,' said Frances.

Henry put his hand in his pocket and touched the wallet, the aged leather smooth against his fingers. When he caught up with Blanche, he, too, was shaken off. She didn't, she told him, want his damn charity.

Wanda cleared a slow path through the crowd, one arm around Doris. Wanda had read what was written on the other side of the key's label. She had to get the Boss home.

Alec gave up trying to restore order. The village was, after all, just a microcosm of the wider world. Every nation was in tumult; why should Ambridge be any different? He lingered by the pond, watching the doors, waiting for Pamela. He felt sure she would quit the hall before the drama died down; she had no appetite for it.

Looking for matches in his pocket, Alec found the picture of a dog. The nice picture of the nice dog. He didn't realize he had hung onto it. Maybe because the nice dog's nice eyes reminded him a little of Hero, who was nosing around the reeds. *I'll bring it with me when I go to war*, he thought.

It might bring him luck.

* * *

The moment shimmers.

The summer solstice is upon Ambridge; Jane has been gone for a year. Everything has changed; nothing has changed. A snake eats it tail.

A hoop and stick sit in an attic.

A wallet is buried in a pocket.

A spade leans against a door.

An opal earring reclines with its twin.

A key lies on a plain wooden table.

There are girls in the graveyard again, washing their faces in the dew. And Frances shouts at them again. She is awake and fuming, knowing she must inevitably air the spare room and put up with Blanche Gilpin for an open-ended parcel of time.

Jack Archer is blank. No cheer, no fear. He tries to sleep, imagining he's in a soft bed at Brookfield and not crammed in with fourteen other male bodies in a tent that feels no more substantial than a dandelion clock.

Pamela pulls on a chiffon nightgown. She smooths it over her spare body. The eagle ring is on a chain around her neck. She can wear it surreptitiously this way, beneath her clothes. But not tonight. She kisses it, unclasps it, and puts it away.

Archie can't drop off. Partly because he is beneath a navy-issue blanket made of, possibly, wire wool. Partly because he misses Blanche. He'll also miss nipping out to meet Terence, that clean-cut RAF fellow and champion kisser, but he won't miss Terence telling him, 'If we meet in the village we don't know each other, got that?'

John and Billy are out and about, as befits big-shot adventurers. They skirt the woods they loved until recently. The trees close over feelings they don't want to revisit.

John whispers to Billy, 'Luca never told on us. He can't be all bad.'

'He's a bleedin' fascist,' says Billy, and that's that.

Bob can't find the sweet spot in his double bed. He pads on bare feet to the small back room, and slips between the clean sheets on Jimmy's narrow berth. The swimming trophy is a bright spark in the darkness; Bob can almost hear the splashing and the cheering as he drops off.

Stan can't sleep. Connie's making a peculiar noise beside him. She's rasping, catching her breath. She hasn't been able to get out of bed since the reading of the will; he is flummoxed by her. Why must everyone provoke Stan? Why does he have the worst luck? Why is he the only suspect when any blood is spilled? *I never touched that Archie fella.* Connie goes quiet; he can hear his own blood rush in the silence. 'Oi!' He shakes her and she wakes with a start. Stan is so relieved he kicks her.

Her last night in Woodbine Cottage and Blanche hears a noise downstairs. She knows it's her imagination playing tricks; there is nobody there. There will never be anybody there for Blanche. She finds herself pitiful; a woman who discovers herself capable of love for the first time in her life with a man who cannot stay. She knows now why they write songs about love. She goes downstairs, to confront whatever ghost is poking around in Doris Archer's house.

Kos shuffles through the arched gates, shoulder to shoulder with men as weary and as dirty as he is. His nose is flat, bloody. He is carried by the human tide, and he carries a new name. He is Bogdan Minko now, according to his identity card. A Jewish tailor, widowed. Kos, or Bogdan – he must remember to answer to that name – feels a scrap of paper fall from his fingers.

He should have burned it, but it helped to feel it tight in his grasp. Now it is trodden underfoot, already in wet pieces, the curling handwriting made nonsense. 'I am yours,' says the little note. Above him, the arch reads 'Auschwitz'.

The women fold linen together, companionable. 'I had a little lass of my own,' says Nanny, 'such a bonny girl. I miss her, but these little darlings will help with the grief.' She gazes through the door at the lamplit dormitory, the parallel rows of orphaned children asleep in their beds. 'Bairns are my life.'

The tug of midsummer magic pulls at Lorna's eiderdown. She turns the pillow so that it's cool. She wonders if her thoughts can rise up through the shingled roof and mingle with Cliff's, like the spectres of Cathy and Heathcliff out on the moors. *Don't be so daft*, she tells herself.

Pamela tiptoes down the hall and finds his room. She slips into his bed. Alec turns to her. Surprised. Sad. Hungry.

Peggy sleeps well as a rule. But tonight she sees her new gentleman friend's face when she closes her eyes. Lovely manners, treats her well, the fancy car one hell of a perk. Her mother asked, 'Is there anything in it, though? What are his intentions?' She is, of course, suggesting that such a man couldn't possibly fall for a Peggy Perkins. *But he has fallen for me, Mum!* Otherwise, why would he give her that exquisite gold bracelet? Peggy will keep her word to Jack Archer, though, and let him take her out like she promised in her letter. Ironic, that Jack's new rival should have posted it after the first evening he and Peggy spent together.

'So, Jane,' says Blanche to the empty parlour. 'What did you do with the emeralds?' She prowls. It's no way to spend her last night in Woodbine. 'Not that it matters.' Blanche raises the glass she has poured to calm her nerves. 'Congrats, Jane. You gambled on my greed and you won. Or I lost. Or both, perhaps.'

The mirror, glinting in the dark, shows Blanche a haggard spectre hanging rootless in space. It's not Jane who haunts Woodbine; it's Blanche. She picks up a vase and throws it. The mirror shatters.

Doris passes the vicarage, and sees the flashing white figures of the virgins dashing among the graves. Doris is practically marching. She should be in her flannel nightie, with curlers in her hair and contentment in her heart. She is wealthy; she has power; she can finance a new herd.

Cliff is out of doors. He won't scold the boys when he finds them; he'll stick John on his shoulders and hold Billy's hand all the way home, even though Billy will protest. He thinks of Lorna as he walks through lanes made strange by the night.

He wonders if their thoughts can rise up and mingle ... *No, that's daft.*

Blanche cuts her foot on a shard of mirror. She watches her toe bleed. She says, 'I'm sorry, Jane,' and to her own astonishment, Blanche means it.

Mr Bigtime has had a long day. He turns off the engine. Opens the glove compartment. And thanks God he did so. He takes out a lipstick. If the wife was to find that, his head would be on a stake outside their Cheyne Walk apartment. Also in the glove compartment is a letter, addressed in an unmistakably feminine hand. 'Sorry, Corporal Jack Archer, whoever you might be,' he says, as he screws it up and drops it into the rainy gutter.

Doris crosses the bridge. One foot in front of the other, she walks into her future, the way she always has.

Alec has forgotten how Pamela snores. He revels in the awful music she makes. He wonders if she knows, as does he, that he'll die on the battlefield. He'll follow Rupert. *But,* he thinks, amending his gloomily comforting outlook of just days ago, *I'll leave a gap.* That makes it worse. Love can, without meaning to, make things worse.

Doris passes the shop. She takes the key out of her handbag. She can simply step into Woodbine. She can sit in the armchairs and pull the curtains and rearrange the silver plate on the dresser.

She is at the door. There is no need to knock. The key is her permission; on the other side of the door is rescue. She turns the cardboard label. Jane's writing: 'You know what to do.'

From the parlour, Blanche jumps at the sound of feet in the porch. She races to the hall, and sees the key drop onto the mat.

In Borchester, a woman says, 'Shush now, you lot!' as she checks up on her furry foster children. The cats meow at her, and roll on their down mattresses in their well-appointed cages. They take the luxury for granted; they have never heard the name Jane Gilpin; they were not present when the anonymous donation of an emerald parure fetched a record amount at auction.

ACKNOWLEDGEMENTS

So many people to thank, and for many different reasons.

My publisher, Simon & Schuster, must be first up, for their enthusiasm and patience and charming way with an email. An especial thank you to Clare Hey, my long-time editor and trusted wingman, and to Laurie McShea in publicity, a ray of sunshine in my garret.

As you can imagine, I kept the BBC's *Archers* team busy with queries and requests about farms and family trees and who lived where. Thank you from the bottom of my heart, Jeremy Howe, Mel Ward, Hannah Ratcliffe and Sarah Swadling. With a special mention for Abigail Woods of Lincoln University who came up trumps on bovine disease.

Plants and flowers loom large in this novel. Thank you, Olly and Janet Ryan-Moore, the husband-and-wife horticulturists who kept me on the straight and narrow.

Thank you to my in-laws, Keith and Jen Strachan, for ensuring my Geordie characters sounded authentic.

Thank you to Pat Cryer, for your fascinating website

www.1900s.org.uk. This treasure trove of social history, of communal memory, helped me at every turn.

Thank you, as ever, to my daughter, Niamh Strachan, for tearing me away from the desk at the end of every day.

Finally, thank you for reading this book, and for making an author happy. ×